A Farewell to Compañeros

Fidel went to them. One was paralyzed from the waist down, his spine shattered. The other had been shot in the head. Both were conscious, quiet, didn't seem to be in much pain. He took their hands, could think of nothing to say. They smiled at him, knowing it was the end. Fidel shut his eyes tightly, made no attempt to stop his tears. Gripping their hands and wrists, he kneeled, wept for them, blessed them, still couldn't speak.

Finally, he got up and managed to utter, "We will never forget you," then left the fort, aware his words were pitifully inadequate. Hurrying across the fields, he remembered that the partisans in *For Whom the Bell Tolls* had left their wounded behind, the book ending with Jordan unable to walk, waiting to die, aiming his rifle at a fascist lieutenant. If it was any consolation, he supposed, it was that Jordan would take some of the enemy with him. *So, Señor Hemingway knew about that too, about men too badly hurt to move, men sure to be murdered,* Fidel thought. *Still, his words do not ease the pain of those who must leave their brothers behind.*

"As events move both men on to their inevitable destinies, the author weaves fact and fantasy into a skillful climax that restores Hemingway's dignity as it humanizes Castro."
— *Library Journal*

Books by Karl Alexander

*Time After Time**

A Private Investigation

Curse of the Vampire

*Papa and Fidel**

*Jaclyn the Ripper**

* A Tom Doherty Associates book

Papa and Fidel

KARL ALEXANDER

A Tom Doherty Associates Book
New York

PAPA AND FIDEL

Edited by James Frenkel

A Forge Book
Published by Tom Doherty Associates, LLC
175 Fifth Avenue
New York, NY 10010

www.tor-forge.com

Forge® is a registered trademark of Tom Doherty Associates, LLC.

The Library of Congress has catalogued the hardcover edition as follows:

Alexander, Karl.
    Papa and Fidel / Karl Alexander. — 1st ed.
        p. cm.
    ISBN 978-0-312-93149-0 : $17.95
        1. Hemingway, Ernest, 1899–1961, in fiction, drama, poetry, etc. 2. Castro, Fidel, 1927– —Fiction. I. Title.
PS3551.L3569P37   1989   88-33281
813'.54—dc19   CIP

ISBN 978-0-7653-2675-1

First Tom Doherty Edition: March 1989
First Trade Paperback Edition: May 2010

Printed in the United States of America

0 9 8 7 6 5 4 3 2 1

For Kateri, love of my life

Preface

Where does history end, fiction begin? It may not matter. What matters is to document the power of hope over despair, the force of imagination, and the sustained power of the written word.

—Stanley Trachtenberg
Los Angeles Times Book Review

Much of fiction is history and vice versa. Ernest Hemingway and Fidel Castro met only once, so the historians tell us, when Fidel won the silver trophy at the 1960 Ernest Hemingway marlin fishing tournament. The historians also tell us that in his last years, Hemingway lost his creative genius, suffered from paranoia, and committed suicide. These are sobering facts, inconsistent with the life and times of a courageous man. Sad, but true, so they say.

The story that follows is what might have happened, what should have happened if Ernest Hemingway and Fidel Castro had become friends.

"Havana, circa 1957"

One

"YOU GOTTA MEET this guy, Hem."

"Meet who?"

"Fidel Castro."

"Heard he was dead."

"Government propaganda," said Matthews, his thin face serious and intense despite the bawdy *élan* that surrounded their front-row table at the Tropicana. "But everyone'll know the truth soon enough."

"Got proof?"

"Pictures."

"Dangerous shit."

"Front page."

Papa just grunted and shifted his chair away from Matthews. He'd heard enough about young "rebels" in the mountains. *Fuck politics, Cuban and otherwise.* He knocked back a shooter of rum and chased it with beer, eyes never leaving the teenaged stripper on stage, now undulating to a raucous version of "Heartbreak Hotel," inviting *aficionados* in Panama hats and one-button rolls to stuff greenbacks between her legs. Papa shook his large, white head and grinned, wrinkles crinkling the way they should when you've had a long and good life. "Will you look at that?" He signaled for a waiter. "Wonder how she does that?"

"Disgusting, if you ask me."

"Yeah, but no matter how depraved the Cubans get, they always seem to have a damned good time."

"What about Batista?"

"He here?" Papa asked cynically.

"He's everywhere."

"What the hell you talking about?" He frowned at Matthews, noticing his friend was still as frail-looking as he had been in Madrid twenty years ago when they were covering the Spanish Civil War. "Don't have to tell me what the gen is around here."

"Been to the Sierra Maestra lately?"

"Nope. Ain't booked reservations, neither."

"The government's got planes, tanks, and three thousand crack troops there right now, and you're not reading about that in Havana." He paused, whispered, "We barely got in and out."

"Damned drunk could get past the Cuban army," grumbled Papa, annoyed by his friend's exploits—jealous, even—annoyed that he really wasn't sure what was going on. What the hell. No one knows anything, what with the lies in the papers, confusion everywhere, and a cop on every corner. Looking. Listening. *Don't want to think about it.*

Finally, a swish waiter minced over, all done up in a watermelon-pink uniform, smiled impatiently. He stunk of Old Spice and Sen-Sens. *"¿Sí, señor? Tienes daiquiris?"*

"Tropicana makes shitty *daiquiris,"* said Papa, fixing him with a hard look. "No *cojones."*

"Sí, señor."

"Need Bacardi, two more Hatueys, and her." He pointed at the stripper—now threatening to smoke a cigarette with her genitalia—then stuffed pesos into the waiter's hand.

"What I'm trying to say," Matthews went on doggedly, "is that this M-26-7 is for real. Castro's either going to be a hero or a martyr."

"So what?"

"Look around you, Hem. He might be Cuba's only hope."

Papa acted as if he hadn't heard and watched the stripper doing circles with her breasts while the crowd howled encouragement. A conga line had started, gaudy *habaneros* and half-drunk tourists snaking around the dance floor, the crap tables, through the slot machines and cigarette haze, past hard-eyed gamblers and gangsters and whores, a mix of bored decadence. His thoughts turned bitter. What the hell does Matthews know about Cuba? Comes down here for a couple of days and thinks he's got all the answers. Shit. I'll tell you about Cuba. First the Spanish come and massacre the natives. Then the Yankees kick the Spanish out, Teddy Roosevelt looking real bad-ass on his horse. Okay. We pass the Platt Amendment, buy up all the land and plant sugar cane. *Cubanos* become tenants on their own soil, and you better pay the rent, boys, 'cause nobody fucks with the USA's sweet tooth. That's the gen of it on this island, he told himself, gazing at the stripper with genuine admiration. Now she was grinding down over a fifty-dollar bill held by a fat tourist from Shaker Heights. Yep, there she is on stage, America's whore, he thought sourly. Stick your hand in the sugar bowl, fella, welcome to Sodom and Gomorrah with a Spanish accent.

The orchestra climaxed with a cacophony of tenor saxes and brass. The sequined curtains closed, and a fast-talking emcee in a yellow suit assaulted the stage. The follow spots made his face beige. While he jabbered on about the next act, Papa turned back to Matthews and said, very simply, "Horseshit."

"I'm telling you straight, Hem, they've—" The waiter came with the drinks, and Matthews paused until he left. "They've started a revolution."

Papa laughed disdainfully, his belly shaking under his white *guayabera* shirt. "Come on, Herb! All you're talking about is a dozen *guajiros machos* in the mountains! You got war on the brain. Covered too damn many of 'em."

"You're no stranger to revolutions, either."

"Damnit, I'm trying to have a good time!"

"Ernie, they're machine-gunning people in the streets, and God help you if you're a student at the university!"

"I've lived on this fucking island for almost twenty years," Papa growled. "They *always* machine-gun people in the streets!"

"This is different."

"My ass."

"Seriously."

"Only thing that ever changes around here is the name on the mailbox at the presidential palace."

"Go up into the mountains, Hem. Go up there and see for yourself."

"I'm working on a Goddamned book!" he roared.

"Okay, okay, sorry." Matthews took the hint, went back to his beer, and began scratching out notes on cocktail napkins.

Angry, Papa chased a shooter with half a bottle of Hatuey. He'd just reminded himself that all was not well at his desk. These days, the words were coming slower, the good ideas fewer and farther between, and he was scared to death he'd lost it. The big book was aching to be written, but he didn't even know what it was about yet, so he diddled with his autobiography. How much had he done this morning, holed up in the tower, the new dog, Machakos, sleeping at his feet, how much? A half page. How many hours had he stood there, staring past the cats on the windowsill at the blue of the Gulf Stream beyond the docks of Cojímar? A fucking half page of distant memories.

Another shooter. He wished he could shut the emcee up, but the man went on and on, making obscene jokes about black girls and snakes. Papa wasn't having a good time at all and was about to suggest they hit the Floridita where the drinks were cheaper and better. But then the stripper swung up to their table wearing fresh lipstick and a mesh get-up that couldn't've used more than ten feet of string. She slid into the chair next to him, her hand going to his enormous thigh. Smiling now, he admired her long, black hair and copper skin. When his eyes got to her belly, she sucked it in and out without moving any other part of her body.

"I can do amazing theengs, señor, amazing."

"I'll bet you can."

Briefly, he forgot his problems with the writing. Hell, even his shot liver and high blood pressure—damn plumbing's gone bad, he'd told himself that morning with a reading of 215/105. Gonna spring a leak one of these days. He nudged Matthews. "Whatta you say, Herb? Wanna take her and a friend back to the ranch?"

"C'mon, Hem, grow up," he said. "You're almost sixty, for Christ's sake!"

"Older the goat, stiffer the horn." He turned to the stripper; her dark eyes held him. *"¿Como se llama?"*

"Sonja."

"Funny. Don't look Swedish to me." He roared with laughter and draped his arm around her.

Now the girl's hand was on his sizable girth, moving down over the large brass belt buckle he'd taken off a dead kraut in World War I, her fingers grazing the inscription, "GOTT MIT UNS." She paused, tugged on it playfully, leaned close, whispered, *"Mi amiga, Rosa, lo va hacer con un perro. Un perro grande. ¿Quieres ir a ver?"*

Eyes twinkling, he turned to Matthews, barely able to contain himself, his belly quivering with suppressed laughter. "Herb?"

He glanced up.

"Wanna see a lady take on a Great Dane?"

"Sure," Matthews replied sarcastically. "Dinner theater?"

"Ain't kidding," Papa deadpanned, making a move to get up. "Hottest show in town."

"You serious?"

"C'mon. Afterward, we'll take the ladies to a *posada*." He patted Sonja on the ass and stood. "C'mon, *vámonos*. Don't wanna miss the first part where she gets Fido real friendly."

Matthews blushed and wouldn't look Papa in the eye. He studied his watch and spoke sideways. Articles weren't proofed yet. Deadlines. Foreign desk closed soon. Little woman back at the hotel. Already late. Plane to catch early. "Sorry, Hem, call me when you get to New York, give my best to Mary." And then he was zigzagging through the tables, sidestepping waiters, hurrying past throngs of tourists feeding slot machines, busting through the endless conga line.

Papa wouldn't let it go. He chased Matthews, his bulk rolling gracefully, finally caught him in the curving mouth of pink tile that was the Tropicana's entranceway. "What's the matter, Herb?" he yelled. "No guts?"

Matthews kept going, out to a line of cabs waiting at the curb, their yellow and green colors glistening in the cool February rain that washed Havana, but couldn't clean her.

"Y'never had the stomach for bullfights, either," Papa

muttered, staying under the overhang, watching his old friend jump into the lead cab. The driver pulled out into traffic, making a U-turn against all odds. Horns blared, brakes shrieked, cars skidded, fishtailed in the wet.

More sad than angry, Papa was already sorry for what he'd said and told himself to send a letter of apology first thing in the morning. While meticulously cautious, Herb Matthews was never one to lack courage.

As he was about to go back inside, Papa saw a khaki-colored Chevy sedan make the same improbable U-turn the cab had done, only this time no one protested. He just stared, a bad feeling welling up inside. Everyone in town knew who drove the unmarked khaki-colored Chevies.

Batista's Military Intelligence Service. The death squads, two to a car, commonly called the SIM boys.

This time, they were after Matthews, his dispatches and pictures from the Sierra Maestra, no question in old Hemingstein's mind.

Papa leapt in the nearest cab, ordered the driver to follow the Chevy. Eyes wide with terror, the driver refused, so Papa handed him a hundred pesos, pulled him out onto the street, commandeered the cab himself. Then he was skidding across traffic, barely missing cars, finally behind the Chevy now two blocks ahead. Hunched bearlike over the wheel, he changed lanes often so they wouldn't notice him. He had no idea what he was going to do, only knew he couldn't let them take out Matthews. We been friends for twenty years, he thought. Boy's a damned fine correspondent too, maybe even better than me, and God knows, the world needs writers more than SIM hit men.

And so the three cars sped west along the boulevard. Papa released a long sigh, grinned slowly, licked his lips. He hadn't had any action in a long time. Too long. Too Goddamn long. His blood sang, the adrenaline tasting sweet and good. His body coiled automatically, just like in the old days, and he almost laughed. He felt strong and alive again.

Since Matthews was staying at the Nacional, Papa figured the SIM boys would stop him in Vedado where the boulevard was quiet and dark, bordered by large trees, their branches hanging over the streetlights, shadowing them. The civilians don't hear too good in this part of town, either, he told himself. Not behind their mansion walls and shuttered bay windows. Got too damned much money.

Sure enough. Just past Treinta y siete, the SIM sedan pulled even with the cab, hovered there briefly, and then Papa saw the glint of a rifle. Immediately, the driver pulled over, the Chevy parking behind, high beams clicking on. The SIMs were out of their car fast, the tall one covering the cab with his automatic weapon while the thick one jerked open Matthews's door and tried to pull him out. He resisted—just what Papa hoped he'd do.

Hemingway double-clutched into second, floored it, waited interminably for the flat-head De Soto six to kick in. Finally, it did, and the cab shot forward, needle jiggling up to fifty. Just this side of the SIMs, he pulled hard right on the wheel and held it. Tires screeching, the cab rocked into a ninety-degree turn, shuddered, flattened out, then slammed broadside into the Chevy, lifting it, jackknifing it against a tree where it did a half spin before crashing to the sidewalk.

The SIMs dove to the ground, the tall one dropping his rifle and covering his head as breadfruit rained down from the shaken tree.

"*¡Vámonos!*" Matthews screamed.

Needing little encouragement, his driver gunned their cab down the boulevard.

The tall SIM came up to his knees, groped for his

weapon, found it, sprayed the boulevard with bullets, but none hit Matthews's cab.

Minutes later, a dazed Papa came around, felt himself being pulled—and pried—out of the cab he'd nose-dived into the SIM sedan. His head had shattered the windshield. Blood from a dozen cuts ran down his face, ruined his shirt, stained the street, then dissolved in the rain. He was vaguely aware they were beating him.

Can't fight back, he told himself. Too banged up, too weak, too Goddamn old. The blows, the curses, the kicks. On and on. The tall one kneed him in the groin. He fell heavily. Before the blackness closed in, his last coherent thought was that they would kill him, here on the street in Vedado. Mercifully, he passed out.

Only to come to an hour later in the bowels of the Bureau of Investigations. He heard screams. The terrible, agonized screams of a man beyond hope that sounded like the shrieks of an animal caught in a fire.

Numb and groggy, Papa pushed up to his knees. His cell was black, but there was a shaft of light coming through a vent in the wall. He crawled to it, peered through and saw the bars, the concrete, the bloodstains on the floor, smelled a decade of vomit, heard the screams again, focused on them. A man was manacled to the wall. Matthews's cab driver. His trousers were around his ankles, and a kneeling SIM sergeant in starched and tailored fatigues was looking up at him from under a gleaming helmet, a Lucky Strike dangling from his lips, asking him why he had run, what he knew of the Sierra Maestra and how many men were there. He shook his head, moaned softly that he knew nothing. The sergeant dragged hard on his cigarette, touched the red-hot ash to the cab driver's balls. He screamed again. Writhed, heaved against the manacles, but there was no place for him to go. At a nearby table four disinterested soldiers played poker, the pesos flying fast, arguing over the merits of American college girls once you got them between the sheets.

Papa watched the brutal nightmare, horrified and fascinated yet detached. Detached until his mind cleared, and he realized where he was and that he might be next. Anger began building in his gut. He shook his head. No, they wouldn't dare, not to you, an honorary citizen. Suddenly, he put his face in his hands, understanding why he was in this holding cell next to a torture chamber. My God, Hem, he realized, they don't know who you are! He remembered his passport on his dresser in his bedroom. He'd been in a hurry, and they didn't check him at the Tropicana, and who would've thought the SIMs were after Matthews, and— He swore silently. Goddamn your skinny hide, Herb, what the hell've you gotten me into?

The sergeant was asking more questions, absurd questions the cab driver couldn't possibly answer. Once again, he hot-boxed the Lucky. Paused. Toyed with it while the cab driver stiffened, twisted, waited helplessly. Then ground it into his testicles and left it there. The screams were hoarse, yet no less horrible. Papa felt sick and looked away, but could smell the stench of burnt hair and flesh. The screams faded, and he heard the sergeant ordering his men to take the cab driver out and shoot him.

Papa looked back through the vent. They unlocked the cab driver. Defiantly, he tried to spit on his interrogator, but his mouth was too dry. A toothy smile from the sergeant. He appreciated the irony and saluted the cab driver with an upraised finger as the soldiers led him away.

A phone on the wall rang. The sergeant answered, identified himself, listened briefly, then hung up and left the cell, door clanging, his spit-shined boots echoing down the corridor.

"Wait a minute!" Papa screamed, "you can't leave me

here, don't you know who I am?" He scrambled to his feet, found the steel door and pounded on it, yelling over and over, "I'm Ernest Goddamn Hemingway!"

No response. Just his voice echoing off the walls. He sat down on the floor near the vent. Alone. Unless Matthews was in a nearby cell. Waiting. Hurting. Cold. Knowing the pain would get much worse. He recalled the time in Italy when he got blown up by incoming from a 420. Almost took his legs off, he told himself, but he made it through.

Now he wasn't so sure. *They're going to come and take you and manacle you to the wall in there and do unspeakable things to you if you don't talk—how can you, you know nothing—and then take you out and shoot you. They don't know who you are. Goddamnit, don't let 'em kill me, I ain't finished yet! You filthy whore, Death, why didn't you take me out back then? When I was young and strong? In a blaze of glorious light?*

You afraid to die, Hem?

He was angry at himself, his blush of fear, then thought, Why should it surprise you, nobody in his right mind would be anything less than afraid in this fucking dungeon. He grimaced. Fear. Another whore in your life, Papa, a new one. *Fear.*

Hours passed, or was it minutes?

Now, through the vent, he heard them coming, their boots ringing on the concrete. That awful moment of truth, and he was not ready. He stood, folded his arms across his chest, hoped that he would live up to everything that had ever been said about him.

Ain't gonna die badly, Goddamnit.

They came into the cell jabbering about women and baseball, their rifles in his face. He told them who he was, asked them to believe him, but they just laughed, sharing a secret joke. Cursing them, he staggered out of the cell, expecting to be taken next door, but they propelled him in the other direction. Oh, shit, the wall, he thought wildly, hating this final journey down the long corridor toward the *paredón*.

But, no.

He was taken upstairs into an office. A large, important office with autographed pictures of presidents and kings on the walls. Off to one side an SIM colonel and the sergeant were standing at attention, sweating nervously, saluting him, yet afraid to look at him. Papa was stunned. What the hell was this?

Behind the colonel's desk was none other than Fulgencio Batista, short and squat, in uniform, dark hair greased straight back, a Latin clone of Mussolini. He was apologizing profusely to Papa, saying the distinguished journalist Herbert Matthews had telephoned from the U.S. Embassy and informed him of Ernest Hemingway's incarceration *hace poco*. It was a disgrace to his regime that the renowned author should be detained by the SIM, and those responsible would be punished severely. After all, Fulgencio Batista, himself, had bestowed the coveted Order of Carlos Manuel de Céspedes on Señor Hemingway just three and a half years ago when Señor Hemingway was vacationing in Spain. Surely he remembered. Now, would Señor Hemingway care for a scotch?

Papa accepted, at the moment SIM whisky being better than none at all.

A white-coated black servant wheeled a bar into the room. Papa thought of Matthews, probably on a red-eye special to New York. Thanks, Herb. Guess we're even now.

Drinks were served, but not to the colonel and sergeant who remained in place, their salutes frozen.

"To your health, Señor Hemingway."

"Amen, General."

Two

PAPA HEARD THE two cleaning ladies whispering just outside the door, groaned and rolled over. Mary's side of the bed was cold, and the servants were wondering what to do since they'd cleaned every room in the house, but couldn't do the bedroom. *El patrón* was still sleeping.

"Jesus Christ, is it that late?"

He sat up and wished he hadn't. His head pounded, and his mouth was dry. The sun streaming in through the window hurt his eyes; they felt scratched. His face hurt too, skin taut and drawn. Jesus, Hem, what'd you do last night? He remembered. Old Doc Herrera had come over for dinner, so he'd been a good boy, but after his friend left, he made up for lost time with straight Haig Pinch and got real melancholy over a box of old letters from before the war. So what? Now you got a giant bull mastodon hangover, you dumb shit.

He rose unsteadily, went into the bathroom, swallowed

four aspirin, then took his blood pressure. Too fucking high. He didn't bother to write down the figures because he didn't want Mary to see them and get all worked up again. Reluctantly, he took his hypertension medication, washing down the pills with a giant glass of water, and hating himself for being so Goddamn old and imperfect.

Normally, he didn't like to make excuses for himself. Pure and simple, he liked to booze it up, but one reason he'd been hitting the sauce extra heavy was that he'd been unable to forget that night at the bureau two weeks ago. For those who asked, he passed the incident off as a casual brush with Cuban marionettes who didn't know who he was. But privately, he wished he'd had the presence of mind, the *guts* to tell Fulgencio Batista to go fuck himself instead of accepting his expensive whisky. The gen of it was he'd lost a little courage in that black cell, waiting, but not ready to die. Very un-Hemingwayesque. Jesus, what would Buck Lanham say, the boy he'd knocked off a bunch of krauts with in WWII? He sure as hell wouldn't laugh. Might understand, though. He'd been in enough "no win" situations. Papa scowled, massaged his throbbing temples. You been scared before—like when that nine-foot grizzly came at you from behind those Idaho pines, and you only had five seconds to drop the monster, but you, afraid? Must come with age. Also very fucking un-Hemingwayesque. Who the hell wants to be an old man? You catch the biggest marlin in the Gulf Stream, the sharks rip it apart before you get to shore, and you know you'll never get another chance. Right, Santiago? He sighed. Do you got it anymore, Hem? Or have you lost it?

He went into the kitchen. A girl he'd never seen before explained shyly that Mary had taken the Chrysler and gone to town for groceries. He nodded soberly and stared out the window at the garden fence posts growing into trees again, their leaves new and fresh and bright in the morning sun. It was time to trim already. Have to get René on it. Wish to hell they'd stick me in the ground, I'd come back young and strong, he mused.

Mary. Hope she had sense enough to go to the local mercado. *Damn gringo place in the city's charging two bucks a pound for steak.*

"*¿Café con leche?*"

"*No, no. Café negro sin azúcar,*" he mumbled, handing her a large mug instead of the usual Cuban demitasse. Good old American-style mud was the only hope for his bad head. Bleary-eyed, he focused on the steaming cup she poured him and left the kitchen without bothering to check out this new girl's stats.

In the living room, he sat heavily in his favorite chair next to the table that had all the hootch on it. While nursing his coffee, he gazed up at the two elands mounted on the wall over the bookcase and dreamed fondly of Kenya. Got to get back over there, too. Before Patrick gets to be a better shot than me, the damned kid.

On the coffee table, he saw the February 28 edition of *The New York Times* plus a manila envelope via the U.S. Embassy from Herbert Matthews. Inside were his articles, published on the twenty-fourth, twenty-fifth, and twenty-sixth, causing a furor in the U.S. Papa felt a twinge of pride. If it hadn't been for him, Matthews would've ended up a bullet-ridden corpse in Vedado, and the world would know nothing of Fidel Castro and his 26th of July movement.

Papa opened the envelope first. He hadn't read the articles yet. They'd been banned in Cuba, so Matthews had sent them in a diplomatic pouch. Rumor had it that an enterprising film student at NYU had flown down with a suitcase full of newspapers, was caught hawking them for twenty-five dollars each, and was gunned down on the steps of the University of Havana. Then on the twenty-sixth, Batista suddenly lifted his censorship, and *The New*

York Times became the hottest-selling item in print since the Spanish translation of *Peyton Place.* Interesting move, Papa thought. The wolves are howling at Batista's back door and he don't want anyone inside to hear, yet he's gotta do something because the USA pays his rent and all the gringos are talking about what's in the *Times* so he lifts censorship to show Washington qua the world that his regime is free and open and the country a place where law-abiding citizens have nothing to fear. Papa chuckled. *Nice move, General. Few more like that, you might get legs.*

He read the articles. They piqued his curiosity, and unconsciously, he added scotch to his coffee. While Matthews was a damned good writer, Papa could tell he was biased as hell and was surprised the editors hadn't been a little heavier with the blue pencil. Matthews let on that these *guajiro*-bozos were young humanist intellectuals fighting for liberty and democracy. Castro's movement was "socialistic, nationalistic, and anti-communist . . . in favor of restoring the Constitution and holding elections."

"Bullshit," said Papa.

Yet, he read on, fascinated by vivid portraits of eager young men, dressed in ragtag fatigues, carrying ancient rifles of U.S. manufacture, all proud to be "one of the eighty-two." The thirty-year-old Castro obviously held them together, reportedly saying after their first disastrous encounter with the Cuban army, "The days of the government are numbered."

Hemingway smiled ironically. "Sonuvabitch'll never see thirty-one, but at least he's got *cojones.*"

More on Castro. ". . . the personality of the man is overpowering. It was easy to see that his men adored him and also to see why he has captured the imagination of the youth of Cuba . . . Here was an educated, dedicated fanatic, a man of ideals, of courage and of remarkable qualities of leadership." Jesus Christ, Herb, you talking about a

Cuban rebel with a scraggly beard and fifteen men? Or George Washington?

Disgusted, Papa put the articles down, opened the current *New York Times*. More stuff on Cuba. The articles had been reprinted along with a statement by Batista's defense minister claiming the interview with Castro was "a chapter in a fantastic novel."

"You wish." Papa chuckled.

For, across the page from the minister's statement was a picture of Matthews and Castro together in the Maestra. The proof he'd been talking about that night at the Tropicana. You sly old buzzard, Papa thought. Scooped 'em all. Just might be the story of the decade.

Wait a second. He looked off and frowned. Sure, the articles were without precedent, but something about them bothered him. He poured more scotch and reread Matthews's account of getting in and out of the mountains. It annoyed him. Don't read like good journalism, Papa told himself, more like mediocre Zane Grey. Seems exaggerated. Overly dramatic. Hell, I may flower things up a bit at the table eating and drinking with friends, but never on paper. *Never*. This shit just ain't true, Herb, it ain't real. Couldn't've been that tough. There's scenes in *The Bell* and *The Sun Also Rises* that sound more honest than your stuff, and they're just stories! Fiction! Next time we get together, I'm gonna call you on it, Herb. Bust your inflated balls. He drained his coffee and got up. To hell with this so-called Cuban revolution.

Though the morning was gone, he decided to go to work anyway, left the house, went down the front steps, paused to admire the great old ceiba tree, its branches shading steps and colonnade. Machakos appeared, tail wagging, head lowering automatically for his master's hand. As usual, Papa's voice was full of love and kindness, the dog answering with playful throat-growls. Then they walked around behind the house to the tower and made the long climb to the third-floor space.

Now standing at his desk, Papa gazed at the palms along the driveway while Machakos settled in at his feet, groaning, shuddering with a great sigh when comfortable. Papa reviewed the half-dozen paragraphs he'd done the day before, made a few changes, then closed his eyes and tried to transport himself back to his salad days in Paris. Nothing came.

Instead, he imagined he was on the Gulf, just drifting, drifting, line out, but no marlin, no sign. Nothing but the blues of sky and water, the gentle swells, the clean taste of a cold Hatuey. A long silence. Only the late morning drone. He relaxed. Cooled out.

The gray and black tom sauntered in, meowed, rubbed against a chair leg, leapt onto the windowsill for a snooze with his brothers. *Damnit, Papa, if they can sleep in the middle of the day, no reason you can't work. Il faut (d'abord) durer. No crybabyismo.*

He forced himself into it. Scrawled down the meandering memories, their sentences made fat and soft by excess words. In his heart, he knew the stuff wasn't perfect, but it felt good coming out, felt good when he typed it, his fingers playing those keys, the carriage bell ringing constantly, the pages stacking up.

Suddenly, he stopped. For the next two hours he did nothing. Just stared at the horizon. His mind was blank, refusing to let him face himself. Finally, he sighed, gave in and read what he'd done. He didn't even bother to correct the typos, realizing sadly that none of it was any good. Sloppy, false prose. Overwritten. Bloated sentences reminding him of retired heavyweights. Slowly, deliberately, he balled up page after page, arced them into the wastebasket by the dog's head. Machakos woke sheepishly, gave his master a sorrowful look, then left his post, something he'd never done before.

Papa didn't notice. Just kept making baskets with the day's work. Thinking, who the hell cares about greenhorn Hemingway—kissing Gertrude Stein's ass while Alice B. Toklas smiles her approval? Who gives a damn about two literary lesbian queens sipping jasmine tea in their salon telling me life imitates art? Horseshit! Sure, it happened, but the only truth to it is emptiness, and I don't want to write about nothing! That damned Matthews ballyhoos his adventures in the mountains, but at least you got action there. Life. Movement. Goddamnit, that's what folks want to read about!

He balled up the last sheet, tossed it too into the wastebasket, strangely calm for an old man in the throes of self-doubt, for the flame still flickered deep in his soul.

So, why don't you go on up there, Hem? he thought, suddenly excited. Take a gander at this Castro fella and his boys. Look around. Get the gen on it. Show 'em you're as good as you've ever been. He grinned and folded his arms across his barrel chest. Might just do that.

A quick frown. But *can* you, Hem? he thought. After all, you ain't exactly eighteen anymore. Think you got the stamina? The heart? The guts? Face it, if you can't even write a decent sentence no more—

That did it. In two giant steps, he was over to the typewriter.

La Finca Vigía, 1 March, 1957

Dear Herb:

How the hell do I get up there without getting myself killed?

Your friend,

Hem.

He knew that's all he had to say. Matthews would make a few calls, and someone would contact him. That's how it would work. He put an airmail stamp on the letter and left his room, pausing in the doorway to savor the cool afternoon breeze. Thunderheads were building over the Gulf Stream, fluffy gray on top, black underneath, heavy with rain. *Chubasco* on the way. He found René closing up the house, gave him the letter, told him to mail it right away. René smiled, gaps in his teeth from chewing too much sugar cane as a kid, nodded and left for town. That business off his head, Papa poured himself a hefty scotch and headed down to the pool, feeling damned good. Thunder rumbled in the distance and the wind picked up. From the steps, he saw gulls circling San Francisco de Paula and the trail of dust from René's old Ford descending the hill.

Mary was already in the pool doing laps. He smiled and admired her body. Still thin, firm, youthful. She liked to swim nude when they didn't have guests around. Not exactly shy himself, Papa shed his clothes, took a gulp of scotch, then dove in, his whalelike form creating a miniature tidal wave. White and nut-brown, massive and petite, they swam parallel, in unison. They were close this way. Silent. Each with his own thoughts, yet together.

He wondered how he'd tell her his latest plans, knowing she'd scream bloody murder the minute he mentioned the Sierra Maestra; she'd try to call in a headshrinker. So, he had to find a way of telling her without telling her so he could get out of the house. No easy task, for she was one smart cookie and always seemed to know when he was scheming. Gotta be a way, always a way, he told himself, the laps piling up. Preoccupied, he didn't realize how tired he was, didn't realize Mary wasn't in the pool anymore.

The twinge of a cramp.

It spread like fire from his foot up into his calf. Grunting, he stopped and massaged it out, looked for Mary, saw her partway up the path. He must've done twenty-two or -three today. Not bad for an old man. Only managed seventeen yesterday. He felt the sting of cold rain on his back and tried to push the last lap, but his arms went stone-dead in the middle of the pool and both legs cramped up. Agonized, he was sinking, lungs about to explode. The water was dark. Going black. He reached back into that primordial oneness, found something and flailed to the surface. One huge breath, half air, half water, and he was sinking again. No. He fought through the water and made the side just as Mary was rushing back to help. Hung there, gasping, angry at himself, relieved that the cramps had let up, but too weak to get out of the pool. Hard rain pelting his bald spot.

Mary offered to pull him out, but he shook his head, growled, and with one great effort, heaved himself over the side.

She didn't say anything. She didn't have to.

Hand in hand, they walked slowly toward the house, past trees, vines, and flowers bent by the rain. Lightning cracked down by the front gate in the mango trees.

In the bedroom, still silent, they dried each other. The urge came over Papa. Not playful. Wagnerian instead. Sober, he embraced her till they both were warm, then led her to the bed. There, stroking each other, she finally spoke, a husky whisper.

"You know, you ought to be more careful, Papa."

"Don't call me Papa. Not now, please."

"Lamb."

"Better."

They made love, the din of rain on the roof muting their

voices, a sigh here, a word there. He was patient with her because she was Mary, unlike any other. The best, hands down. As it should be. He loved her. Even though he didn't always show it and was a sonuvabitch to live with sometimes. He loved her; the true gen.

Then why the others? Pretty faces and nubile bodies flashed through his mind. The star worshippers, the whores, the college girls wanting to compare the real thing with, say, sleeping bag scenes in *The Bell*. None of them in the same class with Mary. Why then? He didn't know. Just like he didn't know why he had pushed himself in the pool. *Or saved himself.* He challenged himself silently. You flat-ass don't know, old man, and never have, but maybe you'll find out in the mountains.

They finished together and lay there barely touching, listening to the rain, softer now, their breathing subsiding.

"I think we should go home, Papa."

"This is home."

"You know what I mean."

"We been through this a thousand times."

"Really, we should leave. Let's fly to New York before things get worse."

"Can't write the big book in New York, kitten." *Can't write it anywhere when you don't know the gen of it yet.*

"I thought you were working on the autobiography."

"Was."

"Wyoming or Idaho, then. You could do some hunting."

"Too damn cold."

"You don't like snow anymore?"

"Not six months of it."

She turned on her side and looked at him, her eyes steady, unwavering. "Well, I'm going. With or without you. I've just decided."

"Bon voyage, kitten."

She frowned impatiently. "Why can't you be reasonable?"

He started to argue with her, saying the situation was under control with the cream of the army in Oriente province, pointing out that the government felt comfortable enough to lift censorship. But he didn't. Just lay there, pondering the question.

"Why?"

"Don't know." He rolled onto his back. "Guess I'd like to get in some decent fishing for a change."

A week later, she was gone. The Finca was quiet, deathly still, the help moving, working, in whispers. Only the dogs and cats acted as if nothing had happened, Papa observed, brooding in the tower. The cotsies either slept, prowled, or played cowboys and Indians with poor, unsuspecting dogs. Didn't mess with the rooster, though. As usual, he was king of the hill, crowing when he damned well pleased.

Papa couldn't work and blamed Mary, missing her, loving her, hating her for leaving him to himself. Like it or not, he depended on her. He considered blitzing through town, making a grand show of *joie de vivre* at all the old watering holes, but decided against it. Havana depressed him now, a modern-day Rome with Batista playing Caligula. The *habaneros* had become subhuman, willing to do anything for the jaded tastes of some Yankee tourists, their decadence counterpointed by rioting students, striking workers, something called rock and roll, and the inevitable khaki-colored Chevy sedans.

He wondered if Matthews had gotten his letter and waited nervously, each day's ritual the same. Up early. Into the tower. Work until two. Accomplish nothing of substance except a few letters. A scotch, a swim, more scotch. He needed a sojourn into the Sierra Maestra. He was all dried up.

He had expected a phone call, muffled voice on the other end telling him to be somewhere at a precise time, but no, they surprised him, appearing in the living room close to midnight during another storm. In ragged khaki pants and rayon shirts, they looked like college students, probably had been, but now their eyes were hard, their voices low and desperate.

He dressed in his African bush clothes, put on his old belt, pocketed his Swiss army knife and lucky chestnut, insisted on taking a flask of Haig Pinch.

They led him outside, got into a Plymouth sedan, shiny in the rain, Papa in back. He knew better than to ask names, just looked back at the Finca's gates, wondered if he'd ever see them again. They pulled onto the highway.

"How the hell we gonna get past their checkpoints?"

The one riding shotgun turned and smiled crookedly. "Checkpoints?" he said in English, shaking his head. "No checkpoints. You are taking us fishing, Señor Hemingway."

Three

"¡*ALTO!*" ORDERED THE sentry, appearing suddenly on the ramp, his cigarette glowing in the predawn darkness, M-1 carbine at the ready.

Papa was jolted even though he knew guards were everywhere these days. "*Buenas,*" he said nervously.

"*¿Documentos?*"

Papa produced his U.S. passport and tried to appear relaxed while being scrutinized. He was used to the ritual, but not comfortable with it, not now with the M-26-7 boys less than a hundred yards away stealing a rowboat from the Club Náutico.

Apparently satisfied, the sentry returned Papa's passport and slung his rifle, eyes once again sleepy under olive-green helmet. "*¿Va a pescar?*"

"*Sí.*"

"*No pescado,*" he said apologetically, stepping out of the way. "*Todo el mundo lo sabe.*"

No shit, Papa said to himself, going by the sentry, down

the wooden dock past yachts and cruisers rolling gently in their moorings. Fishing's been terrible all Goddamn year. The wind picked up. Halyards slapped against masts, lines groaned, somewhere loose canvas fluttered. Peaceful enough sounds, belied by the fact of the sentry. They'd been patrolling the streets and docks of Cojímar for two months now.

Finally, he was at the *Pilar.* She rode high in the water, black hull almost invisible, green decks wet and shiny from last night's rain. The *Pilar,* his forty-foot pride and joy.

Suddenly, Papa stopped, eyes narrowing. The lights were on down below. He heard laughter and the noise of a radio. What the hell was this? He leapt on board, hurried below, went across the galley, and without thinking of who might be there, bulled through the hatch into the stateroom.

"Hey, Señor Papa!" exclaimed Gregorio Fuentes. *"¡Buenas!"*

Astonished, Papa was taken aback. There, in front of him was his long-time first mate, stripped down to his boxer shorts, swaying in a conga line. Behind him was a copper-skinned girl in lavender pedal pushers with matching top, young enough to be his daughter. In front, an aging *señorita* in red, old enough to be his mother. Their clothes were wrinkled, lipstick smeared. Gregorio had a fresh cigar in his mouth, and the room was thick with smoke. Rum bottles and glasses littered the tables.

"Bésame, bésame mucho," Gregorio crooned happily. "C'mon, Señor Hem! You know what they say about *la conga*—longer line, longer life!"

"Fucking *depravada,"* Papa muttered angrily. Ordinarily, he wouldn't have cared, but this morning he had to be out of port before the sun was up. He snapped off the radio and began opening portholes for fresh air. "Get 'em outa here."

"Papa—"

"Get 'em *outa* here, Gregorio!"

"Okay, okay." Fuentes turned, shrugged at the ladies, made a sad face. Already, they were putting their cigarettes away, dancing through the hatch, the songs of the night still fresh in their minds. Gregorio followed them out, offering his regrets, making a date for another time, promising the music would never stop.

In the galley Papa lit the burner under yesterday's coffee, his hands shaky. M-26-7 boys are already on the water, and I gotta sober up Gregorio, he told himself, then checked his watch and scowled. Five minutes at most. He rushed topside and started the big Chrysler engine.

Gregorio was on the dock, kissing his lady friends goodbye.

"Cast off, damnit!" yelled Papa. "Cast off!"

"*¡Momento, momento!*" the mate replied, hurrying to untie the lines. He barely had time to jump back on board, for the *Pilar* was already backing away from the slip. "*¿Qué pasó?*"

No response.

"*¿Vamos a pescar?*"

Papa decided to play it close to the chest. His mate didn't have to know what wasn't necessary. "Yep. We go fishing."

Gregorio was anxious, his party mood destroyed, forehead wrinkling along the tan line from his hat. "But Señor Papa, the engine needs tuning!"

"Sounds fine to me." He switched on the running lights. They had to look normal or the patrol boats would stop them before they got out of the harbor.

"But— We got no ice!"

"So the beer's hot. So fucking what?"

Perplexed, Gregorio rattled on about what wasn't in the galley. Finally, Papa told him to shut up, get dressed, and drink some coffee. Still complaining, he went below, and it was quiet on the bridge as Papa steered through the channel. He kept their speed under five knots, looked for the M-26-7 boys, didn't see them, and grew worried, the sky already gray, the first rays of pink hitting the old Morro Castle at the mouth of the harbor. Then, suddenly, there they were—near a buoy off the starboard side, the larger one rowing furiously. Papa throttled back, let the engine idle. The *Pilar* drifted, rocked on the swells. He threw them a lifeline, dropped a ladder over the side, and they pulled themselves in, climbed aboard, and he helped them load the small boat and lash it to the bow.

"Get below."

They headed down just as Gregorio was coming up to see what was going on. Startled, he looked at them, then to Papa, eyes widening with fear. *"¿Qué pasa?"*

"Old friends," said Papa, hard. "You didn't see nothing, *¿comprendes?* Open your mouth, you're shit-canned."

Gregorio nodded, understood at once, but didn't like it. He put on his greasy Panama hat and squinted at the sunrise on the horizon.

"Get us outa here. Fast."

Silent, Gregorio took the wheel, accelerated to flank speed. The American flag at the stern went straight out in the wind. We get stopped, that'll help, Papa thought cynically. They'll be polite. He sat tiredly in the fishing chair and scanned the water with field glasses for patrol boats. None. He kept looking.

Twenty minutes later, they were in the Gulf Stream, and he finally relaxed, the knot of tension in his gut letting go. So far, no problem, just like his escorts had said. Maybe he could even get in some fishing. It had been a helluva long time.

He took the helm and headed west against the current while Gregorio went below to rustle up some breakfast. There wasn't much food on board, but soon Papa smelled onions and corned beef hash frying, their odors sharp and good. He grinned. Gregorio was the best damned cook in the whole world.

"*Desayuno listo,*" he said noncommittally, coming topside.

Papa went down to eat, wolfed his steaming plate, happy that it was spiked with Tabasco. Then he ambled into the stateroom, nodded to his escorts staring nervously out the portholes, and lay down on a bunk. The smell of Gregorio's girls lingered, a mild annoyance, but nothing to stop him from sleeping the rest of the morning.

He woke fresh and eager, climbed topside and saw that they were far offshore, the tip of Cabo San Antonio barely visible, even from the bridge. Relaxed now, the M-26-7 boys were on the afterdeck, curious, yelling questions about the boat to Gregorio. He asked them their names. They clammed up. Looked at each other. Then one smiled playfully.

"Uno."

The other grinned, pointed at himself. "Dos."

They laughed hysterically, their voices dissolving into youthful giggles from another time, and Papa knew they hadn't had anything to laugh about for a long time. Sad, he thought. They'll grow up old, but that's the damned gen of it when you get into a war. In fact, they'll be lucky to grow up at all.

"*Buenas,* Señor Hemingway," they chorused when they saw him. Now that the situation was less dangerous, they were animated, impressed in his company. Uno had studied English at the university and liked *To Have and Have Not.* Dos wanted free copies of his books for his sister, a cello player in the symphony.

The star treatment. Papa endured it, but was uncomfortable. Don't talk to me of books you ain't read yet, boys, he thought, just get me into them mountains.

The sea was less choppy on the western side of the island

just south of the cape, and Papa decided to try some fishing. He studied the ocean and frowned critically. Normally, when you went out for marlin, you took the Gulf Stream east, but you never really knew where they'd be. Could be blues around here. The thought of bagging a big one in unfamiliar waters excited him. With pole and tackle, he strapped himself into the fishing chair. Gregorio had already netted bait fish, in the tank by the chair. Papa worked a couple of sardines onto his hooks and cast out while Uno and Dos watched, whispering to each other. He let out about three hundred yards of line and tensed for the feel, then the pull of a thousand-pounder, hoping it would come immediately so he could really show these two what an old man was made of. But, no. Nothing. Uno and Dos grew bored, went below for something to drink, reminding Papa he was thirsty, so he called down for *cerveza,* and one of them brought him a beer. He deftly popped it open on his belt buckle. Then drank. Almost hot, the carbonation stunned his nose and sinuses.

"Shit," he said happily, coughing, eyes watering, not feeling the delicate nibbles far below.

The monster took the hook and ran.

Astonished, Papa stared at the line screaming off his reel, but had the presence of mind to set the drag, then yelled up at his mate. Gregorio turned, saw what was happening, instantly cut the speed to a couple of knots, only for pull against the fish, set her on automatic pilot and slid down to help, ready with the gaff. Uno and Dos scrambled on deck, watched in awe. "Blue?" asked Gregorio.

Papa nodded, ecstatic. Felt the enormous strength of the fish, now on a deep, four-hundred-yard run. He grunted and braced himself. *Sonuvabitch's big. Real big. Ain't hooked one like this since Peru. Look at me now, boys, this is what it's all about.* Already, his arms and shoulders ached, but his heart sang.

For the next two hours he played the marlin expertly, letting him take runs when he wanted. Each time, he craftily brought the fish back. Each time, a little closer. Gregorio offered to take the pole repeatedly, but Papa stubbornly refused. *Just keep those hot beers coming, my friend,* muchas gracias *for the wet towels keeping the sun off my head.*

The blue was quiet. Tired. There was no tension on the line. Papa reeled in. Two hundred. And in, steadily. One-fifty. When the fish was a hundred yards out, he tightened the drag and kept reeling, knowing it was over, nodding at Gregorio to get ready with the gaff. His heart pounded. Got you, sonuvabitch, got you.

Suddenly, the blue made a wicked, twisting run that Papa wasn't ready for, coming out of the water for the first time, much bigger than he'd thought, twelve hundred pounds at least, a good fifteen feet long, purple tail flashing, silver sword nosing down. A God of a fish.

"¡Ayyy!" yelled Gregorio.

Jesus Christ, you're big, what the hell am I gonna do with you, I can't put back into port, Jesus Christ, you're the biggest, most beautiful fish I've seen in years! He reached for the drag.

Too late.

The blue dove and snapped the line.

A long, hard silence. Only the sound of the *Pilar* cutting easily through the water and the ensign flapping in the trade wind.

Defeated, Papa didn't move, didn't speak. Stayed in the chair, staring at the nothingness of the waves, the slate-gray sky. Gregorio was there now, making light of it, tying more hooks on the line, but Papa knew what they were all thinking. Ten years ago, that blue wouldn't have gotten away.

Tight-lipped, he fished for another hour and caught a

twenty-pound tuna, but took no joy in it. He thought he'd left his self-doubts back at the typewriter. Just one more thing to prove, he told himself, stowing his gear, going below, cracking open the rum. He didn't want to talk to the M-26-7 boys, so he stayed in the galley. Gregorio was filleting the tuna for dinner, tossing the meat into a large skillet, simmering it in tomato sauce under a low flame. He bitched about the lack of spices, no vegetables, no potatoes, and *Dios* forbid, no garlic or onions left. How was he supposed to cook? "I am insulting the tuna!"

"Shut the hell up," Papa said quietly and went back topside. He sat in the fishing chair and watched the darkness come, occasionally pulling on the rum bottle. For the first time ever, he refused a Gregorio dinner. Just sat there wondering if he could get it back. *What the hell good is a man if he can't do what he loves anymore? Why go on?* The thought sobered him, and it took the rest of the bottle before he could sleep, there in the chair, the wind picking up, the sky clouding over.

Cold rain on his face. He woke to heavy seas, saw that Gregorio had strapped him in so he wouldn't wash overboard. No moon, just the *chubasco*. Uno and Dos were at the rail, seasick, and Gregorio steered through the weather. Papa got out of the chair, went below and fell into a bunk. Groggy, he curled up, hands automatically cupping his balls.

The next morning, the storm had passed, and Papa was in a better mood. He got coffee going, ate some cold fish, went topside and apologized to Gregorio. Then he took the helm so his mate could get some rest.

By midday, they were off central Cuba, Gregorio at the wheel again. They were south of the Gulf Stream now, so there wasn't much chance for marlin, yet Papa stayed in the fishing chair, reminiscing, trying to face the fact that his life was mostly yesterdays.

He heard the drone of an engine. Coming closer. Frowning, he squinted at the sky. A Piper Cub broke out of the clouds and dove at them, the whine taking him back to kraut-strafing runs in the second war, only here, there was no cover. Frozen in the chair, helpless, he just watched.

The plane was a Cuban air force spotter, and made two low passes, prop wash stinging him with spray. What did they see? What do they know? he wondered. Resisting the urge to shake his fist, he turned, watched the plane until it was a speck in the southern sky, then hurried below and confronted the M-26-7 boys. "What the hell was that all about?

"Please, do not worry," Uno said respectfully, but beside himself with excitement.

"What's it mean, damnit?"

"Only that we are getting closer to Oriente."

Indeed, they were. Late that afternoon, the *Pilar* was thirty miles off Cabo Cruz, and Papa saw the top of Pico Turquino in the fading light, ringed by rain clouds. He didn't see any more aircraft, so he assumed boat and crew had passed muster as a genuine fishing expedition. If those boys suspected anything, they would've come back with the P-38's.

When darkness came, he took the wheel from Gregorio and steered toward land, without running lights. His mood kept improving, now that they were almost there, and he wasn't thinking about the giant blue. Well, at least not all the time. About five miles out, off Playa de las Colorado, he throttled back and went down for a final briefing. "After we go over the side," he told Gregorio, "you get your ass back to Cojímar as fast as this old tub'll go."

"Over the side?" Gregorio's face clouded with worry. He looked at Uno and Dos, then back to Papa. *"¿Qué pasa?"*

"You don't tell nobody, either. Not even Señora Mary."

"¿Pero, porqué—"

"Forget it, my friend," he said kindly, "I know what I'm doing." Of that, he was sure.

Gregorio left the stateroom, mumbling sadly that Oriente province was a dangerous place and he'd never see his Papa again, but why waste time arguing with a stubborn old fool?

At 0300 hours, the *Pilar* was a mile offshore, dead in the water, pitching in choppy seas as rain fell steadily. From the afterdeck, they peered at the beach, saw no lights or movement. Satisfied, Uno indicated that they should go now. So, they got the rowboat into the water, boarded, and cast off, Dos pulling hard on the oars.

Papa turned, waved once at Gregorio, then didn't look back. The rain soaked and chilled him. *Good time for a hit on the flask, it's what you been saving it for.* He drank. Again. Right away, the scotch warmed his insides, and he grinned. *Yep. Things gonna be okay.*

They took turns with the oars, Papa insisting that he too row, and after five minutes, he was sweating heavily, but it was good and clean, not nervous and cold. Gonna write about this trip. Gonna get back and pound out five pages a day.

They ran aground in a stand of marsh grass. Papa got out, immediately sunk down three feet in the muck. He cursed. Uno and Dos scuttled the boat, led the way through the thick grass. Papa followed, hating the cold slime that pulled at his boots with every step. Figured we'd land on a beach, he thought. Nope. No beach. Shit, we're in a God-damned swamp.

That went on for miles. He was tired and wanted to rest, but it was worse standing still, wondering what was on your legs, so he kept going and to keep his mind off his discomfort thought of making love with Mary.

Finally, Papa felt something solid under his feet. They

were on a small hillock surrounded by reeds. Uno and Dos crouched and listened. He took another hit off the flask and looked around, unimpressed and disgusted.

"Never thought I'd see the day when a place this fucking miserable could be considered the high ground," he muttered.

Uno shot him a look that said, shut up, Señor Hemingway, please shut up, the enemy is all around us.

Papa scowled, but complied, not wanting to make a fool of himself and get them killed in the process. And then they were slogging along a muddy, runny trail that zigzagged through the marshes. The rain quit, only to be replaced by swarms of mosquitoes buzzing in Papa's eyes and ears, making it a bitch to see, to hear. Cursing under his breath, he slapped at them constantly, to no avail. Whining incessantly, they bit at will, and his face puffed up, numbed over.

By dawn, they were huddled at the edge of a cane field, the mountains less than a mile away, Uno and Dos looking, listening for patrols. This was the critical time, getting across these last, long open spaces. The mountains would be easier. The army preferred to stay on level ground, not far from their jeeps and armor. Uno gestured, and they moved forward at a fast trot.

Suddenly, Uno stopped, whispered, *"¡Baja!"*

Papa dove to the ground and didn't move, his face pushing into the mud. Heart pounding, he waited. Listened. Heard rustling, someone nearby. Close. Too close, now coming through the rows of cane.

"Levantese."

Filled with dread, he looked up slowly. An army corporal stood over him, grease gun aimed at his face. Uno and Dos were gone. He was alone.

"¡Levantese!" The corporal was impatient.

He managed to raise up to his knees. The corporal cocked his weapon, the bolt chambering a round with an ugly, metallic snick. Goddamnit, no! He tried to get up and run, but tripped, pitched forward onto his hands and knees, knew it was over and waited for that short, quick burst to end his life, hoping the world wouldn't judge him badly.

Four

IT NEVER CAME. He heard the corporal gasp, and looked up. Uno and Dos had grabbed him from behind and cut his throat. Blood splashed everywhere as Dos tossed the dying corporal into sugar cane. Mistake. He still had a hold of the grease gun and in a death reflex squeezed off a few rounds, staccato reports breaking the stillness.

Papa stared at his escorts. They heard the shouts of soldiers coming from the north end of the cane field. A jeep started up. No time to think, no time to work it out. They ran. Diagonally across the field toward the foothills, stands of cane in their way, Papa stumbling, refusing to go down or give up, wondering absurdly why the damned field hadn't been harvested, two months past the *zafra*. Never mind meaningless details. Never mind, either run or die.

Three shouts, indignant now, for they'd found the corporal's body. Papa heard the jeep churning in the mud somewhere, yet it was closer, much closer. More shouts off to his right. Now random firing. Soldiers swarming through the field. Angry hornets.

Now caked with mud, the three scrambled up a slope, finally reached the south end of the cane field, and paused. Papa's chest heaved as he fought for breath and wished he knew what would become of him. Death seemed highly probable, but senseless, the worst kind, for he was here of his own choosing. Shit, the rawness of it all, he thought. Did animals feel like this when you hunted them? Hurting, heavy with panic? *Yet they always managed to die so nobly.* He iced his mind. There was no other way to get through it.

Ahead was an open meadow, then trees. Behind, the jeep pushed relentlessly through the cane. The patrols closed in, soldiers calling to each other, coordinating movement. Papa turned, glimpsed the jeep veering off to the left, searching, a .50-caliber machine gun mounted on its hood. He scowled and remembered seeing slugs from a 'fifty knock down full-grown trees.

They sprinted onto the meadow, each man for himself, Uno and Dos rapidly putting space between themselves and Papa. He heard the jeep again, now directly behind, and he could *feel* the gunner swing the 'fifty around, sight over the barrel, brace for the heavy recoil, squeeze the trigger. Not gonna make it! he thought. Can't! He ran harder, harder, his lungs on fire, and that horrible sense of vulnerability spreading from his neck down his back to his legs. He was certain the next moment was his last. The bullets would slam into him like sledgehammers, taking his breath away, and he would sprawl this side of the trees, writhing, unable to shock out the pain, finally dying. Alone. Ignominiously. Unfinished.

Uno and Dos made the trees and disappeared. Papa put on a final burst of speed, tripped on a rock, sprawled into the grass just as the 'fifty opened up, bullets whining overhead into the trees, now behind him spraying mud, the gunner all over hell and gone with the big weapon. A sudden silence. Angry voices. They were arguing, the gunner saying he couldn't shoot on the move, the other saying he couldn't shoot no matter what, then challenging him and jerking on the parking brake.

Papa got up, broke for the trees, dove into them and landed on top of Uno and Dos, their grunts of pain drowned out by the thudding 'fifty, very close, branches raining down. Cursing the machine gun, they crawled through the thick foliage, tree ants attacking them, their bites sharp like needles, but nothing, really. Not when death was missing by just inches.

They made it beyond the trees into a ravine, safe for the moment. There, they brushed off the ants, stomped on them as if they were the soldiers, shook out their clothing soaked with sweat, slime, early-morning wet. They listened. The patrols were still coming. Up ahead were the foothills and more trees. If they hurried, they had a chance. With a nod, Uno set off at a half trot, staying low in the curve of the ravine, Dos right behind. Preoccupied, Papa crushed two more ants he found on his leg, and when he looked, his escorts were fifty yards up the hill. Shit, he muttered, taking off at a brisk walk. They're running. I can't run no more, too damned old and tired. No sense to it. Let the bastards take me. And if they don't believe I'm one of the general's distinguished citizens, then I guess they'll shoot me, and that'll be that. Old Hemingstein, gone. No big book. Just the unknown. The eternal panic. *Homme seul.* Finally.

Uno and Dos were waiting impatiently just over the next rise. *"¡Dése prisa!"*

"Espéreme, Goddamnit," Papa grumbled, trying to catch his breath, gather his strength.

"No!" Uno protested. "The soldiers are all around us, they are coming for us, there will be more and more of them!"

"I'm fifty-fucking-seven," Papa said flatly.

"We want you to make fifty-eight, Señor Hemingway," Uno replied. He turned and was off again, keeping close to the trees, out of the dappled sunlight. Dos followed.

With a huge sigh, Papa went after them, angry at himself, for they were right. Out here age didn't matter. You either kept up—or died.

Soon, they came upon a cattle trail and followed it to a river, swollen with runoff from the winter storms. The ford was washed out, so they had no choice but to swim. Papa was careful and patient, letting the river take him, working the current, the cold waters soothing his tired body. He pulled himself out a half mile downstream, just above some rapids, and felt refreshed; cleansed. He no longer stank of sweat, of crushed insects, of fear.

They zigzagged up a canyon wall, feet skidding on mossy stones, their clothes drying partially only to sag with sweat after a few hundred feet. Then the ground leveled somewhat, the trees thinned, and a breeze picked up. Papa was actually feeling good.

Until he heard the plane.

They broke for the nearest tree line, and this time he wasn't that far behind, but the run damn near killed him, and he lay on his side gasping for breath while his escorts watched the skies anxiously. Spotter planes. Circling low over the trees for almost an hour, their engines sounding like the mosquitoes that besieged Papa. Finally, the planes went away, and they moved on. There were fewer patrols now. The country was too forbidding, almost rebel territory, and the soldiers were afraid. The sky clouded over. It rained the rest of the day, the mud slowing them, yet they didn't stop until darkness, and Papa fell. Half-dead, he slept.

Seconds later, so it seemed, they were shaking him, and he woke stiff and cramped. The rendezvous point was near, Uno was saying, the time close, they had to go on. He tried to get up, but faltered.

Before he could protest, they pulled him up and sent him along the trail with a push. He half turned, intending to shout, keep your Goddamn hands off me, then punch out the one who'd pushed him, but didn't. You could hear jeeps in the distance, the pop of flares, their colors eerie against a full moon. The army was still looking.

Now they were climbing steadily, Papa slipping constantly on the steep, muddy slopes. His usually tough feet were blistered, his hands, raw from grabbing rocks and bushes, his legs, jelly. He was working his way across a slant covered with ferns when his body just let go, and he was tumbling, rolling, bouncing down, down, sliding to a halt in a stream, the water cutting into him at the waist, numbing his legs. He just sat there and felt hollow, too weak to even curse. If he moved, he hurt. He knew he looked foolish, but was too exhausted to care. His dignity was not with him anymore, not here on this patch of the Sierra Maestra. Only pain. He thought of a story he'd written long ago, a fishing story, Nick Adams hiking into the mountains of northern Michigan, resting because he was hot and tired. Papa scowled. How come you didn't write about his pain? he silently raged. You never told how legs could ache, you never said, and you must've known, you had an obligation, but you didn't write it, you didn't put it down the way it should have been. "He was very hot and tired . . ." Big fucking deal. Easy to say, easy to write, but none of the agony comes across. No true feelings there. Just false notes. You should've written it on the river instead of pontificating from a frog hotel room in Paris. Maybe then you would've understood the pain. Robert Jordan, he never knew pain either, going up his mountain to join Pablo's band behind the lines in *The Bell*. Not one damned ounce of pain. Jordan didn't even get tired, and here you are, a broken old man all cut up inside with muscles that refuse to move, cold, miserable, hurting all over, hunted, on the edge of death. You claim what you write is honest and true, yet how can you if your characters don't *feel?* How can you if you've never really done what they have? If you're no longer capable?

"Are your characters bullshit, Hem?" he said aloud, "or are you?"

The question went unanswered, for they were whispering urgently at him to be quiet, pulling him up again, dragging him, and he looked into their hard young faces and knew one reason Nick and Robert hadn't felt any pain. They'd been him in their twenties and hadn't lost the juice, the power that makes you push on. Still, Papa told himself, the characters I write should know such things as pain no matter what age they are, for if there is no pain, there is no joy.

The big book, he suddenly thought. The big book must have both.

On they went. Up, up, rocks, trees, streams, more rocks, trees, their leaves and branches glistening in the moonlight, a downslope, another hill, a rock wall, up, up— Papa fell again, this time facedown in the mud, and when he looked at them, their faces were expressionless. They must know. They must think I'm no longer cut from the same stuff as those whom I write about. Well, Goddamnit, if you punk greasers can make it— If . . . if *Matthews* can make it— He struggled to his feet and moved on, but fell again.

They left him inside a thick clump of bushes. He curled up on the wet ground and just before sleep remembered the line he had given Santiago, the ancient fisherman fighting the giant marlin. "Pain does not matter to a man." One more time, was that bullshit or are you not a man? Where the hell are your *cojones?* he wondered, reaching for them, his hands finding mud instead as the blackness hit.

Hands pulling him up, shoulders under his arms, urgent whispers about another patrol less than a quarter mile away. His eyes were swollen shut, and his face felt as big as a medicine ball, thanks to the swarms of feasting mosquitoes. Yet he realized they were carrying him, and these men were new, smelling more like the rain forest than the nervous reek of Uno and Dos. One complained of Papa's weight. The other chastised him. They were only two miles from the outpost; besides, orders were orders, and Fidel was expecting the *gringo viejo.*

Papa scowled. The only time a man ought to be carried was when he was either gut-shot or dead. He took a deep breath, stood up straight, and pushed away the two surprised rebel scouts.

"I may be old," he growled, "but I ain't no fucking cripple."

With that, he began climbing on his own, ignoring the anxious looks of his escorts, furious that so far on this journey he had come up sadly lacking. Not again. Never. No more crybabyismo. His anger masked his pain, and he reached deep inside and found the strength to go on. He placed one damaged foot in front of the other. Finally, they were beyond the point of no return for the army patrols, and Papa saw his escorts relax a little. A grin here, a nod there, but the pace never slackened because, he supposed, in a situation as fluid and deadly as this, you never really knew. So, he gritted his teeth and kept up, determined to climb to hell, if that's where he'd meet Señor Castro.

Suddenly, fifty yards shy of the summit, the lead scout signaled them to stop, and they crouched in the trees while he scuttled forward silently. Papa heard two low, soft, toneless whistles. A pause. Someone answered, and then the scout was back, gesturing them forward. They hurried to the summit, and, just over the top, passed a crude lean-to with three wispy-bearded youths inside, eyes curious, rifles glinting in the moonlight. They're babies, Papa thought, kids playing cowboys and Indians. How can they be holding off the best Goddamn army south of El Paso? Then he recalled that he too had fought a war at their age, and he and his hadn't fared too badly against the Kaiser's finest, either.

The ground leveled out, and Papa was grateful, for his newfound strength was ebbing fast. *Can't stand much more, feels like razor blades under my feet, but you can't quit now, Hemingstein, all the guajiros machos are looking, you got to keep on and walk into this deal a man, walk until you drop and the old whore, Death, takes you out with your boots on.* He remembered the way Colonel Cantwell had died in *Across the River and into the Trees.* "It" just hit him and gripped him. He didn't hurt at all. Bullshit. *Then you had him lie down in the back seat of the big car and go out calm and peaceful, all the loose ends of his life tied up, body sent back to his lover as it should be, all's well that ends well. Strike up the violins. False romanticism. Bullshit again.*

In the distance, he saw the outline of trees against the sky as the first light came up. They strode by small pockets in the forest, and he was vaguely aware of forms moving around, whispering to each other in the grayness, like game at a water hole before the lions woke up.

Finally, they stopped in a grove, the lead scout spreading a blanket on the ground and telling Papa that Fidel would see him later in the day. Papa grimaced, swayed, had to hold on to a tree.

"*¿Agua dulce?*" the scout asked, concerned, offering a

canteen, reminding Papa of the flask in the side pocket of his bush trousers.

He shook his head, then took out the flask, uncapped it, and drank deep.

"*¿Está bien?*" the scout whispered, still worried.

"Never felt better in my life," Papa replied, putting the booze away, patting the pocket.

He collapsed, out cold before he hit the blanket.

Five

HE LOOKS OLDER than his fifty-seven years, observed Dr. Fidel Castro Ruz, peering down at a snoring Papa curled in the fetal position under a coffee tree, his blanket all scrunched up. What if he dies here? No, no, Señor Hemingway, rest assured, we will take excellent care of you, for there are many things you can tell the world about us, good things, and people listen to you—people who don't trust *The New York Times*—and it would be a disgrace to me, personally, if something happened to you, a true Cuban hero, in M-26-7 territory.

"No, por Dios," he whispered softly, then shrugged and told himself not to worry. After all, Hemingway had made the journey over the most difficult trails in the Sierra Maestra, chased by an entire enemy battalion. How fragile could he be? His escorts, forty years younger, were still recovering in the medical tent. Fidel grinned, lit a fresh cigar, continued staring at Papa, trying to read him as he slept, sensing they were made of similar stuff, not a good

omen. Like himself, Hemingway did not appear to be a man easily won over. In fact, if what he had heard was true, this man wasn't impressed by much more than, say, a beautiful woman or the size of the fish you caught.

Impatient, he checked his watch and cursed under his breath. The morning was half gone, and he had a staff meeting, was supposed to speak to the recruits coming in from Santiago, check on the guns and money from Miami, talk strategy with Camilo and Che. *¡Dios mío!* it never ends. Celia, where is Celia?

Finally, she came with the coffee, careful so metal pot and cups wouldn't clang together, set them down, then left to prepare breakfast. Fidel nudged Papa in the belly with his boot, a playful gesture reserved for his closest comrades.

The old man woke with a start, red-rimmed eyes blinking, focusing on the boot prodding his girth. "What the hell you think I am?" he growled, "a fucking dog? Get your Goddamned foot outa my stomach!"

Fidel backed away, mouthing apologies, astonished, for he'd been taken the wrong way, then laughed nervously, trying to pass the whole thing off as a joke so he wouldn't let his wounded pride come between them.

"How funny you think it'd be if you got a knuckle sandwich?" His face was pale and still swollen from mosquito bites. He struggled up to a sitting position, leaned back against the tree. "Where the hell am I?"

"Near La Plata." Fidel kneeled, poured coffee, handed Papa a cup, then leaned close, put his large hands on the old man's shoulders, looked into his eyes. "Please, please, I'm sorry, I didn't mean to wake you suddenly, Señor Hemingway, but there is much to talk about and so little time."

Papa laced his coffee with scotch from his flask and drank. His color returned, his face softened. He drank again and smacked his lips. "Java ain't bad, no thanks to you."

"It grows here in the mountains," Fidel said proudly. "The best coffee in the world."

"You Castro, huh?"

He nodded vigorously, hands waving, still on the subject of coffee, explaining how the beans were picked, soaked, dried, then going on to the growers who gave M-26-7 the best of their crop and didn't want payment because they supported the revolution like everyone else in Oriente, but he insisted they accept money. The movement respects the people, pays for everything, takes advantage of no one.

Hemingway didn't respond. Just sat there glowering over the canteen cup as if he'd already made up his mind about the revolution.

Fidel smiled to hide his thoughts. Señor Hemingway doesn't like me, he told himself. Not me or anything he sees. He is not as open as his friend Matthews, who accepted us so readily. But he has come, he is here. That is the important thing. And I will persuade him because we are right, *patria o muerte.* "Breakfast, Señor Hemingway?" He offered his hand to pull him to his feet, but it was spurned.

"Don't need no help," Papa muttered, getting up. He swayed back and forth, hung on to the tree, steadying himself. "Goddamned blisters."

"We have a doctor." Fidel picked up his Springfield '03 with the telescopic sight, slung it, reached down for the pot and cups, started off, careful not to walk too fast, for he knew what blisters could do to a man's stride, not to mention his spirit.

"Nice piece you got there," said Papa.

Fidel grinned and was quick to show him the weapon, watched as he aimed the crosshairs at a tree a half mile away, knew he'd be able to see flowers and leaves quite distinctly. "I can pick off their soldiers at a thousand yards."

Papa grunted and handed the weapon back. "Blind man could pick 'em off with that much scope."

Fidel's face clouded over. He turned, moved close to Papa, eyes hard, inches away. "Are you saying I don't know how to shoot?"

Unfazed, Hemingway stared right back. "Lot of folks don't got the stomach for it."

All at once, Fidel grabbed him by the shoulders and shouted. "I don't need a telescope to kill a man!" He jerked out a silver-handled forty-five and waved it around. "I can get them with this, too! Or, or even a shotgun! Yes, give me a shotgun, I'll show you how to shoot!"

Papa smiled slowly. "Don't need no lessons, son. Not from nobody. Can still wing-shoot with the best of 'em."

Fidel stepped back and was quiet, anger replaced by a growing excitement, for suddenly he knew how he was going to win Hemingway over. So you like to shoot birds too, *viejo.* Then, yes, we will have the camaraderie of the hunt and from that common ground will come trust and admiration. From you, the grand old man of letters. Magazine articles will follow, good ones. In, say, *Field and Stream,* they will read a story about a sportsman with a passion for justice and liberty, not a biased political piece depicting a rebel leader that threatens American interests. In, in— Maybe Señor Hemingway will write something for *Life* magazine! Fidel couldn't contain himself and resumed walking at a brisk pace, imagining a photograph of him and Papa on the cover, holding strings of birds and grinning fondly at each other. Millions, millions of Yankees would then ask why their government was sending planes and tanks to Batista, the *asesino,* wouldn't they?

He turned and waited for the old man hobbling painfully after him. "Señor Hemingway!" he called. "In a few days when your feet are better, perhaps you'd like to go hunting?" He swept his arm across the green of meadows and forests that lay before them. "The best quail shooting in all of Cuba is right here in the Sierra!"

Six

"YOU'RE A COMMIE," said Papa, emptying his flask into his second cup of coffee. "A fucking commie."

They were sitting on upturned ammo boxes in a threadbare, two-room GP tent, the ground littered with cigar butts. He had one foot up on a canvas stool being dressed and bound by a rebel doctor with a wispy beard, long, dark hair spilling out from under a beret, and intense, feverish eyes suggesting magic. Castro had introduced him as, simply, Che. His hands were clean, his touch, gentle. Papa felt no pain and wondered how this man could concentrate while Castro stormed about, gesturing, spewing rhetoric, voice high and thin. Guess you get used to it and just turn it off, thought Papa, maybe that's what this guy, Che, does.

The small woman named Celia Sánchez came into the tent carrying a tray of food that smelled hot and good. She had a pretty face, fair skin, black hair to her shoulders, shorter than Che's. Her fatigue shirt was partially unbut-

51

toned so when she bent over and set the tray on Papa's lap, he got a quick shot of her breasts, but found them curiously unsexy. She's a tough little cookie, he told himself, and I'll bet none of these boys're getting any of it, not even Castro. He dug into the spread of eggs, bacon, rice and beans, spiced delicately with fresh mountain herbs and wild onions. Delicious. So she's tough, wears fatigues, and packs a pistol. Ain't forgot how to cook, no sir. Almost in the same league with Gregorio.

"I'm not a communist!" Fidel insisted, hands waving. "I'm a humanist!"

"Horseshit," said Papa between bites.

"He is not good enough to be Marxist," Che said quietly. "None of us are."

"There! You see?"

"At least, not yet." Che smiled, his eyes friendly, but far away.

Papa frowned. "What the hell you talking about?"

"Surely you must know, Señor Hemingway," Che replied. "Your guerrillas in *For Whom the Bell Tolls*—none of them, not even the American, lived up to their ideals, their beliefs, which is why they lost. That was your intent, no?"

Astonished, Papa stared at the philosophical young doctor, considering his interpretation. No, he hadn't planned anything that wise or insightful, but yes, you could read *The Bell* that way, and Jesus Christ, when you think about it for a second, it damn well *works*. He wanted to ask Che how he'd come to that conclusion, but couldn't, for Castro was shouting again, ordering Celia—now typing in the front room—to bring him the two gringo boys.

Ten minutes later, twins strolled into the tent's back room. Tall, well-built, overconfident seventeen-year-olds. Todd and David Blackburn, sons of Captain Willard Blackburn USN, had made their way from the Guantánamo Naval Base into the Sierra Maestra the day after they'd read about Fidel Castro in *The New York Times*. Todd—young, beautiful, striking blond hair and blue eyes, a pampered arrogance in the way he carried himself, a lackey of his more adventurous brother. Papa saw it immediately, nodded slowly. Looks like they ought to be in swim trunks instead of fatigues, he told himself, and carrying surfboards instead of used M-1's. But, no, here they were, all done up for someone else's war. It's a wonder they'll take orders from somebody who don't speak English.

"*¡Compañeros!* Meet Señor Ernest Hemingway!"

He didn't wait for the introductions. "This ain't no game, boys, you *do* understand that?"

They didn't hear.

"The movie version of *To Have and Have Not* was neato, sir," said David, his slang ruining the compliment for Papa.

"We got football scholarships to Yale in the fall, sir," chorused Todd.

"What the hell you doing here?"

"Helping to free the Cuban people," David replied airily.

What the fuck do you know about freedom? Papa almost said, but didn't, letting it go. He turned away and grimaced.

"*Hasta luego, compañeros,*" Fidel said affectionately, dismissing them.

Todd took his sweet time leaving the tent, not really moving until a nod from his brother, David, told him it was okay.

"So you got yourself a couple of Yalies, huh, Castro?"

"They understand," Fidel said vehemently, gesturing after the Blackburns. "They understand that we are only interested in democracy, free elections, and an end to colonialism, and yet your government supports Batista! Why?"

"Maybe Ike gets laid every time he visits Havana," Papa said sardonically. He finished eating, set his tray on the ground, fixed Fidel with a hard eye. "Face it. When him and his boys hear you talking about land reform, they're gonna call you a red. That's the gen of it."

"My revolution is as olive-green as the Sierra," he said stubbornly.

"Don't matter if it's as blue as the sky or how many Ivy Leaguers you sign up. Nobody's gonna listen to you."

"People listened to Matthews."

"College kids, housewives, librarians, and copy editors. Not the government."

Fidel gripped Papa by the shoulders. "Then perhaps you will tell them what we are, Señor Hemingway. They will listen to a Nobel prize winner, no?"

A slow, angry burn flushed Papa's face. He hadn't expected Castro to manipulate the conversation so easily and was embarrassed. He would've walked out of the tent right then except Che was still patching up his feet. "I don't write about politics," he grumbled. "Never have."

"I'm not asking you to write about politics," Fidel replied, totally sincere.

"Fidel?" said Celia, sticking her head through the door flap. "You are supposed to speak to the recruits from Santiago and then you have a staff meeting."

"Okay, okay *bueno. Momento!*" he replied, waving her away.

"You're already a half hour late," she said with irritation, then closed the flap.

"Women," apologized Fidel, throwing up his hands. "Thank God she is married to the revolution." He rose, grinned at Papa and patted him on the back. "We will talk again."

And then he was gone with his beloved rifle, leaving behind a swirl of cigar smoke, slate-blue in the shafts of light that came through holes in the tent.

Papa glared after him. "Sonuvabitch pisses me off."

Che just smiled and chuckled. "The true revolutionary is guided by strong feelings of love. He doesn't know that yet."

"Is he shacking up with her?"

"For the moment, they have separate bedrolls."

"Figures. She probably wants to be on top all the time."

Three days later, Papa was following Fidel along a trail that curved down through trees and brush, wet from rains of the night before. A photographer trotted behind them, complaining about the weather. Indeed, the morning was cold and dark. Their breaths blended with a heavy, damp fog that drifted up from the ocean. Footing was treacherous in the mud. Even Fidel slipped occasionally, and Papa didn't hesitate to laugh caustically. He was feeling pretty good right now, as if rebel youth and enthusiasm had rubbed off on him, lifting his spirit, his step. Not that his opinion of Castro had changed, though. While he hadn't seen that much of the leader since the first morning, their brief encounters so far had ended in Castro-style outbursts of demagoguery. Papa couldn't decide whether the man was satanic or messianic, yet there was no doubt he was political, and over the years Papa had learned never to trust a politician no matter what language he spoke. He was more impressed with Che, the doctor/guerrilla of fortune, a curious combination of a man who killed, then healed while speaking of utopian realities. And Camilo Cienfuegos, the tall, lanky one with the disarming smile and perpetual straw sombrero who'd once played minor-league ball in Texas. They seemed soft-spoken, commensurate heroes, and Papa wondered why they put up with Castro's bombast. Idle questions, for right now he didn't particularly give a damn. He was juiced. Ain't nothing political about wing shooting, he told himself, and I'm gonna kick his ass.

At the edge of the trees where the trail sloped onto a clearing was a crudely lettered sign reading, AQUI NACIÓ LA LIBERTAD DE CUBA, and Fidel wanted them to pose there for pictures, but Papa flat-out refused. Unflappable, Fidel said, perhaps on the way back, and then there was silence. No sounds except the intermittent shriek of a hawk, their boots squishing in the mud. They came to a river, crossed on the rocks. On the other side, the trail merged with a road that went by a cluster of burnt-out huts, black skeletons under sagging, corrugated roofs, the barracks at La Plata. Formerly. Fidel paused to describe the battle, the rebels' first victory. They had attacked at night, but encountered stiff resistance and were in danger of losing until Camilo and Che risked their lives by charging the enclave and firebombing one of the huts. The blaze silhouetted the soldiers, making them easy targets. Soon, they surrendered, and the rebels gained nine more Springfields, a machine gun and ammunition, not to mention self-esteem, and all without losing a man. Papa was mildly surprised. Not once during his account did Fidel raise his voice or wave his arms. Rather, he whispered, and Papa questioned whether he was obsessed by the pursuit of victory or death. There was no bullshit in the man's eyes, not now, here among the ghosts of Batista's finest.

They resumed walking, and fifteen minutes later passed the tiny hamlet of La Plata, just a few palm-thatched huts. In the road, geese honked and a lone rooster picked grubs out of the mud. Undernourished children hid behind their mother's sack dress, stared out at Papa, their brown eyes serious and afraid. An ancient farmer astride a grazing mule waved lazily, confirming that he was going nowhere.

The road paralleled the river for a ways, and Papa tried

to read it, wondering briefly how the fishing would be. Then Fidel angled off the road away from the river, through a grove of coffee trees and finally onto a wide, rolling meadow choked with grass and brush. Bird country. He stopped to drink from his canteen, handed it to Papa. He drank too, watched Castro break open the .410, drop in two shells, snap it shut. He did likewise, heard the faint drone of a spotter plane.

"Now you sure they ain't gonna hear us shootin' and call in the Goddamn air force."

"Bah!" Castro spat and lifted a contemptuous finger to the skies.

"What about the army?"

"They are not within ten miles of here. We have listening posts."

The hunters zigzagged into the meadow, Fidel explaining that they would take turns shooting, regardless of who flushed the quail, and Señor Hemingway would go first since he was a guest of the new Cuba. Papa nodded agreeably, excitement building inside. He raised his gun to the port position, ears perked for the first sign. The fog hadn't lifted, so it was hard to see; he was conscious of Fidel's boots swishing through the wet grass, the photographer's camera clicking.

A sudden rustle.

Off to his left sixty yards away. A buzz of wings. Four of them exploded out of the bush, taking off at different angles, and he slanted the gun down, quick-sighted over the barrels, fired, knew he dropped one but no time to look, swung up, aimed at the others almost gone, fired again, got the straggler. Goddamn, a double, he congratulated himself silently. What the hell, so the bird was fat and slow. A double is a double, and I'll take two for two, not bad for openers, huh, boys? He raised his hand in triumph.

Fidel acknowledged, but did not speak. Tight-lipped, he

removed his horn-rimmed glasses, cleaned them with a bandana, put them back on, continued moving. His turn.

Papa bagged his birds, heard the whirr, looked up just in time to see Fidel shoot, spin, shoot again. One of his .410 loads got two, so three quail fell from the sky.

"Tres," he said happily.

I'll be damned, Papa thought. Fucker can actually shoot. Gonna make it interesting. You bet. Ain't had a match in wing shooting since you went out for pheasant with the boys up in Sun Valley.

"What do you think of *Life* magazine?" Fidel called while reloading.

"Okay rag if you like pictures," snapped Papa, his tone ending any chance of conversation. *Not here to talk, son, here to shoot, here to show you what I learned before you were born. Not in a rocking chair on a porch somewhere dreaming of gone moments or bragging to old cronies. Here for the long haul, and that's the gen of it. The best is yet to come, for that's the only way life makes any sense. The best is—* Quail rustled, then flew out of the grass, veeing apart. He fired, spun, fired again, shots so close together they sounded as one. Four birds dropped. All atingle, he stepped light and young through the brush, then picked up the birds and hefted them before placing them in the bag. He swallowed, his saliva tasting good and clean, then chuckled happily.

"Jeez Chrise, a four-bagger!" he said out loud, "a fucking home run!"

Very impressed, Fidel turned to the photographer—the only other witness—and spread his hands. *"Dios mio,* this old man can shoot! How can he write such beautiful books and still know how to shoot?"

And so it went. The hunters slowly crossed the long meadow, took turns shooting, rarely missed. Occasionally, Fidel asked a question, but Papa didn't answer. He liked to hunt quietly so he could merge with his environs, listen to the brush and grass, sense when the next bird would take flight.

The photographer trailed them, his camera clicking incessantly. Papa was annoyed, and felt exploited, knowing the pictures would be published. The world would see him and Castro hunting together and assume automatically that the distinguished Ernest "Nobel Prize" Hemingway approved of the Cuban rebels. Well, bullshit, Papa told himself. I'll have to make a deal with him. An article for the negatives, straight across. Then do an innocuous piece for someone like *Field and Stream* saying that Castro's a pretty damned good shot for a commie.

He didn't have to. While maneuvering for an angle, the photographer accidentally flushed quail from a briar thicket, and it was Papa's turn. He whirled around, aimed just over the man's head, and fired. Astonished, the photographer threw up his hands, lurched backward, and for an instant his camera was airborne. Papa blew it apart with his second shot.

Fidel guffawed and pointed at the photographer spread-eagled in the briar, making a huge joke of it until he realized Papa had bagged a Kodak instead of a quail. Anguished, he held the ruined film as if it were a dying pet, then turned. "What did you do, *¡Dios mío!* what did you do?"

Papa shrugged, deadpanned, "Looks like I flat-out missed."

The hunt continued. Fidel said nothing, and Papa figured he was mad as hell. True. He missed his next two shots, easy ones, the birds right in his face. He cursed the skies, the earth, the photographer, the birds, Batista even, then lit a cigar, composed himself, finally nodded to Papa.

My turn, and we're all tied up, Papa said to himself. Seventeen each. I can bury him with a couple more doubles, he'll never catch me, he's too pissed off to shoot straight.

"Fidel! Fidel!" someone yelled. *"¡Batistianos!"*

Startled, they turned, and Papa saw a *barbudo* sprinting toward them from out of the trees.

"¡Vienen, vienen! ¡Y rapido!" He ran by a bush. Quail flew out, rising fast and light.

Papa swung his shotgun up, took a quick breath, aimed.

"No!" said Fidel, holding his hand up. "Not now!"

Bullshit, not now, I'm gonna win this fucking *mano a mano*. Papa fired twice, got two more birds, but as he stepped around Fidel, the big man grabbed him, pulled him close, his face intense, inches away.

"¡Estúpido!" Fidel screamed angrily. "The army is coming and you shoot quail? When I said no? You are an old fool, Señor Hemingway, a pigheaded idiot gringo *viejo!"*

Papa didn't care that the danger was real, that Fidel was genuine, just felt his own rage take over, and before he could stop himself, delivered a short, straight left to Castro's bearded chops with all the power of the old days.

Fidel sat down in the grass, blinked, held his jaw, then looked up, strangely calm. "You are too old to fight, Señor Papa, too old."

Astounded, Papa glanced from Castro to his fist and back again, not quite believing he'd just decked the rebel leader, yet overjoyed he still had enough *cojones* to lay out a bigger man half his age. His heart sang. Smiling foolishly, he bent over to offer a hand—to say he was sorry, but nobody talked to him like that and got away with it—when the machine gun opened up, and Fidel pulled him down into the mud instead. Furious, he raised himself up intending to fight, only to see the bullets tattoo the photographer's chest, then slam into the *barbudo*. Both fell dead, and Papa pushed his face back into the mud.

Close by, a forty-five barked twice. No more machine-gun fire. Papa looked up. Pistol in hand, Fidel zigzagged fast toward the trees. Three soldiers appeared, shouted, raised their M-1's. Castro shot one, dropped behind a bush, rolled just ahead of their return fire, shot the other two, was up again and into the trees. A silence. Only the wind sighing through leaves, the distant drone of an aircraft. Then Papa heard one of the soldiers crying in pain, praying to the Virgin Mother, calling for his sister, voice gurgling, a clear sign he would die, and he sounded frightened. Papa crawled over to him, but there was nothing to be done. Half the soldier's back was gone; his life drained into the thick, wet grass. He died badly, face twisted in agony.

Papa shuddered. What had this one left behind? Or was he young enough not to have treasured life, savored its vivid colors, tasted its joys, like, say, the open arms, the warmth of a woman? Disgusted, he turned away, didn't know what to think.

Another shot broke the stillness. Papa dove to the ground. Then, nothing. Slowly, he rose to his hands and knees, listened. The soft wind, water dripping. A bird chattered. Sweating now, he picked up the dead soldier's rifle, chambered a round, metal on metal sounding overly loud. He peered at the dark curtain of trees, bent on defending himself if he had to, feeling naked, the stench of death fouling the sweet air of the green meadow. He imagined soldiers eyeing him, waiting for him to bolt so they'd have the sport of a moving target, his composure coming apart because he didn't know what the fuck was going on, but no, he told himself, don't let it happen, not in these mountains where young men die for dreams. Goddamnit, Hem, you will not be afraid. If they were gonna shoot, you would've been dead five minutes ago.

He stood, faced the tree line, rifle at the ready. Okay, boys, here I am, the real Hemingstein, let's boogie-woogie.

Rustling. He turned quickly, was too surprised to fire, for Fidel came out of the woods *behind* him, leading two prisoners, one so scared he'd shit his pants, the other in shock with a bleeding hand. Grinning confidently, Fidel carried their rifles and was puffing on a fresh cigar.

Papa couldn't help but admire the big rebel leader. Jesus H. Christ, he thought, this *guajiro* ain't no slouch. First, he saves your ass from a machine gun, then takes out the crew, drops three more of Batista's bozos, shoots the gun out of another's hand, captures him and his buddy. Helluva day's work, if I don't say so myself.

He watched Fidel rip the shirt off a dead soldier and use it to bind the hand of his wounded prisoner, all the while talking to both captives of the revolution, imploring them not to fight against something good, just, and necessary. His voice was only a whisper, yet rich and sincere. Transfixed, they hung on every word, exchanged looks of astonishment when he told them they were free to go. Without your weapons, you understand, of course. And, *por favor,* tell your comrades we are not the enemy. *"Es Batista, el asesino."*

Shaken, relieved, in total disbelief—no doubt they'd been told M-26-7 murdered prisoners—they cried profuse thanks, then turned and ran.

Moments later, a squad of *barbudos* hurried across the meadow, anxious for the safety of their leader. He belittled their concern, saying that the movement was all of them, not one. Papa wondered, having seen three wars and a lot of action. What this Castro boy had pulled off ranked right up there with the finest fighting he'd ever seen. No indecision, no fear, no bullshit.

Now Fidel was heading back into the trees, explaining that the presence of the army patrol was a serious breach of their perimeter. Something had gone wrong. They must solve the problem quickly or there would be other patrols. The squad fanned out behind him, moving quickly, silently, blending with the foliage, and had Papa not been so close, he would not have known they were there.

An hour later, they neared an outpost. Fidel signaled the squad to halt. Automatically, the point slithered twenty yards ahead, whistled twice to make contact. The call went unanswered. Frowning, Fidel motioned the men forward. They advanced across a sun-dappled clearing, came to a lean-to built against a giant rock face. Papa heard the buzz of a thousand insects, once again caught the stink of the old whore. Three *barbudos* were sprawled inside, covered with ants and flies, their throats slashed, bodies mutilated, dried blood everywhere. A few rebels turned away and vomited.

"¡Dios mío!" whispered Fidel, "how could this've happened? The sentry!"

Mortified, he went on, followed by the others. Papa stayed with them, also wondering how the soldiers had managed to surprise the outpost without being detected first. What the hell, he told himself, a sentry is a sentry. Normally.

Yet when they reached the sentry's post, they found no sign that anyone had been there. No sign of violence, either.

Fidel turned to the squad leader, his eyes black and hard. "This morning. Who had the watch?"

"Compañero David Blackburn."

The Yankee kid. Trouble in paradise. They all assumed he'd been killed too, but Papa wasn't so sure, given the American mentality. He doubted that the kid had flat-out deserted, for in their own way, West Coast surfer types were just as macho as *cubanos.*

Dismayed, Fidel exhorted the squad to find the gringo body before Batista's soldiers had a chance to show it to the press and claim the *norteamericano* was murdered by M-26-7. "If we must attack, then we will," he said firmly and sent a man back for reinforcements.

The search began. Soon, they left the trees behind. On the edge of the vast, rolling *campo* was a *campesino*'s house. Small, wood frame, thatched roof, chickens and geese in the yard. A goat bawled. Except for the animals, it appeared that no one was there, yet smoke wafted from the chimney. Castro signaled to his men, and they surrounded the place. He walked boldly through the gate to the greasy canvas flap serving as a door, stood there, hands on his hips.

"Buenas."

No answer.

He took out his pistol, eased off the safety, stepped inside. Papa followed. The main room was empty, but a fire smoldered and remnants of a meal were on the table, still warm. Too late in the day for a *campesino* to eat, Papa figured. Hell, he's miles away, working his cattle or something. Then they heard stirrings, light snores from the back bedroom, and went to look.

David Blackburn's rifle leaned in the corner, his boots and fatigues strewn about the floor. Asleep on a straw mat, he was entwined with a buxom peasant girl, his flesh stark white against her nut-brown skin.

The room reeked of sex.

Papa glanced at a curiously impassive Fidel, then looked back at the lovers, shook his head sardonically. Way to go, kid. Way to play vigilant Cuban guerrilla.

Seven

"WHY SHOULD WE bother to give him a trial?" said Fidel, wiping the grease off his beard, reaching for another spit-roasted quail. The GP tent was warm and clean, smelled of cigar smoke, rum, and food. Their faces were orange in the lantern light, and behind them, Celia strummed a lonely guitar. "Why?"

"He's an American."

"Does that make him any less guilty?"

"For someone who supposedly understands politics," Papa responded, "you're sure as hell naïve when it comes to Uncle Sam."

That annoyed Fidel, but he didn't say anything, just continued eating slowly, pausing occasionally to drink rum from his canteen cup while *el viejo* tried to explain.

Young gringos never get laid at home, he was saying. They don't know how, yet are tortured by a society overflowing with sexual innuendos. To make matters worse, American girls dress to tease—tight sweaters and skirts, heavy makeup, their apparent goal to transform boys into perpetual red-faced hard-ons following them around like pets, begging for it while they never come across. In the USA, the only way a guy can get a piece of ass is to save a month's allowance, then find a whore—usually, a Negro—sympathetic enough to let him do it as opposed to having him rolled. So, when you unleash a gringo kid in Cuba or any other exotic locale it's like giving him carte blanche at a sexual soda fountain. Not only are the whores plentiful, cheap, and happy, but *all* the women are willing. Getting laid ain't no big deal down here. Why the hell you think the krauts've always had a love affair with Latin America?

"What does that have to do with your Uncle Sam?"

"Everything." Papa belched, then took a long pull off the rum bottle. "The dumbest thing you could've done was give that kid a uniform and a gun. Of course he's gonna go out and find the *campesino*'s daughter! It's a lifelong fantasy! Like putting on pinstripes and playing for the Yankees!"

"Five of us are dead because he left his post!"

"You think he's gonna worry about his pals when his brains're between his legs?"

Disgusted, Fidel shook his head, spat bones onto his metal plate. Enough of this nonsense, he told himself. Yankee prudishness didn't concern him. Neither did David Blackburn's motives. Pure and simple, the gringo would pay for his crime, and the penalty was death.

"At least give him a trial for the folks back home."

"He should not be treated any differently than a *cubano* deserter," Fidel said emphatically.

"Goddamnit," Papa roared, "he *is* different! He comes from the most powerful country in the world and, right or wrong, that gives him privileges, understand?"

"Didn't some *norteamericano* once say 'all men are created equal'?" Fidel replied caustically.

"That's bullshit, and you know it!" Papa drank more rum, wiped his mouth with the back of his hand. "Maybe I was wrong about you, Castro. You're too damned unrealistic to be a commie."

Fidel leaned forward, eyes afire. "If I let the gringo go free, will your Uncle Sam stop sending tanks and planes to Batista?" He jabbed Papa in the chest. "Huh, Señor Hemingway?"

"Probably not."

"Then to hell with your government!" he said contemptuously, lighting a cigar. "We shall win despite them and Batista!"

"So fucking what?" Papa said brutally, his weathered face tense and strained.

"What do you mean, 'So—'"

"Wait a minute, damnit!" he said sharply. "Just wait a minute and hear me out!"

Fidel glared at Papa, felt that slow, dangerous burn start in his gut, yet held his tongue, puffed on his cigar, and listened.

"There is no perfect way to run things, Castro, never has been, never will. The common people always get screwed, no matter who's in charge. Call the boy on top what you will—king, emperor, president, prime minister, secretary general, chief, generalissimo—nothing changes on the bottom, especially here in Cuba, and that's the straight gen of it."

"I agree with you!" shouted Fidel. "That's why we are fighting, that's why we are here in the Sierra Maestra!" Unable to contain himself, he jumped up and paced the room, speaking forcefully, gesturing broadly as if rehearsing for an opera. "My *compañeros* are not like Batista's butchers! We will not rule by terror, we will not line our own pockets at the people's expense, we will not gun down dissent in the streets, we will not sell our souls to U.S. business interests, we will not kowtow to anyone, we will not be an offshore Yankee whorehouse. Not anymore. Not if I have anything to say about it!"

A long silence, broken only by Celia's soft, pretty voice over the guitar. *"Cuba, que linda es Cuba, que la defienda, que la quiere más . . ."*

The two eyed each other like opponents in the ring. Finally, Papa spoke, his words heavy and conclusive. "Six bits says the boys you put in'll be just as bad as the ones you kick out."

Jolted, Fidel stepped back, couldn't say anything. It had never occurred to him that someone would equate him and M-26-7 with Batista and the SIM, yet he knew Hemingway's statement had the weight of history behind it, the logic being all revolutions were eventually corrupted, so why should his be any different? He didn't have a good answer. Perhaps he should just walk away after they won. Let others chart the course. After all, the only revolutionary heroes he could think of who remained heroes were Martí and Sandino, men whose careers were too brief for the experts to criticize. He paused, examined his cigar butt, flicked it into the dirt, stared at the lantern, then thought, is that why you're doing this, *chico?* To be a hero? Have you put your life on the line to look good in the newspapers, the history books? Why this constant danger, this constant turbulence instead of the *finca* your father wanted you to have? You and your brother would've been gentlemen farmers. Because it's all part of the process, he told himself. Ever since the early days at the university when you stood toe to toe with thugs who called themselves cops, ever since the violence at Moncada, there has been no turning back. They would not've let you. No, you don't oppose them to be a hero. You fight because your alternatives are death or cowardice.

And what of love? He thought of Mirta and his son, Fidelito, now somewhere on Long Island, snug and secure amid Yankee complacency. When he was in solitary confinement on the Isle of Pines, she had betrayed him by going to work for the *asesino*'s dictatorship, and he had divorced her immediately. Often, while doing time in "the humiliation of the shadows," he had heard rumors from his guards that she was coupling indiscriminately with high government officials, and his soul had been scarred permanently. *Es verdad,* he might still long for her, but he would never forgive her. And Celia? Everyone thought they were lovers, but, no, they only lived together because it was expedient. Like her, he was married to the revolution. Now, the only love he felt was that sweet oneness with eternity that touched him every time he sighted an enemy soldier through his scope and squeezed the trigger. No matter how absurd, death remained his love, his moral companion. I kill because it is just. Yet, I want to live because my life too is just.

"We will be the first," he said, squatting on the ammo box. "The first honest government Cuba has ever known."

Papa munched on another bird, fixed him with a jaundiced eye. "Ain't holding my breath, son."

Fidel glowered at the old man, but refused to lose his temper. You can't persuade a stubborn man, he told himself, you have to show him the way, and that too is a process. He poured himself more rum, drank, deftly changed the subject by patting his thick girth and grinning. "Good quail, no?"

"Always thought the best thing about Cuba was the red snapper cooked by Gregorio." Papa swallowed another bite of quail breast, washed it down with rum, licked his fingers, then nodded in Celia's direction. "If I was you, I wouldn't let her out of the kitchen no matter what happened to my revolution."

Fidel laughed, leaned over the lantern, grasped the old man by the shoulders. "Maybe someday I'll taste one of your Gregorio's dinners."

"Maybe." His eyes twinkled. "Got to catch it first, though."

"I'm a better fisherman than I am a hunter."

"So am I, son."

"Then someday we'll have to go fishing," Fidel replied expansively.

"Yep." He drank, then laughed. "'Course your boys'll have to take a seaport first."

Fidel smiled, appreciating the humor. "We'll change our strategy." He waved his hands. "We won't attack any town unless it is a fishing village."

"I'll drink to that." He did.

Is he becoming personable, Fidel asked himself, or am I hearing things?

"Fidel," Celia called. *Es la hora.*

He checked his watch and stood. In ten minutes, he was scheduled to speak to the nation over Radio Rebelde. He had no idea what he was going to say, but that wasn't a problem. The Jesuits had honed his natural gift for oratory when he was just a boy, at school in Belén. Now, he could speak extemporaneously for hours and never once lose the thread, the theme. Even his enemies gave him credit for that.

He slung his rifle, said goodbye to Celia, and left the tent. There were no clouds outside; the stars were bright, yellowish even. Like a thousand cats watching him, waiting, listening. He shivered and assumed it was the cold night air.

Papa followed, bringing along the rum for companionship. "Christ Almighty! Gets downright nippy up here, don't it?"

"We will find you a jacket, *viejo*," he said kindly.

"Don't do me any favors, Castro, I've been a lot colder than this."

Fidel shrugged easily, didn't let the comment annoy him. He was growing used to Hemingway's caustic behavior and wondered again how such a closed-minded person had managed to write so many beautiful books. It didn't occur to him that Papa Hemingway wasn't closed-minded at all. It didn't occur to him that Papa Hemingway was hiding behind an image just as he, himself, became an image when, say, he spoke on the radio. He hadn't lived long enough to separate Fidel, the man, from Fidel, the myth. No, it never occurred to him that behind that legendary toughness, Papa Hemingway was still trying desperately to become what everyone thought he was.

Five minutes later, they came to a black shape that was another GP tent pitched under huge trees shielding it from the sky. The sound of a foot-cranked generator emanated from inside along with a faint glow from a lantern in the back room.

Inside was Che, sharing a bottle of scotch with Camilo and reading poetry over the airwaves while a silhouetted *barbudo* pedaled furiously in the corner. It was a long Pablo Neruda poem paying homage to Jesus Christ, the original revolutionary, the archetype for subsequent freedom fighters, including José Martí, a poet himself. Che half sang the lines, a dreamlike expression in his eyes that never failed to unnerve Fidel because he couldn't figure it out. He glanced quickly from Che to Papa, was about to apologize for this embarrassment when he saw that the old man tacitly approved.

"You see?" he whispered ebulliently to Papa. "There is a place for everyone in our revolution. Even poets."

When Che finished his reading, Fidel sat down in front of the microphone, then proceeded to describe in vivid detail an M-26-7 offensive that hadn't started yet. He spoke for an hour and a half of skirmishes and victories, heroes even, all fancies of his imagination, knowing full well his reports would be published in the newspapers, then denied by the government and—for that reason—believed by the people. At times during the lengthy broadcast, he corrected himself, as if someone were handing him updated dispatches. Out of the corner of his eye he saw Camilo chuckling with admiration and shaking his head. Fidel winked back at his comrade, then concluded his elaborate fabrication with a blur of gestures, a litany of animated rhetoric.

Yes, it was an enormous joke, but not without purpose. He had thought of the tactic shortly after the hoopla surrounding Herbert Matthews's articles in *The New York Times*. Batista's defense minister had called them a "chapter in a fantastic novel," denying that Señor Castro was alive and the existence of the embryonic revolution, touching off a heated controversy throughout the island, showing himself to be a complete fool when the facts proved him wrong. The incident confirmed Fidel's respect for the power of the press—you don't gain recognition by overrunning lonely outposts in the mountains; you do by making the front page of the *Times*. More important, the government's credibility had been destroyed. If they denied rebel successes, which they did blindly, the people accepted them, just as blindly. Truth and falsehood had no meaning. Not according to the press. People believed what seemed convincing or fashionable. Never forget that, *chico*, never. Radio Rebelde is more than the voice of the new Cuba, much more. It is a weapon firing impressions that mold the minds of listeners no matter whose side they're on. And no, you are not deceiving anyone, for the events you speak of are inevitable. He got up, went over to Che, Camilo, and Papa, sat down on a camp stool, used the lantern to light a fresh cigar.

"Where'd you learn to lie like that?" asked Papa, taking the scotch from Camilo, drinking, passing it to Che.

"I went to Catholic school," Fidel retorted with a smile, then leaned close and explained. "You must understand, I was only describing what is going to happen."

"Don't care how you justify it, you flat-out lied," Papa said disgustedly. "How the hell can you talk about an honest government?"

"Sometimes the truth can be deceiving," said Che, "sometimes it plays into the hands of the right wing."

"Ain't interested in left and right. Right and wrong is more my style."

"But your books," replied Che, his eyes bright, intense. "Your books are not real, yet that doesn't make them any less significant, no?"

"I don't pass my stuff off as something it ain't," snapped Papa. "Sure, I write fiction, but damnit, I'm going for, for something truer than reality."

Fidel spread his hands. "That's exactly what we are doing, Señor Papa, only we use the radio instead of a typewriter."

Che interrupted. Impassioned, he spoke of a new, utopian society with none of the constraints found in the world today. Everyone would own everything instead of the majority being slaves for a privileged few. Money would not exist. Goods and services would be free. Relationships would become fluid, families no longer rigid enclaves. Love would take precedence over tradition and an artificial code of morality. Crime and war would cease to exist. Man would be free to create new forms of art and technology. "Work as we know it will become obsolete."

"Sounds great," Papa said cynically. "Where the hell you

gonna find people who'll live in your town without fucking it up?"

"We must make a new man," an unfazed Che replied. "A twenty-first-century man."

"I dunno." The old man remained skeptical. He pursed his lips, stroked his beard, reached for the scotch. "Twenty-first-century man, huh? Don't suppose he could be any worse than the one we've already got."

"Then why don't you tell that to the American people?" said Fidel, his eyes locked on Papa.

He didn't flinch. Just glared back. Finally said, "Maybe."

The conversation drifted to things men usually talked about when they were drinking together. With Fidel's encouragement, Papa rehashed their bird hunt, boasting of his prowess with the shotgun. Then Camilo reminisced about playing ball in the States, unable to speak English, yet understanding the language on the field which was all that was important. It turned out they were all old ballplayers except for Che, who had spent his salad days hitchhiking around Latin America to escape the stress of medical school. They all shared similar tastes in women too, Papa waxing eloquent on his string of wives and lovers. He didn't talk about Mary, though, and Fidel knew why. One never bragged about what was close to the heart, not a real man, anyway. Such memories were either too personal, or too painful. Damn you, Mirta, why couldn't you have loved me as I loved you? They all think I sacrificed you for the movement. They don't know that you cast the first stone. They don't know that I fell in love with the revolution because there was nowhere else to turn. You betrayed me. Yes, you hated me for Moncada, for wrenching your life apart, how could you look your friends and relatives in the eye with a husband in prison, one they called a communist gangster? Will you hate me when I march into Havana and take your former lovers to the *paredón?* I hope so, and for what I do, *la historia me absolverá.* He reached for the scotch, took a long drink, was silent until this talk of women passed.

Much later, Camilo and Che rose unsteadily, apologized for the hour, left for their bedrolls. Papa tried to keep the night going, but had a thirty-year disadvantage aggravated by too much rum and scotch. He rolled off his camp stool, belched, hit the ground out cold, his snores raising small clouds of dust. Fidel put a pillow under his head, covered him with a blanket, then studied him as one would a painting in an art museum. Yes, Fidel thought, he is old and tired, mean and cynical, rude and distrustful. Still, he remains full of life and spirit—why couldn't my father have been like him?

The dawn came, gray light filtering in through the tent seams. Fidel relit his cigar, blew out the lantern, stood, stretched, then left the tent and went back to his hut knowing that Celia would have coffee waiting. As he walked in, he saw that she had cleaned up after him and frowned. Always, she keeps the place spotless, why? She's worse than a mother waiting like a sentinel for you to leave your room so she can hang up your clothes, make your bed, dust and sweep. Defiantly, he dropped his cigar butt on the floor, ground it into the dirt. Why do I surround myself with such stubbornness? "Because she's more loyal than any of them," he said to himself. *"Gracias a Dios,* you are not fucking her—she would demand perfection."

After breakfast, the *barbudos* were waiting for him by the GP tent, loose and relaxed, not in a formation, yet together nonetheless, in unique M-26-7 style. When he stood in front of them, they quieted down automatically. He paused for a moment to look at their faces, each one individually.

Suddenly, Todd Blackburn rushed forward, his face twisted with rage and fear. "Please, Fidel, please! Don't let them do it! Don't let them!" He looked haggard and unkempt and had been drinking all night, his self-assurance lost when he learned that his brother was going to die. Just as he reached for Castro's hand, two *barbudos* grabbed him and jerked him back with the others. He began sobbing and shouting incoherently. "No, please, no, it's not his fault! They, they— The patrol should've been more careful! No, please, no!"

They brought his brother, David, forward, tied his hands, left him in front of the old tree by the tent.

Fidel had planned to make a speech about the responsibilities of a revolutionary soldier, the penalties for misconduct, but decided against it. They all knew it anyway, and the puling display of the condemned's brother was getting to him.

"You can't do this!" Todd screamed. "You're as bad as my father, you—!"

Someone clamped a hand over his mouth. Another *barbudo* pushed him to the ground, and they held him there.

"Who wants to shoot the gringo?" Fidel said flatly.

Rafael Cruz stepped forward, the avowed Stalinist who had gone to school in Moscow with Fidel's brother, Raúl, now a platoon leader. Cruz was a small, wiry man who hated Yankees just because they were Yankees. He looked at Todd Blackburn and spat contemptuously. *"Maricón."*

Then he strolled over to David, took out his pistol, and shot him twice. Once in the face, once in the groin.

The next day, it came as no surprise to Fidel when Todd Blackburn was reported missing.

Eight

"WHAT DO I think of Fidel Castro?" Papa responded, pausing to knock back another *definitivo* and chase it with beer. "I think he's an asshole."

They were in the Floridita at the far end of the dark mahogany bar, near the wall, a fifth of Gordon's in front of Papa. Already he was feeling the hootch even though he'd only had a few, for he'd gone on the wagon since coming back from the Sierra Maestra, determined to whip himself into shape, firmly convinced that that was the only way he'd ever be able to write the big book. So, he'd been swimming every morning, was up to a mile and a half. His weight and blood pressure were down, and he was thinking clearly again. Except he didn't know how to start, wasn't even sure what the big book should be about. When he pushed the recall button, nothing happened. He found himself staring at blank pages, the cotsies, dog, palm trees, overcast sky. To pass the time, he wrote letters, waited for the inspiration, and agonized. Was it even there, in his heart?

The *Atlantic Monthly* called, wanting a contribution for their centenary issue, so he began a memoir of the early days with Scott Fitzgerald, then stopped because it was too personal. He couldn't lie about what that woman, Zelda, had done to one of the most talented writers of the century, recalling that night in the men's room at Michaud's when Scott bared his soul. According to Zelda, he was lousy in the sack and had the smallest cock she'd ever seen. Nope, you can't let the world know that sort of stuff, can't betray a friend six feet under.

Matthews had called then. Was back in Cuba to get more straight gen on the chaos that gripped their paradise. Despite a driving rainstorm and gale-force winds that pasted the trees, Papa met him at the Floridita a half hour later and began drinking immediately, hoping to drown his frustration.

His liver started hurting, just like the doctor said. To hell with it, never liked liver anyway, he told himself and poured another shot. Old Doc Herrera could go to hell too, and now Matthews wanted to talk about the Castro boy. "Surprised they let you back in the country, Herb."

"I'm not."

"How you figure?"

"Ike's still picking up Batista's tab," Matthews replied, sipping his Papa Doble, the drink made famous by none other than the grizzled E.H. And, as long as that were the case, he continued, the general was obliged to pass himself off as a democratic leader with nothing to hide, no reason for censorship, instant visa for the señor from *The New York Times*.

"Ain't you worried about the SIM boys?"

He smiled piously. "Not anymore, Hem. I'm too damned famous to disappear."

Papa roared with laughter and pounded his friend on the back. He was starting to feel good. "I like you, Matthews, you know how to read the minds of small men."

"Doesn't mean they're not listening, though." He nodded in the direction of the restaurant tables separated from the bar by a row of potted palms.

Papa followed his look. One was at a table, nursing coffee, half hidden behind a copy of *Prensa Libre*. The other lounged in the corner by the glass door, gazing out at the rain, checking his watch occasionally, as if waiting for someone. Cuban feds. Hair greased back into ducktails, starched and pressed *guayaberas,* brown pegged pants and mirror shades. Between them, in a booth, a brush-cut tourist wearing a button-down shirt and Bermudas was getting felt up by a lackluster *puta* twice his age while nearby a waiter served fresh oysters to New England newlyweds. The scene didn't surprise Papa; if anything, it struck him as symbolic. All that was missing were the musicians on a cigarette break in the kitchen.

But the feds. He couldn't shake their presence; they made him self-conscious and nervous. He felt guilty as hell even though he hadn't been accused of anything. Jesus H. Christ, he said to himself, can't even relax at the Floridita no more.

"Hem," Matthews said knowingly, jerking his thumb over his shoulder. Papa looked in the mirror behind the bar. Three more feds had materialized at restaurant tables. Grumbling, he stood up and faced them, expecting a reaction. Instead, they looked *through* him, acting as if he weren't even there. Unnerved, Papa turned, ran out the door toward the big Chrysler, both angry and afraid. If he confronted them, they would feign shock and innocence, and everyone would assume he was drunk and crazy, which was worse than doing nothing at all.

Breathing heavily, Matthews caught up with him. "They're not after you, Hem!"

"Don't flatter yourself, Matthews!"

"The joke's on them because they can't do anything to you *or* me!"

"That's bullshit, Herb!" He got into the car, leaving the door open so he could yell at his friend. "There ain't no difference between the feds here and the ones you saw in Spain and Germany except the caliber of their weapons!"

"You telling me I can't have a private conversation in the Floridita anymore?"

"Not about Fidel Castro." Papa tried to shove the key in the ignition, but missed, having had one *definitivo* too many. He slid across the seat to the passenger side. "You wanna talk, you drive."

Matthews climbed in behind the wheel, and soon they were cruising along the Malecón, Papa checking constantly to see if they were being followed. He crossed his legs and winced in pain. The weather was raising hell with his bad knee. Too damned hot and humid for the end of May, he told himself. You'd think the Goddamn rain would make a difference.

"You were saying?"

"No quotes, okay, Herb?"

"Off the record. Completely."

Papa took a deep breath, then sighed. "The man's impatient, arrogant, closed-minded, stubborn, and a fucking genius."

"You describing Fidel Castro or Ernest Hemingway?"

"Watch your mouth, Herb!" Papa growled, then glanced out the rear window again. "The sonuvabitch'll use anyone to get ahead, whether it's you, me, CBS, or *The New York Times.*"

"Does he have a choice?"

"Nope," Papa conceded, "not unless he wants to spend the rest of his days in the Circular."

"He's got a family, he wants to live."

"I'm not so sure, Herb, not so sure . . . He never talked about himself. Only the fucking movement, the people."

"You think he's a communist?"

"Right now he's whatever you want him to be," Papa replied, his face flushed and sweaty. He cracked the window for some air. "Say one thing, though. He's definitely got rain."

"Rain?"

"Juice and *cojones,*" he said impatiently as if Matthews were thickheaded. "When it comes to a firefight, the boy's a natural-born leader." He paused thoughtfully as Matthews pulled into the Hotel Nacional's circular drive and cut the engine. "Dunno if he's gonna win, though."

"The whole country's behind him, Hem!"

"I'm not so sure about that, either. All I know is, if Castro keeps leading his own raids, he's gonna catch one between the eyes sooner than later. He oughta start acting more like a general than a second looey, but he won't listen to no one," Papa stated, his breath fogging the windows. "Too busy flirting with the old whore, and if he ain't teasing her, he's feeding her fresh meat."

Matthews turned slowly and frowned. "What the hell're you talking about?"

Briefly, Papa told what had happened to David Blackburn, a dumb American teenager Castro had no business signing up in the first place. "Kid got caught with his pants down, and the revolution blew his balls off. No phone call, no trial, no Yale, class of sixty-two."

The correspondent listened carefully, pursing his lips, then looked critically at Hemingway. "How's that any different from that SS POW on the Cologne plain who told you you didn't have the courage to shoot just before you blew his brains out?"

"Different," mumbled Papa. He fell silent, looked away, and blushed. You don't understand, Herb, he admitted to himself, I never shot that kraut, never even captured him! That was all bullshit from the Hotel Ritz bar or Rue Scribe or one of those places. A cocktail war story. He scowled, not wanting to be reminded of past exploits—some heroic and true, others false, most embellished—not wanting to face himself, not yet. "Thought you wanted to talk about Castro."

"Just making a point."

"Yeah? Well, you know what, Herb?" he said, his jaw thrust forward belligerently. "I think you're fulla shit!"

Wisely, Matthews didn't respond, except to get out of the car. He paused by the open door, his kind smile saying there was no use in talking further. Not now. "Gotta go, Hem."

Embarrassed, Papa started to apologize, but the door closed with a gentle click. Once again, the booze had spoken. Of course, Matthews had been right when he made the parallel, yet how could he know that some of the Hemingway legend was, at best, mediocre fiction?

He got out of the car, but his friend was already gone. The curved facade of the Nacional blurred, confirming that he was in no shape to drive. He pulled the keys from the ignition, tossed them to the grinning doorman, climbed into the nearest taxi, muttered Finca Vigía. The cab driver nodded and pulled away fast. Goddamnit, he berated himself, how'd you ever get into the habit of flowering things up? No need to. You've done enough, seen enough, fought enough, loved enough for a hundred men. No need for any self-doubt, no need for this absurd comparison with Castro.

As they sped southeast on the Carretera Central, he

gazed at the sky. The storm had moved on; its clouds were over the Gulf now, edged pink by the late afternoon sun. He slid down onto the seat for a short nap. Tired. So Goddamn tired.

The next thing he knew, the cab driver was downshifting through the gate, swinging up the drive to the Finca, past the scarlet bougainvillea, the palms, explosions of white blooms, the rich greens of the mangos. Reassured, Papa was home free, home safe, the entire world laid out before him in a brilliant orange sunset. He tipped the cabby, watched him leave, turned back to the house, now in silhouette. No sounds from inside, no cats by the pillars, the cars were gone, no sign of life, he was alone. Strange. Normally at this time, lights blazed from the house, *cubana* chatter sang from the kitchen along with the mouth-watering smells of dinner cooking. A night bird called, startling him. He swore softly, realizing he had a nagging headache, thanks to his afternoon at the Floridita.

"Mary?"

No response.

"Mary!"

He listened. A breeze sighed through the ceiba tree, black against the sky. He went up the stone steps to the entrance-way, called again. "Mary?"

Nothing. He discovered the screen door unlocked, stared at it. Jesus H. Christ, he thought angrily, I've told her and René, I've told them all, you can't leave the place open, not anymore, not with gunmen roaming the streets, bombs going off everywhere, the police taking people away— Wait a minute! Eyes wide with concern, he hurried into the living room, paused to let his eyes adjust to the dark, remembered the Wehrmacht pistol on his dresser, then the .22 pop gun in the tower.

"Mary?"

Cloth crinkled against cloth.

He spun around, backed against the bookcase under an eland's head, hands searching for something to protect himself with.

Someone jumped out of his chair.

He found an African tribal war club, held it like a baseball bat, hands knuckle-white. "What d'you think you're doing?" he demanded.

A young Englishman of average height and build in a rumpled seersucker suit inched forward, arms spread in supplication. "Ernest Hemingway?" he queried in awe-struck tones.

"You didn't answer my fucking question!" a furious Papa roared, advancing with the club, wondering where the dog was and how come he hadn't been at his post under the tree. "What the hell you doing in my house?"

"It was raining bloody cats and dogs!" He backpedaled across the room, bumping into furniture. "No one was home. I— I didn't think you'd mind!"

"Whatta you *want,* boy?"

"To— To be like you, sir."

Incredulous, Papa stopped, slowly lowered his club. Chest heaving, he studied the intruder in the faint crimson light coming through a window while the young man babbled on about trying to be a novelist and how he'd always admired Ernest Hemingway, wanted to meet him, have a serious chat. Papa just shook his head. He considered the absurdity of the situation. Here I thought the damned feds had nailed Mary and were waiting for me! Almost had a stroke, all on account of some callow limey looking for a shortcut to the Holy Grail. He squinted out at the patio deep in shadow, let the kid prattle on. Should've expected it, he realized. Ever since the Nobel prize. They just keep coming. Mostly tourists waiting at the Floridita for him to make an appearance. But the young ones, hell, they didn't think twice about bothering him at the Finca, messing up his workdays. A month ago, two punks from Princeton walked in on him and Mary swimming, wanted to know what he thought of Faulkner. Then some sissy from Brown came down, touting a bunch of illiterate short stories. And now, a damned limey with an accent so impeccable it sounded fake, shoving a thousand-page manuscript in his face, and he didn't even know where his wife was! "Don't mean to be rude, son," he said solemnly, trying to control himself, "but would you mind getting the hell outa my house!"

Papa ushered him out the door and down the steps. "Be yourself," he said firmly, turning to go back inside. "If you can."

"You mean, you're not going to read my book?"

"I don't have time!" Papa yelled, frustrated.

"Sorry to've bothered you, sir." Utterly disconsolate, he started down the drive.

Papa watched him go, saw that he was crying, felt a tug inside, perhaps from long ago. "All right, for Christ's sake! Gimme the Goddamn book!"

He took the manuscript, quickly got rid of the limey, and in the waning light headed for the tower, wondering if he'd ever get a spare moment to take a look at it. Muttering, he mounted the stairs, hoping there was scotch up top. Once there, he looked out to sea. The sun was gone, the sky, pink again, only a gray residue of light left. Machakos came out of the office barking, tail wagging sheepishly, lowering his head for his master's hand.

"Where the hell were you, dog?" he accused, then petted and loved him anyway, found his coat dry and warm. "Couldn't open the screen door so old Machakos comes up here to get out of the rain, huh?" Papa scowled good-naturedly. "Helluva fine watchdog you are, huh?" He went inside, set the manuscript down.

A note in his typewriter told him Mary was at the

Steinharts' for drinks and dinner. She hoped he hadn't forgotten and would come soon. Love and kisses.

Relieved, he leaned against his desk, gazed at the coming twilight. He chided himself silently. Should've known there was a reasonable explanation. Shouldn't have got so worried and upset. Shouldn't let all the bullshit and confusion on this island get to you. Hell, college kids and limeys aside, things're all right. Like the old days. All you hafta do is cool out and get your ass to work, that's—

A glint off to his left.

Surprised, he peered in that direction, felt his color drain away. There, by the garden behind the house, was the Cuban fed, his mirror shades reflecting sky, then nothing. He disappeared. Ominously so.

Papa knew better than to question what he'd seen or what it meant. Once his shock subsided, he grew angry, clenched and unclenched his fists. That's it, he told himself, I'm gonna go back to the house right now, call fucking Batista and demand to know what's going on. He strode for the door, stopped short just his side of it. Another presence. He crept to the window.

The pool was a black shape merging with the brick, the ground, the dense foliage. He saw nothing there. But near the whitewashed wall was the tourist in Bermuda shorts he'd seen at the Floridita, now without his *puta,* a prop.

Papa backed into the shadows, feeling the cold familiarity of the new whore, Fear. She lingered, cloying, deceptive like poisonous blossoms. Nothing was as it seemed, not anymore, not even at the Finca. That night at the bureau when they didn't know who they'd arrested—easy to joke about at cocktail parties, in retrospect. You skated then, he reminded himself. You remained at large from the mindless swirl of anarchy, a distinguished case of mistaken identity.

Well, Dr. Hemingstein, they know who you are now.

Nine

FIDEL WAS EATING a rare hot lunch of rice, beans, and boiled chicken with Camilo and Che under the trees that shaded the GP tent when the contact man rushed into the encampment. "Prío Socarras has sent another expeditionary force!" he announced between breaths, exhausted from his fast climb. "They landed at Mayarí this morning, and the army is kicking the shit out of them!"

Fidel frowned. The news wasn't surprising. The "leaders in exile" repeatedly sent their men to die, yet always had an excuse for not making the trip themselves.

"We can create a diversion," said Che, lighting a hand-rolled cigarette, "so the survivors can slip into the Maestra and join us. *¿Es verdad, Comandante?*"

"Es verdad," Fidel agreed. *"Por siempre."*

"Bueno," said Camilo. "I was beginning to think we had become *banditos.*"

Indeed, they had spent too much time running, splitting

up, then running again—ever since their upstart victory over the brutal Sánchez Mosquera and his troop. To Fidel, it was demoralizing to win, then fade away, even though he realized the tactic was necessary because they didn't have the manpower for a pitched battle. They were not a unit yet, either. Men would join, stay for a few days, march a few miles and get blisters, eat sparse rations at best, sleep cold on the ground with the constant fear of a hangdog enemy, and that would do it. They'd use any excuse to quit. He made no attempt to stop them, unless they tried to take weapons, figuring it made no sense for someone to risk his life against his will. That made for cowards.

Just yesterday, he'd sent an entire squad back to Santiago because the men weren't ready, mentally or physically; you could see the pattern. They weren't comfortable with being uncomfortable. That left one hundred twenty-seven. Of those, eighty were well armed and prepared, yet their fighting edge was dull, and if they didn't get it back soon, they'd lose it irrevocably. The army kept sending more and more troops to the Sierra. Better troops. Bolder troops. Was Batista's "ring of steel" actually working?

He looked off thoughtfully. It had been three months since *The New York Times* articles had brought them to the world's attention. Since then, not much exposure. True, another gringo had come down and shot newsreel footage for Yankee television, but they hadn't seen any results from that, and Fidel doubted they would. The *barbudos* were no longer headline stuff. But what galled Fidel more than anything was Señor Hemingway's silence. No *Life* magazine article, not even something in *Field and Stream* or *Argosy*. Well, my friends, he mused, now is the time, before things get worse. We'll give them all something to crow about, even Ernesto Hemingway.

"Celia?" he called. "I want to see the staff as soon as possible."

Ten minutes later, they were all crowded into the tent. Fidel stood in the middle, puffing on a cigar, drinking fresh coffee that warmed his bones, waiting for everyone to quiet down. Given the close quarters, he couldn't help but smell them and was astonished at the variety of foul odors, not that he smelled any better. He reminded himself to order them to take baths—after the next attack—then grinned wryly. If *he* were the enemy and smelled them coming, he certainly wouldn't suspect anything human. *"¡Chito, compañeros, chito!"*

Gradually, they were silent. Briefly, he explained the situation, then asked for suggestions. As usual, no one spoke, afraid they would say the wrong thing. As usual, except for Che, a man unto himself. They were in timber country, he said, an area crisscrossed by logging roads, used frequently by the army, whose patrols traveled by truck, giving the illusion they were in control when actually the soldiers never ventured off the roads, making their efforts ludicrous. Already, he had reconnoitered a dozen ideal ambush locations and was recommending that the *barbudos* seize the army's trucks. "We can't lose," he said, eyes shining, "we'll get four or five of them all at once!"

The staff agreed, began whispering sanguinely among themselves until they saw that Fidel didn't share their enthusiasm.

"No, *chico,* no trucks."

"But it makes perfect sense!" Che argued, explaining how vulnerable the mechanized patrols were, how easily they could be taken out, causing a sudden shift in enemy deployment, which was what they wanted, no?

Fidel listened impassively, stroking his beard, but was annoyed. Why does he always have to question me in front of the others, sometimes just for the sake of debate? Why must I convince him at every step? For once, I wish he would accept a plan without holding it up to the litmus paper of his dialectics! Right now, I don't need a philosopher, Che, just a good doctor who can shoot straight.

"No, no trucks," he said again with finality. "Of course, the ambushes are a good idea, but seizing a few trucks means nothing! The press will ignore such an incident or report it as an accident. The people must know we are still here, fighting effectively!"

"Then what do you suggest we do, *Comandante?*" asked Che, clearly not pleased.

"Uvero. We're going to take Uvero," he said, surprised by his sudden choice, for the idea had just occurred to him.

Che gaped at him, went pale, probably the only time Fidel ever saw him genuinely shocked. The others were benumbed. No one spoke. Just a few coughs, boots shuffling, mumbles, whispers.

Fidel smiled, relished the moment, thrilled by his rash decision. Yes, the army post at Uvero and its garrison of soldiers. An outrageous idea, but if they succeeded, the entire country would know within hours, and in his view that was as important as the attack itself. To support the movement, the people must know it exists.

Camilo stood, eyes downcast, fooling with his straw hat. *"Con permiso, Comandante,* but how in hell are we supposed to take a regional army garrison? That's like the Brownsville Blues taking on the New York Yankees!"

"Are you calling the *barbudos* bush league, *Compañero* Cienfuegos?"

"No, *Comandante—*"

"Have your men ready to leave as soon as possible!" He turned, left the tent by the back door, hands shaking. Camilo is absolutely right, he thought, arguing with himself. You've never dreamed of fighting a set-piece battle before, this could turn out worse than Moncada! *Dios,* you know nothing of military science! All you're familiar with is hit-and-run *bandito* tactics! Have you overextended yourself this time? No, no, he shook his head, convinced an attack on Uvero was the right move, *if* it were done correctly. He thought of *el viejo* again, longed for his presence. How many wars had Señor Hemingway lived through? He would know how to take Uvero.

Suddenly, he recalled Papa and Che discussing themes in *For Whom the Bell Tolls*. He vaguely remembered reading the book when he was at the university. Granted, it wasn't von Clausewitz, but it was better than nothing.

He found Che holed up in his chicken coop behind an abandoned farm, cleaning his old machine-gun rifle and drinking maté, seemingly unconcerned over their recent argument. *"Hola,"* he said, grinning. *"Entra."*

Fidel stooped inside the squalid enclosure, crouched over some small hills of ancient dung, glanced around warily, saw that Che kept his meager rations—yes, even his tobacco—in holes long since deserted by mice and snakes. He asked for a copy of *The Bell*.

"A good choice," said Che. He turned to his compact library of peeling, dog-eared paperbacks propped up on a roost, pulled out the book, handed it over.

Fidel thanked his strange Argentine friend, got out of the coop without bumping his head, hurried back to his hut, a palace compared to Che's accommodations, immersed himself in Papa Hemingway.

He read the book in three hours, didn't put it down once, not even for a cigar. The situations were real, the characters, convincing, even for Fidel, not a fan of "make-believe." He was surprised that Hemingway knew about, say, fighting with a limited ammunition supply, or the value of a trusted contact man, or being able to withdraw once you had won, and so on. In a word, the book captivated Fidel, and he finished it reluctantly, wishing the story would go on. He smiled and reflected. Yes, Señor Papa, like your Roberto Jordan, I too have felt "that sudden, rare happiness that can come to anyone with a command in a revolutionary army." In a good mood, Fidel stood, stretched, now lit a cigar, put the book in his shirt pocket as one would a Bible, patted it.

He had come away from *The Bell* with a plan of attack for Uvero.

And that night, after supper, he gave the word. The *barbudos* saddled up and began the long, downhill march, guided by a local sawmill worker who was very familiar with the access roads to the army post. Shortly after midnight, they halted in a draw choked with trees, miserable with flies. Fidel met briefly with his staff and platoon leaders, whispered his orders, sublimely simple: take out the sentry posts, then charge the garrison from the front. The attack would begin as soon as the platoons were in position, just before dawn, to maintain surprise. One last word for Juan Almeida, the Negro. "Good luck, my friend, your platoon has the most dangerous assignment because you are the best I have, so please take care of yourself."

Almeida nodded, smiled warmly, and was gone. A scene from *The Bell*, love versus commitment.

There was some confusion because Uvero hadn't been scouted, so the platoons were late getting into position. From a hill just north of the post, Fidel waited impatiently, cringing every few seconds, for he could hear Sotús's men below him, pushing through the trees, going in circles, whispering to each other. Finally, he couldn't stand it any longer, sighted at the black shape on the telephone pole next to the building, outlined by a starlit sky. He hit it with his first shot, and the attack began, the *barbudos* using the rifle flashes of the defenders to guide their approaches to the sentry posts. Fidel put two more rounds into the telephone box, blew it apart and smiled. *"Adiós,* emergency call to Santiago, just like the book says."

The soldiers put up heavy resistance—there was entirely

too much gunfire. Fidel tried to relax, told himself that once the outposts fell, the outcome was academic—according to *The Bell*. Still, he wanted to rush down into the middle of it all, yet resisted the impulse. Someone had to orchestrate this madness, the book had said, or they would lose. So, he stayed on the hill, got word to Sotús to try a flanking maneuver, sent a message to Guillermo to help Camilo neutralize the post near the shore. And when Juan finally took out the main post guarding the entrance to the fort, he, Fidel, was there on the hill, instructing Raúl to split his platoon and help Amereijeiras with the final assault.

Minutes later, in the predawn light, the white flag went up, followed by a ragged cheer from the *barbudos*.

The sun rose behind them, throwing their long shadows across the field and up the sides of the garrison. The grass steamed; occasionally, a bird called; the dawn was peaceful and quiet, as if nothing had happened here. Fidel strode toward the fort, the crunch of his boots breaking the stillness. He was exhausted, fearful that he'd lost half his men, his face long and haggard. Once inside the gates, the scene did nothing to allay his fears. Bodies were everywhere. The whimpers and screams of the wounded made his testicles crawl. The enemy had fought like fanatics, something he hadn't expected, and now their leader, a bloodied second lieutenant, approached him, holding the white flag and proudly trying to hand over his sword.

Fidel did not allow himself to be overwhelmed. After dismissing the lieutenant, he calmly issued the orders for the withdrawal, was gratified to see Camilo take charge and start loading trucks with confiscated weapons and supplies. Already, *barbudos* were filing back toward the mountains, waving goodbye to a stunned, defeated enemy, singing, disappearing into a misty morning, the stuff of legend.

But there were also five dead and ten wounded.

Fidel found Che in a barracks, helping with the enemy casualties, morose, for out of their own wounded, two would have to be left behind.

Fidel went to them. One was paralyzed from the waist down, his spine shattered. The other had been shot in the head. Both were conscious, quiet, didn't seem to be in much pain. He took their hands, could think of nothing to say. They smiled at him, knowing it was the end. Fidel shut his eyes tightly, made no attempt to stop his tears. Gripping their hands and wrists, he kneeled, wept for them, blessed them, still couldn't speak.

Finally, he got up and managed to utter, "We will never forget you," then left the fort, aware his words were pitifully inadequate. Hurrying across the fields, he remembered that the partisans in *The Bell* had left their wounded behind, the book ending with Jordan unable to walk, waiting to die, aiming his rifle at a fascist lieutenant. If it were any consolation, he supposed, it was that Jordan would take some of the enemy with him. So, Señor Hemingway knew about that too, about men too badly hurt to move, men sure to be murdered, Fidel thought. Still, his words do not ease the pain of those who must leave their brothers behind.

From a knoll, he looked back and saw the first planes circling the skeleton of Uvero. His heart was filled with sadness.

Ten

"WHERE THE HELL'RE you?" Papa shouted into the phone, raising his voice over the static.

"On a sugar *central* outside Bayamo in the 'free territory of Cuba,'" said Fidel with an excited laugh.

"Sounds to me like you're on the moon."

Another laugh. "Considering the differences between us and Batista, you're pretty close, Señor Hemingway."

Papa felt himself grinning, an automatic gesture reserved for hearing unexpectedly from old friends. The grin stayed on his face until he reminded himself Castro wasn't a friend, old or otherwise. Still, he was pleased Fidel was calling, signaled frantically to a passing servant girl who returned moments later with a glass and a bottle of scotch. While waiting for a break in the static—Fidel was almost inaudible—he poured himself four fingers and sipped happily. "So, you're outa the mountains now?"

"Only for dinner." With relish, Fidel described the meal. Filet mignon wrapped in bacon, plantains fried in real butter, *fresh* vegetables and salad, rice pilaf with pork tenderloin, baked oysters in the shell Florentine, three French wines, chocolate mousse, and a brandy VSOP that'd break your heart, Señor Papa. Apparently, the local *latifundistas* were convinced the revolution was going to win, so they'd become very generous, the lavish dinner being the occasion to donate ten thousand Yankee dollars to the movement. "They're worried about land reform."

Papa laughed, appreciating the irony. "Host offer you his daughter yet?"

"Not to my knowledge."

"Hold out for the brass ring, son. Very important."

"Sí, señor."

"Keep an eye peeled for the cavalry, too. Batista's probably eaten at the same table."

Fidel laughed gleefully, sounding much younger than his thirty years. Must be the brandy, Papa told himself, imagining Castro in some planter's library, phone cradled to his ear, cigar in hand, boots resting on a cherrywood antique desk. Already, the big guys are courting favors, and he ain't sure how to handle it, so he sounds like a kid with carte blanche in a candy store. Be careful, Castro. Don't sell your soul before the market opens, you might get a better offer later in the day.

"What did the—"

The static became a horrendous series of clicks and thumps. Papa winced, took the phone away from his ear until it passed.

"What'd you say?"

"Uvero!" His voice echoed, distant and hollow. "Didn't you hear about Uvero?"

"Yeah, I heard about it," Papa replied gruffly, sipping scotch. "Thanks to Matthews. Batista's boys've been making paper dolls outa the newspapers again."

"It was a great victory," he said nostalgically.

"So what?" said Papa. "It happened over two months ago."

"Es verdad, but without your book, *For Whom the Bell Tolls,* I would not have been able to plan the attack."

Papa was stunned, just listened as Castro—fading in and out of the static—quoted from *The Bell* while rehashing the battle. With growing horror and pride, he realized that finally something he had written had actually made a difference. *The Bell* had affected history. Blood had been spilled, lives lost; his fiction, the culprit. *The Bell,* written in part as an antiwar statement, used as a field manual by a brash revolutionary hothead. He wanted to get mad, but couldn't. There was no one to blame, certainly not Castro, who was only trying to pay him a compliment. Certainly not himself, for he'd never intended to publish a blueprint for rebel terrorism. Merely: honest prose creating things truer than truth. Shit, Hem, maybe you oughta start notching your dust jackets, he thought cynically.

"When are you going to visit again?"

"Already told you," Papa said, becoming nervous. He had been on the phone entirely too long, and while he doubted the SIM had gotten around to tapping his line, you couldn't be sure. True, he hadn't seen the feds near the Finca for weeks, but he knew they hadn't forgotten him.

"When?" Fidel insisted. "When?"

"You boys take a seaport," he said with forced bravado, "I'll be there."

Fidel laughed uproariously, and Papa guessed he was on his third or fourth brandy. He heard Mary drive up and park under the ceiba tree, door close, heels clicking up the stone steps. Time to get off the line. For more reasons than one, this wasn't a call he could readily explain. But he wasn't quick enough. She breezed by with groceries, waved, went into the kitchen. Mortified, he hung up instantly, cutting off the bearded one in mid-cackle.

Quickly, Papa padded into the living room, sat in his chair, and waited. Sultry evening haze rolled in the windows facing the bay, adding to his discomfort. "Whole fuckin' summer's been this way," he muttered, wondering what she'd ask, how he'd answer. He couldn't tell her about his association with Castro, it wasn't possible, she'd insist he fly to New York and see a fucking headshrinker.

He heard girlish laughter from the kitchen, reminding him of the old days. Then she came into the living room smiling, looking beautiful, hair done nice and fluffy the way he liked it, curled up in the chair next to him with a glass of cold white wine. Totally disarmed, he grinned sheepishly, guessed she'd question him about the state of whoredom in Havana for openers, wondered what he'd cop to.

"Good day?" she asked.

"Um."

"Who was that on the phone?"

"Nobody."

She arched her eyebrows slightly, flipped through the mail on the coffee table, and that was it. "Rack of lamb and salad for dinner, okay?"

"Fine, just fine," he stammered, amazed she'd let it slide, but what the hell, people called the house all the time, from René's mulatto girlfriend to the American ambassador. "Anything new in town?" he deadpanned.

"You were right about that noise we heard yesterday." She sighed. "Somebody tried to bomb the police station. Now they're saying San Francisco de Paula's become a haven for the underground."

Papa laughed scornfully. "Our town? C'mon! Too damned small for that sorta thing. Where the hell they gonna hide?"

She looked at him, placed her hand over his, spoke softly. "Papa, don't you think it might be wise if—?"

"We'll go when I say so!" he declared stubbornly, then

forced a smile. "Besides, weather's bound to get better, no matter how you look at it."

She thought about his comment, holding her glass to her lips, barely touching, trying to sort through the various levels of conversation. "How're the memoirs coming?"

He looked off and scowled. Started to lie to her, but there was no point. Just as it seemed there'd be no end to the heat and humidity, no end to the Gulf Stream gone flat, empty, and sterile, it seemed there'd be no end to his dearth at the typewriter. He felt squeezed dry. "Not good, kitten." His turn to sigh. "Matter of fact, it's probably worse than the fishing's been."

"I'm sorry," she whispered.

He wiped away angry tears, thought of *The Bell*, recalled flying through it, riding the beast that wanted out of his gut. C'mon, God, give it back to me, just one more time.

"Think you'd do better somewhere else?"

He stared at her, didn't really know, shook his head, regardless.

The dinner was candlelit and quiet, and after a bottle of wine, relaxed, tender even. Papa ate slowly, prolonging the meal, as if his efforts could turn back the clock to a gentler, more productive time. He listened patiently to Mary's chatter, some of it amusing, nodded and smiled frequently.

She came to him in the moonlight on the patio, put her arms around him, held him, and he felt her nude against his back. They made love on the hammock, with some difficulty since the swing was moving side to side and they wanted to go in the other direction. But the chuckles were worth it, especially when they finally got it right.

Later, when the sky clouded over and the wind picked up, they walked hand in hand into the bedroom, curled up together. Close. To hell with the thunder rolling in the valleys, the coming storm, everything was just fine at La Finca Vigía.

Papa lay flat and closed his eyes. For the first time since his nights in the mountains, vivid images were swimming in his mind. Circling. He could almost see them, taste them, smell their freshness. They signaled a new beginning, tomorrow at the typewriter. Was the big book finally taking shape? He yawned, drifted. Was it verdant and fertile like the Sierra Maestra?

He slept.

A hammering woke him around four in the morning. Groggy, he sat up, eyes blinking, looked around to get his bearings. Lightning flashed outside the windows, wind howled, bending the trees, rain sluiced down in sheets. He glanced at Mary beside him on the bed, still asleep despite the storm. He smiled.

That hammering again. At first he thought it was a loose shutter banging, then heard muffled shouting and realized someone was at the front door. He quickly pulled on his trousers, buttoned them, hurried out of the bedroom halfway into his shirt. What kinda fool would get caught in a hurricane this time of night? Must be an emergency. Accident down on the highway or something. Or maybe— Maybe somebody died. He fumbled for the lamp in the living room, was surprised it went on. They still had power, of all things.

More hammering, shaking the bookcases in the entranceway.

"*Momento,* for Christ's sake!" He crossed the room, stopped in mid-stride when he saw the door buckling and splintering, heard a string of Spanish curses, could not believe his eyes. Someone was breaking down the door! Your pistol, top dresser drawer, bedroom, no time— already the wood was splitting along the hinges. He looked around frantically. In a glass case on a bookshelf was the Smith and Wesson .32 revolver his father had shot himself to death with, a gift from his mother. He lunged for it, too late. The door crashed open, and they were inside, five of Batista's brownshirts, trousers bloused into knee-high jackboots, one, a mestizo sergeant with a forty-five leveled at Papa's face.

"*¡No te vayas!*"

Papa turned slowly, looked into the cobalt-blue muzzle and gulped. The sergeant ordered him against the wall, hands on his head, mouth shut. He did as he was told. Rain dripped off the sergeant's helmet and poncho, staining the floor. He stared impassively at Papa, nodded imperceptibly, turned, shouted orders out the broken door.

More shouts from outside as men spread out, began combing the Finca grounds.

The sergeant pointed this way and that, spoke sharply to the four behind him, and they trotted off to search the house. Papa heard them opening doors, cabinets, pushing furniture over, breaking things, violating his space, his life. Rage built inside. A helpless, useless rage, for he knew this spit-shined marionette was just waiting for an excuse to snap off a few rounds. He studied him, recognized the haughty smile, the flush of quick, early success. The sergeant's night was going well.

There was much Papa could've said, wanted to, but it had all been said before and never made a difference. Like all fascists before him, this mestizo pig had his instructions and that was that.

"We will find them," he said in broken English, removing his poncho, settling in for a time.

"Who?"

"You know who, *Señor maricón,*" he said contemptuously, "and then you will die. All of you."

Screams. Then high-pitched laughter. They had found Mary. Papa stiffened, clenched his fists. In response, the sergeant tilted his pistol, making sure it was aimed right.

Two of them prodded her out of the bedroom as she struggled into her housecoat, across the living room and into the entranceway. They leered at her, exchanged knowing expressions—not bad for an old lady, not bad at all, who gets her first, before the dance of death?

Papa saw the terror in her eyes, wished he could help, wanted to desperately, but wisely did not move.

"What do they want?" she whispered tremulously.

"They think we got people stashed here."

"*¡Silencio!*" the sergeant screamed.

Papa looked at him closely, sensed a crack in his veneer. He moved restlessly, head swiveling back and forth, things weren't happening the way they were supposed to. No shouts of triumph, no bedraggled fugitives brought forth like wet rats. Only the storm, shrieking around the Finca, tearing at the house, the fences, the trees.

The moment was tense. Charged. On edge. Papa had been there before. He rolled up on his toes, waited. No matter how it goes, he told himself, I will not be humiliated, I will not die badly.

Outside, someone was yelling and running, coming closer. The sergeant motioned for one of his men to cover Papa, stepped out under the colonnade. A terrified soldier sprinted past the ceiba tree, his helmet and rifle gone, turned, threw up his hands, was knocked to the ground by a snarling black apparition. Machakos. He had the soldier by the throat and was shaking him.

Papa felt his fierce pride well up inside. "Get him, Machakos! Get the sonuvabitch!"

Cursing, the sergeant jumped down the steps, started kicking the dog.

"Wait a minute, Goddamn you! *No!*" Beside himself, Papa shoved past the soldier guarding him, went outside, grappled with two more who blocked his way.

Growling, Machakos charged, lunged at the sergeant, but

the mestizo was braced, had his forearm up, and as the dog slammed into him, sank in his teeth, he shoved his pistol between the brown eyes and pulled the trigger.

Machakos yelped once, dropped to the stone. Gone.

"No!" Papa screamed. *"No!"*

He threw himself at the sergeant, but the soldiers pinned his arms, held him back, so he spit, hitting the mestizo on the diagonal strap of his Sam Browne belt. *"Hijo de puta!"*

The sergeant backhanded him hard across the mouth. Once. Twice. Nodded at his men. They heaved Papa into the bushes, and he expected the bullets then, was resigned, but no firing, no blaze of glorious light.

They left, double-timing down the driveway toward their personnel carrier.

Papa scrambled up, wet, muddy, bleeding, went to Machakos, cradled his still-warm body, and wept for the dog's love, his courage, his final act of fealty. He stood, looked up at Mary, now under the colonnade, hugging herself, tears streaming down her face. He would get a shovel from the tool shed, dig the grave before dawn, bury Machakos next to Black Dog by the swimming pool.

Still holding the dog, he turned to go, stopped. One last look at the house, a warm light from inside promising shelter from the storm when there was none, not anymore.

It was time to leave Cuba. He disappeared into the rain and wind, filled with despair and anger, not certain he'd ever see his beloved home again.

He dug the grave quickly, methodically—short, choppy strokes with the shovel—then gently placed Machakos into the ground and covered him with the wet earth. He started for the tool shed, stopped suddenly and shook his fist at the raging sky.

"Goddamn you, Batista! Goddamn you, Castro! Why can't you sons of bitches leave my island alone?"

Eleven

A COLD RAIN hammered down as the deuce-and-a-half ground up the twisting road to the Angel Castro y Argiz plantation. Riding shotgun, Fidel squinted out the side window, but couldn't see anything. Then, as the truck took another curve, its headlights swept across a stand of burnt sugar cane alongside the road, and he felt both dread and nostalgia. He hadn't been home in almost ten years. Until now, he'd had others make the trip to the farm to pick up the arms shipments from Ramón, his older brother. This night, though, was his mother's birthday, and Celia had made a present, something special. Fidel found himself smiling foolishly. *Mamacita.* He remembered her Rubenesque frame, her round face, stern yet kind, her long dark hair, her brown eyes that could shine with such happiness when her sons pleased her. What did she look like now? he wondered, fidgeting on the seat as if he were twelve, hoping she'd be the same, assuming so, how could she change, she was his mother.

He studied his younger brother fighting the wheel, straining to see the road through the downpour. Raúl. He reminds me of a gopher, Fidel told himself, laughing inwardly. Beady eyes, sunken cheeks, small, hard body. Yes, a skinny rodent wearing a cowboy hat over his ponytail, unable to grow a beard. But he was smart and tough and loyal. Fidel smiled ironically. The others called him "little helmet" because he had a small man's complex and lacked a sense of humor. No one particularly liked him or his politics, and once Che had asked why he was made a platoon commander. He does what I want, Fidel told himself. He follows orders without question, and when unpleasant tasks have to be done, Raúl is always there. If I ask it, he will die for me, and how many men can say that of a brother?

He lit a fresh cigar, unmindful that the smoke further impaired Raúl's vision, tried to relax as the truck crawled up the final hill. When he saw the lights glowing from the house, his heart surged and he recalled the early years, the sweetness of cane cut fresh in the field, the mouth-watering smells from the kitchen when Mamacita and his sisters cooked, the flush of pride when he shot his first bird in a remote cane field just after the *zafra.* Then the problems with *padre,* stern, unforgiving, iron-willed, insisting he should not go to school, an unnecessary frivolity. He tried to remember how he'd talked his father into it when wind buffeted the truck and swept away the bittersweet memories.

He pointed. "Ramón'll be at the barn."

Raúl nodded, downshifted, drove behind it. The door was open, and he backed inside.

Fidel swung down from the cab, took two giant steps and embraced his older and shorter brother, Ramón, who was apprehensive in the presence of a half-dozen *barbudos* scrambling over the tailgate of the deuce-and-a-half.

Eyes twinkling, Fidel stepped back, held him at arm's length.

"Hey, *chico,* what happened? You got old and fat!" he said, raising his voice over the din of rain on the roof.

Ramón merely nodded.

Fidel read his nervousness. "Don't worry, Ramón, we will only be here a short while."

"Rurales," he whispered, "they were here two days ago."

Fidel frowned, turned to his men, ordered half of them to form a perimeter outside, then directed Raúl and the others to load the cases of weapons as quickly as possible. Yet, he had lived with danger for years and it wasn't going to prevent him from surprising his mother. He'd been gone too long. From the cab, he took a brightly wrapped package, waved to the *barbudos,* trotted to the house, hunched against the stinging cold of the rain. The years seemed to recede as he splashed through mud puddles. He remembered being a big, ungainly kid, too outspoken for his own good, loving his mother intensely, demanding her time, furious and hurt when she denied him. Still, there had always been something precious between them. He knew he was her favorite and longed to see her joyful expression when he strode into the house, now a man, now savior of their country. Eager, timid, he tiptoed across the veranda to the door, knocked softly, shifted his bulk from foot to foot, heard the muffled voices of his sisters telling each other to see who had come, the chore passed down to the youngest.

Finally, the door opened. *"¡Dios mío! ¡Fidel!"*

"Shhhh!" He raised his finger to his lips, for a moment not sure who this lovely young woman was. "Juana?"

She nodded.

He gave her a bearlike hug, but felt her stiffen and grow cold, then push away from him. Her face blank, she asked him inside, playing courteous country hostess. He was about to question her aloofness, but she was gone, the years had passed so quickly, and now he was a stranger in the house he'd grown up in. Big, bushy, red-faced, he stood in the living room contemplating the porcelain nativity scene on the mantel, the mahogany candlesticks, constant troublemakers because he was always running into the room, knocking them to the floor. Awkward, he faced the windows, staring out, not knowing what to do with his hands, his gift, his hat. He wanted to smoke, but knew instinctively Mamacita would disapprove, so the cigar stayed in olive-green pocket. Glancing down, he wondered about his boots and whether he'd tracked mud in.

"Fidel!" she gasped.

He turned and was shocked. Her hair, my God, her long dark hair, it's white! She seemed smaller in stature too, a shadow of her former self, and behind her, his sisters had ahold of her in case she fainted. She didn't. Tears streaming down her wrinkled cheeks, she ran to him, threw her arms around him, embraced him fiercely, whispering his name over and over. He closed his eyes, buried his face into her shoulder, not wanting anyone to see the warmth, the love he felt. Oh, Mamacita, I love you too, but there is so little time, maybe when the war is over we can reminisce, oh, Mamacita, I am your Fidel, always, no matter what they say about me. Her grip loosened, so he stepped away, grinning sheepishly, glad his sisters had left the room, not yet understanding why.

"Mamacita, it's—"

She slapped him hard across the face. "The rebel underground burned our cane fields! Why?"

Bewildered, he could not think of a reasonable explanation. Except the truth. Anything to hurt the Batista government, disrupt the economy, and bring the army to its knees. But he couldn't tell her that, not when the boys from Santiago in the name of Frank País had cost her and

Ramón thousands of pesos. Nor could he say that he believed if one should suffer, all should suffer, including friends and family, if it would hasten the fall of a repressive regime.

"Why!"

"Mamacita—"

"You look terrible! Why don't you cut your hair and shave? Take a bath? You smell like dirty socks!" She turned away and wrung her hands. "Have you forgotten everything we taught you?"

"Mama, please, it isn't easy in the mountains."

"The mountains!" she snorted. "Didn't you go to school to become a lawyer? Why aren't you working in Havana instead of running through the hills with a bunch of criminals?"

He didn't know what to say. Just stood there growing more and more uncomfortable while she berated him, repeating her complaints over and over as was her custom, making sure he'd remember. "The neighbors," she was saying, "always yelling at me about your *banditos* burning cane fields, blowing things up, ruining lives, shooting policemen, causing riots in the cities, you and your people turning the country into a, a—cemetery!" She paused. "And Ramón! He risked his life to get a message to you that your father had died, and you couldn't even come home for the funeral!"

"I was in Mexico, Mama."

"I don't care where you were! When a man dies, his sons should be there to bury him!"

Padre. Please, Mama, he said silently, don't talk to me about Padre. He used to whip me with his belt if I went hunting before the firewood was cut, my back, my legs, my feet, the welts are still there, burning inside.

She stepped back and looked him up and down. "At least you haven't lost your appetite."

"Feliz cumpleaños." He handed her the present.

Briefly, her face lit up. Wreathed in smiles, she thanked him, started opening the package, talking constantly, her tone a little kinder now, asking if there weren't some way he could sit down and talk with the government so the war, the deaths of so many fine young men, could stop. He thought of telling her what the army did to the bodies of his rebels, but there was no point, she was upset enough, so he just shook his head, no, Fidel Castro will never talk to Fulgencio Batista.

Frustrated, she gave him a disapproving look, yet by then had finished unwrapping her gift, a shawl handmade by Celia, red and black, with "M-26-7" across the center in white. Fidel smiled proudly.

"¡Qué lindo!" she said, before realizing the garment she held was, in reality, a knitted flag of her son's movement. Then horror crossed her face, and she dropped the shawl as if it were diseased. "I can't wear that!"

"Why not?" he cried, beginning to get angry. "Celia worked on it for months!"

"That whore who lives with you in the Maestra?" She shrank away from the pile of wool on the floor. "Take it back to her! Have her use it to cloak her shame!"

Amazed, he stood rooted, feeling the fury build inside while she railed at him once more, somehow back on the subject of his father and how terrible it was for Fidel to miss the funeral. Tight-jawed, he bent over, scooped up the shawl, flung it loosely over his shoulder.

"How can you call yourself a son of Angel Castro?" she cried. "You're a disgrace to the family name!"

Humiliated, he turned and left the house, slamming the door, unmindful of the continuing downpour, the shawl dragging behind in the mud. Padre. He couldn't get away from the subject. Her only man, that's all she can think about. A tyrant of a father. Well, Mamacita, I'm glad he is dead, he cannot torment me any longer. Why couldn't Padre have been Papa, he asked himself. A big-hearted, generous old man with a penchant for good humor, good liquor, a man whose sardonic nature was tempered by the wealth of adventure and success he'd experienced. Why had Padre been so mean and obsessive? I tried so hard to love him!

"Chingas tu padre!" he screamed, his voice swallowed up by the howling wind. He threw the shawl into the bushes, squared his shoulders, lifted his face to the rain, then told himself, the movement has become your family, *chico*. Your life. Mamacita is a memory now.

He strode around the barn, saw they hadn't finished loading. "Can't you work any faster? The *rurales* are coming!"

Raúl shot him a look of hangdog apology while trying to manhandle a case onto the truck. His expression was so pathetic Fidel would've laughed, had he been in a better mood. Mamacita, oh, Mamacita, how you can hurt. He walked around the truck, climbed into the cab, pressed his face against the cool of the window, filled with the pain of the moment. Finally, he heard them finish loading, then shutting the tailgate and getting aboard. And then Raúl was behind the wheel, pausing before he started the engine.

"Mama," he whispered, "how is she?"

"Shut up!" Fidel roared. "Get us the hell out of here! *Now!*"

As the deuce-and-a-half lurched away from the barn, he stared out at the blackness, doubting he'd ever see her again.

Twelve

THE BODY HUNG from the ceiba tree in the middle of the Cotorro village plaza, swinging back and forth, sometimes spinning when one of the boys hit it with a stone. The mestizo sergeant who had shot Machakos, Papa observed, watching the scene without any particular sense of vindication. Uno and Dos had asked him down, excited with the news that the locals had taken the police station for the night and were paying the bastards back.

Now the boys were maiming the corpse, a lesson for the uniformed thugs when they returned to Cotorro. Imitating their favorite major-league pitchers, they took turns hurling stones, laughing and cheering when someone hit the body in the balls. Each time they scored, they saluted Papa, these, the same young men who'd played little-league ball for him years before.

He folded his arms across his chest, watching a rangy black kid do "Satchel Paige," throwing side-arm with blinding speed. The stone hit the former sergeant in the

111

face and flattened his nose with a resounding splat. The crowd whooped its approval. Papa remained impassive, listened as Uno and Dos told the others he was a "man of courage" for returning to Cuba, for watching them mutilate the pig of a policeman who had dared to shoot Ernest Hemingway's dog. Courageous? he thought, scowling. Just because I came back home? It doesn't have a damned thing to do with courage, boys. The true gen is, there's no place left to go.

After the brownshirts had ransacked the Finca and murdered Machakos, Mary had finally convinced him to return to the States, and they'd gone to New York City, but he'd only been able to tolerate it for about a month. The older he became, the more he hated the city with its arrogant salesclerks, nasty taxi drivers, condescending receptionists, hostile bartenders, even. What the hell was the world coming to when you went into the West End on 114th Street, ordered scotch straight up, and the fucking bartender asks you where you got the Hemingway costume? The hell with New York, he told himself. Maybe those Russkies'll drop an A-bomb on it and somebody in Des Moines'll publish the rest of my stuff. He scowled. Write or die. Every morning, two hours in the pool, then up in the tower to work. Mindless work. Going back and forth between the sketches and the novel. A bad novel. Graphic sex scenes with Mary on practically every page. He grinned in spite of his moroseness. If Charlie ever publishes it, your own wife'll probably sue for libel. Mary. He wondered why she stayed with him. They rarely spoke. And when they did it was trivial. Yet she stayed, blindly pursuing the colonial good life, the endless shopping trips, daily lists of chores for the servants, while the fabric of society, not to mention their own relationship, unraveled around them. Danger was rampant, everything was out of control, while at the Finca life retained its surface calm. Maybe that was why she stayed, except she had no delusions, for she was constantly badgering him to pull up stakes and get out of Cuba while the getting was good. Seemed like every time she mentioned it, another storm would roll in from the Gulf Stream and kick hell out of Finca Vigía, underscoring her advice. Well, he wasn't going. Not till he got it back. He figured if he couldn't find it here in paradise, he wasn't going to find it anywhere else. If only the fishing would get better, he lamented, reminding himself he hadn't caught a marlin in a year and a half.

He looked up at the corpse, now black from the stoning, uniform tattered, dripping bodily fluids. *If only they'd stop killing each other.*

He wondered what Castro would think of this if he were here. Papa snorted. Probably, he'd make like Bob Feller and get in a few high, hard ones just to keep the locals stirred up, the bearded asshole. He turned away, sick of the spectacle, only to see the crowd looking to him expectantly, smiling, the atmosphere, carnival. Uno stepped forward, offered him a primo stone, almost perfectly round.

He shook his head vehemently. "Too old to throw, kid."

"Then perhaps Señor Hemingway would like to bludgeon the mestizo's body in memory of his faithful companion?" Dos offered a club.

"No thanks, boys, it's past my bedtime. Besides, the feds're gonna be back any minute with some cavalry, and if any of you *guajiros* got a brain in your head, you'll get the hell away from here." He climbed into the big Chrysler and drove away, the ugliness of the scene making him queasy. When he got back to the Finca, it took two glasses of scotch before he was unwound enough to go to bed. Lying there, hands behind his head, staring at the ceiling, he heard the wind pick up again, whistling through the mango trees, the rain at first gentle, then hard and driving. Like sex. Like the smut spewing out of his typewriter every morning. For

God's sake, when you gonna write something *noble* again? He felt the warmth from Mary on the other side of the bed, an exotic mixture of perfume and woman smell, was tempted to wake her, but, no, she'd only get mad, and he doubted he'd be able to do anything, anyway, what with the images of the sergeant's body fresh in his mind. Mercifully, sleep came.

At first light, he roused Mary, ostensibly to go fishing. She was annoyed, then over coffee—surprised. Happy and smiling, since they rarely did anything together anymore. He kept silent during the short drive to Cojímar, not telling her why he really wanted to go out, for she might say the wrong thing or look the wrong way at the sentry on the docks, and then there'd be trouble with the authorities. Bad trouble. He'd debated with himself about taking her along, except this had to look like a typical Ernest Hemingway fishing trip or they'd suspect something.

While Gregorio steered out of the harbor, he made the obligatory move into the fishing chair, accepted his first drink of the day from Mary, listened to her enthused chatter, watched for patrol boats. Maybe this trip would relieve the pressure. Help him shake his paranoia.

They crossed the Gulf Stream. Gregorio looked at him imploringly, but he just frowned and nodded, indicating that the *Pilar* should continue on course. At ten miles, Mary stopped talking, realizing that something was up. She didn't want to ask, not yet, just prowled the deck, making herself obvious like an unanswered question. Papa had no desire to explain things to her and didn't; his task was personal, she was not part of it, and when the job was done, he would come forth with the necessary rationalizations.

"Papa, where on earth are we going?"

"Fishing, kitten," he replied calmly, "like always. Would you bring me another Haig's?"

At fifteen miles out with no other boats in sight, Papa

signaled Gregorio to throttle back, looked at the sea behind them through field glasses just to make sure, got out of the fishing chair.

He told Mary to take the wheel, went below with Gregorio and began upending everything. Cabinets, storage bins, the bunks, even, revealing hidden compartments that contained caches of automatic weapons, belts of ammunition, and hand grenades.

"All of it." He gestured toward the side. "Overboard."

They carried the arms and explosives to the stern and tossed them into the sea, Papa feeling more and more relieved as he disposed of the old Q-boat arsenal left over from World War II when his boat had served as a submarine chaser. Quite frankly, he'd forgotten about it, but the swirl of recent anarchy had increased his fears and convinced him that if he were going to stay in Cuba, he'd better make sure his own house was clean. The specter of the mestizo sergeant's mutilated corpse, a symbol of so much mindless violence, had prompted him to make the move. Nobody's gonna shoot up the countryside with these babies, he told himself, tossing a grease gun over the side. Not the general's bozos, Castro's boys, or anybody else.

Yet he knew his gesture was pathetic because it wouldn't change anything. He also knew that what he was doing was pure bullshit. He wasn't dumping his stash of weapons to stop the violence, he was doing it because he was out-and-out scared.

Gregorio passed him a wooden box of grenades. With a grunt, he heaved them overboard, watched them swallowed up by the great mother ocean, receiver of all things, giver of life, of death.

"Any more?"

"*Sí. Mucho.*"

The parade continued. Shotguns, pistols, M-1's, more grenades, submachine guns, a bazooka, even. Should've

115

done this a long time ago, he told himself, sweating now, throwing the weapons over the side as fast as his mate could pass them, feeling exposed. He worked faster and faster, anxious to get it over with, hating the thought of getting caught red-handed, angry at himself for being so chickenshit.

"Ernest?"

"Jesus Christ, *what?*"

"Look." She pointed off.

He glanced up quickly. His heart stopped. On the horizon was the unmistakable silhouette of a patrol boat, low in the water, cutting toward them at flank speed.

"Goddamnit, Gregorio!" he screamed. "All of it! *Now!*"

He hurled the last of the weapons over the side, so rushed he even scuttled Gregorio's flare pistol and some of his old fishing tackle.

They were putting the bunks back together when the patrol boat hove to, and a young ensign boarded the *Pilar,* brass gleaming, shoes spit-shined. He saluted Mary correctly, heels snapping in unison. *"Buenas, señora."*

Papa sagged, had to sit down, couldn't fake it, put his face in his hands. All he could think of was they'd made it. Just barely. Too close, too fucking close, I can't take any more of this! What the hell's this seagoing marionette want, you know damned well what he wants, Hem.

"¿Pesca?" the ensign asked.

Papa nodded tiredly.

Then why isn't anyone in the chair, the ensign was saying, and aren't we a little far out for marlin, you don't mind, of course, if we look around, there is so much smuggling going on and turbulence fomented by the communist bandits. *"Documentos, señor, por favor."*

Papa was so paralyzed, he couldn't stand, but managed a quick nod to Gregorio, who handed the *Pilar*'s log and papers to the ensign. They were, thank God, in perfect order.

"So you are berthed at Cojímar?" the ensign remarked, his English perfect, a broad smile on his face. "Fantastic parties at the Club Náutico, enh?"

Then he and his men proceeded to search the *Pilar.* Thoroughly, with precision, yet courteously. After all, these were well-to-do Americans.

Papa stared at Mary, sensed that she was unconcerned, didn't realize she could coat the worst feelings in the world with a look of serenity. "Don't you understand what happens to me, what happens to our lives, if they find one fucking bullet?" he whispered, but she didn't hear. Furious, he could do nothing except sit and act innocent while the ensign and his men continued hunting for contraband. He agonized that he'd forgotten something, waited helplessly for that sharp voice of discovery and accusation.

They were on the boat for two hours and found nothing. Smiling thinly, the ensign apologized for the inconvenience, wished them good fishing and a happy Easter, saluted, and left.

Papa watched the patrol boat throttle away, did not move or speak until it was a speck on the horizon. Then he ordered Gregorio to take the helm, went below, poured himself rum, gulped it down, refilled his glass.

Mary appeared in the hatchway. "Ernest, we're going to be late."

"Late? For what?"

"The new Trader Vic's is opening at the Hilton. We're supposed to meet the Steinharts there."

"We almost get busted," he exploded, "and you're worried about a Goddamned Trader *Vic's?*"

"Papa," she said quite sensibly, "if we can't live here the way we want, what's the point in going on?"

117

Thirteen

JANUARY 1, 1959

"HUYE BATISTA, HUYE Batista, huye Batista," the bearded announcer repeated over and over into the Radio Rebelde microphone.

Fidel nudged him, handed him a statement saying that the Comandante would address the nation tonight from Santiago, then left the tent, lit a fresh cigar, met with his staff, ordered his columns to descend on Santiago. Not that he expected a fight. Batista had fled, the army had all but given up, the war was over, M-26-7 had won, Cuba was his—if he made the right moves. He threw his rucksack into the back of the jeep, wedged his rifle in by the door, was about to swing into the driver's seat when he saw Celia. He grabbed her by the shoulders, lowered his face to hers, whispered, "No one knows it yet, but we are marching to Havana, and I want my son along for the ride, so when you get to Santiago, find a phone first thing and call New York, *muy bien.* I don't care what you have to say or promise or what it costs, I want him here, *¿comprendes?"*

118

She nodded firmly.

First, we will take Moncada, he told himself as he drove off, recalling the bitter defeat five and a half years earlier. We will take it with a vengeance, he vowed, his only concern being the sobriety level of his troops in the caravan behind.

It didn't matter.

The five thousand soldiers garrisoned at Moncada had already stacked their arms and were seated on the parade ground, waiting, when the *barbudos* approached the large, square archway. Fidel's lips quivered. He felt a rush of emotion. July 26, 1953, he'd sped toward these very same gates at the wheel of a brand-new Buick followed by his desperate, hard-eyed companions. He remembered the soldiers firing at them, and—absurdly—the Henry J. parked there, then running one soldier down, the Buick stalling, diving for cover behind it as he realized that Raúl and the others were *not* attacking through the back gate. He and his men were alone, and then it was too late, the soldiers were everywhere, killing them, smashing their skulls. The years of prison, humiliation, and exile had begun.

Now he parked his jeep by the barracks headquarters, got out, and—hands on his hips—surveyed the scene, suddenly annoyed the army had surrendered, realizing he'd wanted a fight, a chance to redeem himself and undo the one colossal failure of his life. *Pero, no,* it wasn't to be.

Cheering civilians surged through the gates after the rebel column, and Fidel watched impassively while his more sanguine men duckwalked the Moncada officers down the steps and threw them into the crowd whereupon they were jeered, spit upon, and torn to pieces. He made no move to stop the violence. Let the people vent their fury, he decided, let them remember their sons hanging upside down from street signs. Woe, he thought, to the captain or major who does not burn his uniform as soon as he can find something else to wear. Papa, yes, Papa, you should be here observing your words becoming reality once again. Didn't I read this scene in *For Whom the Bell Tolls?* Only you could appreciate these ritual killings, no one would understand better than you. Yes, let them become a mob, let each one taste the violence, for then they have committed themselves, they have joined the revolution.

From atop his jeep, he waved his fist and declared Moncada liberated. While the crowd roared its approval, he slid behind the wheel and continued the journey into Santiago.

As the shadows lengthened into twilight, he found himself at the microphones in the plaza addressing the nation, the world, calling for a general strike, naming Manuel Urrutia as provisional president, and proclaiming Santiago the new capital of Cuba. The crowds went berserk, rushed the platform wanting to touch him, while Gonzáles— appointed head bodyguard just that morning—frantically orchestrated his men to keep the people at bay.

"Daddy, if Santiago is the capital now, how come we're going to Havana?" asked Fidelito as the jeep cruised slowly along. He was tall for a nine-year-old, thin, fair-skinned, but with the same dark, piercing eyes of his father.

From behind the wheel, Fidel looked askance at his son, thought before answering, waved to the people alongside the highway tossing flowers and kisses at them as his column neared Holguín, a dusty cowboy town about one hundred miles north of Santiago, then smiled and shrugged. "Simple. When we get to Havana, Havana will be the capital again."

"But how can you do that?" the boy cried, astonished. "Even the President of the United States can't do that!"

"The President of the United States is not Cuban," he said flatly.

"But, Daddy—"

"Sh, sh, sh, Fidelito, don't worry about such things, you are too young." He patted the boy on the head. "Relax and enjoy the trip."

"How long before we get there?"

He started to reply, but an old woman ran in front of the jeep, and he had to hit the brakes. She came to his side, reeking of onions, hugged and kissed him, hung a crucifix around his neck, made the sign of the cross. He thanked her graciously, as he did all women in all things, drove on, turned to Fidelito with a sudden burst of laughter. "At this rate, maybe a year or two, maybe never, enh?"

The helicopter following them hovered close when they reached the outskirts of Holguín, its noise making conversation impossible. The crowds, now thick on both sides of the highway, were cheering wildly, waving M-26-7 flags. Fidel's throat went dry. He felt he was dreaming, sleepwalking through a scene he could not even have imagined when cold and hungry and scared and surrounded in the Sierra Maestra, his men numbering twelve, Batista, fifty thousand plus, the odds, impossible. Yet we won, he thought, still amazed. We beat them simply because we didn't want to die. Of course, I had my doubts; of course, I knew the situation was always desperate; of course, it could have—should have by all the laws of probability—gone the other way, except I was always prepared for death, and they weren't. He recalled Batista bragging about his "campaign of extermination" and those hard, tense days when the army threw everything they had at his minuscule forces.

Well, he thought, you can't hit what you can't see, and we never faced the beast until he was exhausted, and then we were everywhere, coming from all directions, and the beast was running, staggering out of Oriente, jeeps, trucks, armor, artillery, all of it heading north; you would've thought the U.S. Marines were on his tail.

Then the lightning strikes by Che and Camilo as they surprised everyone and took Las Villas province away from the army, the surprises continuing with Raúl's successes in the Sierra Cristal, and the underground making the cities undeclared war zones. And then the tyrant up and flees just when I was ready to slug it out. I don't know whether to be joyful or pissed off, come on, *chico,* how can you not be happy? He tooted the horn, waved, pounded on the steering wheel.

And then the tyrant up and flees.

In the Holguín plaza were the requisite microphones, the platform, the battery of correspondents, the crush of people buzzing with excitement. He stopped his jeep, intent on giving another speech despite his raw vocal cords, but found himself held up by the famous, distinguished journalist from the *Chicago Tribune* asking him what he was going to do for the Cuban people.

"There will be a new ministry," he said, "the Ministry for the Recovery of Stolen Property, which will redistribute the island's wealth so that everyone has a share."

"Does that mean your revolution is socialist," came the inevitable, "and that Fidel Castro is a communist?"

Fidel smiled patiently, then replied diplomatically, "The Communist Party supported Batista during the war, enough said, señor?" As the interview continued, Fidel surveyed the vast crowd waving flags, now chanting his name, a collective joy he could not fathom, the same scene as in Santiago. He was tempted to feel invincible, yet realized it would end soon, and he would have to do something about running a country, a sobering thought. No one knew anything! All the bureaucrats were swimming to Miami, and the only ones left with any sense of organization were—the communists. *¡Dios mío!* Jolted, he stepped back, turned away from the *Chicago Tribune.* The communists. The enemy. The red menace who would do anything to become part of the revolution. He smiled, finished his interview with the usual, the pat "freedom with bread, bread without terror," then checked his watch, excused himself, saying absurdly he was late, knowing full well that time had stopped as long as the celebration continued.

As he swung back into the jeep, he saw Matthews trapped behind the pack of reporters, so he had Gonzáles escort him over.

Wreathed in smiles, the intrepid Matthews shook his hand vigorously. "Congratulations, señor!"

Fidel shrugged. "Happy New Year, Señor Herb."

Matthews gestured north. "What kind of government are you planning?"

"A humane one," he replied, hoping he didn't sound glib. His son was listening, and Fidel wanted to impress him, wanted to make him proud of his father.

"How long will Urrutia be president?" Matthews was scribbling notes in shorthand, not even looking, years of experience behind him.

Fidel shrugged again. "As long as the people want him."

"You mean, you're going to hold elections soon?"

"The people will decide."

"How?"

"They are the revolution."

Confused, Matthews nodded anyway, perspiring now. "Isn't Urrutia a little to the left?"

Fidel grinned, his eyes lighting up. "Perhaps, but we're

thinking of José Miró Cardona for Prime Minister, and you know where he stands."

Clearly startled, Matthews stopped writing. "But he's a conservative!"

"I studied law under him, Señor Herb, he's a good man."

"What about you?"

Fidel laughed. "I guess I'm unemployed, no?"

Matthews was bewildered. "But—"

Fidel started the jeep. "When you get a chance, call Señor Papa and tell him it's safe to come home, okay, *bueno?*"

He drove away, slowly through the town, picking up a little speed on the long, straight run to Camaguey, passing arid countryside dotted with scrub, cattle grazing in dry pastures, a sugar *central* in the distance, occasionally the palm-thatched house of a *campesino,* sometimes a pig in the yard, always chickens, always the bright-green vegetable patch, then the dry savannah again. Someday there'll be water here, he told himself, and everything will be green. Like the Sierra Maestra.

He glanced at his son. Fidelito seemed unhappy. "What's wrong?" he asked, concerned.

"I thought you was gonna run things," he said disconsolately, staring off. "I told all my friends back home we was gonna be rich."

"Rich?" Fidel replied, suddenly thinking of *his* father, hating him abstractly. "We'll never be rich."

"How come?"

"No one is going to be rich."

"What if you work real hard?"

Fidel tried to think how Che would put it. "Everyone has to learn to work hard, not for money, but for the revolution. Rich people don't work at all, they live off the pain and sweat of others; your own grandfather ruined lives and families, Fidelito! To work hard is to be morally pure! The

Banco Nacional charges too damned much interest, rent is too high, Cuban Telephone, all of them are making money for doing nothing! It will change, and soon the day will come, my son, when nobody needs any money, and everyone will be free, *¿comprendes?"*

"Money," he stated five miles up the road. "We will abolish it someday. Yes. In a few years, it will be a crime to carry pesos."

"Speaking of money," said Celia, in one of her less than tactful moods, "who do you think we should name as minister of finance?"

"How the hell should I know?" he shouted over his shoulder. *"¿Qué me importa?* Find someone qualified!"

It took them all week to get to Havana.

On the outskirts of the old city, a Sherman tank joined the column, and they rumbled into Havana. Fidel was pleased with the millions cheering him, flattered by the longest conga line in history snaking behind his men, appreciated the mangled, twisted parking meters they passed, hated symbols of oppression, was satisfied with the smashed windows and looted shops owned by *Batistianos,* pleased with the way his climactic speech was received at Camp Columbia, delighted with the white dove perching coincidentally on his shoulder when he spoke of peace, but the real warmth inside had come when he'd seen the pure joy on Fidelito's face as he'd lifted him onto the tank for those last triumphant miles. He would never forget that look, for it was the first sign that his son might grow to love him.

Five weeks later, Miró Cardona resigned and fled to Miami, claiming the communists had taken over, the standard, ritual cry of the political exile.

In the Palace of the Revolution, Fidel broke away from a knot of admirers, headed for the broad, marble staircase, laughing inwardly, taking a bottle of Bacardi from a bartender in black tie and tails at the foot of the stairs, leaving guests and reception behind, his first state affair after ceremonies naming *him* prime minister, though he preferred "premier" and the faded fatigues molded to his frame. Miró Cardona, bah! He didn't leave because of the communists, he left because he couldn't get anything done! Yes, he was a good man, but the times passed him by, and the student becomes the master. A twinge of guilt stabbed at him as he reached the second floor. Why appoint Miró at all? You knew what would happen. You knew you were the only one who could accomplish things, yet you stepped away from the government when you were the leader all along. It had to be that way, he confessed to himself, it had to. You had to appear innocent of wanting anything more than liberation, you had to keep your hands officially off, you could not merely seize power like just another Latin American dictator! After all, you do have ethics. Principles! Neither you nor the ministers will change one word of the 1940 Constitution, not after all the years of death and sacrifice. You will rule, yes, but only by popular acclaim, otherwise you will become a bearded Batista. He shook his head, took a long pull off the rum bottle. No, Miró Cardona left because I was in the streets making things happen, and he was here and could do nothing.

Sadly, he recalled the last incident, the one that had angered his old professor so much it had caused the resignation. Near his temporary residence, the Havana Libre qua Hilton, a bus had stalled and was blocking the street, creating a massive traffic jam so he couldn't get his jeep out of the driveway. Not even the incomparable Gonzáles could clear the street. Annoyed, Fidel berated the hapless bus driver, a sweaty fat man who sat cross-legged on the pavement with a near-empty toolbox and stared at his stricken engine. "Don't you know what's wrong with it?" The man shook his head. *"No sé, Comandante."* "Have you called your supervisor to send a mechanic?" He shook his head again, explaining, "There aren't any at the shop no more, they all took their money and went to the States and're opening Spanish-speaking Sinclair stations, so all the buses are breaking down. I'd go to Miami myself, but they don't need any drivers there." Then he shrugged apologetically, adding, "You know how it is." Angry, Fidel stripped off his shirt, grabbed a screwdriver, slid under the bus, started poking around while criticizing the man for lacking revolutionary consciousness. "If you truly supported the new Cuba," he said, "you would stop dreaming of Miami and pick up a book on auto mechanics. *Por favor,* a nine-sixteenths socket wrench." His hand shot out impatiently, took the wrench from the slack-jawed driver, went back to work. "As a matter of fact," Fidel continued, "that's how it's going to be in the revolution, anyone who chooses to serve his country by driving a bus damned well better know how to repair the engine." He slid out from under, grinning now, a glint in his eye, wiped his greasy hands on a rag, reached for his shirt. "The distributor was loose, *compañero,* and one of the wires wasn't connected anymore. You tell your supervisor if he doesn't start a training program for his drivers, he'll hear from me, personally!"

Well, the supervisor had been affronted by orders from a lowly bus driver and fired him. When Fidel heard of it, he removed the supervisor and gave his job to the bus driver, offending the minister of transportation, a close friend of Miró Cardona. When the minister complained, Fidel got rid of him too, and Miró packed his bags. Of course, it wasn't just a broken-down bus. Similar things had been happening every day, and Fidel's direct approach to the people's problems had paralyzed official channels, already clogged by years of neglect and mismanagement.

He took another long pull off the bottle and wandered down the hallway, passing the open door of Celia's office. When she saw him, she left her desk with a stack of documents, asking him to please read and sign them. "Not now, Celia, not now." He waved her away, continued along the corridor, drinking more frequently, feeling tired suddenly, realizing he hadn't slept in days, hadn't gotten more than two hours a night since January first. He smiled grimly, musing. Who needs sleep when you're living your dreams?

He entered the Salon of Mirrors, a long, empty room, walls and ceiling covered with glass. Finally, he was alone, facing himself. Shut into a room with his own image, an endless reflection, everywhere and nowhere, like a demigod.

Another drink of rum. He frowned. *And then the tyrant up and flees.* Why couldn't there've been a battle? he asked of the man in the mirror. The battle of Santiago, or better yet, the battle for Havana? Why did he have to run, leaving me to win by outmaneuvering the others? Damn you, Fulgencio Batista, damn you!

Except he only saw himself, every turn, every movement reflected endlessly. You are no hero, Señor Premier, he shouted, you are a fraud. No matter what they say, Señor Premier, your presence here is a miracle. You didn't win, he quit. He turned to avoid his image as tears came to his eyes. He longed for those glorious moments in the Sierra, the purity of a dangerous, yet brave move, like saving Papa Hemingway's life.

He was sobbing now, fearful he had lost some of his soul. *¡Dios mío! chico,* you are only thirty-two, but already middle-aged! Does Che feel this way?

He drank more, calmed himself, disgusted with his maudlin display. He turned to again face his image. Okay, okay, he said, ready to debate the point. So you didn't get your battle. Make up for it. Give yourself to this island. Completely. Make a better life for everyone. He frowned again. Is that bullshit, *chico?* Can you really do it? He didn't really know—the rum was talking.

He postured to the mirrors as if he were giving the speech he was supposed to deliver that evening in the Plaza de la Revolución, imagined the millions assembled, the statue of José Martí in the distance, even the gringos watching him on television, those in power labeling him an *enfant terrible.* They know nothing. The cameras show them everything, but they don't see, they don't understand what is happening here, they don't take us seriously, they can't believe we haven't shaved and put on coats and ties, those mantles of respectability. Well, go ahead, gringos, he thought, call me what you want, *enfant terrible* is better than puppet, and if that's what you see, I promise you, I'll rewrite the definition. He laughed morosely, his mind suddenly detached, observing his gestures repeat themselves to infinity, making him a parody of himself.

And then the tyrant up and flees.

Burning with shame, he was transfixed by his endless reflections. Yes, Señor Premier, you are like the wind, you are everywhere and nowhere.

Nowhere and everywhere.

His eyes narrowed. He hated himself for the way he had arrived. It was Papa's fault. *Hold out for the brass ring, son. Very important.* Papa, his words of caution. If I hadn't listened to him— He paused. *Momento, chico, momento.* You're drunk. Without *el viejo*'s advice, maybe there *would* have been a coup d'état, maybe you would've fought a war for nothing. He shook his head furiously, knew he could not change history, no, Señor Premier, he thought bitterly, there are no second chances.

Suddenly his frustration overwhelmed him, and with a burst of motion his gestures segued into a lanky pitcher's windup. He threw the bottle as hard as he could, and it shattered the mirrors on one entire wall, his multiple image disappearing in pieces as shards fell to the floor.

Fourteen

AS SOON AS he finished the conference call with his editors at *Life,* Papa phoned George. "Get your ass over here, partner!"

"Ernie?"

"I'm going hunting, George," he stated, in a good mood. "Cutting out in a half hour with or without you."

"Reckon I'll be there."

Papa hung up, went upstairs and dressed for the snow, very pleased with himself. Finally, he had a good idea. *Finally.*

The day had started inauspiciously enough with coffee and brandy, and him longing for the sweet summer of his youth, those innocent, passionate salad days when his juices flowed like fresh mountain streams. So hard was his nostalgia that he hadn't made the obligatory move to his writing table with its stack of flaccid prose ironically depicting marathon sexual fantasies. Instead, he'd dallied over the Sunday *New York Times,* saw an item in the sports section announcing the long-awaited *mano a mano* between Luis Dominguín and Antonio Ordoñez, Spain's finest matadors. The years evaporated as he transported himself back to those marvelous times on the bullfighting circuit, the women, friends, wine, dust from the bulls in the arena, orange sunsets behind *"las estocadas,"* the glory of death in the afternoon, the— He paused, benumbed as the idea took shape. Why not, he thought, a sequel to *Death in the Afternoon,* you could do worse, that was one helluva book. You can go back, Hem, next summer, you can write your impressions of the greatest *mano a mano* in history, you can turn back the clock, what a great fucking idea! Moments later, he was on the phone, laying out terms the editors graciously accepted.

Better believe, Papa thought joyfully, shucking into his hunting vest, *Old Man and the Sea* sold over five million copies for those boys. Made 'em a damned fortune. Flexing his hands, he went downstairs into the storage room, took the Winchester pump out of the gun cabinet, transferred a box of shells to his vest.

Upstairs, he fried eggs and bacon, made sandwiches, wrapped them in wax paper, filled his flask with scotch. When George pulled up and tapped his horn, Papa put on his coat and hat, pocketed the sandwiches, and was out the door, a huge grin on his face.

"Papa, wait!" Mary appeared on the deck. *"Time* magazine on the phone."

Sonuvabitch. He told George to hang fire, then went back upstairs, approached the phone in the living room as if it were diseased. Mary must've sensed his trepidation, for she'd left a fresh glass of Haig Pinch and lime juice on the coffee table.

"Hello?"

It was a lady reporter, some hysterical bitch with a Smith

College accent wanting to know how he felt about the turn of events in Cuba.

His mind wandered. So many people had called the past two weeks. At first, he had been grateful. René, in the middle of the night with the news that the general was on a plane to Ciudad Trujillo with his family, top murderers and thieves, not to mention eight million in gold stolen from the treasury. Batista, gone. The Finca, fine, the staff, happy and eager for Ernesto and Mary's return.

He wondered when they'd go back. While Mary hadn't said anything, he knew she didn't want to, and that saddened him, for he considered the Finca home. Maybe he could talk her into it, though. Sure, they'd left under trying circumstances—he'd told his buddies that Cuba was no longer "suitable for work or play"—except now a new era had begun, one that promised excitement, if nothing else, one that piqued Papa's curiosity, it was sort of like finally getting to see what would've happened had the Loyalists won the Spanish Civil War. Yet he knew as soon as he raised the issue, maybe even getting the luggage out of the closet, she'd start bitching about a bunch of young, unkempt beatniks who'd taken over her island and were threatening to expropriate everything American, right down to the Chesterfields sold at the Hilton gift shop.

He sighed heavily, his ear weary of the *Time* magazine reporter and her incessant inquiries. Grunting again, he produced enough sound to get her going on another long-winded question, this one speculating that Fidel Castro would apply to Eisenhower for commonwealth status like Puerto Rico. Papa almost laughed. Fat fucking chance, lady, he thought to himself. If Castro wants anything from Ike, it's gonna be an honorable discharge from the gringos, no strings attached. But he didn't say that, not to *Time* magazine. Instead, his answer was a remarkably noncommittal "news to me," and the interview dragged on, Papa resisting the urge to insult the lady and hang up so he could get out on the meadow before the sun got too high.

"So then you approve of the Cuban revolution, Mr. Hemingway?"

"Delighted with the change. Yep. Island's got a halfway decent future from the looks of it."

Mary gave him an icy look, put her finger to her lips, but that only made him bluster on, saying more than he should just to defy her.

"I dunno, though, they're up against Yankee interests, and that means a helluva lot of money, ma'am."

"You're glad General Batista has fled the country, I take it?"

"Sic transit hijo de puta."

"I'm sorry, Mr. Hemingway, would you mind translating?"

"So passes the son of a whore, lady." He hung up.

"Ernest, my God!" Mary was livid. "You were talking to *Time* magazine!"

"So? Let 'em print the truth once in a while."

He walked out of the house, leaving her wringing her hands, for once more worried about his image in the press than he was. He knew she didn't love him anymore, was supportive purely for the sake of appearance, held him in contempt. When had it started? He took a pull off his flask, went down the snow-covered steps. It's the Goddamned writing, he told himself, if it were going well, kitten would be purring like crazy.

To hell with her. No one tells old Hem what to say to the press or anyone else. This is gonna be a good day, you better believe. He climbed into the pickup, strapped the Winchester into the gun rack, greeted his old friend with a playful punch to the shoulder.

"What we lookin' for today, Ernie?"

"Moose," he said abruptly, figuring the game ought to match his expansive mood.

"Reckon we ought to start in the high country, then," said George, nodding.

They took the highway east, turned north onto a series of snow-covered roads, eventually ran out of pavement. George stopped the truck, got out, changed the axles into four-wheel drive, got back in, and then they were grinding up an old fire trail that switchbacked through stands of stunted pine and aspen, passing granite formations lit hard by the morning sun. Papa was silent, his mind already composing sentences he hoped would equal, say, the beauty of Antonio making a pass with cape and muleta, the purity of a clean *recibiendo*. He would do his damnedest, and while the articles for *Life* might not be the big book, they were a stepping stone, a warm-up for that one, last magnificent work lost somewhere in his soul.

He braced himself as the pickup bounced over rocks, then hit a series of huge potholes, the studs of the tires spitting mud and ice. George cursed the trail and the Idaho forestry service. They drove past the bad spots, over a hill, inched down the other side. The trail, barely visible under the snow cover, leveled out onto a long, white plain, and George appeared to relax.

"What d'you think of all that hootin' and hollerin' down in Cuba, Ernie, you spent some time there."

His reverie broken, Papa frowned, didn't want to comment and maybe ruin the hunt, knowing where his friend stood, but felt he had to say something. "I just read the papers, George. Watch the news."

"According to them reporters, you'd think there wasn't nothin' going on anywhere else in the world."

"Agree with you there."

"Don't know about that Castro, Ernie, him and all them executions."

Papa gazed out the side window at the cold, blue sky. He knew about the executions, he'd seen them, written about them at length in *The Bell*. You can't blame a father for shooting the man who tortured his son to death, he thought. Still, you gotta feel for the poor bastards kneeling in the dust, shaking with fear and bewilderment, maybe lucky enough to envision a beautiful woman at the instant their brains are blown apart. The unfortunates are the ones in the wrong uniform at the wrong time, the ones who don't deserve it. He shook his head. Bad stuff. Like rotten fruit. Nobody won in the execution business, and that was the straight gen of it.

He recalled Castro shrugging, deadpanning to the TV news: if we don't kill the *Batistianos,* somebody else will. The dumb shit thought the gringos would understand too, which just goes to show you he's still a kid playing marbles in a grown-up world. Makes you wonder if he's taken leave of his senses, Papa thought, or if he's just making damned sure he gets all the bad guys before they get him. One thing was certain, however. The blush was off the Cuban revolution, Castro's *barbudos* seemingly quite capable of imitating their predecessors.

"Where d'you stand on Castro, Ernie?" George asked as they got out of the pickup at the high end of the meadow.

"Don't think he's got a snowball's chance in hell," he grunted, hoping it wasn't so, annoyed by his own reservations because he knew in part they'd been shaped by the gringo press, which was giving Fidel a veritable pasting, but with just enough hard facts to make you wonder.

"He sure can talk."

"Yep."

They drank the last of the coffee from George's thermos, Papa lacing his with scotch, then started along a dogleg that dropped down into trees and a broad valley several miles long where they might find moose. Papa moved slowly, boots crunching on iced-over snow, fading from shadow to shadow, noting that moose had stripped the bark from the trees as high as ten and eleven feet. Must be some real beasts in this herd, some kings. He shuddered with excitement, a good feeling.

"So, you don't think Castro's gonna last?"

He scowled. Goddamnit, George, he complained to himself, you want to hunt or talk politics? He'd thought about Cuba enough for one day, enough to get righteously homesick, for he wished he was there, writing in the tower, or out on the *Pilar* playing a thousand-pound marlin while the turmoil swirled around him, and he could draw from it like he always had in the past. But, no, here he was trudging through the snow, and, yes, he loved to hunt, yet he didn't particularly care for the bone-cutting cold, it made his joints remind him of his age. Annoyed, he kept silent, kept walking, but couldn't get George's question out of his head. Castro had surprised the entire civilized world. Against all odds, he'd snookered his way into the presidential palace as the youngest, most outrageous prime minister in recent history. Mighty impressive. Kid must've changed, must've shit-canned some of that greenhorn idealism he was ranting and raving about in the Sierra Maestra. Hell, maybe he actually listened to me.

The thought stopped him in his tracks. Jeez Crize, Hem, he said to himself, don't tell me it's partly your fault that bearded youngster is calling those insane shots down there! He quickly shook his head. Naw, come on, old man, quit tooting your own horn, the kid just got lucky. Or did he?

No way of knowing, he thought, resigned. Have to wait and see what he does, maybe you can go home before you have to leave for Spain, spend some time at the Finca. Finally, he turned to George, said truthfully, with finality, "Don't know about Castro, too early to tell."

End of conversation, Papa deliberately moving away

from George so there wouldn't be any more questions. He put a huge boulder between them, and was grateful for the sudden quiet. As he labored through a drift of powder, he heard the lonely cry of a hawk, reflecting the absence of life, the winter. Clearing the boulder, he saw George again, fifteen yards off to his left. They nodded to each other, kept going, crested the rise, started down the other side.

There.

Papa stopped. Blinked. Two hundred yards away, standing on a knoll in front of a granite slab, was the largest bull moose he'd ever seen, nine feet at the shoulder, antlers, eight feet across, at least twenty points, Jesus Christ, what a rack! He took a deep breath, raised the Winchester, got the beast lined up in his sights, exhaled slowly, concentrated on the massive head, the alert, frozen, dark eyes staring back at him. Time stopped. He squeezed the trigger.

Suddenly, his mind switched. A *Look* magazine photograph of Raúl Castro directing a firing squad segued into a Cuban television film clip of a *barbudo* comandante shooting a Batista colonel in the head, cephalic mass splattering all over the small screen.

He jerked the shot, and the round hit the granite over the bull's head, ricocheting off with a high-powered whine that echoed for miles.

Instantly, the moose was gone. Slack-jawed, George stared at him, unbelieving.

"I missed, okay?" Papa growled furiously. "I just fucking missed!"

Fifteen

A SHOELESS FIDEL had been up since six, reading diplomatic cables from socialist-bloc countries, while his bodyguards moved him into his newly borrowed house in Cojímar that overlooked the sea. Since he owned no furniture, they had brought an assortment from the Havana Libre, none of it matching. Celia protested, saying this wouldn't do for the Premier of Cuba, but he overruled her, went back to his dispatches, and she contented herself by scolding the bodyguards for not wiping their boots before they came inside.

Guardian wandered into the room. He was the two-month-old German shepherd Fidel had purchased because a house was not a home without a dog around. Tail wagging, he waddled over to his master, licked his hand. Fidel looked up from a rather boring cable about Soviet quotas for Romanian black caviar, grinned, playfully nudged Guardian with his foot whereupon the dog began chewing on his sock. Laughing, the Prime Minister sparred with his puppy until the razor-sharp teeth started to smart. He pushed him away, put his feet up on the glass coffee table out of the dog's reach, ignored him. Discouraged, Guardian walked away, claws clicking on the linoleum, and his master continued reading.

"No," Celia shouted. *"No!"*

Startled, Fidel looked up. Celia slapped the dog across the nose, shoved his muzzle into a puddle of urine in the corner. Yipping, Guardian ran out of the room, tail between his legs.

"Don't be so hard on him," said Fidel, spreading his arms. "You'll break his spirit."

"You clean it up, then!" She stormed into the kitchen, started unpacking pots and pans, deliberately banging them.

Women, Fidel sighed as he got up, glanced around for something to wipe up the mess with. That morning's *Prensa Libre* was on the table, but he hadn't looked at it yet, so, without thinking, he used a half-dozen East German state papers and a couple of UPI dispatches. There was no wastebasket, so he left the crumpled and sodden business of foreign relations in the corner.

Gonzáles walked in hefting two hundred pounds of barbells as if they were feathers. *"¿A dónde?"*

"The bedroom, *chico,* the bedroom."

He left, followed by two others carrying armloads of scuba gear. Fidel opened the newspaper. On page 3, he saw a picture of Señor Papa and his wife surrounded by reporters at Rancho Boyeros airport, the caption announcing that the distinguished Nobel prize-winning author had come home, appropriately, on Easter Sunday. Fidel smiled, pleased he was back, wondered how long it had been since they'd seen each other. A year? Two years? No, it couldn't have been that long! Yes, *chico,* two years ago in the Sierra

Maestra, the day Rafael Cruz shot the gringo deserter, that was the last time you saw *el viejo, es verdad.*

Suddenly, he sprang out of the chair, strode from the room through the kitchen and screened porch, out to the hill where his son was trying to fly a homemade kite. "Fidelito!" he called. *"¡Vámonos!"*

Three minutes later, Gonzáles was impatiently herding the bodyguards into the Prime Minister's fleet of Oldsmobile Delta 88's, four to a car, submachine guns poked out the windows, ready. Fidel gave the word, and they took off, drivers accelerating to seventy-five. When they turned onto the main highway, the cars formed a phalanx around Fidel's, forcing all other traffic off the road, horns blaring, drivers feinting like boxers, swerving at trucks or buses that came too close, bodyguards shouting threats at the bewildered citizens. As the road narrowed, the 88's intermeshed into a column, and then they were zooming through San Francisco de Paula, ancient, beshawled women watching curiously from the steps of the church, barefooted children waving. The drivers braked fast at the gates to La Finca Vigia, turned, shot up the long, curving driveway, and Fidel admired the variety of mango trees in the orchard, craning around to see after they'd passed. In front of the house, the Oldsmobiles circled and parked, but all at different angles so every car had a straight run at a fast getaway. Instantly, the doors swung open, and the bodyguards were fanning out around the house and grounds.

"Where are we, Daddy?" asked Fidelito, confused by all the hoopla.

"At Señor Papa's house, don't tell me you haven't read Ernest Hemingway yet!" He didn't wait for an answer, having seen *el viejo* in clean *guayabera* shirt standing under the arched colonnade observing the scene with consternation. Grinning, he strode up the stone steps with outstretched hand. *"¡Buenas!"*

"What the hell's this?" asked Papa. "An advertisement for General Motors or an invasion?"

Fidel shrugged. "They insist on it."

"Who's they?"

"Gonzáles, Celia, the staff," he said impatiently, "you know how it is."

"Looks to me like you're scared you're gonna get bumped off."

For a moment, Fidel was jolted, then, growing annoyed, shoved his face close to Papa's and started in. "No, no, *viejo*, you're dead wrong, why should I worry about something as absurd as an assassination? The people adore me, can't you see it? You read, you listen, you watch TV, where did you come up with such a ridiculous notion? You don't understand, our enemies are demoralized, on the defensive, there is a spiritual regeneration going on here, no one is against me!"

Papa pursed his lips, squinted at the Oldsmobiles, then grinned, eyes twinkling. "C'mon inside before you get shot." He went into the living room, headed straight for the table with the liquor, poured rum over ice, handed his visitor a glass. "Have a cold one. Enjoy it while the Frigidaires're still working."

"Why are you trying to insult me?" said an affronted Fidel, sorry he'd come. "Okay, *bueno*, so the security's heavy, so what? If that's what the people want, that's what they'll have! But, rest assured, no one is going to shoot me! I don't deserve it!"

Chuckling, Papa held up his hand. "Take it easy, son, don't get so damned riled." He settled into his chair, raised his glass. "Cheers."

"Compai."

They drank.

"Looks like you gained a whole bunch of weight. Guess they serve some pretty good eats in the palace, huh?"

Fidel blushed, smiled in spite of himself. He'd forgotten *el viejo*'s caustic edge, wasn't sure he appreciated it, was about to comment on Hemingway's bulging waistline when the old man changed the subject.

"What the hell you doing here, anyway? Don't prime ministers work nowadays?"

He shrugged. "Everything happens at night. Or before dawn."

"Russkies must love that," Papa said, bemused, "they ain't worth a shit before ten or after two."

"I have nothing to say to the Russians."

"Good for you."

At least, not yet, viejo. "And how is the writing coming, Señor Papa?"

"Goes fine till the work-killers show up."

A chilled pause. Is he asking me to leave? Fidel wondered, feeling like a small boy chastised for wanting companionship at the wrong time. Apparently not, for now he was commenting on some "pretty shrewd broken-field running," alluding to his circuitous route to the Prime Minister's office, though the "double-cross" pulled on Miró Cardona seemed pretty damned cold, was that an example of "humanism"?

"Obviously, you don't like what's going on," Fidel stated flatly. "What would you do differently?"

"Don't ask me about politics," growled Papa. "Horseshit belongs in pastures, not in friendly conversations between men."

Fidel spread his hands. "This is a friendly conversation?"

Surprised, Papa roared with laughter, nodded approval at the witticism, refilled his glass. "It is now."

Fidel laughed too, also helped himself to more rum, sat on the couch across from Papa.

"Just keep it all in perspective, son. Hang on to your sense of humor, and you halfway got a chance."

"What are you saying?"

"Men think the same way they live. Including you."

"What do you mean exactly?" he said slowly.

Papa affixed Fidel with a critical eye. "Listen, kid, and this ain't no bullshit, everybody knows that right now the hottest-selling item in Havana is a one-way ticket to Miami, and as them of the bourgeois persuasion cut and run, your boys with the beards are moving into those empty Vedado mansions with the swimming pools still clean, air conditioners still working, plenty of hootch behind the bar, even some hundred-year-old French cognac, plus a Caddy in the garage with a full tank."

"So?" he said defensively. "The spoils of war."

"C'mon, Castro, cut the crap! You take someone used to hiding out in the mountains and stealing chickens to stay alive, label him a hero and drop him into a fourteen-room estate he can call home, something's gonna *happen,* y'know what I mean?"

"What's going to happen?"

"Well, in the first place, things're gonna start breaking down, and nobody's gonna know how to fix 'em, so if I was you, I'd have the rebel army round up all the folks in conga lines who forgot New Year's was over and send 'em to technical school. Secondly, your boys in the mansions are gonna get used to satin sheets, silk pajamas, and late nights at the casino, and pretty soon, the peasant with seven hungry kids and a pregnant wife ain't gonna seem so important. So, you can go ahead and rename the Hilton the Havana Libre, but that don't change the fact that you got the entire twenty-third floor to yourself whenever you need a place to stay in town. What's more, next thing you know, this island's gonna run out of canned ham and Champion spark plugs about the same time you run out of rhetoric for the world's press, and I sure as hell wouldn't want to be in your boots then, Castro. That's what I mean by 'men think the way they live,' and if you want my advice, I'd be damned careful when they blow the whistle for the second half, 'cause it kinda looks like Uncle Sam might be coaching the other team, y'know?"

A silence. The old man took a swallow of rum and eased back in his chair. Behind him, cats padded through the room, rubbing themselves on the bookcases as they went out, and a warm breeze signaled the approach of a *chubasco* over the Gulf Stream.

Fidel felt burned and shamefaced. "Don't you see what we've done, *viejo,* or are you as blind as the rest of the gringos? Already we have reduced rents, cut utility rates, lowered food costs, increased salaries, Cuban Telephone is now controlled by its workers, we are planning agrarian reform, now the casino profits are paying for low-cost housing instead of lining the pockets of New York gangsters. You, you talk about Vedado mansions, Señor Papa," he said finally, index finger stabbing the air. "The Ministry of Recovery is giving Cuba back to *cubanos!"* He paused, then, "You see these?" He gestured with the collar of his fatigue shirt. "Fidel Castro will always wear olive-green, he will always be at one with the people, and so will his ministers! I tell you, the revolution is working!"

"What happens when you run outa spare parts?"

"We will manufacture new ones."

"Ain't holding my breath, son."

Fidelito came into the room, his face long. "Daddy, there's nothing for me to do. Is it okay if I go down by the pool?"

"Fidelito!" he said expansively, forgetting the state of the revolution. "I'd like you to meet Señor Ernest Hemingway, one of the greatest writers of all time!"

Papa shook the boy's hand. Studied him and smiled. "You know what, son?"

"What?"

"Baseball season opens in a week and a half. Think Larsen's got another perfect game in him?"

Fidelito looked down shyly, fidgeted with his hands. "I dunno. Who's he?"

Fidel and Papa exchanged looks of disbelief.

"You don't know who Don Larsen is?" exclaimed Fidel, bending over, peering into his son's eyes.

"No."

Chagrined, Fidel turned to Papa, threw up his hands. "I don't believe it! The boy grows up in the shadow of Yankee Stadium, and he doesn't know about Larsen!"

Papa laughed, but not at the boy's expense; instead, he was pointing at Fidel. "You ain't never going to live that one down, Señor Prime Minister."

Annoyed, Fidel glared back at *el viejo,* then grabbed his son by the shoulders. "In 1956, Don Larsen pitched the only perfect game in the history of the World Series."

"Oh."

Bewildered, Fidel realized the boy didn't comprehend the enormity of such an achievement, and then—*¡no me digas!*—it gradually dawned on him that the kid didn't know anything at all about baseball. He squatted in front of Fidelito and spread his hands. "Tell Señor Papa what your batting average was last year."

"Didn't play," he said, his voice small. "Mama didn't want me around the Puerto Ricans."

Fidel was stunned. *"¡Dios mío!* how could she do that to him, what's the world coming to when a kid doesn't get to play ball in New York City of all places, he could've been a bat boy for the Giants or even the Dodgers, you see what happens when sons grow up without fathers!" He ran outside screaming for Gonzáles, who was dressing down a frightened bodyguard for flirting with one of the Finca's servants. The Chief sprinted over, moving with amazing speed for his size, drawing his pistol, ready to shoot the problem, even if it was a Nobel prize winner. "No, no, no, Gonzáles, we're going to play some baseball. I want bats, balls, gloves! *¡Tan pronto posible!"*

A car was dispatched to the nearest sporting goods store and returned with a trunkload of equipment. Already, Fidel had his shirt off, folded up on the driveway as a makeshift home plate, couldn't wait to get Fidelito's hand into a glove, found a good fit, grabbed a ball, started warming up, scowled when he saw his son throwing like a girl.

"No, no, no, you stride when you throw, and pivot, pulling your chest around with your left arm, your right arm becoming a whip, and then you follow through, okay *bueno?"*

He kept glancing at Papa and Gonzáles playing catch a short distance away, was ready to attack them for any desultory remarks, but they remained silent and ignored him. Occasionally, Papa bitched about his aching joints, yet he threw gracefully for an old man, and Fidel was surprised. "Watch *el viejo,"* he murmured to his son. "He throws correctly."

The boy got the hang of it quickly, and Fidel was pleased. *"¡Todos!* Look at him! He's a natural, he can play for the Cojímar Lions this season!" He paused. "What position will you try out for, enh, Fidelito?"

"Pitcher."

"Sí, sí, sí, pitcher!" He laughed with delight. "Like father, like son, *¡es verdad!"*

"What the hell you yelling about, Castro?" said Papa.

"You don't know, *viejo?* After the university, I had a tryout with your Washington Senators!"

"No shit?"

"De verás. Except Señor Calvin Griffith said I didn't throw hard enough, *qué será."*

"Smart man."

Fidel shrugged, then winked. "Maybe, maybe not. If he had signed me, there might not have been a Cuban revolution." He turned. "Gonzáles! We need a catcher!"

Compañero Rafael was given a catcher's glove, and the requisite sixty feet were paced off. Fidel began throwing in earnest, the balls cracking when they hit the catcher's glove, that sweet sound of a live, albeit slow fastball. Delighted with himself, he stopped, wiped sweat off his brow, handed the ball to his son, watched him throw for a while, not noticing the black clouds overhead or Gonzáles warily glancing skyward.

"Okay, *bueno,* Fidelito, *bueno.*" He took the ball back, gripped it loosely, his index and middle fingers split over the seams, rotated it back and forth. "This is how you throw a curve."

"Wait a minute," said Papa, stepping forward. "I dunno where you learned to pitch, but that ain't how you throw a curve at all, and if you got cut by the *Senators—*" He held his ball up, gripped it tightly, fingers together, perpendicular to the seams. "This is how you're supposed to hold it."

Fidel frowned, paid no attention to the thunder rolling through the valley below. "Okay, Señor Papa, you know so much about it, go ahead, show me."

Papa toed the line in the dirt that was the rubber, wound and threw. The ball roundhoused into the catcher's glove.

"You call that a curve?" the Prime Minister exclaimed, spreading his hands. "I'll show you a curve!" He turned to his chief bodyguard. "Get a bat, Gonzáles!"

When the big man was at the plate and ready, Fidel stepped to the rubber, stared hard at his target, unmindful of the large raindrops kicking up puffs of dust here and there. He went into an elaborate windup, leg kicking high, came over the top and threw, snapping his wrist.

The ball didn't break.

Gonzáles, a pretty fair country ballplayer himself,

stepped into the pitch and belted it. Awed, they turned and watched the ball carry a good four hundred feet before bouncing to obscurity, below in the streets of San Francisco de Paula.

No one said anything.

The skies opened up, rain coming down in sheets, soaking everyone in seconds.

And then Fidelito was giggling, that joyful look on his face again, laughing uncontrollably, and now his father was laughing with him, and soon everyone was laughing, even Gonzáles, and Fidel couldn't remember having ever been quite so happy.

"Calvin Griffith was a fucking genius," said Papa, heading for the house.

Sixteen

FROM ATOP A knoll in Central Park on a cold April night, Papa watched the neophyte Prime Minister performing for 30,000 midtown New Yorkers and other curiosity seekers. Castro had come to the States at the invitation of the American Society of Newspaper Editors, was determined to make friends and good impressions, and seemed right at home in the middle of the vast plain of dead grass, his shrill voice and accompanying gestures eliciting enthusiasm from the crowd—small by Cuban standards, but enough to upstage Broadway. There were the usual liberals in the front rows—secretaries with sack dinners wearing "JFK" buttons, bespectacled, pipe-smoking Columbia and NYU students with hair over their ears wearing turtlenecks and cord jackets with leather patches, doing their "poly-sci" assignments. A tiny group of suburban pickets bussed down from White Plains marched off to the side, their slogans ranging from "Better Dead Than Red" to "Don't

150

Ban the Bomb, Ban Castro." As always, the New York City
mounted police kept the assemblage orderly. One of their
trusty steeds punctuated a Castro commentary on agrarian
reform by lifting his tail and fertilizing the grass. The
pickets cheered.

Papa heard laughter behind him, moved closer to the
trees, pushed his Stetson low over his eyes, hunkered down
into his leather vest. Dressed like a Wyoming cattle baron,
he didn't want anyone recognizing him. He'd been in New
York a week now getting ready for the trip to Spain, was
sick and tired of people accosting him, was sick and tired of
the city, annoyed that Mary liked it so much. New York's
an abomination, he told himself, living proof of man's
inhumanity to man; no wonder they're fascinated by
Castro, he's describing another world.

Four young blacks in shiny jackets and porkpie hats
sauntered up the hill near Hemingway, were about to slide
into the bushes when one noticed Castro, nudged his
partner.

"Say, brother, check it out."

The partner stared and blinked. "What he talkin', man?"

"Trash."

"Say, dig it. Cat look like a puppet, man, a mothafuckin'
jive-ass puppet!"

Convulsed with laughter, they boogied off and disappeared, four shadowy testaments to alienation.

Shrewd observation, Papa thought. Castro did resemble
a marionette, a dancing-bear character singing for his
supper. Everyone rises to the occasion in this zoo of a
town, even brand-new heads of state.

"¡No se apuren, mis amigos!" Castro shouted. "American interests in Cuba will be protected, the revolution will
always respect the rights of private property, we want
nothing more than freedom and justice for the Cuban

151

people, we want nothing more than the right to chart our own destiny without outside interference! Freedom with bread, *mis amigos,* bread without terror!"

The audience applauded and cheered wildly. The liberals danced and chanted, "Viva, Fidel!" Thousands joined in. There were even choruses of "Olé!" with no one except old Hem appreciating the irony.

Papa waited patiently while the festive mood ebbed and the crowd slowly dispersed, then started down the hill, observing the pack of reporters hound Castro, the body-guards pushing them away, the mounted cops enjoying the show. After everyone had left and the Prime Minister was angling toward the limousines, Papa crossed the dead green, saluted Gonzáles, who was complaining about his frozen feet and cursing the weather, and approached Castro.

"Not bad, son, not bad at all. You had some of the nastiest people in the world eating out of your hand."

"Papa!" Fidel whirled around, his face lighting up. He embraced Hemingway, stepped back, held him by the shoulders and gazed at him—a long-lost friend in a strange land. "I heard you were here, but I had no idea how to find you! How have you been?"

"Homesick."

"Tell me about it." His dark eyes shifted in all directions. "Nueva York, *¡ayy!* I could never live here, *viejo.* Listen, why don't we have dinner together?"

Papa shook his head firmly. "You think I want to be seen at . . . at Toots's with a bunch of *barbudos?"*

Fidel shrugged dejectedly. "There is so much I want to tell you, and so little time. Tomorrow they have me speaking at City Hall and the United Nations. Then I'm supposed to say nice things about Picasso at the Museum of Modern Art." He frowned. "To hell with Picasso and his squiggly lines, what about tomorrow afternoon?"

Papa pursed his lips, thought quickly. He too wanted to

talk, but was supposed to board the U.S.S. *Constitution* at noon for the trip to Spain. Except the ship didn't actually sail until after six. He grinned. "Why don't we take in a ball game?"

Fidel beamed. *"¡Perfecto!"*

Papa held up a restraining hand. "No bodyguards, Castro. I ain't gonna be on public display for you or anybody else."

Fidel winked conspiratorially. "I'll come, how you say? Incognito?"

"Is that possible?"

"¡Claro! I just change clothes and disappear!" He laughed. "It drives Gonzáles crazy!"

"Can't imagine why." Papa shook his head. "The game's at two-thirty."

The two left Central Park by different routes, Fidel leaning out the window and waving as his limousine pulled away.

They didn't see the brush-cut man in a trench coat half-hidden in the bushes on the knoll, his binoculars reflecting the park's streetlights.

"¡Mucho gusto!" exclaimed Fidel, jamming the rest of the hot dog into his mouth, spilling some relish and mustard, washing it all down with huge gulps of beer, wiping his mouth on his sleeve.

They were in Yankee Stadium behind third base watching the Red Sox go down in order in the top of the fourth. True to his word, Fidel had come without his bodyguards and in disguise, wearing dark glasses and a seedy overcoat.

What with his scraggly beard and hair, he looks just like one of those beatniks, mused Papa. We should've gone to the Village, he would've fit right in.

"When I was in Washington, I talked to your Señor Nixon."

"Yeah?"

Fidel grinned sheepishly, smacked fist into hand. "I almost hit him."

"Oh, Jesus." Papa put his head in his hands, listened soberly as Castro described the encounter, gradually growing louder, gestures becoming more intense, annoying the Puerto Ricans sitting behind them.

"His dog, Checkers, was there beside his chair, farting in his sleep, the smells consistent with what he was saying, can you imagine such rudeness? He advised me to start cooperating with the señor in your State Department in charge of Cuban affairs, I think the words he used were *muy pronto*. And when I replied—with a certain amount of irritation—that I was, in fact, the Premier of Cuba and did not wish to consult with a foreigner about the affairs of my own country, he got angry, called me a threat to the stability of Latin America, a 'comsymp' radical in danger of coming under Soviet influence!" He paused. "Well, I already *have* talked to the Russians, Señor Papa, and you know what they tell me? Slow down, comrade, be careful, your agrarian reform proposals are too extreme, get rid of that Guevara, he talks like an anarchist, be sure to maintain a dialogue with the United States, but must I sit there drinking weak coffee while Señor Nixon humiliates me and his dog keeps breaking wind? And when I protest, he gets enraged, jabs at me with his finger and threatens to end trade and cut off the sugar quota!"

Castro paused again, drank more beer. "So, I stood up too, I mean how much can a man take, and said, *'Chinga a tu madre,'* then I walked out!"

Papa stared. His mouth fell open. "You told the Vice-President of the United States to go fuck his mother?"

Fidel spread his hands. "What else could I do?"

"Jesus H. Christ and John R. God!"

"Of course, the man doesn't speak a word of Spanish so I doubt that he understood me."

Unchecked, the grin spread across Papa's face, and he realized for the first time he actually *liked* this boy. Yeah, the kid's got elephant *cojones,* he told himself, but unfortunately, that ain't gonna cut it. "Something bad's gonna happen."

"What d'you mean?"

"C'mon, Fidel, don't act so fucking dumb. Richard Milhous Nixon has risen from the ranks of the rattlesnakes! He's the one who inherits the throne from Ike come November, he's gonna be the most powerful man in the world." He paused, raised his eyebrows, gestured. "You tell him to go fuck his mother, you think he's gonna write you a check?"

"I did not come here asking for Yankee dollars!" he replied indignantly.

Papa sighed, looked back at the field, saw Whitey Ford give up back-to-back singles in the Red Sox's fifth.

"How much money you figure the gringos got tied up in Cuba?" he asked, chin in hand, still watching the game.

"Eight hundred fifty million dollars."

The next batter moved the runners to second and third, and the crowd started rumbling.

"Dunno about you," Papa said gloomily, "but I'd hate like hell to be up against that much cash and be in the ring with Mr. Nixon."

"American interests in Cuba will not be touched, Señor Papa, but our revolution insists upon a free Cuba, an honest government, a return to the Constitution of 1940, and for all *cubanos*—"

"Shut up, for Christ's sake!" Papa was on his feet. "Can't you see who's coming up?"

As the lanky ballplayer ambled out of the dugout to the

155

bat rack, the announcement came. "Now batting for Boston . . . number nine . . . centerfielder Ted Williams!"

Yankee Stadium rocked with boos and raspberries.

Fidel stood too, sensing that the moment was infinitely more important than deteriorating U.S.-Cuban relations.

With first base open, the catcher signaled for an intentional walk, and Whitey threw the first pitch way outside. The boos increased, mixed with catcalls, number nine being the man they loved to hate in Yankee Stadium.

"The cowards are putting him on," complained Fidel.

"Wouldn't you?" growled Papa, appreciating the move, but pissed off because he loved to see Williams swing.

"No *cojones,*" Fidel said sadly.

Williams took three balls. Whitey wound and threw what should've been ball four, but Ted stepped *across* the plate and belted the pitch into the upper deck. The crowd went berserk, bombarded him with cups of beer and other debris as he circled the bases, but Williams merely smiled and lifted his middle finger to the outraged Yankee fans.

Papa was laughing so hard his sides hurt, and he doubled over. Fidel was jumping up and down, pounding Papa on the back, unmindful of the icy Puerto Rican stares.

Later, as they left the stadium, Fidel was still grinning from ear to ear. "If they made Señor Ted Williams ambassador to Cuba, our countries would get along fine."

"Forget it, my friend, you want to survive, join the Republican Party and the Kiwanis Club, marry an Irish girl from New England, send Fidelito to prep school, root for the Washington Redskins, change your last name to Casper, and for God's sake, *shave!*" He hailed a cab.

"You are trying to belittle me," Fidel said flatly, climbing in after him.

Papa ignored the remark. "Listen, son, if you're planning to go at it with Nixon—or whoever ends up as the champ—lemme give you some advice."

"I've had enough of your advice, *viejo!*"

"Yeah? You ever been in the ring?"

"No. We always fought in the streets."

"Then you don't know shit from Shinola, boy, and I'm gonna tell you something you'd best not forget. You remember the second Louis-Schmeling fight?"

Fidel looked dubious.

"Naw, you were too damned young, but Joe decked him in the first round 'cause he knew how to counterpunch, understand? So when Uncle Sam nails you with a hard left hand—and he will—come across the top with a right cross. *Always* hit him harder than he hits you. That's the only chance you got, believe me."

Within minutes they were at the docks on the Hudson River, but Papa made no move to get out of the cab. Instead, he gazed at the ship he was due to board, the U.S.S. *Constitution,* which gleamed white-pink in the late afternoon sun. Hundreds of people lined the decks throwing kisses, ticker tape, and confetti to well-wishers seeing them off. There it was, the first new American luxury liner in quite some time. No expense had been spared on the proud white knight of the oceans. "That's exactly what you're up against, son," he said quietly, "that kind of money, that kind of mentality."

"Hey!" said the cabby, switching off his meter, turning, his hand out for six-fifty, expression never changing—he could've seen God and it wouldn't have made any difference. "You guys fuckin' mind gettin' outa my fuckin' cab, already? Gotta go, got a fuckin' fare in Queens, c'mon now!"

Grimacing, Papa dug into his pockets, but wasn't used to being on his own where he couldn't run a tab, and could only come up with two dollars and thirty-five cents. "You got any cash?"

"Money?" said Fidel, astonished. *"Soy poco ordenado."*

"What's he talking about?" said the cabby suspiciously.

"I know you're gonna find this hard to believe," Papa explained, "but he's the Prime Minister of Cuba, and he ain't got a dime."

"Why should I find that hard to believe?" The cabby reached for his radio. "Fuckin' Puerto Ricans're always broke, too."

"Momento, momento," said Fidel, leaning forward, "let me explain something about money to you!"

While Fidel lectured the cabby about the necessity to demythicize money and *not* rehabilitate it, so that eventually all goods and services would be free, Papa slid from the taxi and hurried toward the gangway, intending to borrow the fare from the ship's steward and be right back. Chuckling, he glanced over his shoulder and saw Fidel wagging his finger in the cabby's face, haranguing him as if he were a delegate to the United Nations. Boy's got rain, he told himself, enough rain and *cojones* for a Goddamn regiment.

Seventeen

THE HELICOPTER WAS high over the island, heading south at flank speed, Fidel strapped in the copilot's seat, on his way to La Plata to sign the agrarian reform bill. He was followed by two more helicopters carrying ministers, bearded dignitaries, and state security to witness and rubber-stamp the historic occasion. He'd worked long and hard on the new legislation, fighting compromise, making sure the bill didn't allow the peasants to get screwed again. Che had been so happy with it he suggested the ceremonial signing be staged in the Maestra. Why not forever bury Cuban feudalism where we picked up the gun? he'd said. In La Plata, the site of our first victory.

Yet they weren't going merely for symbolic reasons. Fidel hadn't relaxed in a long time and saw a chance to get in a few days of bird hunting before returning to the sleepless rigors of Havana, the endless phone calls, the long lines of envoys and functionaries, the disorganization of state affairs.

Finally, the helicopters touched down in the Oriente foothills, Gonzáles and the bodyguards on the ground before the engines were switched off, pushing back a small crowd of curious peasants.

A caravan of jeeps waited, now filling up with officials; bodyguards sat on the bumpers, hoods, and fenders, weapons at the ready. Fidel frowned. No, no, this will never do, as Che advises, there will be no carte blanche to pomp and circumstance.

"Get out of the jeeps, *compañeros,*" he yelled. "We walk to La Plata!"

The ministers exchanged looks of disbelief, grumbled, but obeyed, and the trek began—up steep switchbacks into the mist-shrouded Maestra. Although surrounded by the obligatory security, Fidel was happy, recognized landmarks, remembered incidents, ambushes. Oh, how he longed for those desperate, yet simpler times. For him, these mountains were sacred, a Cuban holy land, and the long march to La Plata, a pilgrimage. The act symbolized the revolutionary ethic, *his* determination never to separate his values from those of the working class.

A half mile farther along, the road got steeper. A switchback higher, he was huffing and puffing, unable to talk. He realized he was out of shape. He scowled, sucked in his belly that rolled over his pistol belt, but that didn't help his overworked lungs. Worse, his legs were turning to jelly, and—*¡Dios mío!*—blisters on his feet! Angry at himself, he remembered escaping from Sánchez Mosquera's troops, running for two days on trails much steeper than this road, using the pain as a force, a conditioner. "We've forgotten how to be hard," he said to no one in particular. "We've forgotten how to be hungry."

With that, he ignored his pain and picked up the pace, eliciting from the others mutterings of "Jesus Christ, Fidel never changes," and *"¡ay, mi madre!* just like the fucking old days." Gritting his teeth, he pushed himself over the summit into the heart of the Maestra. By the time he got to La Plata, he was limping and staggering, his breath coming in tortured gasps, his uniform ringed with sweat stains. Not wanting anyone to see him in such condition, he skirted the small valley to the old *barbudo* encampment and entered his GP tent through the back flap, thanking God he'd made it.

The army had been shuttling peasants up to La Plata all day long, so there was a respectable crowd around the temporary stage when the ministers straggled onto the scene. By then, Fidel was rested, wearing cleaned and starched fatigues, and moving around on bandaged feet. From his tent, he made a grand entrance to waves of applause, took the stage with a vengeance, raised his arms in triumph.

"*¡Compañeros y compañeras!*" he shouted into the microphones, eyes fixed hard on the TV cameras. "The plantation system has finally been destroyed, *¡Que vaya con diablo!*"

"Fidel, Fidel, Fidel, Fidel!" they began chanting.

He waved for silence, went on. "The Yankee landowners and businessmen will say that the new law will ruin the economy, that we have robbed them of their property, yet mark my words, *compañeros,* this day will live in history as the day you, *los pobres,* were unshackled and set free!"

More applause.

He lectured extemporaneously for three hours, gesticulating, his voice modulated—so it seemed—by the swirls of mist as the morning waned. Then concluded: "Let *diez y siete de mayo* live in your hearts! Cuba is beginning a new era!"

Once again, they chanted his name while at a long table the ministers dutifully signed the reforms, making them gospel, creating the monolithic Instituto Nacional de la Reforma Agraria. Then, the crowd's enthusiasm channeled young and old into an elongated conga line that snaked and sang through the village and down the road, an undulating flow of peasants. The new Cuba, Fidel thought and smiled, no longer a nation of slaves, or, as Papa might say, a place where people don't play bush league anymore.

It started raining. Fidel retreated to his tent, followed by his ministers and friends, some complaining about the elements, not remembering the war years, the roots, when it didn't matter what the weather was like. Thunder. Lightning. Quick, get inside. Nervous laughter. Brandy passed around. The tent rapidly filling with cigar smoke. *Comandantes* unwinding among themselves. Toasts to the old days. War stories and lies exchanged. More brandy.

Soon, the storm settled into a steady downpour. Fidel stared out at the sheets of rain and wind bending the trees. No, *chico,* there will be no hunting today. *Caramba.* He sighed, it was always something, then heard the familiar click of dominoes. He shrugged, why the hell not, he hadn't played in ages. Camilo was shuffling the dominoes, the only one at the table, the others waiting—in deference—for Fidel to take a chair. He obliged them, sitting with his back to the door so he wouldn't be distracted by cronies entering or leaving. Given the weather, though, no one was going anywhere. In fact, the tent was crowded, the air, humid, foul with smoke and the smells of sweat. At the end of the first hand, won by the mayor of Havana, Camilo Cienfuegos took off his shirt, opened a bottle of Bacardi, drank deeply. Fidel noticed his comrade had gotten fat. He frowned pensively, remembering his own struggle walking up to La Plata earlier in the day. They say he's in the casinos night after night, a glamorous woman on each arm, consorting with gringo playboys, gambling heavily, drinking heavily, wearing out the mattresses in the *posadas.*

Bourgeois tendencies. The "dolce vita" disease. Others you can warn, but Comandante Camilo Cienfuegos? He is the darling of the rebel army, the people love him almost as much as they love you, you cannot say anything to Camilo. Besides, he is your friend! Still, someone must talk to him, he's setting a bad example. Fidel stroked his beard, nodded as the inspiration came. Raúl. Of course. The original harbinger of unpleasant tasks. I'll have him give Camilo the word.

Fidel looked around the table, realized they'd *all* grown fat and out of shape. *¡Dios mío!* half of them have shaved, and in the city they've taken to wearing coats and ties. Look at the chairs they're in, he observed, forgetting it was his tent. Cushioned! What was so bad about sitting on a log or ammo box? I'll have to have Raúl talk to *all* of them. The easy days are gone, he thought sadly, we are no longer united by the fear of death. These men, they are changing.

Except for Guevara, that recalcitrant soul. Fidel glanced at Che lounging on a bunk in the corner, still dirty and unshaven, still lean and hard, still as uncompromising as ever, still with the courage of his convictions. Reading. Always, he reads! Stendhal again, this time, *Le Rouge et Le Noir,* in French, of course. He frowned again, turned up his dominoes, studied them. Yet, you can't come down on him, either. Face it, you love him, even if he does make you feel inferior at times, you need him. He sighed, pinched his belly. You too have gone soft, Fidel.

He left his thoughts unfinished, signaled for a bottle of brandy, concentrated on the game, finally began to relax.

"*Seis,*" said Camilo, placing a six on the table.

"*Bichocabrón,*" muttered Rafael because he had no play.

"*Yo paso,*" Raúl entoned in his nasal flatness. He too was blocked.

The mayor tried to lay off a five on a four, but a sharp-eyed Fidel caught him cheating. "No, no, no, no!"

He grabbed the nearest Hatuey and poured beer over the mayor's head, a childish gesture, but one that had everyone in the tent roaring with laughter—even Guevara— everyone appreciating the fact that the Prime Minister of Cuba was still one of the boys.

Fidel's turn. He matched Camilo's six, leaving a one.

"Paso," said Camilo.

Raúl dropped a one and a deuce. No one had another play except Fidel.

"Hey, *chico,"* he said to Camilo, matching the deuce, "you never were any fucking good at this game."

"Speak for yourself, *Comandante,"* Cienfuegos replied, pulling on his rum, playing his next to the last tile, leaving a blank.

All around the table, eyes shifted from Fidel to Camilo and back again, measuring the tension between them.

Absorbed, the Prime Minister took stock of the game. He held a blank-seven and a blank-three, counted all the dominoes on the table, then played the seven, figuring he was safe.

"¡Ayy, mi madre!" Camilo laughed delightedly, matched the seven and went out, winning the game. He slapped his belly as if he'd just eaten a good meal.

"Now I know how you won all those battles," Fidel said darkly. "Fucking luck."

"Some of us got it," Camilo replied, eyes twinkling, "some of us have to work for it." He left the table with the Bacardi, went out into the rain, jumped into a jeep, took off for a tryst with a local lass, never looking back.

"Gonzáles!" Fidel shouted, annoyed, and pointed at Camilo's vacant chair. "You take the *compañero*'s place!"

The game turned into a marathon, and when the players were too tired or drunk to continue, others took their turns. Except Fidel, who was at the table for the entire time, trying to make up for the embarrassing string of losses started by Camilo.

PAPA AND FIDEL

No more good-natured banter. Serious drinking, serious dominoes. On into the night. No breeze. Air heavy with cigar smoke and humidity. Fidel lost a close one to Raúl, not a very good player. He seethed. Another loss. Finally, a third one even though Raúl had made an artless attempt to throw the game.

Fidel exploded, screaming, *"¡Chinga está a tiempo!"* He upended the table and stomped off to a cot. It was five A.M.

An hour later, a refreshed Fidel was fully awake, picking dominoes out of the dirt, stacking them on the uprighted table. It was still raining. He sat down, briskly rubbed his hands together, demanded coffee, breakfast, and players. Exhausted, bewildered, several ministers dragged themselves to the table while an eager Fidel mixed the dominoes.

The rain never did let up, so the game continued for two more days until the Prime Minister had to return to Havana, but he left the Maestra reluctantly, on a hot streak of thirty-seven straight wins, in an excellent mood, his only concern the ministers. As their girths grew, or so it seemed, the less they were in touch with the peasantry.

There must be something you can do, he told himself, taking the palace steps two at a time, so they will not forget where they came from. Papa would have an answer, but he is in Spain, chasing the bulls.

A frazzled Celia was already on the phone. Rather than disturb her, he went straight into his office, sat behind his desk, was intimidated by the stacks of paperwork, wondered where to begin, stared out the window. Why should you be faced with all this crap, doesn't anyone else know how to make a decision, *¡Dios mío!* we've been running the country for over five months! The intercom buzzed.

"Tu madre, Fidel, creo que sí."

He picked up the receiver. *"¿Teléfono?"*

Yes, it was her, there was no mistaking her voice coming at him over the long-distance lines, bitching about the agrarian reform law, saying that already INRA bureaucrats had confiscated the family's land. "What is going on with you?" she continued. "How can my son be doing these things, giving away the country to *los pobres* who deserve nothing, they will always be ignorant and lazy. I am beginning to believe what I seen on American television and in their newspapers, they think you are turning into a dangerous and irresponsible dictator! My friends won't speak to me anymore, Fidel, at least give me compensation for the land you grew up on, the ranch you would have inherited!"

"You have been paid in freedom, Mamacita," he said flatly, then slammed down the phone, sprung out of his chair, and went across the office into the hallway, his nerves shattered. He asked the guard to bring him brandy. "You'll find me in the Salon of Mirrors." Mamacita. Bah! He threw up his hands. She was too old and narrow-minded to understand what was going on.

He entered the salon. The glass had been cleaned up from his last tirade, but new mirrors hadn't yet been installed. The effect was disturbing. No longer was his image reflected to infinity. He had to be content with either an endless profile or view from the front. He frowned, uncomfortable with himself. Am I really as bad as what I read in the Yankee newspapers? he thought, examining his image in the mirrors. How can Mamacita—how can *anyone*—take them seriously? Is it my fault that the *norteamericanos* raped and robbed this country for over half a century? What do they expect me to do, turn over and take it in the ass, the way the rest of Latin America does? *"Never!"* he screamed at the mirrors.

Except he could not fight them and win, he knew that,

Papa was right, he had to keep them permanently off balance. Che and Raúl kept telling him to start a dialogue with the Russians, they may need them someday, but, no, they were wrong, the Soviets will need Cuba because it was no longer a Yankee satellite. We should prepare, he thought. We should teach every man, woman, and child how to defend himself. In case they send the Marines. *Sí, sí,* we must establish the people's militia—Raúl and Almeida, they'll love to get that going—but we'll need weapons, of course, we can't buy them from the United States, and if we go shopping in Eastern Europe, Ike and Nixon are sure to send down the Marines and then— He smiled. Belgium. Of course. They make the best firearms in the world, anyway. *"Sí,* Belgium!"

He shook his head, turned to go. All this trouble just because *el pobre* should have a piece of the land he farms. "Fucking gringos! All they care about is money! Why should the well-being of the entire Cuban population be less important than their material wealth?"

He left the room. The guard was waiting in the hall with the head of the kitchen staff who explained, very nervously, that there was no rum or brandy in the palace, though it had been ordered some time ago.

"Well, then, go get it from the casinos!" he shouted, gesticulating. *"¡Sangre de Cristo!* you have a brain, *compañero,* use it!"

He turned and stormed off, saying to himself, "You should've never left the mountains, *chico!"*

Celia hurried up behind him with papers to sign and a list of phone calls he was supposed to return. "Fidel—"

"¡Ahorita no, Celia, ahorita no!"

Minutes later, he was in his car, hurtling through Havana at seventy-five, the phalanx of Oldsmobiles around him, going home to more paperwork, dreading it. Along the way, he caught glimpses of threadbare workers sweeping the streets, mostly Negro, some barefoot. Although he'd seen the same scene countless times, now it finally registered, and he was stunned. They have no shoes, and Camilo spends a fortune in the casinos; Rafael goes to Moscow once a month, I think that's where he goes; Raúl and Vilma plan a huge wedding reception at the Havana Libre. They have no shoes, and I drive by in new Oldsmobiles with thirty bodyguards, I take three helicopters for a pickup game of dominoes. He frowned and felt a guilty flush spreading across his face. Such inequities. Do you deserve the red-carpet treatment when they have so little, Señor Premier? You complain about the ministers losing touch, what about yourself? The question worried him, gnawed at him, made his gut sour. It wasn't like this in the mountains, he recalled unhappily, for then you were one with them, you shared their pain, promised liberation, and now—

¡Momento! You can still be like them, you can make everyone like them, you can work alongside them! He leaned forward, tapped his driver on the shoulder, ordered him to take them to the helicopters. Riding shotgun, Gonzáles swiveled a quick look at him.

"We are going to Matanzas, Gonzáles! To cut cane!"

From the chopper pad, he called Celia and told her to have all the ministers, anyone who was anything, the Havana press corps, even, in the Matanzas cane fields as soon as possible.

It took them a while to find fields that hadn't already been harvested, but there were some, cane left to grow for seed, and soon Fidel was sweating hard, whacking away at the tough, wizened stalks. He kept at it for hours, cutting, throwing the cane back for the women to stack and cart away. Unaccustomed to stoop labor, his back screamed in pain, so he had difficulty straightening up, moving from row to row, and despite the heavy leather gloves, his hands were raw and bleeding, yet he persisted, determined to cut twice as much as anyone else, his only consolation being that his ministers were hurting worse than him. This is no mere publicity stunt, *chico,* this is how you will stay in contact with the people.

To set an example, Fidel insisted the ministers go the distance with him, so everyone was in the fields for two full weeks. Except for Señor Premier, the only one who enjoyed the experience was Gonzáles, working his machete with a vengeance, as if the gnarled stalks were potential assassins. An enthused Gonzáles, nodding vigorously when Fidel told them all that the hard work was good for their souls, would cleanse them, keep them honest and humble. Equal.

Surprise.

Unlike the other *macheteros,* precisely because he *was* in the fields, Fidel became a smash hit in the international news, the original celebrity *pobre,* the story of the month. He hadn't thought the press would make that big a thing out of it, yet it wasn't just them. Ultimately, the people were responsible. Lining up along the road, waiting hours just to see him, to touch him as he passed by at the end of the day. He realized he had been wrong. He could never be just another *machetero,* could never be like them and vice versa. Why?

Power.

Given to you—and only you—by them. They *expect* the cars, the helicopters, the entire twenty-third floor of the Libre, the villa on the Isle of Pines, the house at the beach, state security, after all, you are their leader!

Power makes men unequal. Never forget that, *chico.*

As he waved to the crowds, climbing in the jeep for the ride to the helicopter and back to a life these people would never know, he felt satisfied, pleased with himself, but not because of a two-week symbolic gesture. He'd worked his ass off and was especially proud of his callused, filthy hands.

Hey, *chico,* how many other heads of state can say they've just cut over a hundred hectares of cane?

Eighteen

FROM BEHIND THE mango trees under unusually warm November skies, the young Englishman watched the Finca, frequently mopping sweat from his face, attired in the same seersucker suit as when he'd forced his thousand-page manuscript on Hemingway two years ago. Then, he'd been an aspiring novelist moonlighting as a spy. Now, his priorities had shifted. He no longer viewed his position with the firm as temporary. He supposed the change had come when Hemingway returned the manuscript to his London post office box, saying it didn't ring true and was in sore need of *cojones*. Humiliated, he hadn't written a word since.

He scowled at the memory; he didn't like to be reminded of dreams locked away in a trunk, back in a country he no longer considered home. Quit mucking about in the past, he told himself, his eyes narrowing. You've got a job to do, a right and proper one.

When he saw Hemingway's wife leave in the big Chrysler, he hurried toward the house, automatically keeping to the trees and bushes. Certain that the staff was in the kitchen, he ran across the driveway—a flash of nontropical color—dashed up the steps, slipped into the house, and went silently to the telephone. Quickly, he had the cover off, the electronic device attached, the whole thing back together again in minutes, was out of the house and gone from the Finca grounds.

No one the wiser.

Papa finished work for the day, came into the house from the tower, was about to pour himself a drink when the phone jangled. "Hello?" he half whispered, not realizing that lately his voice had quieted with age.

"Is that you, Hem?"

Papa glared at the receiver. Who the hell did he think it was? "Was the last time I looked, Herb."

"Okay, okay," Matthews said apologetically. "Listen, I'm in Havana to interview Castro again. Thought maybe we could get together."

"Um."

"Lunch?"

"Drinks."

"The Floridita?"

"Gimme an hour or so." Papa hung up, did not associate a static click with the bug that had just been planted on his phone.

He went into the bedroom to change, sipping his drink, telling himself the diversion with Matthews would be good. Since coming home a couple of weeks ago, he'd been pretty much holed up in the tower, churning out the *Life* stuff, page after page of his five-month bullfighting junket in Spain.

He got to the Floridita early, started easy with a beer,

looked around warily, then relaxed. The place was almost empty, and the bartenders moved like shadows. He smiled. Matthews was gonna want to know how Spain was these days, how she'd changed. His face crinkled with pleasure as he recalled last summer and turning the clock back to the old days. The drama of the *mano a manos,* Antonio Ordoñez and Luis Dominguín making suicidal moves, working the crowds to orgasms of *olés.* Hands down, he'd witnessed some of the best bullfighting in history and would never forget that one special day in the Plaza de Toros when everyone waited for his judgment of the performance, even the president, who wouldn't give the matador the bull's ears until Papa stood and waved his handkerchief. And between the *corridas de toros,* a perpetual party along the circuit, Papa accompanied by his own *cuadrilla.* Old friends from his salad days in Europe, friends from the States along for the ride, Mary of course, new friends, and lovers taken here and there, usually left behind.

Except for Melanie.

He'd been holding court at some bar, pissed off because Mary had been calling him petulant and childish, when this young "journalist" sallied forth asking for an interview. Interview, my ass. With a large gourd of wine, he spirited her away in his week-old Lancia to the river Iratos, was pleasantly surprised when she suggested they go skinny-dipping, not thinking there was reason behind her wiles—everyone knew he'd been married four times and from all appearances was casting around for number five. They ended up on the other side in a stand of beech and alder, cool in the dappled sunlight, her hands quick on his loins. Touch me, she whispered, kneeling in front of him on the moss, kiss me all over like Jordan did Maria in the sleeping bag. No, no, that's not possible, daughter, it's

Across the River nowadays, starring Colonel Cantwell and Renata.

And so the summer became an absurd quest for the fountain of youth, Papa dragging his *cuadrilla* everywhere, pontificating, boasting, making damned sure he lived every minute, Melanie always at his side, now his "secretary." He rarely slept, was never without a drink in hand, unless in the arms of his nubile lover. The parties didn't end, just segued into alcoholic picnics, then treks to the bullrings.

His pursuit took its toll, though. One day after bragging to Melanie about his prowess as a swimmer, he almost drowned in the Mediterranean. And then, on the way to Madrid, showing off for her, playing "Grand Prix," he stacked up the Lancia. Luckily, they walked away. The incidents sobered him, but not as much as the news—when he got back to Málaga—that Mary had up and left for Cuba. The party was over, and he was alone, feeling sick and frail and defeated. Father Time held all the hole cards. The *mano a manos* had been cut short too, Dominguín ripped open by another bull and in the hospital; Antonio, suspended for cursing out the officials. Not the kind of ending old Hemingstein would've written.

Papa had no choice except to go to work. He'd planned to write the articles in Spain with the magical countryside as a backdrop, but when rumors came that Mary was intending to leave him, he booked passage on the *Liberté,* not ready to trade his wife in for a newer, sleeker model. He needed her mind, her advice and support, was halfway tired of the dumb-shit stuff that came out of Melanie's mouth, was bored with the prospect of having to explain himself all over again to a girl young enough to be his granddaughter.

Home. Patched things up with the missus. Ate plenty of crow. Promised her everything, watched her hire more servants, then go shopping. Women.

He grinned, shook his head, signaled the bartender. It had been one helluva summer, though.

"¿Sí, señor?"

"Another Hatuey." Then he hesitated. "Might as well bring the Gordon's too, son."

Some things never change, he thought, one of them being your drinking habits. He glanced around. The Floridita's stayed pretty much the same too, despite the face-lift that Castro's boys had given Cuban society. When were you last here, anyway? Way back in March, lunch with Ken Tynan and that faggot playwright, Williams. Sad case. Little guy actually was a bullfight *aficionado,* could've been a helluva man except his mother cut off his balls before he reached puberty. Mothers, he mused cynically, cracking open the Gordon's, pouring himself a *definitivo.* They're the storm troopers of the female race.

Matthews came in, was about to apologize for being late, stopped short, just stared.

Papa scowled right back. "What the hell's wrong with you?"

"You been sick, Hem?"

"Bad cold a few weeks ago, but a man really doesn't have to worry till his liver's shot."

"Looks to me like you ought to slow down on the sauce," Matthews remarked quietly.

"Didn't know you were an M.D.," Papa said disdainfully, annoyed by his friend's concern. "We've both seen better days."

Matthews looked away, then turned back and changed the subject. "Understand you saw Fidel in New York."

"Yeah, we talked."

"What'd you think?"

"He'll be lucky to make thirty-five," Papa said morosely, hoping he was wrong. "The motherfucker don't pull his punches."

Matthews wasn't so sure. Castro's resilience impressed him. The agrarian reforms were still in effect despite sabotage attempts and constant threats from the United States. Half the ministers had resigned, the chief of the air force had defected, President Urrutia had dropped the proverbial me-or-you glove on television and lost, counter-revolutionary bands were springing up in the Escambray, Huber Matos had been arrested for conspiracy, yet Fidel was more popular and powerful than ever before.

"What happens when Ike and his boys cut off trade? Officially?"

"He'll have the economy turned around by then."

"I dunno." Papa stared at his beer.

"What d'you—"

"Listen to me, Herb." He paused, grimaced, steadied himself. "Okay, Castro takes over, lowers rents, utilities, food costs. Raises salaries, starts all kinds of public works projects, increases employment, and suddenly everyone's got pesos to burn, and nobody likes creature comforts more than Cubans, right? Okay, there's huge surpluses in the stores—cars, TVs, hi-fis, refrigerators, jewelry, furs, you name it, the consumer goods for colonial gringos who've taken the boat back to the heartland. So the revolution becomes an orgy of consumption despite the moralists and spartans and commies, and everyone's happy. Restaurants, nightclubs, and casinos do a land-office business while the baby-sitters've got *American Bandstand* on the TV. But nobody seems to realize that the gringo ships ain't unloading cargo in Havana harbor no more, nobody seems to realize that overall production is half what it was before the war. *Half!*" He drew himself up and spread his arms, imitating a facile Cuban bureaucrat. "What's that, you say? No more beef? Go ahead, *compañero,* slaughter the herds of breeding stock, we want steak in the restaurants, maybe someone will ask the Venezuelans for more cattle, you know how it is."

"Yes, but—"

"Listen to me, Herb!" He leaned toward Matthews and glared at him. "The true gen is conditions are worse than they were before the revolution. The party's over, my friend. The gringos are pissed off and spoiling for a fight, and Cuba's running on empty."

It was a sentiment echoed when he got home, confronted himself in the mirror, and saw what Matthews had seen. *He* was running on empty. White hair thinning to beat the band, sallow complexion, permanently bloodshot eyes resembling road maps of, say, Pennsylvania. He looked fragile, a porcelainlike figure in danger of shattering. Might as well know the worst, he told himself. With shaking hands, he took his blood pressure. Grimaced. 210 over 140. He imagined capillaries popping right and left in his brain, reached for his medication, figuring maybe if he doubled up on it, the old pipes would quiet down.

Hem, you gotta get yourself back in shape, gotta start taking care of yourself again or you won't even make it through the bullfight articles, let alone the big book. So resolved, he went down to the pool, swam through the sunset into twilight, finally pulled himself from the water, exhausted, yet satisfied he could still do a mile or so. And that night at dinner, he passed up booze in favor of wine, ate quietly and listened to Mary for a change, bringing hopeful smiles from her, the first in a long time.

He was up at six in the morning, in the tower banging out the pages, his mind clear and sharp, last summer piling up alongside the typewriter. Yet he knew he'd let himself slide too far this time, and was conscious of the old whore waiting, hovering nearby, anxious to take him out unfinished.

"You had your chance, bitch," he said out loud, facing her down and disturbing the cats on the windowsill. "I had my pants down for five months."

Right then, he knew what he would title the articles, and with a raspy chuckle, penciled "The Dangerous Summer" on a sheet of paper, taped it to the window above his typewriter.

A week later, Papa was sick of the bullfight articles, knowing deep inside they were becoming overblown, pretentious, and arrogant.

So it came as a welcome relief one dull afternoon when he heard the roaring engines, looked out the window and saw the Oldsmobiles parking askew, raising huge clouds of dust, brakes squealing, the bodyguards out first, as quick as ever. Skeptical, yet eager, he eased down the steps, started toward the house. Fidel met him on the path, made a great show of welcoming him back to Cuba, shaking hands, pounding him on the back and all, but Papa read sorrow in his eyes. He looked downright terrible. "What's wrong, Castro?"

"Camilo."

"Shit, I shoulda known." Papa winced, nodded once, stuffed his hands in his pockets, started for the house. He'd heard about it on the boat. Camilo Cienfuegos, second or third most important man in the Cuban revolution, took off from Camaguey in a light aircraft, was never heard from again. *Granma* and *Prensa Libre* reported that because of a severe storm, the plane was lost at sea, although no wreckage, no bodies were found, and the Cuban coast guard had stopped searching. The American press, on the other hand, blamed Fidel Castro for eliminating a "rival" in his government.

At the bottom of the steps, Fidelito approached Papa shyly. "Wanna play some catch?"

"Later, son, me and your old man got some catching up to do." He turned, saw René trimming a bush. "Hey!" he yelled and gestured. "Get a glove and play with the kid!"

"Mucho gusto," said René, dropping the clippers.

"He hates garden work," Papa exclaimed. "C'mon inside."

In the living room, he broke out a fresh bottle of Haig Pinch, in deference to Camilo's memory, ushered the Premier out onto the porch where they sat, drank, watched the boy throw.

"Want to talk about it?"

Fidel shrugged. "We were very close," he whispered, his voice cracking. "I keep hoping—"

"They say in the papers—"

"I know what they say in the papers!" he shouted angrily.

Papa looked away, was sorry he'd brought it up. The tragedy in Fidel's eyes was all the proof he needed. There's no way this man could've "arranged" the disappearance of Camilo Cienfuegos. That just doesn't happen between close friends. An important observation, he told himself, something worth writing about someday. Better do it soon, though, because you yourself ain't got much depth left on the bench in friends.

They didn't say anything for a long time.

"See where your boys're trying to ban Santa Claus," said Papa, trying to lighten the mood. He was referring to a campaign in the local press to replace the venerable Saint Nick with a rotund revolutionary figure, one Don Feliciano. "You'd think a fat man dressed in red would be pinko enough for them."

Fidel merely shrugged and watched his son pitch.

"Jingle Bells, Jingle Bells, always with Fidel," Papa sung, then laughed. "Somehow I don't think it's gonna catch on."

"*¡Basta, basta!*" Fidel exploded. "I can't be responsible for the idiots who run the magazines! I can't be everywhere!"

"Hey, take it easy, son, I just wanted to see you smile before your face breaks."

They lapsed into silence again.

Fidelito was really firing now, reaching back, coming over the top, the ball cracking into René's glove. Papa smiled. Though it was November and soon he was leaving for the winter hunts in Idaho, the sounds of a pitcher warming up always reminded him of early spring, of hope, young girls, the sweet smell of new grass, trout fishing in icy streams, life waking up.

"Kid's got one helluvan arm."

Fidel nodded.

"Wouldn't surprise me if he tossed a couple of shutouts next season."

"A change-up," Fidel said solemnly. "He needs to learn a change-up."

Papa sipped his scotch and agreed. "A slow curve coming behind one of them fastballs would sure pick a lot of pockets, you're right about that."

"If only I had the time to teach him, *ay mi madre*, there is so much to do!"

"I'll show him how," Papa said emphatically. "When I get back from Ketchum."

Fidel smiled for the first time. "You are a good man, Señor Papa, very kind." He leaned forward. "You know, sometimes at night when I put him to bed, he asks, 'When are we going to see Grandpapa again?'" He chuckled. "What a thought, no?" He looked down at the boy. "He will be very happy if you coach him. Very."

Indeed, from a distance they could have been mistaken for father, son, and grandfather enjoying a moment, a rare time together.

Papa settled back in his chair, comfortable with Castro, savoring the warm glow emanating from the scotch in his belly.

"This has been the hardest year of my life," Fidel said abruptly.

"Understandable. Lot of bad weather." He drank. "Saw where you named a Negro as head of the army."

Fidel's face clouded over. "What difference does his race make, don't tell me you—"

"Didn't mean that, damnit!" Papa interrupted, frowning. "I was gonna say, it took guts to do that. Even here."

A long pause. They both softened, having understood.

Fidel smiled, winked conspiratorially. "And next week. You know what happens next week?"

"Shoot."

"Che will be named director of the Banco Nacional."

Astonished, Papa stared at Castro. "Are you outa your fucking mind? Guevara's a philosopher with a license to practice medicine, not a financier, for Christ's sake! He oughta be making house calls!"

Fidel spread his hands. "What am I to do? He is one of the few honest ones left with any brains."

Good point. Indisputable. Papa pursed his lips, folded his arms. For all their arguments, they agreed on the basics, honest government and fiction being two of them.

"What are you writing nowadays?" he asked softly.

"Bullfighting articles for *Life.*"

"Do you really believe, my friend, that a man hasn't lived unless he's been in the ring with a bull?"

"Metaphorically, you bet your ass, son." Papa grinned, his eyes twinkling. "I mean, you oughta know—you got your own little *mano a mano* going with Uncle Sam."

Instead of laughing, Fidel leaned forward, put his hand on Papa's knee, and started in.

"Planes. They bomb our cities, then drop supplies to

counterrevolutionaries in the Escambray. Why can't the U.S. stop those attacks, *viejo,* the planes take off and land in Florida! We intervene ranches, confiscate land that rightfully has always been ours, offer the gringos reparation which they indignantly refuse, calling me a communist! Ask yourself, Señor Papa, ask yourself what is so bad about communism when the *anti*communists and the counter-revolutionaries are often one and the same, *¿sabe?"* He paused and looked off, forlorn and hangdog, then threw up his hands.

"Such lies they speak of me, *viejo!"* he exclaimed, turning back, aiming his finger at Papa's chest. "One of these days, I'm going to sit down and write the truth, the way it actually happened." He grinned slyly. "I mean, I'm no Ernesto Hemingway, but since I can't get him to write the story, perhaps I'll try it myself."

Wham.

Papa almost fell out of his chair, gaped at Castro, his jaw slack. "Jesus H. Christ and John R. God," he said quietly. "That's it!"

The big book.

The main one, the big one, the idea, pristine and clear, as massive and breathtaking as a fifteen-hundred-pound marlin. Why the hell didn't you think of it before, your books've all been based on your own experiences and relationships, why should the big one be any different? He was thinking fast and hard, his mind focusing, inspiration blossoming into full-blown story. Father-son, the classic, quintessential relationship. His heart sang.

Okay, Hem, okay, ride the beast, the way you did *The Bell* and *OMATS.* Here we go, this is for you, Scott, and all you other guys who couldn't go the distance and got kayoed into eternity. Main characters. Me'n Castro, one step removed, father and son. Kid saves his country from a horrible dictatorship, makes sweeping changes, declares himself a permanent revolutionary, buries his mother, rejects his father. Eventually, father redeems himself, atones for his sins, has a reconciliation with his son, then—

The muse vanished.

Papa scowled. Fickle bitch, that damned muse, gives you a taste and then disappears. He shrugged. What the hell, how can you know what happens next when it ain't in fact happened?

After Fidel left, Papa hurried back to the tower, roughed out the structure for the first two chapters, writing furiously until his fingers were numb, his hand cramping up. Bottled up for so long, his juices were boiling over, flowing freely, he couldn't stop himself, not even at dinnertime, not even after Mary had come home, ventured with trepidation onto the landing, peeked into his hallowed space, and asked hesitantly if he were all right.

"I'm fine," he grunted. "Don't bother me."

She left, and he kept working, now seeing the logic of the story, some nuances even, the characters in all their glory and frailty.

An hour later, he paused. Sighed with an exhaustion he hadn't known in years, a good, sweet feeling. His thoughts wandered. Mary. Don't tell her what you're doing, she'll say you're fucking crazy, she'll want to bring on the headshrinkers, and this one last time it's gonna be pure Hemingstein, from the heart, don't care if kitten likes it or not.

He went back to the page, pencil poised, then stopped suddenly, looked up alertly. Night. Pitch-black outside, no stars, the sound of rain, the wind began to howl. So what, champ, you're in Cuba, remember? Except he sensed something else. Saw it in the restlessness of the cats, tails switching, yellow eyes staring balefully, wondering why he was still in the tower long past sunset.

The new whore. Fear.

Coming up cold in his gut, threatening to consume him again. You gonna live long enough to write your book, old man? You gonna make it? Or have you burned it too close?

He tightened his jaws, looked inside himself, and faced down the new whore. "Fuck you, bitch," he said aloud. "I ain't going out unfinished."

Then, for a glorious hour, he worked on the first pages of prose, not quitting until the words were swimming in front of him and his brain needed recharging. Tomorrow, old man, *mañana,* he thought, this book is between you and the rest of your life. He leaned back, let his mind drift. Oughta be damned glad you met that Castro boy, damned glad you climbed the Sierra Maestra. Remember what you told yourself then—that the big book must be truer than true, must have both pain and joy?

"You've got plenty of both now," he said slowly, "plenty. And if you listen to your heart, you ain't gonna write nothing but the truth."

Nineteen

"TELL ME, WHAT was it like, fighting for Castro?"

Todd Blackburn had been asked that before and was ready with an elaborate set of lies. "I remember La Plata," he said, "when me and my brother, David, were down to our last two clips of ammo—"

"Bullshit," Becker said quietly, ending the conversation.

And shattering Todd's surface calm. Fingering his dark-red tie, he twisted in the chair and watched the man read his dossier. H. Russell Becker, assistant director of Latin American affairs. An older dude, Todd observed, late forties, salt-and-pepper brush cut, OSS in WWII, Dartmouth BA on the wall, reputed to be one of the originals. His face was cut square, like his shoulders, like his hands; gray hair crept out of his nostrils; his ears seemed too big.

"Smoking lamp's lit, son," he said as an afterthought and continued reading.

Todd took out a fresh pack of Pall Malls, opened it, fired one up, inhaled deeply, then checked out his light-blue summer suit to make sure he hadn't dropped ashes on it. The cigarette gave him something to do, but didn't quell the gnawing in his belly or stop the nervous sweat that stained his button-down shirt. He had no idea why he had been called back to headquarters and could only speculate the worst. The age thing, he told himself, it had to be the age thing.

He thought of David and tears came to his eyes, tears he wiped away surreptitiously. It had only been two and a half years, yet it seemed like a lifetime since Castro's *barbudos* shot him in the Sierra Maestra. The bastards. They killed him just because he went off to get laid; they blamed him for their own failings; somebody *else* should've spotted the army patrol, yeah. Damnit, what was the point of fighting a war if you couldn't get laid? To the victor belonged the spoils.

Todd recalled that *he* hadn't gotten laid in the Sierra Maestra, though he would never admit that to anyone and had been making up for lost time ever since with weekend sexual forays akin to bird hunts.

After David's execution, he ran, afraid for his own life, but as it happened, getting out of the mountains and back to Gitmo had been a snap. All he had to do was show his USN dependent's ID to the first Batista army patrol he encountered, and he was home free, but no hero's welcome for him. The next few months were pure hell, "Captain Dad" blaming him for David's death, condemning him for running off to join the *barbudos* when it had been David's idea from the start. Every night after a few drinks, his father would call him worthless and spineless and "the runt of the litter," not caring if he woke up the entire household. Todd had hated Captain Dad ever since.

"No, Dad, I can't go to Yale," was the first serious

decision he made after David's death. "Well, you have to go somewhere, son, you sure as hell can't stay here." His second decision was to join the CIA, a choice his father heartily approved, for it dispelled rumors that Todd Blackburn was a Fidel Castro spy. The only problem was his age. So, Captain Dad spent one morning on the phone pulling strings in Washington, and a few weeks later, Todd was three years older, with a new birth certificate, passport, and plane ticket, not to mention an interview with the head of personnel at Quarters "I".

He was accepted, made it through the firm's rigorous training, was sent to Panama for his first tour of duty, assigned to a cryptographic desk. The humdrumness had been good for him, allowing him to seal himself over, ice his emotions and mask his pain. From then on, he hid behind a happy-go-lucky facade that made fast friends and turned on the chicks. His skeletons were closeted. Permanently.

The radiator clanked. Outside the window, it was snowing. He crossed his legs, shuddered and felt cold. Christmas was just a few days away, yet he was still dressed for the tropics. They hadn't even given him time to change or pack a bag. As soon as the word had come down, he was whisked out of the Zone, the only passenger on a MATS C-123 transport back to Andrews. Goodbye, ten-cent drinks at the Fort Clayton "O" Club, so long, mother-daughter two-for-one nights at the best whorehouses in Panama City, see you later, alligator. Goodbye, summer, hello, winter.

Why? It had to be the age thing. Except why would they fly you all the way back to CONUS just to shitcan your ass, Todd asked himself, why the big deal when all they had to do was send you a form letter and severance pay?

Finally, Becker looked up and smiled, mouth curving into a straight line.

"You got quite a history for someone twenty-two years old." He took Todd apart with his cobalt-blue eyes.

Todd gulped. He's playing with me, he's being sarcastic just like Captain Dad, the son of a bitch. "Yes, sir," he stammered.

Becker held up some papers, gestured with them. "Your section chief in the Zone thought quite highly of you. Damn fine-looking fitness reports."

"Thank you, sir."

"How're the martinis at the club nowadays?"

"Good, sir."

"Old Juanito still behind the bar?"

He nodded.

"Then they're the best damned martinis in the whole damned world." Becker looked off reflectively, then returned to the dossier and chuckled cynically. "Got more ass than a toilet seat down there, huh?"

Todd blushed, stared at the floor, didn't know what to do with his hands, so he lit another cigarette without realizing he still had one burning in the ashtray. What the hell's he want, what's he driving at? He stood. "Excuse me, sir, but—"

"Zip it up, Blackburn, I'm asking the questions!" Becker paused, started tapping a pencil on the dossier, his eyes scathing. "You know why they shot your brother?"

Todd sat down heavily. He gripped the chair, his knuckles going white. He couldn't bring himself to speak.

"He deserted his post," Becker said flatly.

"Yes, but—"

"The same fucking thing would've happened to him in any man's army. He got what was coming to him."

A slow burn crept up the back of Todd's neck. His face twitched. For a moment his mind slipped and Becker became Captain Dad and he almost lost control and lunged at him. He looked away and bit his lip. His heart was pounding.

"You understand that?"

"Yes, sir," Todd lied, his voice a whisper. He took a deep breath, exhaled slowly, felt his resentment sink back slowly into his loins. He ran his hands through his closely cropped blond hair.

"Okay," said Becker. "Okay. Just making sure we got all our ducks in a row." He smiled and slid an embossed folder on top of Todd's dossier, then opened it. "I don't think you can handle the assignment, but *c'est la guerre.*" He looked off and frowned. "I don't have a choice."

"Handle what, sir?" Todd was truly perplexed.

"You weren't flown up here because you're a fucking cryptographic genius, Blackburn, that's for sure." He held up more papers, his mouth off and running. "Here's a three-page memo from Nixon to Eisenhower," he explained, "written just days after the Vice-President met with Castro last April, then had yours truly shadow the son of a bitch in New York City. A three-page memo that describes him as a very dangerous character, a lighted fuse in search of a Spanish-speaking time-bomb, definitely an unstable influence in the South American sphere. Nixon strongly recommends the President consider 'normalizing' things down there, except it takes our leader seven indecisive months to pull his head out of a Georgia sand trap and give the word to the director."

Still another sheaf of papers was lifted, gestured with. "This is 'Project Cuba,' son, a brand-new, special team of field operatives, and you're going to run it for me."

"Me, sir?" He was amazed and couldn't stop the foolish grin from spreading across his face.

Becker frowned contemptuously. "Don't get fat-headed, Blackburn. You happen to be the only white man in the firm who can say he fought with Castro. The in-country boys'll respect that because a lot of them did, too. They'll trust you, and if you don't fuck up, you'll have a shot."

"I won't screw up, sir."

"I certainly hope not, Blackburn." He shuffled papers like a magician working a deck of cards, glanced at one document in particular, then grinned. "If you happen to run into a gentleman named Flynn, you should know that he's on our side."

"Flynn . . ." Todd nodded. "Um, if you don't mind, sir, what exactly am I supposed to do?"

"Sabotage the Cuban revolution."

Todd gaped at him.

Becker leaned across his desk, dropped a box of research material onto Todd's lap. "Memorize this stuff, okay? I don't want you embarrassing us."

"Yes, sir."

"Oh, by the way." He stood and extended his hand. "Merry Christmas."

Twenty

DECEMBER 31, 1959

FIDEL STOOD AT one end of the bar, detached from his guests by several bodyguards, sipping Dom Perignon, courtesy of the French ambassador, gazing at his city from the twenty-fifth floor of the Havana Libre in the *"cielo"* room. There were no walls, just windows all the way around, making the view spectacular. He turned, looked out to sea, appreciated the rich, orange sunset, shafts of golden light shimmering off the ocean. To the east, the skies were already dark, rumbling with an approaching *chubasco*. The waves, slate-colored whitecaps, and on the horizon, the gray speck of a Yankee destroyer on patrol.

"Gringos, always the gringos," said Che, coming up behind him, pointing at the ship. "They are like circling sharks."

"Sí, compañero. Worse than Batista ever was. Far worse."

"Hopefully, they will send in their Marines," said Guevara, his voice taking on a religious fervor.

Fidel looked at him askance. *"Caramba,* what are you saying? That's madness!"

"No, no, *Comandante,* don't you see?" Che's eyes sparkled. He leaned close. "A Yankee invasion would galvanize the island and simplify things! Restore the clarity and order and unity we left behind in the Maestra!" he exclaimed jubilantly.

Fidel backed away, averted his face. As usual, Che hadn't bathed, and his breath stunk of garlic. At a loss for words, Castro shrugged and dismissed the notion, even though he recognized the brilliance of it. Taunt the gringos, make them so angry they send in their troops, thereby saving the revolution and turning world opinion against them. No, no, no, he told himself, you must try to placate them, they buy our sugar. Disgusted, he shook his head and walked away. Guevara, he marches to his own music, even signs our banknotes with his nickname. If only he weren't so pure, so Christ-like. Sooner or later he'll have to leave, *es verdad.* He deserves a country all his own.

The room was filling up, conversations becoming louder, more animated, *compañeros* already celebrating. Indeed, it was New Year's Eve, and his government was one year old. As they exchanged *abrazos,* pounded each other on the back, Fidel viewed them all with a jaundiced eye, wondering if any of them knew how lucky the government had been to survive—"escape" might be a better word—1959. We named it "the year of the revolution," he mused cynically, but we should've called it "the year of disorganization." So many mistakes had been made. The *zafra* was half what it should have been, the Yankee *centrales* stole us blind, no one checked their figures. We bought Czech tractors, they sent us wheat threshers, the port authority blithely accepted them, how much wheat is grown in Cuba? We gave the Chinese advance payments for rice, we got a load of condoms instead, do they think Cubans would rather fuck than eat?

Morose, he looked out the windows again. Things must change drastically, he thought, or our revolution will never see New Year's Eve, 1960.

"Fidel?" called René Vallejos. "He is here."

Fidel looked to the entrance, forgot his troubles for the moment and smiled. His honored guest had arrived. Still handsome and well-built for a man past his prime, he cut a dashing figure in a beige silk suit and wide-brimmed Panama. Former heavyweight champion Joe Louis came into the sky room, and was immediately surrounded by well-wishers. Fidel parted his bodyguards, strode across the room *politico* style, a word here, a smile there, always making the guests feel important, indispensable, special to him. A space cleared, and then he was pumping the "Brown Bomber's" hand. Flashbulbs popped by the dozens.

"Buenas, champ, *bienvenidos."*

"Good to be here, Mister Premier," Louis replied, his voice soft and quiet.

"Call me Fidel. Everybody calls me Fidel."

"Sure enough, Mister Fidel, whatever you say."

Castro led him to a table near the windows, got old Joe talking about his fight career, truly admiring this man who had won so many and lost so few. Louis dwelled on the second Schmeling fight, a high point in his life, and Fidel recalled his conversations with Papa Hemingway last April. Interest stirred inside, interest that went far beyond the mechanics of a boxing match, even such a famous one.

He leaned forward. "Excuse me, *compañero* champ, what did you hit Schmeling with?"

Joe lifted his fist and grinned happily. "A right cross."

Fidel made like a boxer throwing a punch. *"After* he hit you with a left?"

"Yessir, Mister Fidel, that how it happen."

While Joe rambled on, Fidel was absorbed by his thoughts. So Papa was right, Louis had beaten a much bigger and stronger man by counterpunching. Except how many more Yankee punches can you duck, how much longer can you dance? Unlike Louis, you cannot retire, you are condemned to fight them forever.

He glanced around the room, saw that now Guevara was lecturing a knot of eastern European diplomats, their faces rapt as they hung on his every word. Why don't you talk to them too? Fidel asked himself. You don't have to beg the fucking Yankees to buy Cuban sugar!

A dialogue with the Soviets. The unthinkable. He warmed to the idea. Why not? he thought. When their first deputy, Mikoyan, comes, after the *de rigueur* ceremonies of state, tell the world you're having serious talks, a summit meeting of sorts, shout it to the rooftops—the gringos and their friends have labeled you a communist, anyway. He chuckled gleefully. Can you imagine Señor Nixon's outrage?

He signaled for more champagne, the possibilities exciting him. Maybe you don't have to spar with the gringo Goliath any longer, *chico,* maybe a fresh and eager Russian bear is willing to take your place. He laughed, rubbed his hands together. *Gracias,* Ernest Hemingway and Joe Louis, your counsel has been most valuable, I will never forget the wisdom of counterpunches.

The band kicked off with a medley of Latinized rock 'n' roll, brass and bongos transforming the guests into a mass of hand-clapping dancers. Fidel had to lean close in order to hear the "Brown Bomber." Curiously, he was talking about tourism now, a sore point, for the industry had all but gone belly-up since the *norteamericanos* stopped coming. The Joe Louis publicity agency could help, he suggested, if the Cuban government were willing to give them a contract.

Fidel put his hand on the champ's shoulder. "How much?"

"A quarter of a million ought to get it going, Mister Fidel."

"Make it three hundred thousand," Fidel said generously. "Talk to Garcia at INT, tell him you spoke with me, personally, and you shouldn't have a problem."

Then he was out of the chair, in a good mood, mixing with his guests, making intimate small talk, bragging about the revolution. Champagne, rum, and brandy flowed, the platters of food were heaped with steak and lobster, fresh fruit and vegetables. The night was, indeed, a night for celebration. No one paid any attention to the *chubasco* that had settled over the city, the rain sluicing down, lightning, rolling thunder, winds that buffeted the hotel.

At eleven-thirty, Fidel took the microphone and serenaded his guests with a litany of their struggle. "Our past glories are the touchstone for tomorrow's victories, on into 1960, *compañeros!*"

"Fidel, Fidel, Fidel!" they chanted, applauding wildly.

The band segued into a rumbaesque "Auld Lang Syne," a conga line formed, the revelers singing along, dancing around the room, oblivious to the storm that pounded Havana.

The power went off.

Apparently, lightning had hit the recently intervened Cuban Electric Company, so they said. Or was it a bomb from "Air Eisenhower"? No one seemed to care. The band kept playing, unamplified guitars and voices, brave whispers. Candles were lit, the conga line continued swaying on into the night, all of them chanting revolutionary slogans to a rock 'n' roll beat.

Hasta luego, 1959.

Twenty-one

"HOW YOU FEELING, kitten?" asked Papa, padding into her bedroom, drained after another long stint in the tower.

She was in bed reading, housecoat on under the covers because the Finca was unusually cold, even for January. She looked up at him, smiled, put her book down, half lifted her elbow, broken in a fall on the iced-over slopes of Ketchum two months ago. "Almost chipper."

They'd been getting along well since coming home, better than in years; they were lovers again, and Papa was being a considerate husband. He knew it was the book. With the pages stacking up, his typewriter machine-gunning them out, he felt marvelous.

"How about yourself?" she asked.

"Yep." Tired, he sat heavily on the bed.

"You're awfully late again."

"Can't stop."

"You writing articles, Ernest, or just words?"

He looked away, didn't want to lie to her, just shook his

head. She'd know of the book when he was finished. Not before. "You mind if I bring Melanie over?" he asked. "She can edit the articles and answer the mail." Actually, he wanted her to finish the damn things, so he was free to work on the big book.

Mary smiled again. "Why should I mind? Whatever you need, you should have."

"Thanks, kitten." He sighed with relief, leaned forward, kissed her, saw that her housecoat had fallen open, slipped his hand inside.

She laughed low. "You'll never change."

Habits, no, she's right about that, he told himself, but you should see the life blossoming inside my head, it's like a Goddamn orchid jungle in there, the old brain feels like twenty-five again. He grinned. "That an invitation?"

"I've only got one hand."

He undressed, climbed in alongside her, and they made love, patiently, understanding of each other, gentle, and as usual, the experience enveloped them with closeness, gave them a reason to go on. Lying next to her, hands behind his head, he thought, no wonder she says okay to Melanie or whoever, she's got them all outclassed, even with one hand. Just don't let yourself become too damned dependent on her—that'll be the kiss of death. He stared at the ceiling, listened to her breathing subside. The moonlight streaming in the window suddenly went dark as the clouds closed in. Raindrops began tattooing the roof.

"Christ, another norther," he said softly.

"How long you think we'll stay this time?"

He frowned, didn't want to face it. "We're home, kitten."

"You know what I mean."

She was talking about the changes, billboards formerly displaying Lucky Strikes and Coca-Cola now replete with revolutionary slogans; murals on buildings depicting bearded heroes; everywhere, the graffiti, CUBA SÍ, YAN-QUI NO; the columns of blue-shirted militia marching off for weapons training; the emptiness in the casinos; people always watching for behavior lacking solidarity, even waiters in the restaurants. "At the Morro this morning, Ernest, I had to wait in line, and when I got to the counter, they had no steak."

"What was wrong with the chicken we had tonight?" He turned on his side, stared off. "Don't need steak all the time."

"There were lines at the Casa Recalt, too."

"C'mon, kitten, one thing this island'll never run out of is booze," he said without conviction, raising his voice over the hammering rain. "Next time send Juan or René. No reason you should have to stand in line."

He got up, went into the living room, poured himself scotch, sat in his chair and wondered. He had been calling this place home for over twenty years. He loved it here, he had always gotten along with the locals, they'd always liked him. Hell, he might as well be *cubano*.

Except he wasn't.

You know it, they know it, he told himself. Sure, they wave and smile when you drive by, sure, they're still friendly, treat you the same, but this "Yankee go home" fad looks like it's pretty much caught on, and where the hell does that leave you? A man without a country? A troubling thought. A possibility he could do nothing about.

He drained his glass and headed for the bedroom, already steeling himself for tomorrow. He'd get up with the sun, swim for at least an hour, until his arms and legs were like lead weights, convinced that he had to stay in shape if he wanted the book to be taut and hard, too. It was a state of mind, he'd always written that way, the good ones, anyway, just never was conscious of it before. Soft body, soft head, flaccid prose. Avoid at all costs. He slept well.

A week later, Melanie arrived. From the amount of luggage René and he stacked into the Chrysler, Papa could tell she hadn't come down with work in mind, so he was quick to tell her she'd been hired as an editor, nothing more, nothing less. And when he installed her in the little house, he gave her the voluminous stack of unfinished articles, told her to go through them, and if she had any questions, she could ask them the next day over lunch. Then he was off to the tower again, already dreaming of scenes, too preoccupied to appreciate her slack-jawed bewilderment. He skipped dinner, worked until midnight, was up with the sunrise and into the ice-cold pool, swimming lap after benumbing lap, convinced he was sharpening his mind for the work that lay ahead. Then he was back in the tower with the magnificent sight of a Gulf Stream morning calm, and the sleeping cats disturbed and annoyed. The book, the big book was before him, gathering steam, hurtling along.

After lunch in the middle of a father-son scene—just before the father runs off, leaving the son stranded under the umbrella of the upper class—he suddenly derailed. The pampered sons of the rich who grow up without fathers become pansies, he told himself, not tough revolutionary leaders, at least that's how it has to work in fiction. Sure, there's exceptions, but reality doesn't have to explain itself. In a story, you have to motivate change, action, direction. Plant the seeds. What's the psychology behind a situation like that? He had no idea. Frowning, he stared out at the palms swaying languidly in the afternoon breeze. Desperately, he tried to transport himself into the middle of the scene, the emotions of a boy deserted by his father.

The whisk of a sweater coming off, the unsnapping of a bra, the rustle of skirt falling to the floor, swish of panties over creamy thighs, sandals kicked away, mischievous giggle: none of it registered. And then he was startled by her breasts pushing into his back, lips on his neck, hands snaking around for his penis. He jerked away and turned. Melanie. In all her dark-haired loveliness, tipsy from too much wine at lunch, nude except for a pearl necklace— and fresh lipstick.

"Surprise!"

Her presence angered him. She had violated his space, his privacy. She had no right.

"Do it to me," she whispered. "Here. Now. In this room where your heart lives."

He took her by the shoulders, held her at arm's length, peered into her eyes. "Listen, daughter, and listen good," he said as gently as possible. "Take your clothes and get the hell outa here, ¿comprendes?"

Her shock came when she saw that he was serious. Awkwardly, she began to dress, a picture of woman-child confusion.

"Never come in here without knocking. As a matter of fact, don't come in here at all."

Choking back sobs, hand to her mouth, she ran out and down the stairs.

He was immediately sorry and knew he'd have to make up to her; but damnit, he thought, if a woman tempted a man in the throes of creation, he'd never get it done. Back to the kid and his old man.

Nothing.

His concentration was shattered for the day. Grumbling, he went up to the house, told Mary not to hold dinner for him, grabbed a couple of cold beers out of the refrigerator, and left, wondering about the souls of young boys. He couldn't quite get back that far in his own life, his mind playing out with fogged memories of teenaged fishing trips and early sexual encounters. "You want to know how a kid thinks, old man, go talk to one."

And so he found himself aiming the big Chrysler toward

Cojímar and Castro's house on the hill. It had been months. Too long.

He parked in front, crossed the lawn, zigzagging through the fleet of Oldsmobiles. The bodyguards at the door frowned, stiffened, barred his way with their tommy guns. A television set blared from inside.

"Ain't here to see the *Jefe*, boys," he growled, "just want to talk to the kid."

"Grandpapa!" said Fidelito from behind the screen door. He came outside grinning, genuinely pleased, shook Papa's hand.

"You get any taller, son, we're gonna have to turn you into a basketball player."

"Hey, you wanna throw some?"

"Hell, yes, I want to throw some," Papa said happily. While Fidelito ran back inside for gloves and a ball, he sat on the steps, remembered he'd promised to show the kid how to throw a change-up. His face crinkled into a smile. On the street, a trio of dark Cuban beauties swung by— supposedly on their way to the beach. Behind Papa, the guards relaxed, lit cigarettes, exchanged lewd opinions.

Fidelito returned, gave Papa a catcher's glove, and they warmed up.

"Take it easy on me, son," he warned, easing into a squat. "I'm too old to get loose."

The boy began throwing in earnest, but was consistently wild. Soon Papa was sweating, working hard and annoyed. He lunged for one on the dirt, stopped it with his shins, winced, cursed the world, stood up slowly. "What the hell's the matter with you?"

"Sorry, Grandpapa, I haven't been practicing. My dad doesn't have time anymore."

"Well, take a little off the ball, then. At least till you can put it where you want."

The kid settled down, threw strikes, hit the glove right on

the money, and Papa was satisfied. Then he stopped, called Fidelito over, and showed him how to throw a slow curve with the same motion as a faster one, the killer pitch, the equalizer if he got it down right. A hesitation.

"Can I ask you a personal question, son?"

Fidelito nodded soberly.

"How would you feel if your father just up and took off? Left you all alone?"

The question startled the boy, yet he thought it through, finally shrugged and smiled. "Could I come and live at La Finca Vigía?"

Papa's heart surged. He was deeply touched. *Jeez Chrize, what a thing to say, there is so much innocence and goodness in this kid, what a thing to say.* "Sure you could. For as long as you like."

They went back to playing catch, and Fidelito tried the change-up, but lost control again, this time throwing one that veered off sideways and smashed through the living room's large bay window. An instant commotion inside. Obscenities, shouts, alarms. They thought someone had thrown a bomb. Gonzáles was out the door first, grease gun leveled. Perplexed, he glared murderously at Papa roaring with laughter, arm around a scared Fidelito.

Disheveled, Fidel came out next, in fatigues and bedroom slippers, cigar in his face, state papers in his hand. He took it all in, understood at once, started laughing, too. "Hey, Señor Papa, if that's how you coach, maybe Fidelito needs somebody else, no?" He gestured. "Come inside, I'll show you around."

Later, they were on the veranda, tall glasses of dark rum and ice by their chairs, watching the boy cavorting on the hill with the dog Guardian in sharp contrast to revolutionary slogans about discipline.

Fidel shook his head. "I have to do something about that dog. Last week when I tried to give him a bath, he jumped out of the tub and ran through the house, shaking." He laughed gleefully. "If Celia had had her pistol, she would've shot him."

Papa leaned forward, spoke confidentially. "What was your old man like?"

Fidel frowned darkly, turned sour, glanced warily at his guest. "He's not worth talking about."

Papa was puzzled. He sipped his drink, was about to ask another question, when suddenly he realized Fidel's terse remark said it all. Castro didn't get along with his old man, he thought, sure, that's the answer. So, in the book, have your kid motivated by hatred to turn his back on his heritage and when he's old enough, he picks up the gun.

Pleased with himself, Hemingway enjoyed the moment, the salt-air breeze, the distant sound of the surf, the bittersweet taste of the rum.

"And *your* father, señor?" Fidel said harshly. "What about him?"

The question surprised Papa, caught him off guard, and before he could stop it, his brain conjured up a vivid picture of Dr. Ed Hemingway—old, in failing health, henpecked—pistol to his ear, blowing his head off. A coward's way out. No grace of a happy death there. A pathetic end to a ho-hum life. He shuddered, wondered fearfully if such an act were hereditary. Worse, he knew deep down that he, himself, might be considering suicide if it weren't for the big book.

Slowly, he turned to Fidel, fixed him with a hard look. "My old man?" he deadpanned. "No *cojones.*"

Twenty-two

MILLIONS OF YOUR countrymen could, ah, appreciate coffee from Oriente province, Señor First Deputy, should your government choose to purchase some," said Fidel.

Anastas Mikoyan chortled at the possibility, eyes darting around the stately palace chamber with its high ceilings, arched windows, glassed doors opening onto marble balconies. An illicit chortle, the sound of a man sorely tempted who knew he was in the wrong hemisphere, yet longed for its proverbial forbidden delights. He lit a Winston, jiggling the medal on his lapel. "What about the United States?" he asked, his voice a Draculian lilt.

"They are not the only country in the world," Fidel said easily.

The chortle again, accompanied by hands rubbing together briskly. "We would pay handsomely for such a coffee."

"Perhaps the Republic of Cuba and the Soviet Union

have something to discuss, then." ·

"Perhaps."

Fidel listened carefully as Mikoyan hinted at future alliances. Normally, he would've drawn the line at ceremony, but just a few days ago, his G-2 had reported that the Eisenhower administration was asking its Congress for the power to lower sugar quotas "in an emergency." A declaration of economic warfare. Last year, even with the chill in relations, ninety-five percent of the *zafra* had been exported north. Without that market, the Cuban economy would go belly-up. Fidel grimaced, hating the reality of running a one-crop nation.

Mikoyan went to the old Spanish sideboard, poured himself vodka, drank, then nibbled on a piece of sugar cane.

"Delicious," he murmured, his face lighting up. "Absolutely delicious."

"It's only the best in the world," Fidel said offhandedly, spreading his hands. "Like our coffee."

"The Americans have surrounded us with missile bases," the Russian said dourly, pouring more vodka, not really changing the subject. "And God help us if they elect Richard Nixon."

Nixon, Fidel thought, resisting the urge to smile, how I would love to see his face when he hears I am meeting with Mikoyan. "I sympathize with your position, Señor First Deputy, I only wish Cuba could help, but we are very small and poor, we have practically no resources, we are insignificant."

"Au contraire, my friend," Mikoyan replied, happy again, beaming. "An island ninety miles from American shores is hardly insignificant."

Fidel stroked his beard, lit a cigar. *Cuidado, chico,* Mikoyan is looking to build dachas in the Caribbean. If you become dependent on the Russians, you merely exchange one form of economic tyranny for another. Trade with them, yes, but don't expect something for nothing or this island will lose its identity.

Ultimately, he agreed to sell the Soviets five million tons of sugar and two million tons of coffee and tobacco over a five-year period if the USSR would lend Cuba 100 million dollars—no rubles, *por favor,* not yet—and sell her oil. Cuban cane for Russian crude, not to mention cash, the details left to the functionaries. Prime Minister and First Deputy shook hands, grinned at each other, exchanged toasts, moved slowly onto the balcony, Mikoyan volunteering memories of his early years in the Soviet Ministry of Food.

Fidel tuned him out. The deal they'd roughed out seemed simple enough, but what of Uncle Sam? While the official press releases would say the agreement symbolized Cuba's determination to trade with the entire world, he realized there would be serious repercussions, especially when the Russian tankers started arriving. All our refineries are owned by the gringos, he told himself, and it doesn't take a genius to see that, say, Shell or Esso or Texaco will refuse to process communist oil. So what will you do? He raised his fist to the skies. *¿Qué más?* Intervene the refineries. Counterpunch! He dreamed of the succession of headlines while trading blows with the Goliath to the north. U.S. CANCELS SUGAR QUOTA. Fine, *yanqui,* go ahead. CUBA NATIONALIZES SUGAR MILLS AND BANKS. Take that. U.S. IMPOSES ECONOMIC EMBARGO ON CUBA. Okay, *bueno,* how about this? CUBA LIQUIDATES ALL MAJOR U.S. INVESTMENTS. So there. U.S. BREAKS DIPLOMATIC RELATIONS WITH CUBA. *Hasta luego,* gringos, we're teaching Russian in the schools now, to hell with you.

Celia crossed the balcony, interrupting his thoughts and Mikoyan's ramblings. *"Teléfono,* Fidel."

He frowned. "I told you—"

"He insists." She turned and walked away.

Annoyed, he apologized to the First Deputy, followed

Celia back inside the palace, strode into his office, picked up the phone. "This had better be important!"

"Castro, you know your kid's got a game tomorrow?"

Papa. Fidel winced, pierced by an image of a forlorn Fidelito in search of a father, dropped into his desk chair. "He didn't tell me."

"You gonna go or not?"

"I— I'm sorry, Señor Papa, why don't you take him, I won't have the time."

"Whatever you say, Señor Premier, but just so you know, that boy misses you a lot."

Guilt raced through him, bringing angry tears to his eyes. "Don't you think I'd spend more time with him if I could?" he shouted into the phone.

"Sure, sure, forget I said anything."

If only, Fidel thought sadly, if only there were less to do, weren't stacks of paper everywhere—

"Listen, can we get together soon? I got a million questions about your mother."

Jesus, he knows how to twist the knife, this old man, he doesn't pull any punches, why isn't he telling me stories of, of shooting Nazis in Europe or hunting lions in Africa like before? Must I endure this, too? "You know I don't like to talk about my personal life."

"Already know about you," came the gruff reply, "have to get a handle on her. She's a damned important character."

"And Mirta?" he said sarcastically. "I suppose you'll want to know about her, too?"

"Who's she?"

"Fidelito's mother."

"Naw. Anyone who'd marry you's got too many problems to make for believable fiction."

Astonished, Fidel just stared at the phone, blinking, finally responding when he heard the dial tone and realized

Papa had hung up. Cursing, he slammed down the phone, left his office. *El viejo* knows too much about human frailty, he told himself.

He returned to Mikoyan on the balcony. "Ernesto Hemingway was on the phone." He forced a grin. "Sometimes even *he* needs help."

Twenty-three

"WHAT DO YOU think about that Fidel Castro signing a trade agreement with the Russians?" Melanie asked petulantly.

"It's the equivalent of Ike and his boys getting caught with a hard left hand," said Papa.

"Huh?"

He squeezed her knee, patted her thigh. "Don't sweat it, daughter, private joke."

They were sitting in the bleachers at the Little League field near the Club Náutico on the third-base side, waiting for the game to start, watching Fidelito getting in his last warm-ups, Papa nodding, approving. The kid's throwing hard, but holding back a little, just so the other team don't see everything. Smart. He learns fast, already knows how to finesse his opponent; it must run in the family.

The Cojímar Lions took the field, Fidelito striding to the mound, fingering the resin bag, looking in to his catcher while the lead-off batter rubbed his hands in the dirt, picked up a bat and trotted to the plate. He was wiry and little, light and springy, and, according to pregame rumors, had hit safely in his last seventeen trips.

The crowd settled, and the umpire yelled, play ball.

Fidelito wound, threw a blistering fastball that cut the outside corner. A called strike.

The batter stepped out. More dirt on his hands. A deep breath. He stepped in again, choked up on the bat. Ready. Fidelito threw the same pitch, and the kid swung hard, barely missing.

Papa nudged Melanie. "Watch this. He's gonna pull the fucking string."

Indeed. Fidelito delivered his next pitch with the exact same motion except it *crawled* through the air, floating along, and the batter had already swung himself into a human corkscrew before the ball even got to the plate.

The kid struck out the side.

Delighted, Papa cheered enthusiastically, especially when the Lions scored two in the bottom of the first, three more in the second, and Fidelito still had a shutout going in the third.

Just before they started the fourth, Papa saw Uno and Dos slouching alongside the bleachers, looking hard and cool in militia khaki and blue, cigarettes hanging from their mouths. They'd been glancing in his direction ever since the game started, stealing eyefuls of Melanie when they thought he didn't see, flashing *guajiro macho* signs when they were caught looking, their expression saying, hey, *chico,* if you're man enough for a *jovencita* young enough to be your granddaughter, then you're okay *bueno* with us. He grinned, acknowledged them with a nod and thumbs-up gesture. He wondered briefly what their real names were, but preferred to think of them as simply Uno and Dos, his guides into the Sierra Maestra, the ones who had accompanied him on the first leg of a long and painful journey he sensed would be over soon, ending in a triumphant blaze of glorious light. Yes, sir, a fond place was reserved in his heart for Uno and Dos.

Melanie noticed them too, turned to Papa, concerned. "Those two men over there, they keep staring at me. Makes me feel creepy."

He patted her leg again. "Don't worry, daughter, they ain't gonna bother you."

She frowned, confused. "Are they friends of yours, or something?"

"Sort of."

"Oh." She was relieved. "They look dangerous."

"They are," he said. "Very."

She snuggled up to him, her eyes saying most of it. "I'm so glad you're you."

He smiled, pecked her on the lips, then nuzzled her neck and caught a faint whiff of her scent, that fresh, yet musky sensuality not quite washed away by her morning shower, so pungent last night in her bed.

He closed his eyes briefly, recalled the scene, just before midnight. He had knocked on her door with trepidation, for they hadn't spoken since her humiliation in the tower. The door opened a crack, she peered out, and right off he knew she'd been crying. Profuse apologies got him inside, mea culpas locking the door, smoothing the path into the bedroom. It ain't just you, daughter, he explained, nobody's allowed in the tower except me and the cotsies— and them, only because they don't talk. If people come in and out all the time—especially someone as pretty as you—I'd never get a damned thing written, understand? Apparently, she did, for she threw herself at him with a passion he hadn't seen in her before. No calculating, no "maybe he'll marry me next" stuff here, just pure lust and need, the tears persisting for a while, giving way to blissful cries after she hit it the first time. The pace slowed, became patient, tender. He held back, played her like an instrument, enjoying her sounds, the taste of her loins, her smell permeating everything. Slowly, he took her higher, riding the beast in her, until it almost hurt, then finally let go. She knew exactly when, collapsing into soft whimpers and dreamy smiles. Normally, he would've quit, but the time was too special, so their lovemaking continued, and he savored it all, made damn sure every touch, every kiss, every stroke was registered in his brain before staggering back to his own bed, a spent old man.

Life goes on. The Lions were leading 9–0 in the top of the seventh, and Fidelito was showing no signs of tiring. Indeed. He struck out the side again, the Lions winning the game easily.

Papa and Melanie drove the boy home, listening as he retold the game in detail, explaining how he felt in each situation, the errors he made, the superior play of his teammates. A put-on modesty. He was rehearsing, of course, for his father, but when they got back to the Cojímar house the fleet of Oldsmobiles was gone. The boy's face fell.

"If we play for the championship," he said wistfully, "maybe he'll come then."

"Take it easy, kid," said Papa, tousling his hair, "your old man would make all of 'em if he could."

Fidelito smiled sadly, got out of the car, walked to the house, twirling his glove, dragging his bat.

When they got back to La Finca Vigía, Papa found the place in an uproar. Servants dusting, sweeping, picking up, polishing windows, even. The kitchen was a maelstrom of activity, Mary in the center, directing, as he walked in.

"The Russian Embassy called!" she exclaimed. "He's due any minute!"

"Who?"

"Anastas Mikoyan, and we don't have any hors d'oeuvres!"

Papa smiled. "Let them eat ideology."

Moments later cars began arriving. Six of them, Papa counted, standing at the top of the steps, and more Russkies than you could shake a stick at, half of them gaping at a freshly made-up Melanie as they approached the house. And finally, the First Deputy: short, ebullient, springing up the steps, looking very un-Russian in a tailored summer suit and narrow tie.

They shook hands, then went inside. Introductions were exchanged, Papa immediately forgetting everyone's name except Mikoyan's. He broke out the vodka and, after a round of toasts, sent one of the servants for more bottles. Mikoyan took an oblong box from an aide, gave it to Mary. Wooden dolls from the Ukraine, a Soviet cliché. Papa looked away, almost blushed. He had almost admired this Russkie for having some class, until the dolls; until you saw the hero medal on his jacket. The hell with it, he thought, more vodka and these boys won't seem so bad after all.

The First Deputy pressed him to autograph Russian translations of his novels, and he obliged, knowing full well Mikoyan hadn't read any of them. Another philistine, he thought, resigned to it. They rule the world.

Papa retired to the fresh air of the patio, saddled by a real buzz from the vodka. Mikoyan followed him, and a servant brought another bottle, placed it on the table, left discreetly. The First Deputy offered to fill his glass, but Papa declined. The Russian shrugged casually, made a joke of it, poured himself more, always talking.

"So what do you think of the Cuban revolution?"

"Jury's still out," said Hem.

"Fidel took us around the island," Mikoyan said enthusiastically, ignoring Papa's skepticism.

"He shoulda been a tour guide."

"We went to La Ciénaga de Zapata. Do you know? They're building a Cuban Yalta there."

"So?"

"It's a government retreat, a perfect place to refresh one's spirit. The food is delicious, too. Have you ever had a corvino baked in guava leaves?"

"Skip the menu, my friend, do they have indoor plumbing yet?"

"Mr. Hemingway, we are in the third world."

"No shit."

"Which means you are an American living on unfriendly soil."

"Was friendly when I moved in."

"Will you leave, then?"

"Don't talk to me about politics," he growled. "I'm too old."

"Age and politics, a fascinating topic, one worth considerable discussion," the First Deputy rambled on. Papa was only half listening until Mikoyan revealed that he would be sixty-five in a few months, felt better than ever, was planning on at least another ten years in the Politburo. Sixty-*five*? Papa was jolted; he stared at Mikoyan, analyzed him. Trim, full of energy, thick black hair, unwrinkled face, clear brown eyes. *Holy Christ, Hem, he's got almost five years on you and the sonuvabitch looks forty! And you? Hair gone all white—what there was left of it—face ravaged, wrinkles, creases, age spots. Sure, you've lost weight and can swim miles, but this constant weariness, this, this deterioration— Maybe you should go see old Doc Herrera, make sure you're up for the late innings, wouldn't hurt, might give you some peace of mind.*

He knew he wouldn't. Nope, don't have time, he told himself. Fighting the old whore is a solitary business, goes hand in hand with writing the book. With each sentence, you are reborn, with each chapter, you prolong life, you become immortal.

"You know what amazes me?" Mikoyan was still rambling on with his impressions of the Cuban revolution, chortling between sentences, a man about to share illicit secrets. "There is no bureaucracy here!"

Papa laughed cynically. "You're right about that, Mr. First Deputy, but it's only because nobody knows how to establish one."

Twenty-four

AT THREE A.M. off the coast of Pinar del Río, a submarine surfaced, cut slowly through choppy seas under a starless, black sky. Dressed in frogman gear, Todd Blackburn emerged from the hatch, braced himself on the conning tower, read the beach through infrared glasses, but saw no militiamen patrolling the shore. Too late, too cold, too wet for them, he told himself. The Cubans'll always be creatures of comfort no matter who's running the show, even the fucking commies. Always a party, a carnival, then the *posada,* a bottle of rum, a naked lady, a warm bed, the proverbial rumba.

He took a flashlight from his belt, signaled the beach with quick flashes. Near an inlet where the water was calmer, his signal was answered. He went below, nodded to the lieutenant commander at the helm, synchronized watches with him, slipped scuba tanks onto his back, climbed topside again, pulled on a mask.

He went over the side.

Six feet down into the Caribbean, he was swallowed up by the blackness. He'd done this dozens of times off the coast of Florida, had developed an internal sense of direction, didn't really need the luminous compass on his left wrist. He swam steadily, conservatively despite his eagerness, knowing he should have plenty of himself in reserve when he got to shore. His rigorous training had shaped him permanently, he hoped. In this underwater limbo, he took stock of himself, examined his feelings, centered his purpose. Nothing pleased him more than the thought that he, Todd Blackburn, was going to screw up the Cuban status quo. He owed it to memories: his brother's bleached bones somewhere in the Sierra Maestra, a debt of love; his father's condemnations echoing in his soul, a debt of hate.

He felt the pull of a gentle surf, reached down, touched rough coral sand, crawled out of the water, a dark, ominous shape. They ran to him, five of them, helped him off the beach into some trees, then out of his wet suit. As per instructions, his gear was cached—except for his map case and the eighteen-inch survival knife he sharpened obsessively—and covered over with branches. Then they gave him the humble clothes of a *campesino,* and he changed quickly.

The trek began. He was content to follow, even though he had memorized the maps and aerial photographs showing the way into these mountains, the Sierra Escambray. Moonlight broke through the clouds, giving him a chance to size up his companions. Four were boys, too young, a disquieting fact. The apparent leader was in his thirties, stout and hard, a malevolent glitter to his eyes. Todd recognized the familiar sign, was relieved. At least one of them was capable.

They came to a road. A canvas-backed truck was stashed in a ramshackle barn. They piled in, Todd hiding under a tarpaulin in back. The truck took off, belching smoke, engine coughing, in bad need of a tune, a testament to the *mañana* syndrome that had gripped the island since the departure of gringo influence. Yet, the malaise has always been there, Todd thought, it's in their blood, you can smell it when the flamboyans trees bloom, when overripe mangos fall to the ground and decay, when unwashed whores strip languidly and spread their legs.

That will never change, no matter what Castro does, he told himself. The Cubans have a subservient mentality, they need a strong foreign presence, a guiding hand, not a bearded maniac giving Uncle Sam the pinko finger. And here I am, blazing the trail. *In blood.* He placed a reassuring hand over the sheath of his knife, then squeezed his cock and grinned. Yessir, this time I'm gonna have a ball, because this time I'm calling the shots instead of the spicks, and that's the way it should be.

The truck ground up the hill, transmission howling for oil, freewheeled down the other side, in neutral to save gas. They slowed as they came to Guane, the only town on the route, went around a curve.

Stopped.

What the fuck they stopping for? he thought, panicked. We're not supposed to stop!

"*¡Documentos!*"

Holy shit, a checkpoint, a Goddamn checkpoint, he thought, disgusted. Becker said there wouldn't be any, and now here's some FAR corporal all excited about a curfew violation in a military zone, demanding papers. Christ, I hope the one driving knows how to handle it, I hope he's cool—

He wasn't.

The crack of a pistol shattered the night, the driver firing a round between the corporal's eyes, but he hadn't seen the other one in the shadows who opened up with a grease gun, killing him instantly, bringing cries of terror and surrender from his brothers in the cab.

A silence. Heart pounding, Todd listened as they climbed out of the cab. Someone ordered them to spread-eagle on the ground. They obeyed. Footsteps. A blinding flashlight lit up the back of the truck, flushing the other two counterrevolutionaries outside. Only Todd remained un-detected, shivering under the tarp, realizing he had just a few minutes before the truck was searched thoroughly. His "compatriots" would be dealt with first. He strained to hear more sentries. Apparently, there were none, so remote was the checkpoint. A solitary voice full of scorn, insulting the *"gusanos,"* telling them they would suffer much worse deaths than their bandit *compañero,* his body half hanging out of the cab, fluids staining the mud.

Todd took a deep breath, eased out from under the tarp, tiptoed to the tailgate, his skin all atingle, mind buzzing, painfully aware if the truck bed rocked even slightly, he was a dead man. He slid his knife from its sheath. With a hang-ten lean, he was around the side, throwing left-handed, a blur of motion, the knife flashing in the moon-light. It went completely through the sentry's neck, just as he was turning to fire. Eyes bugging out, he made a horrible choking sound, fell to his knees, gurgled, pitched forward facedown in a mud puddle.

Todd retrieved his knife, cleaned it, turned over the corpse, went through its pockets, found identification, read it, was startled. This man had been a captain in the Cuban Intelligence, not exactly your ordinary sentry. No, this one had been the real thing, a G-2 "Jiménez," which meant Todd was in a critical area, a dangerous place. Even now, he heard the whine of an FAR personnel carrier coming down the hill. He glared at the four standing passively in front of him, barked a command, started trotting away from the town. They followed, but soon were gasping for breath. His pace was relentless; justifiable. The zone would be crawling with FAR patrols before long. They had to get to the drop point by first light and make contact, then hole up for a while, until pressure from the army abated.

Soon, they left the town behind and were moving along a ridge line that paralleled the highway below. Todd heard the FAR down there, speeding back and forth in their vehicles, looking aimlessly, horns honking in frustration and anger. Already, he'd stung them, and savored the image of the Jiménez gagging on his knife as if a large bone had caught in his throat. There will be more, Todd vowed to himself, many more.

An hour later, they were deep in the Escambray, the country too forbidding for FAR jeeps and personnel carriers. Yes, the rebel army would come after them, but on foot; and already, they were miles behind. In a clearing near a stream, Todd called a halt so the others could rest. He watched them drop and lie staring at the sky, chests heaving, their ordeal over for the moment. He turned, climbed a rise, sat down with map and compass, oriented himself, then shot azimuths to the surrounding peaks, triangulated and found his exact location. He checked it against the coordinates of the drop point, calculated they were a half hour away, looked at his watch. Despite their dangerous brush at the checkpoint, they were ahead of schedule and looking good. He returned to the clearing.

The three young ones had their boots off, pants rolled up, were soaking their feet in the stream, whispering about their dead cousin and what to expect next. Todd sat down next to the one in his thirties who was smoking reflectively, with his back against a tree, his legs straight out in front of him. They shook hands, talked quietly for the first time. He was Ricardo Martínez-Díaz, one of many Jehovah's Witnesses opposed to the revolution on religious grounds, one of the few with guts enough to leave his village and take to the hills. He nodded toward the others at the stream. His sons. He knew they were not old enough to fight, but so few had joined them, the people were so afraid, the government propaganda so powerful, even here in the obscurity of the Escambray.

"The one driving. Was he your son, too?"

"Bueno, no," Martínez sighed, *"todavía no, gracias a Dios."*

A silence.

"So, it's going badly, then?" asked Todd.

Martínez thought for a while, then shrugged. "Castro started with twelve, and he didn't have the help of the USA."

Todd smiled with satisfaction. That said it in a nutshell.

Just before dawn, in the middle of a field where oxen trails crossed, he spread out an iridescent "X." Moments later, a plane droned overhead, circled once, dipped as cargo was shoved out the side door, then leveled off and flew away. The stuff parachuted down, landing easily in the grass and mud. Weapons. Explosives. Rations. Martínez's sons jabbered enthusiastically as they opened crates, pulled out rifles and machine guns coated with cosmoline. Todd found the M-26 radio, quickly made it operational, called the firm, waited.

A ciphered message came back confirming his arrival. He laughed with excitement when he read the last of his unscramblings: "Win this one for the Gipper."

Twenty-five

MARCH 2, 1960

CARS.

Painted gaudy colors, sporting flowers and palm fringes, bangles and crepe paper, jammed with festive people, traffic stopped dead along the Malecón. It was carnival time, and the sweet smell of spring was in the air. From behind the wheel of the big Chrysler, Papa gazed at the revelers, impressed they were having such a good time going nowhere, everyone honking their horns, radiators shooting off like anxious teenagers. He'd forgotten. When the party bell rang in Havana, all self-respecting *habaneros* took to the streets, nobody giving a damn how long it took to get anywhere. Right now, in the massive tieup, a long look, lingering smile, ardent gesture, and consenting adults exchanged back seats, making their cars sexually compatible. No big thing, turn up the radio, this conga line goes all the way to Veradero, *compañero,* keep smiling, you might be next.

"We're going to be late," said Mary. She was staring straight ahead, trying to ignore the din and crush of carnival, as if it offended her sensibilities.

"So's everybody else, kitten," Papa replied, placating her.

They were on their way to the Nacional and a cocktail party for Jean-Paul Sartre and Simone de Beauvoir, celebrity guests of the revolution, in March 1960. The only reason Mary had agreed to go was the fact that Havana's American and European cliques were sure to be there in spite of what she termed the *verde olivo* of swaggering *comandantes*.

Surprise, the cars actually began moving forward, fazing no one, least of all a half-naked couple doing the rumba atop a stalled '47 Caddie. They didn't miss a beat. One for the memory, Papa thought, fun without reason, love without commitment, joy out of desperation. This is it, folks, Cuba, 1960, people dancing on their cars and fucking in the back seats, that's the gen of it, the soul of this revolution, no creeping politics around here, bring on the rum and Cokes qua Cuba Libres.

Papa laughed, craning around for one last glimpse of the girl's bouncing breasts and swollen nipples before the Chrysler inched around a curve in the street. *Love without commitment.*

"I suppose you're thinking about Melanie," Mary said coolly.

Actually, he wasn't. Aside from the carnival, he was wondering why he had always felt compelled to marry the women he'd loved instead of committing himself to something more lofty or permanent. Except you can't get much more permanent than Mary, he told himself. Looks like she's gonna go the distance regardless of Melanie or anyone else. Does that mean she's calling the shots now? He scowled. Hell, no, Hemingstein, not as long as you can get out of bed in the morning, swim a couple of miles, keep going on the big book. Just don't let her take over. Then again, don't drive her off, either. The days're getting shorter, the nights longer, and sometimes an old man gets lonely.

"I think it's time for her to leave," Mary said politely.

"I thought you said it was okay."

"It isn't anymore."

"She ain't finished with the Goddamn articles!" *And I'm not finished yet, either!*

"If that's all she was doing," Mary said, tight-lipped and hot, "she could stay until doomsday!"

He stared out the side window and did not respond. His kitten was snarling, and he had no desire to get scratched, not when he was in a good mood and curious to see how Castro and his boys mixed with the distinguished, dour-faced French playwright and philosopher. Especially since Sartre and Simone had taken Havana by storm, becoming so popular there was already a drink named after them at the Tropicana.

At Paseo del Prado, Papa foolishly turned inland to detour around the traffic jam and ran into more people and another conga line. He threaded his way through the mass of dancers only to encounter a roadblock and glowering FAR sentries telling him to go back where he came from, their voices muted by a million bongo drums, their stances in sharp contrast to the ambience of fiesta. Sweating now and muttering curses, Papa dug out the engraved invitation to Sartre's reception, hoping it would get him past the roadblock. The Nacional was less than a mile away.

Suddenly, the dancers started chanting, "*¡Uno, dos, tres,*

*Sartre y Simone, ten cuidado, aquí venemos! ¡Uno, dos, tres,
Sartre y Simone, ten cuidado, aquí venemos!"*

Everyone picked up the beat, and then miraculously the
enormous conga line split off to the sidewalks, clearing the
street. The chant became, "Fidel, Sartre, and Simone, look
out now 'cause here we come! Fidel, Sartre, and Simone,
look out now 'cause here we come!"

"Well, I'll be Goddamned," said Papa, laughing again,
"will you look at that?"

Mary gasped.

At the wheel of his jeep, Fidel was tooling down the
street, grinning and waving to the crowd. A scowling
Gonzáles rode shotgun, unhappy because there was little or
no security. Jean-Paul Sartre and Simone de Beauvoir were
in back, also waving to the crowd, the little man throwing
kisses enthusiastically, his Coke-bottle glasses fogged with
humidity. Between them sat a wrinkled and unwashed Che
Guevara, arm around each, the Argentine philosopher in
hog heaven.

"Take me home!" Mary demanded.

"What the hell're you talking about?"

"Jean-Paul and Simone are one thing, but I have no
intention of hobnobbing with Fidel Castro!"

"What's wrong with him?"

"What's *wrong* with him?" She drew herself up and gave
Papa a withering look.

"He's a damned sight better than Fulgencio Batista."

"What will you do when they take the Finca away from
us, Papa?" Mary smiled bravely, but her lips were quivering. "What will you think of Fidel Castro then?"

Papa gazed at the conga lines and was silent. He couldn't
conceive of losing Finca Vigía, yet couldn't ignore the
sinister reality of muddy boots on imported carpets,
barbudos evicting gringos despite Castro's reassurances
that Yankee property rights were being respected. He

supposed his personal friendship with Fidel would exclude the Finca from repossession, but how long would that last?

At this rate, not very long at all.

Now Castro's jeep was not moving, trapped by a crowd of adoring people. Gonzáles was standing on the hood, gesticulating with his automatic weapon and screaming at them to get out of the way, while the soldiers from the roadblock were trying in vain to push them back. None of it bothered Fidel who was—absurdly—introducing Jean-Paul and Simone to those closest to his jeep, shaking hands, touching, letting himself be touched.

Papa was awestruck. Look at him, he thought, blessing his people, his disciples. God, does he really believe his image as the omnipotent, invincible Prime Minister of Cuba? Does he see himself as a visionary? Does he really think there's a moral order protecting him? Doesn't he listen to Gonzáles anymore? Doesn't he see the concern, the terror in his chief bodyguard's actions? Doesn't he realize the danger?

Just one crazy here or in the Plaza de Revolución or *anywhere,* one kamikaze, that's all it would take. Castro dead, and then *hasta luego,* Pearl of the Antilles, not to mention Finca Vigía. All the joy, all the promise, all the changes, all the experiments. Gone. Guevara's shot at the twenty-first-century man, forget it.

The island up for grabs. Chaos. The butchers coming back from Miami, the pretenders knee-deep in blood, machine-gunning each other. Sure, he can tell the world that should harm befall him, Raúl will take over, he can name all the successors he wants, but the end result will be a tropical slaughterhouse. *One way or another.*

Finally, Gonzáles got the soldiers to form a wedge, then pulled his *jefe* out of the driver's seat and took his place. He revved the jeep, leaned on the horn, popped the clutch, and they jerked forward. The people scrambled and dove out of the way, realizing that Gonzáles wasn't going to stop for anyone. Soon the jeep was in third gear and then gone, a conga line forming in its wake.

Papa was shaking. He wished he hadn't seen Fidel mobbed in the open by crazed *habaneros,* for it was a premonition that things could not go on as they were, a sign that they were all vulnerable.

"Somebody's gonna kill him," Papa said flatly.

"Don't you think you're being a little paranoid, Ernest?"

The thought *had* crossed his mind.

"I mean, I'm no fan of Dr. Castro's, but the people love him dearly. You just saw it for yourself."

He couldn't argue with her; he couldn't explain himself, either. Perhaps he was being paranoid—that would account for the cold, sick feeling in his gut, wouldn't it? Grumbling fearfully, he backed the Chrysler away from the roadblock, turned it around.

"What are we doing, Papa?"

"You wanted to go home, didn't you, kitten?"

Twenty-six

IN OLD HAVANA, Todd Blackburn left the safe house by the back stairs at precisely 3:30 A.M. coming out onto a narrow alley that curved down into the ancient city. He moved easily, but was alert, always looking for sentries and the unseen eyes of the militia, yet he seriously doubted he'd come across anyone, since the carnival was in full swing. Partying and vigilance did not exactly go hand in hand. Trash was everywhere, broken rum bottles glittering, limp strands of wet crepe paper looking like snakes in the darkness.

He turned a corner, stopped. Up ahead, a De Soto was parked alongside a building, and all the windows facing the street were shuttered tight, no lights anywhere. He came up behind the car, heard snoring, peeked inside, smelled stale alcohol. A man was curled up in the passenger seat, leaning against the door, sleeping off the carnival. Todd smiled. This guy wasn't gonna wake up. Too much party.

He glanced in all directions, then opened the door and slid behind the wheel, nose wrinkling at the rancid miasma surrounding the man. Ignoring it, he pulled the wires from behind the dash, cut two of them, touched the bare ends, hot-wiring the car. It started instantly, and he took off, driving farther away from the safe house, deeper into the Colón district where whores, pimps, faggots, thieves, and black marketeers were still plentiful. Two blocks away from a particularly run-down intersection, he floored the De Soto so by the time he got to the corner, he was doing fifty. With one hand, he reached across the seat, opened the passenger door, then jerked hard on the wheel. The car lurched into a screeching, tire-smoking turn, the momentum throwing the man out into the street. Todd glanced in the rearview mirror, saw him tumbling, rolling, arms and legs akimbo, head finally smashing into the curb, splitting open. No, he wouldn't wake up. Not now, not ever.

Involuntarily, he squeezed his crotch and discovered that he was hard. He stroked himself and smiled, drove around the block and headed back the way he'd come, singing the latest Everly Brothers tune that had been playing when he'd left D.C. He couldn't get it out of his head. "Dre-e-e-e-am, dream, dream, dream, dre-e-e-e-am . . ."

Several blocks later, he turned up the alley, slowed, parked behind the safe house close to the old stucco wall. The back door opened immediately. Ricardo stepped outside, confusion in his eyes.

"No taxi?"

"Nope." He popped the lid of the trunk. "Cleaner this way."

Ricardo said nothing, began loading their equipment into the trunk.

"If you call a taxi," Todd explained, lending a hand, "there's a record of the dispatch. You have to dispose of the driver's body too, and then there's the chance one of his buddies'll recognize you on the street. A hot car is much slicker." He grinned. "By the time it's reported, we'll be long gone, buddy."

They went inside, sat facing each other at a table, bare light bulb hanging overhead, and ate breakfast. Cold roast beef sandwiches, tasteless Cuban oleo on the bread, but with the salt shaker, they were okay. And the coffee was thick, steaming hot. Good shit. Some muscle in it. They didn't talk; there was no need. Normally, Ricardo's sons would've been jabbering away, but they'd been left behind in the Escambray. This was a job for two alone.

Todd refused another sandwich, not wanting to feel heavy, not before. Afterward, he'd have plenty of time to eat, drink, celebrate. Not now. This was a time to center, to make sure all the pieces were in place. He read his companion's face, was reassured. No apprehensions there, just raw commitment. The tight jaws chiseled, a hardness in the dark eyes. Ricardo was A-okay. A good man for the job. Both checked their watches, got up from the table, and Todd turned off the light.

0400.

They were out the door, into the De Soto, right on schedule, backing into the street, cruising off.

Twenty minutes later, they turned onto the Malecón, going by the perpetual traffic jam of carnival, ghostly now, most of the revelers passed out on back seats or sleeping it off on the sidewalk. Incongruously, a Miami Spanish-speaking station coming over a radio left on in some car filled the silence, the commentator's virulent anti-Castro rhetoric falling on deaf ears. At the end of the Malecón, Todd spun the De Soto around, parked, got out, opened the trunk, quickly changed into a wet suit, then lifted a partially inflated bag containing magnetized strip blocks of C-4, detcord, nonelectric detonators and blasting caps, twenty-five pounds in all. He carried the bag down to the water, patted it affectionately, went back to Ricardo who held his air tanks while he slipped into the harness. Then he put on his flippers and waited, gazing out to sea in search of his target, yet barely able to make out the dark form of the old Morro Castle at the end of the harbor. Finally, in the gray first light, he saw it. The silhouette of a freighter outlined by red and green running lights being pulled into the channel by tugboats. He nodded to Ricardo who helped him snap on his equipment belt. A thumbs-up to his partner. He duck-walked down the rocks, eased into the water towing his bag of explosives made almost weightless by the air pockets, dove to his customary six feet, began swimming on a collision course with the ship. The approaching thump of the giant propellers was music to his ears.

Halfway across the channel, he surfaced, pushed his mask up and looked. The sky was considerably lighter now; he had no problem reading the name high on the freighter's starboard bow. *La Coubre*. Cutting straight toward him, a mere hundred feet away.

Mask in place, he dove to fifteen feet and waited, the pounding of her screws thundering in his ears. All at once, there she was, huge black bottom coming over the top of him. He flattened out, swam on his back parallel to the ship, matched his pace with her three knots. You don't want to get too far astern, he told himself, anywhere close to her screws and you can cash in your chips, yet you gotta make sure you wire this sucker where the ammo's loaded so when she goes there isn't anything left but fucking shrapnel.

Midships.

Once there, he switched on his light, took suction cups from his belt, attached them to the hull, hooked himself to them so he could work without having to swim. From his bag, he pulled out the strips of C-4, fashioned a large circular ribbon charge against the hull, magnets securing it. He dovetailed the ends, shoved in the blasting caps, cut three fifteen-minute lengths of detcord, tied them to the caps, thus tripling his odds, wired detonators to the other ends, unhooked himself. He checked his watch, pulled the detonators, turned off his light, then shoved off the hull and swam hard, very aware of the propellers churning a short distance away. He felt their pull, swam harder, using all his strength, and did just slide underneath them, death inches away.

Gasping, he surfaced, watched the ship moving down the channel, her flag limp in the early morning still. A calm settled over him, then came a sense of personal loss he didn't immediately understand. He dove again, headed back the way he'd come.

It was over.

He had done his bit, his nonplace in history was about to be recorded, *La Coubre* was about to go sky-high, and he would get away scot-free. Big fucking deal.

He was anonymous.

No one would know. No one, not even Captain Dad who *should* know, who should sweat and worry that his sole surviving son was dangerous, was someone to be reckoned with. *Todd Blackburn was anonymous.*

And that wasn't enough. He deserved more. He touched the rocks, pulled himself from the water, climbed up the bank of the channel. A grinning Ricardo helped him out of his gear, stowed it in the trunk. Another thumbs-up. Todd broke out the M-26 radio, got it cranked up, sent in code, "The Irish have it." Moments later came the reply, "Way to go," then instructions. At 0400 the following day, he was to rendezvous with a submarine at coordinates 02193768 off Cabo San Antonio, close to his original staging point.

Todd stared off, thinking hard, ignoring Ricardo's urgent

whispers that they had to get away, soon the ship would explode, and the harbor would be crawling with militia.

God damn the firm, he thought, defiant. God damn them to hell, they want you to pull out clean so they can send in a new guy for the next deal. Well, they can't do that, not to you, David means too much, you haven't satisfied the memory, you haven't buried Captain Dad. He shook his head resolutely. Nope. You're not gonna make their fucking rendezvous.

He checked his watch. Three minutes to six. Ricardo was gesturing frantically, white with fear, now waiting in the car. The radio crackled again. Why hadn't he acknowledged their last transmission? Todd picked up the radio, his mind made up. To hell with the firm. He was going back into the mountains with Ricardo. We'll bring down the revolution on our own, he told himself, then threw the radio into the channel. He watched it sink, ran back to the car, jumped behind the wheel, started the engine and took off.

Twenty-seven

WHAM.

The explosion rocked the city.

Fidel was out of his chair instantly, over to the window, astonished, gaping at the ugly brown mushroom cloud rising over the early-morning Havana skyline. Foreign Minister Raúl Roa and Celia Sánchez joined him seconds later. Not a word was spoken.

Immediately, the phone began ringing. Celia went for it, but Fidel got there first. *"¿Digame?"*

"They have blown up *La Coubre!*" shrieked Pepín Naranjo, the pudgy little mayor of Havana. "There is nothing left, Fidel! The dock is gone too, the stevedores— we don't know how many are dead, but there are bodies everywhere, many, many casualties, nobody knows what is going on, we need help!"

Fidel ordered him to mobilize the police, hung up, returned to the window. Now the cloud was huge, blocking out the sun, casting a dirty, acrid light over the city. Sirens wailed, coming from all directions. He turned to Roa, glared at him.

"And you talk of negotiating with the gringos," he said scornfully, gesticulating. "Well, take a good look, *compañero,* there is the language they speak."

"*¿Creen que es norteamericanos—?*"

"Who *else,* Roa?" he exploded. "They were the ones who refused to sell us arms in the first place! Who else do you think would sabotage an arms shipment? Who has been bombing our cities with leaflets and burning our cane fields? *Sangre de Cristo,* Roa, how can you be so naïve and a communist, too?" He spun around, his face full into Celia's. "Call Gonzáles! We are leaving *en seguida!*"

He stormed out of the room, went down the hallway toward the stairs, cursing under his breath. The explosion was an act of war; *La Coubre's* cargo had been the 40,000 rifles and machine guns purchased from Belgium. An act of war, yet economic too, for the FAR still needed arms— arms his government could no longer afford. You must retaliate, *chico.* He thought furiously. You must hurt them worse than they've hurt you, but how can you, that is like taking the proverbial piss in the Gulf Stream.

As he reached the bottom of the stairs, Celia called from the balcony. "All the phones are ringing, Fidel! Where are you going, anyway?"

"To talk to Bonsal!"

Then he was outside and into the waiting Oldsmobile, saw his bodyguards in the rearview mirror piling into their sedans with unusual snap and speed, doors slamming shut with authority. No, he wasn't the only one aware of the tension, the electricity in the air. The *compañeros* were with him.

Gonzáles heaved his bulk into the front seat, rocking the car, and turned. "*¿A dónde?*"

"The gringo embassy," he replied, appreciating the murderous fury on his chief bodyguard's face. Everyone knew what had happened. Everyone had heard the explosion, had seen the mushroom cloud. Everyone was waiting for Fidel.

"*¡Vámonos!*" Gonzáles said savagely.

The driver stood on the accelerator, and the fleet took off down Paseo del Prado, turned onto the Malecón doing sixty, tires squealing and smoking, the drivers adroitly swerving through the traffic, most of the time half on the sidewalk, leaning on their horns, barely missing stunned *habaneros* watching the skies who scattered at the last possible moment. Fidel caught glimpses of their sad faces; the carnival had become a funeral, the revelers, tragic clowns. He grimaced, vowed revenge—not so much for himself, but for them and their spoiled party.

The closer they got to the U.S. Embassy, the angrier he became. He hadn't anticipated the *La Coubre* incident, was furious with himself for not seeing the Yankee perfidy, realizing too that had he known, he still would not have been able to prevent it.

Swearing, he slammed his fist into the door, denting the carpeted paneling. What good would it do to lodge a formal protest with the gringo ambassador and his cohorts? They would merely deny responsibility and offer condolences, their blue eyes mocking him all the while.

At the west end of the Malecón on the edge of Vedado, the phalanx of Oldsmobiles stopped in front of the embassy, a large mansion with vast expanses of lawns, gardens, a curving brick driveway, the Stars and Stripes hanging sedately from a flagpole over the entranceway.

Its gates were closed.

Fidel took a deep breath, exhaled slowly, swallowed hard, controlled himself, finally nodded to Gonzáles when it was clear that the gringo Marine in dress blues was not going to open them even though the Prime Minister of Cuba desired entrance. Gonzáles got out of the car, strode to the gates, faced down the Marine through the iron bars, spoke. Intimidated, the Marine said nothing, responded with nods and gulps, went into his guardhouse, picked up the phone with a shaky hand, dialed. A brief conversation. He returned to Gonzáles, gulped again, shook his head, assumed the position of parade rest.

Fidel stared at the scene through the car window, eyes blinking. For a moment, he could not believe it, a foreign embassy does not deny entrance to the head of state of the host country, it's unheard of. Gonzáles turned, looked back at the car, anger and confusion clouding his features. He didn't know what to do.

Muttering, Fidel got out of the car, walked to the gates, glared at the sentry, waited. The man stood rock-still. "Do you know who I am?" he demanded.

No response.

"Open those gates," he screamed, livid, arms waving. "Open them immediately!"

The sentry did not move.

Fidel stepped back, cupped his hands around his mouth, yelled at the mansion, aware he was making a spectacle of himself, but too angry to care. "I want to talk to you, Bonsal! I want an end to this insanity! I want to send a protest to Washington!"

On and on he shouted, for a good fifteen minutes, complaining about Yankee arrogance, insisting they take full responsibility for *La Coubre* and stop their subversive attacks on the Republic of Cuba. His words echoed across the manicured lawn. Nothing happened. The sentry was unmoved.

Never before had one of his impromptu lectures fallen on deaf ears. Infuriated, he jerked out his forty-five, aimed at the gate, emptied the clip into the lock.

Astonished, the sentry turned, started to raise his rifle, but Gonzáles had his pistol out, aimed at the man's face.

A brief tableau.

The smell of powder hung in the air. Then a determined Fidel was swinging the gates open, muttering under his breath.

"Cuidado, Fidel," said Gonzáles.

He looked up. A platoon of Marines decked out in full combat dress was double-timing across the lawn, rifles at port arms. They fanned out behind the gates, locked and loaded their weapons. Fidel glanced at Gonzáles, then the Marines, his fleet of Oldsmobiles, his bodyguards, ready, the Marines again, waiting. Obviously, if he walked or drove through the gates, war was declared, and like it or not, he might not survive the first skirmish. Okay, *bueno,* but these gringo Marines are going to sweat for a moment, they are going to seriously consider dying absurdly on Cuban soil, protecting nothing more than the cowardice of their ambassador. Deliberately, he took out a cigar, lit it, puffed, then hacked and spit at the feet of the terrified sentry, brown saliva splashing on spit-shined shoes.

"Tell your Philip Bonsal he hasn't heard the last of this." He nodded toward the platoon of Marines. "And tell your comrades that when the invasion comes, they will die hard at the hands of the people's militia."

He went back to his car. Gonzáles followed. In concert, the drivers turned around and sped off down the Malecón, Fidel strangely calm despite the humiliation, for he knew how he was going to respond. So the Yankees sabotage an arms shipment, then refuse to talk to you, he thought. Guess what happens next, gringos. Cuba will not buy any more guns from Belgium. No, no, no, you might blow those up too, and you can talk the British and French out of selling us arms as well, but what about the Russians? We've signed a trade agreement with them, we've already purchased Soviet oil, why not their weapons? He smiled. So, go ahead, gringos, blow up a Russian ship in Havana harbor and see what happens.

If you got the *cojones.*

"A dónde?" Gonzáles asked.

"The harbor," Fidel replied automatically, intending to take charge of rescue operations for the survivors of the explosion. He was not planning a publicity stunt. Becoming involved—getting his hands dirty—was his way of relieving the helpless feeling in his gut.

Yet when he was in the middle of all the smoke and chaos, directing the ambulances, then watching the militiamen line up burnt corpses on the street, he realized the most effective way he could respond to this madness was through the press, the TV cameras. I will speak at the funeral, he told himself. I will speak of sacrifice and strength and commitment. And I will pledge to them, *¡patria o muerte, venceremos!*

Twenty-eight

THE CROSSHAIRS CENTERED on a tall, handsome black man some six hundred yards away in a clearing dotted with open-air classrooms, talking to a group of students, most of them female, mist-shrouded trees behind them. The place was Topes de Collantes, recently hacked out of the Sierra Escambray, a training center for the vanguard of the national literacy campaign, and Todd Blackburn, in a thicket by a jeep trail, was about to bag his first school-teacher.

He took a deep breath, exhaled halfway, slowly squeezed the trigger. Suddenly, the black man turned. Todd almost jerked the shot, but controlled himself. Wait till he turns back, wait for a clean hit, he told himself, be patient, you want to put one between his running lights, by the book. His loins stirred.

The teacher was smiling now, reciting from a book, and Todd imagined him soft-spoken, modest, reasonable. Unsettling thoughts, for he had come expecting a fanatic proselytizing the pinko faith to round-heeled minds. Not so. The book was *La Gramática Modernade Español,* and the students appeared animated and curious. Why the hell wasn't the dude reading Marx to a bunch of zombies? Another deep breath. C'mon, ace, don't chicken out, what the fuck difference does it make?

He shot him between the eyes.

Todd melted into the trees, followed by Ricardo and the others, started up a steep mountainside at a swift pace, his mood deteriorating. He had hoped the killing would raise his spirits, but it only showed the impotence of his counter-revolutionary band. While the men behind him could joke all they wanted about a dead teacher with *tres ojos,* the fact was they were limited to isolated acts of terrorism. They didn't have enough people to take on the FAR patrols, and weren't likely to get more recruits since the peasants were scared to death of them.

He reached the high ground, called a break, sat on a rock and lit a cigarette to discourage the mosquitoes. Gazing at the black trees and gray overcast, he reflected on his decision to toss that M-26 radio—and his career—into Havana harbor. He figured it would be worth it if he could bring down the revolution, yet that seemed impossible. He'd thought about it a lot the last few weeks, and decided the only way was to assassinate Fidel Castro. But how? No one could ever get close enough—not even a kamikaze could get past the bodyguards and Jiménezes.

Todd finished his cigarette, field-stripped the butt, gave the word, and they moved out across a broad meadow. Ricardo asked him what was next, and he just shook his head, his frustration increasing. "Forget it, *amigo,* forget it for a while, when we get back to camp, post sentries, eat, get drunk, but no fires, the FAR's gonna be out in force the next couple of days." You too, ace, he told himself, forget it for a while, go see Rosa, the *campesino's* daughter, fourteen years old with a body going on nineteen, the one you'd met in the forest picking berries just a week ago, Rosa, with full lips and lush smile. She'd taken to sex like a cat to cream. The thought of her made him anxious, so anxious he didn't bother to look behind him before going into the trees and missed seeing the glint of field glasses far across the meadow.

A half hour later, they were at the camp. Todd filled his canteen with rum, got a fresh pack of cigarettes, left Ricardo in charge, and hurried off through the rocks, keeping to the lengthening shadows of afternoon, switchbacking his way to the top of a ridge line, then down the other side. He followed a goat path through trees, up another hill, down to a small clearing. The *campesino's* thatched hut was at one end next to an empty corral, a wisp of smoke rising from a hole in the roof. Out front, chickens pecked in the dirt, and geese honked at his presence. He went no farther, stayed hidden by the trees, knew better than to mess with them. There was her father, too. When you popped a girl's cherry, you turned her old man into a wounded beast, and Todd wanted no part of him.

The geese kept it up, but didn't advance beyond the corral. Peering through the branches he saw her come around the hut calling, *"¿Quién es?* Is that you? My father is gone, he will not be back until tomorrow!" In rough cotton blouse and skirt, she looked childlike, the clothes concealing her figure. He stepped into the clearing, still leery of the geese. Another chorus of honks. She shooed them away, then turned, her round face blossoming with a smile. She looked down shyly, folded her hands, came at him sideways. Her hair was pinned up for work, but curls fell down here and there, limp with perspiration. Her arms were dusty, her skirt stained from kneeling in the garden.

Alone until tomorrow. *"Buenas, querida."*

243

"Buenas," she whispered, playing in the dirt with her toes.

He lifted her chin, kissed her tenderly. Her mouth was sweet, tasted of banana and sugar cane. She went soft against him, trembling as his hands slipped inside her blouse and worked their magic. Then she pulled him toward the canvas flap that was the front door, her shyness gone.

In her small room with the crucifix and picture of Castro on the wall, she let her hair down, undressed quickly, lay down on the broken mattress by the window, her curls falling over the edge onto the dirt floor in the shape of a flower.

He took off his clothes, kneeled over her, admired her firm breasts, her tight, supple body not yet ruined by the daily struggle for existence in the Escambray. The sheen of hair on her legs, the tufts of it starting under her arms like new grass. An unsullied beauty. His. He smiled sardonically. In five years she'll be just another Cuban mother or whore, with wrinkles and sagging tits. He glanced up at the picture of Castro and almost laughed. Watch me, you bastard, watch me fuck the daughters of your precious revolution.

He kissed her thighs. She hadn't bathed and smelled faintly of dead sperm from two days ago when they'd done it in the forest on a bed of decaying leaves.

Excited by her various scents, he took her savagely, and she responded just as eagerly, surprising him, her eyes black and unfathomable. Like it, don't you, you little tropical slut?

Right then, he hated her. His mind slipped, and he imagined his sperm—almost, almost there—burning through her insides like acid, purifying her. Then he lost control and buried his face in her hair. Her moans and whimpers filled his senses, her teeth in his shoulder, her hands clawing at his back. Grunting and sweating, he was totally gone.

Unaware of the *campesino,* home early, drawn to the window by his daughter's cries, unaware of him cursing, racing around to the door, jerking out his machete, coming inside.

When he finally sensed danger and saw the *campesino* raising the machete, Todd couldn't stop, it felt too good, he was frozen in an awful moment where bliss touched death. His own.

A pistol shot rang out.

Astonished, the *campesino* dropped his machete, fell, was dead before he hit the floor, a small hole in his forehead.

Todd rolled off the girl, backed into the wall, heart pounding, wondering what was happening. Confused, she sat up, looked at him blankly, then the body, recognized her father, gasped, eyes widening with horror, hands covering her face. A long, anguished scream.

Todd saw him in the window then, a ruddy, blue-eyed man wearing bush clothes and a straw hat. Todd glanced at his knife sheathed in his boot across the room, but the man read his mind.

"Wouldn't attempt it, mate," he said cheerfully, brandishing a .38 special. "If you get my drift."

Grief-stricken, the girl was crying hysterically, shaking her father's body as if to give it life, then glaring hatefully at Todd and the man in the window, spewing out foolish accusations, foolish because the instant she mentioned the local militia, the man shot and killed her, too.

"Wha— What the fuck?"

Now two corpses were twisted together, the stench of death permeating everything. Already the flies were there, buzzing, settling down on the eyes.

Todd gaped helplessly at the man in the window.

"Get your togs on, mate, we've got a bit of catching up to do."

In seconds, Todd was fully dressed. He ran out of the hut and would've kept going except the man was waiting in front, one hand tossing bread to the geese, the other loosely holding the .38. He stopped short.

The man looked him up and down. "Well, now, when you're in a hurry, you don't mess around, do you?"

"Who the fuck are you, anyway?"

"Name's Steve Flynn." He grinned and extended his hand.

Flynn, Todd told himself, shaking the man's hand automatically. So this is the firm's resident vagabond in Cuba. I wonder if we're still on the same side?

"Took a bit of mucking about to find you, Blackburn. I must say, you and your lads handle yourself quite well in the bush." He gestured with his pistol, indicating Todd should go first. "Dinner's just around the corner."

Todd started down a rutted ox trail into a deepening twilight. Apparently unconcerned about patrols, Flynn wouldn't stop talking. Now he was analyzing the scene back at the *campesino*'s hut, praising Todd's sexual prowess, though he found it quite remarkable that the act of ejaculation had proven stronger than Todd's instinct for survival. Was that a noteworthy masculine characteristic among Yanks or merely an aberration? he asked.

Todd grimaced. "Don't you ever shut up?"

Flynn just laughed, enjoying himself.

They left the trail and pushed through a mile of thick underbrush—hot, sweaty work, hard to see, gnats, flies, and mosquitoes constantly in Todd's face. Finally, they came to a well-hidden cave.

"Relax, mate," said Flynn, indicating a camp stool. He got a small fire going, broke out C rations, offered Todd some. He refused them. Flynn ate anyway, smacking his lips, wiping his mouth on his sweaty sleeve. "In case you hadn't guessed, I'm with the firm. Been on board for five years, learning the business from the inside out so my books'll read like the real thing."

"Books?"

"Right, mate, I'm a Yank now and someday I'm gonna write the great American novel." He poured Johnny Walker into a canteen cup. "Whisky?"

Todd nodded, took the canteen cup, drank deep—once, twice—in awe of the situation and this Steve Flynn.

"The firm's quite happy with *La Coubre*, Blackburn. You're still on the payroll, all you have to do is keep in touch."

Todd looked at Flynn with a jaundiced eye. "Bullshit."

He didn't act surprised. "Figured that's what you'd think," he said, dropping an envelope in Todd's lap.

It was his bank statement from Dade County First National, showing deposits in March and April totaling five thousand dollars. He was amazed.

"Looks like they've given you a bit of a bonus too, hey, mate?"

"Jeez!" Todd bubbled with laughter, felt good and warm inside for a change, not realizing half of it was the whisky.

"So what do we tell them?"

"Huh?"

"What's next, Mr. Blackburn? They're all ears."

Todd held out his canteen cup for more whisky. When it was refilled, he drank again, stared blankly at Flynn. "What's next is the final solution."

"The final solution?"

"Castro. His head on the proverbial spear."

Flynn chuckled. "How poetic."

"I wanna kill the motherfucker," he said defiantly, thinking of David, shot in the face and groin.

"Any particular reason?"

"I don't like his politics."

Flynn stared at him, then smiled slowly, realizing Todd wasn't going to talk about his reasons, personal or otherwise. As if it mattered. "Well, you have my blessings. And the firm's." He paused, drank from the bottle. "Unofficially, of course."

"What the fuck's that mean?"

"They'll pay the bills, but if we get caught, we're freelance chaps without a country."

"We?"

Flynn nodded. "I've been trying to get Castro for a long time, mate."

"You don't like his politics, either?"

"I could care less about his politics," Flynn said matter-of-factly. "His scalp will look good on my service record. I'm here for the duration, mate."

As the sun dropped behind the mountains turning the sky orange and pink, they passed the bottle back and forth, kicked around the monumental task before them. In Flynn's opinion, the problem was Castro's inaccessibility, compounded by the fact that no one knew where he would be at any particular time. He didn't keep to a schedule. Not even Celia Sánchez knew his plans, and she lived with him. "So, we must never waste time trying to guess his movements."

"How else we gonna do it?"

"We track his friends, someone he's likely to see occasionally and relax with when there's not so much heavy security and the Jiménezes're half asleep."

"How're we supposed to do that?"

Flynn patted Todd's knee, said confidentially, "They're all wired, my friend. I know who he calls and when he calls. I have a network in Havana—everything is logged."

"Yeah, but that has to be a lot of people."

"True enough, mate, except we hold out for the right

one." He folded his hands, pursed his lips, a messianic look in his eyes. "Back in fifty-seven the firm had me interview a distinguished Yank expatriate suspected of giving aid and comfort to the rebels. I gave him my first novel, a spy thriller, to explain my presence in his living room. Six months later he sent it back, wishing me the best of luck with it."

"Who the hell're you talking about?"

"Ernest Hemingway, old chap."

Todd gasped. "I met him in the Sierra Maestra!"

"I know." Flynn smiled and nodded. "And yours truly bugged his phone. So when Castro calls—or vice versa— we'll hear. And if the time and place are right, we make the hit, mate."

Twenty-nine

WHEN THE FIRST pink rays of sunlight glanced off the Finca, the veteran rooster perched in the mango tree outside Papa's window hopped to the ground, ruffled his feathers, and crowed, just as he had been doing every day for the past twelve years. Grumbling, Papa rolled up, threw on his robe and slippers, left the bedroom ignoring his fatigue. Outside, at the top of the steps, the morning chill opened his eyes; he savored the freshness, knowing it would burn off soon. Yawning, he went down the path to the pool, moving gracefully for a man his age with all his aches and pains and scars and ailments.

Out of the robe and into the water, the cold bringing him fully awake and alert. Lap after lap he swam, half of them beneath the surface, his strokes practiced and efficient. He was proud how quickly he'd shaken off the disruptions and fears surrounding the *La Coubre* incident and gotten back into his regimen. The blood pressure was down, weight just under two hundred, and he was swimming better than ever.

Here, in the pool every morning, he shed his years, performed like a thirty-year-old, staying in shape for the late rounds. He wasn't so worried these days, the new whore hadn't been around lately. As long as the book flowed and he took care of himself so he was equal to the task, he would finish and finish strong. Life at the Finca had not changed; he could still write here, thank God. Even the chaos outside the gates seemed to have settled into a routine, suggesting that Castro's revolution might actually be working.

An hour later, he pulled himself from the pool, sat heavily on the edge, exhausted. He buried his face in a towel and waited for his breathing to subside, then—groaning—stood up and put on his robe.

"I'm sorry, Ernest," said Mary. She was behind him at the glass patio table, had brought down a tray of hot coffee, rolls, and fresh fruit.

She looked beautiful in the early morning light, and his heart surged like it used to when they first met almost twenty years ago. "Sorry for what, kitten?"

"Well, I haven't been a very nice person to live with." She began serving them breakfast.

"Who has?"

"Melanie, perhaps?"

"She's a pain in the ass," Papa growled.

Mary started crying, her tears falling on the mangos she was spooning out so carefully. She tried to pour the coffee, but spilled it because her hand was shaking. "That's not what the girls in the kitchen are saying."

"You believe them or me?"

"I—I don't know anymore, Papa."

"You trying to tell me something, Mary?" Suddenly, he felt deadhouse tired and wasn't sure he was up for this conversation, but knew he couldn't avoid it. Not if he wanted to stay on his feet and go the distance. He stared at the demitasse of strong Cuban coffee, then tossed it down in one huge swallow and met her eyes. "You trying to tell me you're gonna leave?"

"No, no." She shook her head. "I'm trying to tell you that I don't want to leave!" She dabbed at her tears with her napkin. "But I'd like some consideration! I'd like to be able to hold my head up when I walk through the house!"

"Nothing's going on between me and the daughter." He sighed heavily. Not that he didn't *think* the clothes off her when they were alone. All his energies were channeled into the big book. "Nothing. Not anymore."

"I wish I could believe that."

He squinted at the gray sky over the Gulf Stream, pink where the sunrise lingered. "When the articles are ready to go to New York, Melanie goes with them," he stated flatly. "End of story."

"Thank you, Ernest," she said, her voice quavering.

"De nada," he murmured, still looking off. Right then he knew that he would spend the rest of his days with her, for better or worse. It meant giving up his well-cultivated roving eye and the possibility of hooking up with an angel somewhere along the line, but curiously, he felt no resentment. Are you losing it, Papa, he asked himself, or merely retiring into the convenience of a lasting marriage? He bristled at the thought, but didn't fight it. There was a more important battle going on up in the tranquility of the tower.

"I won't bother you about leaving the Finca anymore, either. If you want to go on living here, then I'll stay here and take care of you." She gave him a radiant smile, picked up the tray, and started back toward the house. "I love you, Papa."

He turned, was about to tell her in no uncertain terms that he didn't need *anyone* to take care of him, but she was already halfway up the path, chattering over her shoulder about a shopping trip.

"Christ," he said, pouring more coffee, getting ready for the climb to the tower, "Christ on a crutch."

The morning went well, the pages coming quick and easy. He was nearing 67,000 words, well beyond the half-way point, up to the funeral scene where the revolutionary hero buries his mother, rejects his penitent father. He paused, tried to focus on the psychology of it. Nothing came. He scowled, realizing the funeral scene was pivotal and couldn't be adequately written until he knew how the book would end. Would there be a reconciliation between father and son? If so, would it be tragic, reflecting the gritty realities of the Cuban revolution? He had no idea.

Sighing, he left the tower, went up to the house, intending to call Castro and ask him how *he* would end the story, but when he dialed the presidential palace, no one answered, not even a secretary, and after twenty rings, the line went dead. Papa shrugged, glanced at the receiver. Maybe Castro doesn't pay his phone bills, he thought, then called the house in Cojímar.

A tape recording of Celia Sánchez answered. "If you are calling to discuss a personal matter—about a home, an intervened farm, a house at the beach, furniture, refrigerators, automobiles, accessories for the same, scholarships, exits from the country, or prisoners—direct yourself to the appropriate organization. I do not work in any of those departments, and neither does the Prime Minister. After seven o'clock at night, do not call us. If it is not urgent, *do not call us.*" Click, dial tone.

Papa glared at the phone, then slammed it down, bewildered. Now that's the most ridiculous thing I've heard in a long time, he told himself, it makes absolutely no sense at all. How in hell does she know whether or not it's urgent if a tape recording answers?

Knowing that work for the day was finished, he gazed out at the Gulf Stream, dreamed of taking the *Pilar* out. Ought to call Gregorio, leave before noon, except— Holy Christ, how could he forget! Fidelito and the Lions were playing for the championship! He checked his watch. In ten minutes!

He took off in the Chrysler, turned onto the highway, immediately got stuck behind a stake-bed truck loaded with chickens on a curvy section of the road. Frustration rankled him; Cuban highways did not have turnouts; there was nothing he could do. Suddenly, he heard the roar of high-speed engines and a chorus of horn blasts. He looked in his rearview mirror, was shocked. The phalanx of Oldsmobiles was coming up behind, straight at him, two abreast, with no intention of slowing down. He pulled hard on the steering wheel, gunned his car off the road just in time. The truck went the other way, ending up in the ditch, cages springing open, chickens flying through the air, feathers everywhere as the Oldsmobiles zoomed past, then nothing, just the whine of the *Jefe*'s fleet receding in the distance.

"Asshole!" Papa screamed, shaking his fist.

He went to help the chicken farmer. Distraught, the man was trying to capture his hens, a fruitless endeavor, all the while muttering about his cousins in Miami, the lucky bastards, but the wife, she is a judge on the people's court, what can I do, you know how it is.

Papa didn't get to the ball game until the last inning. Angry, he strode past the haphazardly parked Oldsmobiles, went directly toward the cordoned-off bleachers intending to give Castro a piece of his mind, but ran into Gonzáles who just shook his head and crossed his huge arms.

Unmindful of his stance, Papa jabbed him in the chest with his finger. "You tell the Premier that *el viejo* wants to talk to him, *¿comprendes?*" He turned on his heel, walked around to the other side of the field, found a place to sit—in time to see Fidelito hit a two-run double, breaking a 3–3 tie. Then the kid struck out the side in the bottom of the ninth, and Papa's anger was swept away with the crowd that surged onto the diamond to congratulate the Lions.

At the center of the mob, Papa discovered Fidel himself, hugging his son, was surprised, but before he could say anything, was overwhelmed by the joyful Prime Minister.

"Hey, *viejo,* there you are, I've been looking all over for you, where have you been?" He did a little dance with Fidelito, tousled his hair. "What do you think of him, huh, *chico?* In five, maybe six years, he'll be ready for the majors, maybe I should call Calvin Griffith, no?" He threw his other arm around Papa. "We must celebrate, okay *bueno?*"

An hour later, they were ensconced in the Floridita, Papa and Fidel at a table in the corner, Fidelito and the Lions at the bar drinking Papa Dobles without the rum, joking nervously about the security. Indeed. Gonzáles had stacked the place with his hard-eyed *hombres,* intimidating the tourists, a tour group from France who left without finishing their drinks.

Strange bivouac, thought Papa, nursing a beer, not exactly the way the Floridita ought to be remembered. He observed the bartenders—mute, overly preoccupied with washing glasses. They wouldn't look him in the eye. C'mon, fellas, he wanted to say, I'm the same old Hem, nothing to worry about, and this Castro boy's really okay, he's just like you 'n' me when all these bone-crushers ain't around.

"So what did you want to talk to me about?" Fidel asked six drinks later, showing no ill effects.

Papa confessed that he was having troubles with the book and waited—not for a lengthy answer, just a phrase, a word to trigger his own imagination hung up in the wings.

Incredibly, all he got was a shrug and a blank stare. This, from the world's foremost orator, the man with a corner on the rhetoric market.

"Huh?"

"How should I know, *viejo?"* he said impatiently. "When a story is over, it's over, maybe you've finished already, and that's all there is to it, you work too hard, anyway." He leaned forward, grabbed Papa by the shoulders, smiled with enthusiasm. "I have a great idea, my friend. Become a Cuban citizen, join the revolution, and I'll make you ambassador to the United Nations, then you won't have to worry about ending your book." He chuckled gleefully. "Can you imagine what Señor Nixon would say?"

Papa frowned, pulled out of Fidel's grasp, annoyed by what he considered an offhanded response to a dead-serious question, but didn't say anything, finished his beer instead.

A waiter materialized, smiling formally, all squared off. *"¿Otra vez, compañero?"*

He was about to say yes, but noticed a red star on the waiter's lapel. Astonished, he leaned on the table, chin in his hands. Jesus Christ, a card-carrying commie waiter working at the Floridita. What a fucking contradiction, what the hell was the world coming to?

"¿Con permiso, compañero, otra vez?" Without flourish, he took the empty Hatuey bottle, hesitated.

"No, damnit," muttered Papa, needing real painkiller. His all-time favorite watering hole had changed, and he didn't like it one bit. "Gordon's," he said emphatically, adding the passé *"señor"* instead of *"compañero."* "A fifth of Gordon's and a coupla shot glasses."

Still smiling, the waiter shook his head. *"Lo siento, compañero, no lo tenemos."*

"What?" growled a shocked Papa. "You're telling me you don't have no Gordon's gin? This is the Floridita, for Christ's sake!"

"Lo siento, compañero," the waiter repeated. *"No lo tenemos."*

"Rum, then, anything." He threw up his hands, scowled at the waiter, then Fidel. "What's happening to this island, anyway?"

Affronted, Fidel immediately started in, hands waving, dark eyes burning at Papa. *"¡Momento, viejo, momento!* If it weren't for the United States, there wouldn't be any shortages. How can the revolution plan an economy when the Yankees plan an invasion, how can the Cuban people work if they constantly have to watch the skies, the beaches, each other, how can the government worry about trade when its first concern is defending the people, how can I be bothered about Gordon's gin at the Floridita when the Yankees are blowing up ships in Havana harbor?"

"Well, somebody oughta be, son!"

Fidel banged the table, rattling the glasses. "The gringos say we are only ninety miles away from them." He wagged his finger at Papa. "The problem is, if you want to know the truth, *they* are only ninety miles away from *us!"*

Normally, Papa would've let it slide, but not this time, not when he was deprived of his favorite sauce for political reasons. "Yeah? Well, you know what I think? I think you've tossed out the baby with the bathwater!"

Fidel ignored the remark, was off nonstop on Yankee imperialism. "Your planes drop leaflets and bombs! Napalm our cane fields! You give sanctuary to counterrevolutionaries, your government encourages criminals to plot against us, your Congress threatens not to buy our sugar.

And all because we have the audacity to seek independence and nonalignment! Why, I ask you. Why?"

"You know damned well what the problem is," Papa declared. "You got commies coming out of the woodwork and messing everything up."

"¡Dios mío!" He touched his forehead, then spun his hand around his head, imitating a swarm of hornets. "Everybody badgers me about the communists! Even you, Señor Papa! I wish the word had never been invented!" He shoved his face across the table, arms flying up behind him. "You talk about communists, what about the accomplishments of the revolution? Are you color-blind? We have eradicated poverty, racial discrimination, illiteracy! Our people are well fed, they all have shoes, a roof over their heads, there is full employment, decent medical care, soon everyone will be able to read, education is free, so is rent, salaries have been raised, prices and costs reduced, we are industrializing, diversifying, building a new society, yet all the gringos can do is talk about communism!"

Papa sighed heavily. "Y'know, Señor Prime Minister, if you could sell words, Cuba'd be the richest country in the world, and you wouldn't have to worry about the economy."

Fidel frowned darkly and sat back, displeased. "Never have the Cuban people been better off!"

"Then how come I can't buy a fucking shot of gin?" said Papa, bringing it home, then burying it. "God forbid I'd want scotch. Probably have to swim to Miami to get it."

Fidel was cut to the quick. For an instant naked, all the successes of his revolution compromised by one simple fact: the cupboard was bare. Then he covered with a sweeping gesture and a huge burst of laughter. *"¡Ay, mi madre!"* he exclaimed, loud enough for everyone to hear. "What does this old man know?"

Papa gripped the table with both hands, felt the heat rising into his face. His breath hissed out slowly. *The fucker's trying to belittle you, Hem, he's trying to make you look like an old fool.* "Maybe I don't know nothing about running a country, Castro, but it looks like nobody else on this island does either, and if you don't get some answers soon, you might as well petition Uncle Sam for statehood."

Fidel leaned close, eyes feverish, sweat beading up on his forehead. "I have the answer, *Compañero* Papa," he whispered intensely, "and it's not communism. Not capitalism. Certainly not Yankee imperialism." He paused. *"Socialismo."*

"Aww, horseshit!" Papa remarked scornfully, his voice ringing through the bar.

Not a sound.

"Listen to this old man, will you?" Irritated, Fidel waved his hands, raised his voice for the benefit of state security. "Is that any way to speak to the Prime Minister of Cuba?"

Nervous laughter.

"Watch what you say, *viejo,* you don't want to get into trouble." With a patronizing smile, he reached across the table, patted Papa on the cheek, then mussed his hair, uncovering his bald spot. "You shouldn't talk about what you don't know, people will think you've become feeble-minded."

"Don't you touch my head!" roared Papa, leaping up. *"Nobody* touches my head!"

He upended the table. Candle, ashtrays, and glasses flew through the air, shattered on impact, and an astonished Fidel was left with a table in his lap, his fatigues soaked with Papa Dobles. Hemingway had his fist back, intending to throw a left hand, but was suddenly pinned by three bodyguards.

Gonzáles shouted orders.

An explosion of movement. Bodyguards had the kids outside and pulled a screaming, gesticulating, red-faced Fidel from the place in seconds.

Papa was left with the bartenders frozen in amazement, the pinko waiter cowering in the corner. Just for the hell of it, he took a warm bottle of beer off the bar and pitched it through a window.

"Scratch what could've been," he said to the emptiness of the Floridita while walking out.

Never to return.

Thirty

FIDEL BRACED HIMSELF under the barbell, lifted the weight off the rack, eased it to his chest, sucked in a huge quantity of air, exhaled sharply, bench-pressed 250 pounds. Once. Twice. Ten times before he stopped and rested, gasping for breath. He was in the bedroom of the modest Vedado apartment he rented for a peso a year from the Ministry for the Recovery of Stolen Property. The louvered windows usually let in a pleasant breeze. But today the air was dead, the humidity almost unbearable.

Weight lifting cleared his mind, released tensions that invariably built up before official state functions. He grimaced, took a deep breath, grabbed the bar again, lifted. Just three days ago his government had established formal diplomatic relations with the Soviet Union, and this afternoon at the Palace of the Revolution there was a reception for the Russian ambassador who'd arrived late the night before, drunk out of his mind, and had to be helped from the Aeroflot turboprop.

He was not looking forward to it. So much was expected of him, more than just his presence at the affair. The world was watching. He must act enthusiastic, warm, friendly, eager for close ties with the Eastern bloc when he wasn't at all sure he wanted them.

He didn't even *like* Russians. All they did was drink, talk about machinery, five-year plans and quotas; they were alien to such pastimes as hunting and fishing, had never even heard of baseball, and he didn't know one *guajiro* who could honestly say he'd gotten all the way through *War and Peace.* He paused. Well, maybe Guevara.

He pushed the barbell up again, straining now, muscles quivering. So now he must dance with the Russians and hope they would not make unreasonable demands in return for their aid and support.

Such as Cuban sovereignty.

He shook his head furiously, the sweat flying. Don't lose control, *chico,* whatever you do, he told himself, the stakes are too high. If Cuba loses her independence, the revolution means nothing, and you have failed.

Cinco . . . seis . . . His left arm started to go, and the weight listed in that direction. He clenched his teeth, forced it, neck bulging, arms shaking. *Siete . . . ocho . . .* Come on, just two more, you can do it, you can do anything, never forget that. *Nueve . . . nueve . . . ¡diez!* He let go of the barbell, and it dropped into the rack with a resounding clang. He just lay there. Panting. Arms limp, jellified.

Finally, he sat up, watched his sweat pooling on the linoleum. *Madre de Dios,* it was hot! He should've stayed at the beach. He frowned, stared out the windows at the thick, green mass of breadfruit trees and bamboo, dazzling in the sunlight. No. Cojímar reminded him of *el viejo* and that awful scene at the Floridita.

Papa. The name was a reproach to himself. You should telephone him, *chico,* even though you have nothing to apologize for. No, no, no, don't waste your time, he is a cynical old man who is losing his mind, he will not even listen to you. Fidel scowled, knew he was placating himself. Undeniably, Papa was stubborn, churlish, rooted in the past, hiding behind his myth, but he was also very much in touch with reality. Hard realities that sometimes you can't bring yourself to face. There is much wisdom in his counsel, you should telephone him—

"Fidel?" Celia called from downstairs. "We should leave in twenty minutes!"

"Está bien," he grumbled, *"está bien."*

He started for the bathroom, undressing as he went, letting his sweat-soaked clothes fall where they might, turned on the shower, tested the water. Cold. He turned the hot up all the way, waited a good five minutes, had to settle for lukewarm. Irritated, he stepped into the stall, soaped his body, made a mental note to speak to the building manager and tell him to fix the hot-water heater *muy pronto.*

As he turned into the spray to wash the soap off his face suddenly it became a trickle. Briefly, he stared at the shower head, looked down at his lathered frame, then back to the shower head. No water pressure. What the hell is going on around here? he wondered. Some housewife has probably thrown in a load of diapers down in the basement, *you know how it is.* The spray slowed to a drip.

Angry, he got out of the stall and tried the water in the sink. Nothing there either, so he began wiping the soap off his body, accepting his plight stoically, until rivulets of sweat mixed with soap ran down into his eyes. Howling with pain, he buried his face in a towel, wiped his eyes clear, left the bathroom, vowing to send both the building manager and the superintendent at the water company either to technical school or prison.

Feeling sticky, he put on his underwear, looked around

for a clean and starched set of fatigues, but on the bed, Celia had laid out a dark blue uniform of lightweight gabardine with silver piping and gold epaulets, a matching tie, light blue shirt with diamond cuff links, spit-shined shoes, knee-length nylon socks, a gold-braided hat with patent-leather visor. *¿Qué es esto?* Astonished, he held up the jacket. Four rows of medals were already pinned above the left breast pocket.

"Celia?" He hurried to the door. *"Celia!"*

She appeared at the bottom of the stairs, very feminine and stateswomanly in a dark blue three-piece Paris original, coiffured hair and makeup. Very self-conscious, too.

"What the hell is this?" Fidel shouted, holding up the uniform jacket.

She looked down, half turned away. Shrugged.

"¡No me digas! Another shrug? Doesn't anybody on this island know how to do anything except *shrug?"*

No response.

"¿Qué se significa esto?" he screamed.

"I—I thought you might want to look a little more formal for a change." She walked away, teetering in high heels.

He bounded downstairs, making furious connections between his appearance and the purity of the Cuban revolution, caught Celia in the kitchen, was about to grab her by the shoulders, but stopped. He'd never seen her in a dress before.

"What is wrong with my fatigues? I told you, I told everybody in the Sierra Maestra I was comfortable in fatigues, that I would die in fatigues! I have no desire to look like—like a Brazilian generalissimo!"

"But, Fidel, the Russians—"

"What *about* the Russians?" he exploded.

"They—". She blushed crimson. "They sent a note asking if the Prime Minister might be persuaded to wear something more in keeping with a reception for an ambassador from the Soviet Union."

He stepped back, leaned against the door, eyes blinking, mouth agape. The Russians, already they— "Telephone their embassy!" he ordered. "Immediately!"

"Sí," she replied, picking up the phone.

"Tell them if they want friendly relations with Cuba, they'd better not ask *this* Premier to look like a marionette out of the Grand Guignol!"

"Sí."

"Fidel Castro will not choke himself with a necktie for *anyone!"*

Thirty-one

A COLLECTIVE GASP.

All the Cubans near the entranceway to the Palace of the Revolution stopped talking when Papa and his companion were introduced, stole glances in his direction, exchanged whispers of amazement. The Russians and East Europeans figured they were showing deference to the renowned, Nobel prize-winning author, but Papa knew otherwise.

Leopoldina was on his arm.

The willowy, exotic Leopoldina was resplendent in a backless saffron gown split up the sides and matching her skin color so at first glance she didn't appear to be wearing anything except turquoise eye shadow. Leopoldina, "formerly" Havana's most notorious prostitute.

Grinning, Papa patted her on the hand, strode into the room, nodding to those he recognized. Leopoldina wagged her fingers and winked at men she had known. Those closest tried to shrink away and act nonchalant at the same

266

time, sudden movements causing spilled drinks and jostled matés.

Papa had been surprised when he received an invitation to the reception, hadn't planned on going, had no desire to shake hands with droll Russian diplomats, knew better than to ask Mary, then by chance ran into Leopoldina while on a nostalgic visit to the Tropicana. And, ten drinks later, what do you say, *hija*, want to go play footsie with the Russkies next Friday? She agreed instantly, the prospect of offending official Cuban sensibilities appealing to her as much as it did to him.

In the corner, a tuxedoed string quartet tried Tchaikovsky in honor of the occasion. Nearby, Papa spotted Che Guevara lecturing a group of Russians. In contrast to their dark suits, the enigmatic Argentine's fatigues were wrinkled and limp with dirt, his shoulder-length hair greasy, his boots pooled in cigarette ashes, his body odor obvious ten feet away. Needless to say, he hadn't bathed, changed clothes, or slept in days, but the fire was still fresh in his eyes, for he was arguing philosophy with the Russians. In French.

"Your position is not realistic for twentieth-century man," said their spokesman.

Che smiled, lit a cigarette from the butt of one smoked down to his untrimmed fingernails, then inhaled deeply. *"Je vous demande pardon, messieurs,* but I am only interested in the twenty-first-century man, a new man created simultaneously with a new economic base, and before you object, let me explain that the new man will not be governed by material incentives such as we see in the mistakes of your country. Rather, motivations will be of a moral character. The new man will develop a higher consciousness of himself and others; he will free himself from alienation through work. You see, *messieurs,* man is basically good, society is basically good, and as long as we believe that, no struggle is too great."

The Russians frowned and mumbled, looked to each other for a way out of Guevara's intellectual clutches. Finally, the spokesman smiled. "You sound like a Chinese communist," he said.

"Hasta la victoria siempre," Che replied. He turned, winked at Papa, then strolled toward a side door, waving aside the palace guards.

"Wish he'd stick around," Papa said wistfully.

"He is too radical," observed Leopoldina. "Even for the *comandantes."*

They got into the reception line that curved around the hall, Papa stopping a waiter for a couple of daiquiris, but declining hors d'oeuvres. There was black caviar and crackers from Romania, cold Polish sausage, Bulgarian herring, et cetera; nothing Cuban anywhere, not even pickled *malanga,* staple of the *barbudos* in the Maestra.

Leopoldina nibbled on caviar, a faraway look in her eyes, a dreamy smile on her face. "Remember the old days, Ernesto, the days when the gangsters ran the casinos and you could get anything you wanted?"

"Yep."

She sighed. *"Muy depravada."*

"Were you happier then?"

She pouted at him, struck a pose, hand on hip, eyes stormy over the daiquiri glass. "Of course not," she protested, "how could anyone be truly happy when such decadence was in vogue and we were all exploited by the capitalists, forced to do unspeakable acts in order to survive? Now things are much better, the streets are safe and clean, there is much solidarity," she said with a knowing smile.

"Amen," he said soberly. "Drink up before Bacardi closes its doors."

"You know how it is."

"So what're you up to these days?"

"Casi lo mismo," she said vaguely, fluttering her hand, the smile blossoming. "I get by." She glanced around the room, affecting boredom, checking out the potential, then came back to him. "And you, Ernesto?" She patted his leg. "How've you been lately?"

"Can't complain."

"If you ever need a new old friend," she said confidentially, "someone who knows . . ."

"Worth consideration."

"We could . . . reminisce?"

He roared with laughter, thoroughly enjoying the moment, for now they had reached the raised platform, the smiling Russians and Fidel. Here goes.

"May I present *Compañero* Ernest Hemingway," Fidel said smoothly, avoiding Papa's eyes.

The Soviet ambassador nodded politely, sweating in his ill-fitting wool suit, eyes like stoplights reflecting a bad hangover.

"And this here's Leopoldina Maximilian," Papa replied, ushering her forward, relishing it.

The ambassador took one look and almost fell off the platform. Fortunately, his wife was with Celia and didn't see his reaction: the dropped jaw, hard swallows, quivering hands, eyes fixed on Leopoldina's décolletage. Smiling, she turned, giving him quick shots of her breasts.

Fidel was smiling too, almost laughing, his eyes twinkling mischievously. "Ah, *Compañera* Leopoldina," he said expansively, "so nice to see you again." Fidel put one arm around her, the other around the ambassador, walked *out* of the reception line to the rear of the platform! Bewildered, the other Soviet dignitaries hesitated, not used to breaks in protocol, then followed the power. A sober Fidel began telling them all about Leopoldina's "war

record," how she single-handedly took on an entire company of Batista's soldiers and did them all in, no prisoners, no
quarter, earning the highest order of the revolution. Indeed. He asked innocently, "Why aren't you wearing your
medal, *compañera?*"

"It didn't go with the dress," she said modestly.

"Ah, yes, female sensibilities." He laughed, then continued performing for the fascinated Russians.

A flabbergasted Papa couldn't believe what was happening. He had meant to embarrass Castro fawning in front of
his new lord and master, but it wasn't like that at all. Jesus
Christ, he's got them in the palm of his hand. Don't look
now, gringos, but those Russkies have just become *his*
puppets!

"Cuban women are as beautiful as they are tough, no?"
said Fidel.

The ambassador mumbled something lecherous in Russian.

"Leopoldina is reeducating the lumpen proletariat now,
why don't you tell our honored guest about your program,
chica?"

He practically pushed them together. They left the hall
arm in arm while Fidel went on bullshitting the Soviet
entourage about morality in the new Cuba.

Yep, sorta looks like he's got some rain after all, thought
Papa, maybe the Pearl of the Antilles *ain't* gonna roll over
and spread her legs for this bunch of Rasputins. He
wandered through the great hall, just marking time, wondering if he should say something to Castro.

When someone caught his eye. He was a red-faced man
engaged in easy conversation with a Canadian diplomat.
Papa knew instantly the man didn't belong. He had a tan
line across his forehead indicating he spent all his time in
the sun, and there were too many wrinkles in his suit. He
was definitely not a diplomatic functionary. And there was

something else. He'd seen this bozo before, but where? He moved closer for a better look when some half-drunk East Germans were pushed in front of him by a blond-headed waiter Papa hadn't seen. He sidestepped them, looked again.

The man was gone.

Frowning, Papa went in search of him, telling himself to be careful, the guy might be trouble, and you ain't got no weapon, old man. He crept through the palace, found nothing but empty rooms and offices. No trace of the red-faced man. Papa returned to the reception intending to ask the Canadian diplomat for an ID, but he was gone, too. The crowd of guests had thinned out considerably, and he was left with a coldness inside, a visit from the new whore. He scowled. Aw, come on, like Mary always says, you're just being paranoid, forget it, you're making something of nothing, nobody could've got past security without an invitation and papers! Yet he knew he had seen the man before.

Nervous, he took a daiquiri off a tray, decided to leave, headed for the entranceway. As he rounded the corner, he ran into Castro coming down the staircase—curiously alone.

A pause.

At precisely the same time, Papa and Fidel apologized to each other, and the knot of fear and anger dividing them dissolved into warm laughter.

"No le creo, Compañero Papa, bringing Leopoldina!"

"Yeah? Well, I don't believe you either, telling the Russkies she was a war hero."

He shrugged in spite of himself. "The Russian ambassador will be my friend for a long time."

"How about his wife?"

"Russian women are all grandmothers," Fidel said glibly. "She won't be threatened."

They appropriated a tray of daiquiris, strolled out onto

the balcony, each very aware of the other, cautious, not wanting to say the wrong thing and shatter a fragile truce.

"Daiquiris aren't bad," remarked Papa.

"They're not as good as Papa Dobles."

"Tell the chef to hold the sugar."

"I'll call him tomorrow."

A silence.

"You know, I've been thinking about your book," Fidel said tentatively.

"Yeah?"

"Do you want the father and son to, ah, reconcile their differences?"

"Maybe," Papa said carefully.

"Then why don't you have them go fishing?" he exclaimed, spreading his hands.

"Not very exciting."

"It's a common ground!" Fidel argued. "You can—"

"Listen, Castro, the problem is I can't write something until it happens, that's the way it's always been, I gotta live it, then write it and make it true. Maybe I never should've asked you in the first place."

Fidel understood, looked off pensively. "Then maybe we really should go fishing, maybe that would help."

"You been threatening to do that for a long time."

"You know how busy I get."

"There's always the tournament next week."

"The Hemingway, *sí.*"

"Your boys over at the tourist bureau keep calling me up and asking dumb questions. Surely there's someone in the government who knows how to organize a fishing contest," he said caustically.

"Please, no more arguments, *viejo.*"

"Anyway, I was planning to sit this one out." Papa finished his daiquiri, squinted at Castro. "But I'll enter if you will, and may the best man win. Got the *cojones?*"

"Tengo los cojones."

"You're on." Papa grinned. "Who knows? You might even get some decent press for a change."

"I'll take the boy!" Fidel said eagerly. "He'll love it!"

"Oh, no, you won't," Papa said sternly, folding his arms. "The kid goes on my boat. Don't want him picking up any bad habits."

Thirty-two

THERE'S TOO MUCH brass, Todd Blackburn thought, twirling the pretty blonde in a chiffon formal across the floor, too much brass and not enough violins. The Club Náutico orchestra was attempting Percy Faith's "Theme from 'A Summer Place'" for the dance contest's finale, and the air was heavy with the scent of jacaranda and night-blooming jasmine. Memories were alive on the faces of the spectators lining the waxed parquet. Dreamy smiles and teary eyes. Most of these people're convinced they won't be here next year, Todd mused. Well, me and Flynn might have something to say about that.

In front of the judges, he spun the girl out, brought her back, turned himself, a graceful merge of light-gray seersucker with organdy. A bend, and then he was up again with the music, causing a gasp of delight from his partner. He just kept smiling into her large blue eyes, her heart-shaped lips forming an O. Just kept on dancing.

He'd only known her for about three hours. They met at

the patio bar while he was observing the pretournament boat auction, this one with an unusual amount of activity since the high rollers wanted to unload their yachts before the revolution considered them donations. Her name was Lynne Jameson, she'd just finished her freshman year at Goddard, Daddy was an Esso vice-president, one of the last in Havana. They'll probably send us to Venezuela, she'd said, I hear Caracas is absolutely divine, then introduced him to her boyfriend, a junior down from Dartmouth, talking funny on his second gin and tonic, so Todd kept buying him drinks, and they carried the lad off before dinner. Embarrassed, Lynne had been on the verge of tears until Todd graciously offered to fill in as her escort for the evening.

He had trouble getting through dinner without letting his boredom show, for the level of conversation never got beyond what a gut course "soc" was, but he needed a cover, a reason to be here. Flynn hadn't been too concerned, not spotting any Jiménezes among the guests, but you never knew. Not that they expected Castro to show up. Even if he did, to kill him in the club would be suicide. It was the next morning they'd been thinking about—ever since reading in the papers that the Prime Minister was entering the fishing contest.

Ever since listening to the bugged phone conversation between Hemingway and Castro when they agreed to meet on the docks between five-thirty and six A.M.

On and on they danced, Todd thoroughly enjoying himself. He didn't even mind the leers from Flynn, always in the shadows. Eat your heart out, Steve, he thought, you never touched a chick as fine as this one, you couldn't even score unwashed pussy in the Escambray.

Two more couples were eliminated, and Todd knew they had won. He closed his eyes, imagined he was flying, imagined David cheering him on. Another triple twirl, then a final bend climaxing with the music. They bowed, and the crowd applauded wildly. The lights came up, and the smiling judges handed them trophies as the flashbulbs popped. Todd took Lynne by the hand, escaped to a table in the corner with a view of the harbor. The orchestra swung into a rock 'n' roll medley of "Blue Suede Shoes" followed by "You Send Me," and "Bird Dog," almost unrecognizable in instrumental form.

"Everything okay?"

She laughed, covered his hand with her own. "Todd!" she cried. "It's perfect!"

He signaled a waitress, ordered mai tais. When the drinks came, he sipped his, relaxed while Lynne yakked on and on about school. He surveyed the crowd, noticing for the first time the curious mix, not just the well-to-do elite of the Club Náutico. FAR soldiers were among the guests. Cuban workers too, and even a few *campesinos*. Castro had insisted a lot of quota-filling *macheteros* be allowed to try their hand in the tournament, yet—strangely—the club seemed as prestigious and exclusive as ever, despite blue collars, fatigues, and boots on the dance floor eclipsing the narrow ties and suede shoes of colonialism.

He checked his watch. Almost midnight. If he wanted to score, he'd better hurry. The party would be over at two. "Want to catch some stars?"

She giggled. "Why not?"

He escorted her out to the balcony, his arms going around her waist. She leaned her head against his chest and sighed. He closed his eyes, placed his hands over her alabaster breasts, felt himself grow unusually hard. He hadn't had a white chick in a couple of months, was about to kiss her when she moved his hands back down to her waist.

"Now, now," she scolded.

Mortified, he frowned impatiently, knew that he could

sweet-talk his way between her creamy thighs in a matter of minutes, but didn't want to take the time. He'd rather rip her dress off, smack her smug face, and just take what he wanted. He glanced over the balcony. Sure, man, he told himself, go ahead and fuck her, then break her neck and dump her into the bushes, they'll never find her. As he reached for her dress, he felt a hot spasm in his groin and hunched over.

"Is there a Todd Blackburn out there?"

He stiffened.

"Phone call for you at the bar, mate."

He told her he'd be right back, strode across the balcony. "Goddamn you, Flynn," he whispered, going inside. "Goddamn your—"

Suddenly, he was jerked through a door onto a landing in the stairwell, found himself face-to-face with the angry limey.

"What the hell you up to, mucking about with a prom queen? When we've got a job to do, don't you think you ought to keep it in your pants?"

"You— You touch me again, motherfucker, you're a dead man!"

Flynn just smiled. Todd shoved him out of the way, went up the stairs to the door leading to the roof. Ignoring the No Entrada sign, he jimmied it open, then taped the latch so the door wouldn't automatically close and lock, ensuring they'd have a viable escape route in the morning, one that state security wouldn't immediately suspect since the club didn't open until eleven A.M.

On the roof, they removed the components of the lightweight sniper's rifle taped to their bodies, and Flynn assembled it, making jokes about Todd dancing with a rifle scope between his legs. "What if you'd gotten the bird to lift her skirts and given her quim a load of cold metal?"

"She was only a cover, for Christ's sake!" He wouldn't

admit to himself that since the *barbudos* had executed David, he had unconsciously linked sex and death. Wouldn't admit that in the Escambray, he'd found it particularly satisfying to shoot someone, then score some tail. Or vice versa. No, he wouldn't admit to himself that the idea of raping and murdering Lynne Jameson was so exciting he had come in his trousers.

Not to be. Frustration rankled him, but it wasn't just his near-miss. He sensed that Flynn was trying to take over. "You understand," he said testily, "that this is my deal. I mean . . . since you blew it at the reception."

"How was I to know Hemingway would be there?"

"You're the one who's got his phone tapped!"

"Would've been suicide, anyway."

"Then why the fuck were we there, *huh?*" Todd punched his finger into Flynn's chest. "You oughta be thankful I pushed those krauts in front of you before Hemingway recognized you and blew the whistle!"

Flynn glared at Todd, then shrugged and backed down. "Get some sleep, mate," he said, handing him the rifle, "get some sleep so you can bloody-well shoot straight."

Todd turned his back on the limey, stared at the lights of the boats moored along the Barlovento marina, then went to the edge of the roof and paced it, looking for the best firing position, judging all the angles. When he thought he'd found it, he lay down nearby, tried to sleep, but couldn't. Thoughts of David filled his head, bringing tears to his eyes. He twisted on the hard surface, listening to the noise of the party below, the orchestra segueing into "La Bamba" and the thump of a conga line, the guests saying goodbye, laughing, car doors slamming, then long silences broken by nightbirds calling, an occasional militia patrol, wind in the palm trees. Finally, he slept.

Only to be awakened in the predawn light by voices. Frantically, he looked behind him, but no one else was on the roof. Except Flynn, wide awake too, signaling for quiet. They stared at each other, the moment an awful eternity, until realizing the voices were *below* them, yet too close to be drifting up from the street. Cautiously, Todd peeked over the edge.

One story down, two men on extension ladders attached the end of a huge banner to the balcony railing while others unrolled and stretched it across the street, intending to secure it to a lamppost by the ramp to the marina. Greatly relieved, Todd watched idly for a minute, then went to the other side of the roof and urinated.

0530 hours.

Won't be long now. He returned to his firing position, lay on his back, inspected the rifle, stared at the gray overcast. Pistol drawn, Flynn half crouched by the door, should someone come onto the roof prematurely.

Todd heard the fleet of Oldsmobiles several blocks away, right on schedule. He swallowed hard, tensed and waited. Closer. Closer, the engines whined. Then screeching brakes, doors opening and slamming, orders shouted, boots ringing on pavement as the bodyguards fanned out. One thousand one. One thousand two. Castro would be on the ramp.

Sweet revenge.

Now.

He rolled up into the prone position, shouldered the rifle and sighted all in one smooth motion, half squeezed the trigger, stopped.

The banner blocked his line of fire.

11th ANNUAL ERNEST HEMINGWAY MARLIN TOURNAMENT, it read in Spanish. He couldn't see a fucking thing through the scope except the words! Up and running to the other end of the roof, raising the weapon. Too late.

Castro was already on board, below decks, and *Cristal,*

the Prime Minister's intervened yacht, was throttling away from its moorings, out into the channel on its way to the starting line. He set down the rifle and put his face in his hands.

"Well, mate," Flynn said sardonically, "you had your shot now, didn't you? Looks like it's my turn."

"After we get Castro," Todd said murderously, "I want Hemingway. I want him bad."

Thirty-three

THE GULF STREAM was narrow and close to shore that year, compelling most boats to bunch up and fish in each other's wakes. Not Fidel Castro in the *Cristal*. On the first day, he boldly sailed twenty miles out, and when Papa radioed to tell him he didn't know what the hell he was doing, he replied blithely that no self-respecting marlin would stay in waters clogged with fifty-some fishing boats. Bemused, Papa turned to Fidelito and said, "That's his first mistake. You watch, he ain't gonna catch nothing. Everyone knows that marlin only run in the Gulf Stream."

Except, on that first day, Fidel landed a forty-six-pound sailfish and a fifty-four-pound marlin, and Papa was shut out. Back at the mooring, adding insult to injury, the Prime Minister bragged to reporters about the two big ones that got away. "Yeah, we've all heard that one before," someone shouted, whereupon Fidel pointed to a cameraman, yelled back gleefully, "It's on film, *chico!*" then got into his Oldsmobile and took off.

They turned to Papa, asking, just what does the Nobel laureate think of Castro's fishing prowess?

"No comment," he grumbled, heading for the club bar and a therapy of *definitivos*. It was going to be a long night.

The second day of the tournament came much too hard and early for Papa. Bleary-eyed, yet tight-jawed and determined, he eased back on the throttle, let the *Pilar* nose to the starting line at the mouth of Havana harbor alongside the other boats in the contest, rolling gently in the early morning calm, the pink traces of sunrise streaking across the ocean. From the old Morro Castle, a cannon boomed, signifying the start of the day's fishing, and the boats headed out toward the Gulf Stream.

"Gonna be a good day, son," he said to Fidelito standing near the helm, then squinted at the horizon. "We're gonna catch us some big ones."

"Like Daddy did?"

"Bigger."

"Hope so."

"Don't worry, he just got lucky."

Yet like every angler that's ever held a pole, from greenhorns to seasoned veterans, Papa second-guessed himself. Maybe Castro knows something nobody else does, he thought, steering the *Pilar* across the current, away from the other boats, following the *Cristal* and her sister ship, *La Luna,* carrying the ministers, their wives and/or lovers. Face it, Hem, you'll never be too old to learn something new about going after marlin.

As they cruised along, Papa entertained the boy with an endless string of fish stories, each one having a lesson.

"Sometimes it's good not to tie more than one hook on your line, if you're going for a real big one, a record breaker." He paused, cleared his throat. "I remember being off Peru a few years back, hooked a twelve-hundred-pound blue. Man, he was a beauty. Played him good for a couple of hours, had him surfacing fifty feet off the stern, was real close to reeling him in when *another* big one took the second hook, almost jerked me out of my chair."

"Did you catch *both* fish?" asked the boy, awed.

"You kidding? They broke my line. I was only using thirty-pound test."

The delicious odors of breakfast cooking wafted up from the galley. Frying onions, peppers, and garlic in butter, tomatoes stirred in, salsa for the eggs, and later, fresh snapper poached in beer. Papa's mouth watered. He turned to go below—just as Gregorio came topside and handed him a mug of coffee.

"*¡Buenas!*"

"*Todo está listo,*" Gregorio said, expressionless, then went back to the galley.

Papa grinned, took a slug of coffee, the warmth dissolving his hangover. "You'll want to find a mate like Gregorio, too. He has connections. Can get you the best bait in town, every time."

The breakfast was superb, the finest Papa had tasted in months, and Fidelito ate so much, he had to lie down. "Just don't tell your old man about Gregorio," Papa said, wiping his plate clean. "He'll take him away from me, make him head chef at the palace."

An hour later, Papa was in the chair, fishing seriously, Gregorio at the helm as the *Pilar* trolled the open seas. The *Cristal* was five hundred yards off their starboard side, shadowed by two Cuban gunboats, gray hulls inconspicuous, merging with the haze. Trailing behind was *La Luna* and the faint sounds of music and partying as the ministers hooked into *la dolce vita,* forgetting the affairs of state.

Papa squinted at the *Cristal,* thought he saw Castro in the chair, then heard a distant whoop echoing across the water, the splash of a fish jumping, followed by laughter, cries of excitement, another jump. Silence. Maybe the sonuvabitch lost him, he halfway hoped. Then the radio crackled, and Gregorio answered, listened, called down.

"Es Fidel."

"What's he want?" he asked, already knowing, not wanting to hear.

Gregorio queried, listened again, reported apologetically. "He says he just caught another marlin and wants to know how *Compañero* Papa is doing."

"Tell him I'm doing just fine," Papa growled, glaring off at the *Cristal*. Just when he was starting to feel good and easy in the chair. He reeled in his line; the bait was taken. Annoyed, he wondered why he hadn't felt any nibbles, threaded fresh sardines onto the hook, cast out, let the line drop a few hundred feet and waited, this time tuned to the feel of pole and tackle.

Nothing.

The sun burned the haze off, turned the water a brilliant deep blue etched with whitecaps. He began sweating, mopped his brow with his forearm, was about to yell up to Gregorio when Fidelito appeared at his side with an ice-cold Hatuey, surprising him.

"Jeez Chrise, son, thanks!" Beaming, he took a long pull off the bottle. "How'd you know I was thirsty?"

"I dunno." The kid shrugged. "You looked it."

"Want to take a turn in the chair? I ain't doing so hot."

"I'll wait," he said quietly. "You need to catch one first, Grandpapa."

Papa smiled, genuinely touched by the boy's kindness, glad he'd decided to bring him along on this, possibly the last fishing trip. Tears welled up in his eyes, of joy, of sadness, and he looked out to sea so Fidelito wouldn't notice, then scowled at his show of emotion. Don't get maudlin, you grizzled old bastard, all things must pass, even your fishing days, face it, sooner or later the lights go out, even yours, at least you got someone to pass on your secrets to, the boy here, you're close to him, you— Cut it out, Hemingstein, you don't need to think of inevitabilities right now, you're in the fishing chair with your line out, for Christ's sake, just wait for the nibble, set the hook, and have a grand old time, there *are* marlin in these here waters.

The high-speed whine of an aircraft.

Papa glanced skyward, saw a plane with Cuban air force markings go into a steep bank. To lighten his mood, he pointed it out to Fidelito. "Know what that is, son?"

The boy shook his head.

"A Corsair. Marines use 'em for close air support. Back in WWII, we—" Wait a second, he thought, growing cold and fearful, the Cubans don't have any Corsairs, they can't afford them!

Confirming it, the plane dove, came in low over the water, opened up with quad fifties and strafed the *Cristal,* rounds tattooing her gleaming white hull, shattering her windows, kicking up spray on either side, bodies flying, some overboard, appearing miniature and unimportant from a distance. The Corsair nosed up sharply, climbing vertically, and Papa heard the popping of AK-47's from bodyguards still alive, the thump of antiaircraft fire from the gunboats—black puffs against blue skies—horrified screams from those on board *La Luna.* It seemed unreal, almost— Holy Christ, he thought, they're trying to take him out! Stunned, he watched the plane level out and bank. The fucker's gonna come around again, he told himself, just to make sure. Goddamn Sam, this can't be happening!

"Daddy!" screamed Fidelito. "They're shooting at Daddy!"

Papa dropped his pole, was out of the chair fast, grabbed the boy by the shoulders, shook him roughly. "Get below, son."

"They've killed Daddy!" he cried. "They've—"

"I said *get below!*"

Papa shoved him down the ladder, turned, vaulted onto the bridge, pulled an astonished, paralyzed Gregorio away from the helm, slammed the throttle all ahead flank, spun the wheel, headed straight for the *Cristal,* his mind clear and sharp, filled only with the moment and the way things were arranged.

The aircraft slid into a steep dive, came over the water at a different angle, machine guns blazing, raking the yacht. The return fire was more accurate this time, knocking out one engine and damaging a wing. A wounded bird, the Corsair struggled valiantly for altitude, then exploded in a ball of fire as the Cuban gunners found their mark. Smoking debris rained from the skies, hissing when it hit the water, some pieces landing on the *Pilar.*

Seconds later, Papa cut the engines, spun the wheel ninety degrees, let his boat drift sideways toward the *Cristal,* listing now, slowly sinking. The carnage was eerie. At least six bodyguards were dead, two hanging over the side draining into the sea, another decapitated by a .50-caliber shell, two more with torsos shot away, the deck awash in blood. In the middle of it all was Gonzáles, wounded in three places, but alive.

The fishing chair was empty.

"Where's Castro?" shouted Papa.

Dazed, the chief bodyguard pointed at the water.

With no second thoughts, Papa pulled off his shoes, dove over the side into the cool blue water, stroked down a good ten feet, kept going. If those boys're professional enough to call in a Corsair, he reasoned, they'll be coming from all directions, and while Fidel Castro ain't no fucking angel, he's better than all the other thieves who've ruled this island, he doesn't deserve to go out this way. Nope, not if I can help it. And personally speaking, Fidelito's too nice a kid to grow up without an old man. Who the hell's gonna teach him how to throw a knuckler when his arm starts to go? Old Hemingstein ain't gonna be around when that day comes, nosiree.

He was under the *Pilar* now, kicking hard for the white, blurred shape that was the *Cristal,* feeling good and strong, never better, unafraid, the new whore transcended forever. He saw Castro near the stern of the boat, holding onto the screws, waiting for someone to dive and signal that the plane was gone so he could surface.

Too late.

Off to the left was the ominous presence of a submarine. Closer, two frogmen in scuba gear and tanks—armed with high-powered spear guns—swam relentlessly toward the Prime Minister. One wore no hood, his blond crew cut bright against the ultramarine water, and Papa recognized him from long ago, from—

No time.

No escape.

Frantic, Castro tried to put the boat between him and them by pulling himself underneath the shelf of the hull and spread-eagling against it. Papa swam even harder, confident the assassins were unaware of him, yet worried that Fidel would panic and break for the surface, giving them sure-kill shots. Time was frozen, the moment charged with Castro's awful dilemma. Does he drown or commit suicide?

About thirty feet away, the blond-headed frogman wheeled up, aimed too quickly and fired. The spear leapt through the water, hit the *Cristal's* hull between Fidel's legs, ricocheted, and Papa retrieved it. Sonuvabitch aimed for the *cojones,* ain't that something, he told himself, changing direction, circling the frogmen, closing the gap, thankful for all the hours in the Finca's pool and the power of his lungs.

Now the moment seemed an eternity, a dream. There was no age. He was young and supple again, yet old and wise. His mind was filled with light and energy. That blaze of glory was before him, within reach, finally, again.

He was going to take it. Hold it. Savor it.

He was behind them now. Swimming closer. Twenty feet away. Fifteen. The blond one drew a long knife that glinted in the blue, nodded to his partner. They separated, waited for Castro to choose which way he would die, their air bubbles singing death's siren song, mocking their prey.

On came Papa. Ten feet. Five . . . He raised the retrieved spear.

Fidel pushed out from under the shelf of the hull and broke for the surface, the agony of no air etched on his face.

The one with the loaded spear gun took deliberate aim at point-blank range, but that was all.

With an enormous strength, Papa shoved his spear into the man's lower back. It went completely through him, came out his stomach, blood exploding. He dropped his gun, clutched at himself, kicking spasmodically, drifted up, just floated there in a cloud of his own blood. Papa turned, saw Fidel fending off the lunges and slashes of the blond one. Like an old bull walrus, he hit the assassin from behind, clamped one arm around his neck, with his other hand jerked the hoses out of the tank. A huge rush of bubbles, then no more air. The man kicked and thrashed, dropped his knife, with both hands tried to free himself from Papa's grip.

Fidel broke for the surface again.

Another form flashed by overhead. Papa glanced up. A great white was swimming away with the first assassin's leg in his mouth. The man vomited, choked, ripped his mask off, breathed in water, convulsed. Up close, Papa recognized him. Flynn, the young Englishman who had visited him at the Finca, the kid with the thousand-page manuscript and no sense of self, the man at the reception who had disappeared suddenly. Now his face was bluish-white, twisted with terrible pain and confusion—what happened, what went wrong—questions never to be answered, for another shark slammed into his midsection, and Flynn was no more.

No time for astonishment, no time to wonder why or how it went back that far, the water was murky with blood and danger, get the hell upstairs. Papa let go of the blond assassin, roughly shoved him away, kicked for the surface, tingling with vulnerability.

Air.

Huge breaths.

Hands, many hands pulling him onto the boat. Excited voices all around, fading. He lay on the deck gasping, chest heaving, staring at the sky, grinning foolishly, head filled with song. Sorta sounds like a conch shell, he thought, the myth of eternal ocean inside. A sweet symphony. Tears rolled from the corners of his eyes. You are filled with legend, old man. In your guts, your balls, your soul. Finally. You did it, you don't need no image, you are who you are, call it myth, whatever the hell you like, that's the gen of it.

"Jeez Chrise," he said happily, as a dozen voices started screaming in Spanish.

Gunfire. Off the port side. Papa raised his head. A submarine—the "USN" on its conning tower painted over—had surfaced. Two sailors were frantically pulling aboard the unconscious blond-headed assassin while the gunboats closed, machine guns blazing. They got the blond one down the hatch just before a burst of fire blew them off the deck and into the sea. The sub dove immediately, leaving bubbles and a small oil slick.

Papa's good feelings were replaced by an awful sense of foreboding. It wasn't over yet. One of them got away clean.

Thirty-four

HELLUVA WAY TO end a book, thought Papa, not bad, not bad at all.

He'd been up since four, making changes here and there, going over the last few pages. Satisfied, he sat back, sipped lukewarm coffee laced with Pinch, ran the ending through his head just to make sure. Father saves son from assassination attempt, redeeming himself, atoning for abandoning the kid years earlier, and they are finally united—*not* because the son has arrogantly accepted the old man, a pathetic finish. Rather, the psychology of it is the father has finally accepted and loved the son, which is what the kid wanted all along. *Write what you know, Hem.* Damn straight. And this one was in the "belle époque" league. All the old tautness was there, the quick rhythms, the easy flow. His heart sang. There is no greater feeling than to go the distance and come out on top, he told himself, ladies and gentlemen, the winner and still champion of the world . . .

Chuckling, he neatly stacked the manuscript, boxed it, took his coffee, padded to the office window, gazed up at the ridge line edged by the early morning Idaho sun, remembered the aftermath of that fateful day over a year ago.

There had been no accolades. State security didn't want anyone to know how close Castro had come to getting knocked off, figuring the news would only encourage other attempts. Papa agreed—for a different reason. He didn't want his name and picture plastered on the front page of every newspaper in the world; he had enough trouble hanging on to his privacy as it was. So, there was just the warmth between the two men—genuine, mutual gratitude for saving each other, physically and spiritually, and that was enough.

The mechanics of it: Helicopters airlifted the dead and wounded while the survivors were taken on board *La Luna.* The badly listing *Cristal* was scuttled, and her name painted over that of her sister ship, no one the wiser. The tournament continued as if nothing had happened. Except on the last day, four gunboats shadowed *La Luna* qua *Cristal,* and Uncle Sam sent a note to Havana asking why a Cuban patrol boat had fired on a U.S. submarine, May 14.

Papa grinned. The kicker was that Castro won the fucking tournament. He had 268.8 points with a catch of five marlin, talk about your lucky streaks. And he'd never forget the moment he handed Fidel the silver trophy, the strong, firm handshake, the love in his proud, dark eyes, the whispered, *"Gracias,* Papa," a huge understatement.

He coughed. His condition had deteriorated since then, one reason it had taken so long to finish the book. Kidney trouble, enlarged liver, too many years of *definitivos.* He'd lost too much weight, and the blood pressure refused to stay down. Kinda looks like the fight is over, he told himself, and the old whore is waiting in the dressing room.

Yet he had emerged victorious, and when he did slide into that proverbial saddle, he was going to give her a ride she'd never forget. Amen. He was finished. True to himself and his dreams. Time to write Scribner's and drop the big book in the mail, the one they didn't know about. A Cheshire cat grin spread across his face. The big book, done in silence because they all would've thought he was crazy writing a story one step removed from himself and Castro.

It hadn't been easy, though, pulling up stakes from La Finca Vigía a couple of months after the tournament; giving in to Mary's laments that all her friends had left the island, her hysterical concerns about conditions in Cuba. Sure, they were bad. Guns, uniforms, and eyes everywhere, half the fucking U.S. Navy off the coast, nothing in the stores except Chinese condoms and plastic purses from East Germany. Still, he considered the Finca home, and— sadly—had the distinct feeling he'd never see his farm again. Uprooted to a nondescript apartment in that hell-hole, New York City, stealing time to write, then on to Spain, going through the charade of final edits on "The Dangerous Summer," Melanie's prose being as overblown as her wardrobe. Waking bad and lonely every morning, working hard, even though his body was unraveling. Seeking respite at the Callejón, a small, intimate restaurant, where he had lunch almost every day, always complimenting the chef on his excellent cuisine. It was there, halfway through a dish of rabbit simmered in red wine, that he heard Spanish spoken with a Cuban accent, looked up curiously, saw the assassin with the blond crew cut in a waiter's uniform, taking an order three tables away, glancing sideways at him and smiling, eyes cold. Dead.

The one that got away.

It came back to him in a rush, four years ago seeming like four centuries. In the Sierra Maestra. The blond punk talking of freeing the Cuban people before matriculating at

Yale and becoming a football star. The blond punk cutting and running soon after his brother had been shot for leaving his post to score a piece of ass. The blond punk, switching sides, his destiny driven by vengeance and a hard-on for death, the worst kind of gringo. What the hell was his name? Papa could not remember.

He left the restaurant immediately, went back to the Suecia, locked himself in his suite. Refused to see anyone, worked feverishly on the book until he could get a plane back to the States; left under the cover of night four days later, landing at Idlewild the next morning. The blond crew cut was there too, dressed as a skycap, out of step with the frenetic pace of the city, biding his time, letting Papa know.

In the cab, Mary hadn't understood his anxiety, then his stubborn refusal to leave the apartment, his insistence they get the hell out of New York, go to Ketchum as soon as possible. *No one understood.* They all thought he was losing his mind, turning paranoid. When they asked what was wrong, he said the Goddamn feds were after him, but couldn't say why, except to give them lame excuses about the IRS, customs, and immigration. He *couldn't* tell them the truth! Quite simply, who would believe him?

He'd spotted the blond crew cut a third time, at a family steakhouse in Sun Valley, went home and broke out a shotgun, intending to carry it as a sidearm. His friends thought he was contemplating suicide and took the gun away. Mary and Doc Saviers shipped him off to the Mayo Clinic, which was okay because he was safe there and could hammer out the book undisturbed except for sexy nurses and shock treatments—amazing how they burned the cobwebs out of your brain. He worked every day until deadhouse and made good progress, just like old times. His cheerfulness convinced the doctors he didn't need to be hospitalized in spite of his physical ailments. So, he went back to Ketchum, shut himself up in his office with the last few chapters, emerging only for meals and terse conversations.

Occasionally, he took long walks in the mountains, his checkered cap bright against the snow. One day he caught the glint of field glasses reflecting the sun from the ridge line a half mile away. The blond crew cut was there too, wearing a white ski suit.

They took the shotgun away from him again, wouldn't listen to his protests about the feds. They'd heard it all before and told him he "needed help"—a euphemism meaning he was off his rocker—then shanghaied him back to the Mayo Clinic. On ice again. He felt like he was in one of those new Hitchcock films where the main character is the only one who knows what's really going on and, ironically, has no control over his fate.

Regardless, he finished the book, a triumph of the spirit. Why must the greatest successes come in the midst of adversity? he asked himself. Or is it the adversity that forces us into greatness?

They let him out again. The long drive to Ketchum. Sad dreams of the Finca and the *Pilar* and— Talking to bears in Wyoming and Montana, Mary and those of the human persuasion not comprehending him anymore. A quick polish on the book.

Satisfaction.

He went downstairs, refilled his mug with coffee and scotch, returned to his office and typewriter, started the letter to his editor.

Dear Charlie,

Hope the wife and kids are doing just great.

Listen, I've known for a long time that you and the boys at Scribner's have thought that old Hemingstein is over the hill, that he cashed it in with OMATS. Well, the enclosed is what the champ has been doing in his "spare" time for the past year and a half. I am anxious for your opinion, but not worried as I—

Dogs started barking. He glanced at his watch and frowned. Somebody here at seven o'clock on a Sunday morning? He hadn't heard anyone drive up. He crossed the room, peered out the window into the dappled sunlight. A flash of colors in the cottonwoods down by the river. Another in the sagebrush to the east, or had he just imagined it? No, movement in the cottonwoods again. A chill shot through him; he knew instantly. They're coming for me, he told himself, Jesus H. Christ, they're coming for me.

Thirty-five

TODD BLACKBURN CROSSED the river where it was shallow, ran over the rocks and was into the cottonwoods again, his breath coming hard and fast. He stopped, pulled out a .44 Magnum revolver, checked it, then patted his pockets making sure he'd brought some fast loads in case six rounds weren't enough. His hands were shaking. He swallowed hard and tried to calm himself. The excitement was almost too much for him. He had waited a long time for this day, the day he was going to kill Ernest Hemingway.

He took a deep breath and moved forward, angling through the trees away from the tranquil sound of the river. The sweet taste of rum was still in his mouth from the night before. He and Ricardo had stayed up late at the TraveLodge in town drinking toasts to each other and this moment. He smiled bitterly. The same Ricardo he'd hooked up with in the Sierra Escambray when the firm sent him to blow up *La Coubre*. The same Ricardo now approaching the Hemingway place from the other direction.

Keeping inside the line of cottonwoods, Todd worked his way closer to the house. The memories came flooding back. Being pulled into the submarine after failing to assassinate Castro and almost drowning, no thanks to old man Hemingway. Recovering at Walter Reed, unable to score with the nurses because they saw failure written all over him— or so he thought. Then the final humiliations when he went home to see his dying mother, Captain Dad heaping abuse on him and his already checkered career with the firm.

Days later, upon returning to Quarters "I" for a new assignment, he resigned from the CIA—joining it was the only decision he ever made that Captain Dad approved— and vowed that he would get even with those who had screwed up his life. Finally, he was on his own. He was horribly free, a well-trained, unemployed assassin. He made a list, put Hemingway at the top, then hired himself. With his savings account, he sprung Ricardo from Cuba and outfitted their mission, but Ricardo balked when he found out their target was the famous, Nobel prize-winning author. When Todd explained that Hemingway had saved Castro's life, Ricardo changed his mind, agreeing that Hemingway deserved to die. And so the hunt began.

Todd caught up with Papa in Spain, probably could've killed him then, but was leery of the Spanish police. Besides, he wanted the old man to be afraid, to live in terror until his painful, ignominious end, thus making a mockery of his myth and the heroes he wrote about. Todd tracked him back to New York City, then Idaho. Along the way, he watched the old man's paranoia fester and grow as he worked desperately to finish the book he'd talked to Castro about on the phone. Now the time was right. Todd wanted his kill, he wanted Ernest Hemingway's blood on his hands.

He sprinted up a hill out of the trees, then onto a meadow straight toward the house. As he broke into the open, he expected, *wanted* Hemingway to start shooting. *Make it interesting, you fucking has-been, make it a dream come true!* When no gunshots came, he figured he'd catch the old man in bed, sleeping. That's okay, too, he told himself. After you're done with him, you can rape his wife. Empty your pistol into him, then empty your sperm into her. No, no. He caught himself. Not this time. Better to take his book so the world will never know. That way, you rape his soul.

His mind slipped. The early morning sunlight glanced off the windows of the house into his eyes, and briefly, he saw stars. His image of Hemingway was replaced by one of Captain Dad. His father's face was twisted and ugly and pathetic. He too deserved to die.

Thirty-six

PAPA RUSHED DOWNSTAIRS, thinking wildly about saving himself, about escape, realizing that Mary had locked up all the guns in the storage room over six months ago, yet knew the key was on the windowsill in the kitchen. He found it, hesitated, parted the curtains, saw the swarthy, stocky one approaching from the south. Two of the bastards. His heart sank. At least two, but in all likelihood more because the feds never take chances, never give a man an even break. No way out, he told himself. If you opt for a shoot-out, Mary'll get hurt, and there ain't time to call the cops. They're probably in on the deal anyway. After all, you saved the life of the man they love to hate. He chuckled cynically. Two of the bastards, my ass, he thought. There's probably a dozen. You don't have a chance, Hem. Not a helluva lot of time, either.

He hurried down into the storage room, unlocked the gun cabinet, paused, stared at the weapons, finally chose the double-barreled shotgun he'd used for pigeons and pheasants. He cracked the breech, slipped two shells inside, snapped it shut, ran back upstairs. Breath coming hard, pulse hammering. He looked out the living room windows. The blond crew cut was crossing the meadow now. He had his pistol out, and it looked like a .44 Magnum. What the hell does he think you are, a Goddamn redwood tree?

Final decisions.

You know you're dying. Mary, Doc Saviers, the staff at the clinic, they never say anything, but their silence is deafening. You know you're dying. So why give these bozos the satisfaction of a cheap-ass revenge? Let them live with one more failure. You've always known that the only man good enough to take out old Hem is Hemingstein himself.

He cocked the hammers on the shotgun.

Wait a minute, damnit! You're a man of letters, of words, for Christ's sake!

He leaned the weapon against the wall in the entranceway, rushed up into his office, moccasins silent on the stairs, grabbed a sheet of paper, scrawled, *Man Can Be Destroyed, But Never Defeated,* placed it on top of the big book. He gulped. His heart surged. The tears came quick and easy. All the years of hard work, sacrifice, frustration, good times, rewards, you deserve all of it, you took it, if you had to do it over again— Hell, yes, wouldn't change a Goddamn thing. Goodbye book and books, may you live forever.

Downstairs again, mind free, floating, filled only with the ritual before him. He placed the shotgun butt on the floor, pressed his forehead against the coolness of the barrels, felt the metal cut into his skin, smiled. Fate is just another whore, Papa, she can be had, too.

He heard a window opening in the kitchen, heard

someone coming up the steps, raised his eyebrows, saw the door handle turning.

He pulled both triggers.

One last blaze of glorious light.

"La Finca Vigía, circa 1961"

Thirty-seven

"OKAY *BUENO, CHICO*, I'll be there." Fidel hung up the phone, dropped the state papers he'd been reading onto the linoleum, put on his fatigue shirt, buttoned it, tucked it in, lit a cigar, donned his hat, strode through the kitchen onto the veranda.

"Fidelito!" he shouted, raising his voice above the wind. "Come, come, come, *vámonos*, we must pay our respects!"

Compañero Dr. Luis Herrera had just called, head of the FAR medical section and an old friend of the Hemingway family. Apparently, Señora Mary had returned to Cuba to wrap up Papa's affairs and take his things back to the United States, but was having trouble with officials at CNC. Well, Fidel wasn't about to tolerate bureaucratic bullshit, not when it came to the memory of Señor Papa.

El viejo's death had deeply saddened Fidel. Puzzled him. At first, the reports said that Papa had accidentally killed himself cleaning a shotgun, but Fidel found that hard to

305

believe—the old man had always been so good and careful with weapons. Then the wire services were saying Hemingway committed suicide, which confused Fidel even more. Suicide was anathema to *el viejo,* even though he hadn't been in the best of health, even though he knew his days were numbered. They'd had discussions about it, both agreeing that the act was a coward's way out. He remembered Papa commenting on his own father's suicide: no *cojones.* They'd talked just days before on the phone too, and *el viejo* had seemed in excellent spirits. So none of the reports made any sense to Fidel. Why? he kept asking himself, there was no reason.

Nevertheless, the old man was gone, his death tragic, sudden, absurd, and Fidel would carry the sorrow in his heart for a long time. Like a son grieving a father.

Now the fleet of Oldsmobiles was speeding out of Cojímar onto the *carretera central,* heading toward the Finca. Fidel observed that his new bodyguards took their jobs very seriously, leaning out the windows, slamming on the doors and making threatening gestures with their automatic weapons to get traffic out of the way, hurling insults at those who didn't move fast enough. *A savage breed, where does Gonzáles find them, we didn't have such barbarians in the Sierra Maestra, did we? Maybe you should start screening the recruits yourself, except where would you find the time?*

On a dirt side road, *macheteros* and workers from a sugar *central* climbed aboard an already crowded bus, arms and heads hanging out the windows. It pulled away, belching black smoke, leaving a cluster of old women behind. Dusty and hot under the fierce August sun, they started walking, then stopped to stare at the Oldsmobiles racing past. Their wrinkled faces were long and tired, their backs stooped from stacking cane. Fidel scowled. Where were the new buses the English had promised him for futures in Cuban rum and tobacco, why weren't the new buses here? He almost told Gonzáles to stop so he could offer *las viejas* a ride, then realized there was no room. The cars were filled with bodyguards. You must do something, he told himself and shook his head, knowing that already there was too much to do and no one to do it. *Except him.*

The cars braked as one, turned at the Finca gates, went up the long driveway, passing the mango trees Fidel admired so much, now heavy with fruit, ready for harvest. They parked in front of the house, and he saw that Señora Mary had the Finca staff lined up on both sides of the stone steps, an old-style, formal welcome, a carryover from Spanish colonialism. *Qué va,* he should have been annoyed, but was touched instead. Then he was out of the car, smiling and waving. As the bodyguards fanned out, he shook hands with the servants, gardeners, and others—a show of solidarity—while mounting the steps to the house. Mary was by the door.

"Ah, Señora Hemingway." He bowed courteously, removed his hat. *"Mucho gusto."*

"Bienvenidos," she said graciously. "Won't you come in?"

"Hey, Dad!" cried Fidelito from the driveway. "Can me and René play some catch?"

The Prime Minister looked to Mary. "Is it all right, señora? I mean, if the *compañero* has work to do—"

"No, no," she said emphatically, then called down. "Go ahead, René."

They went inside.

"Señor Papa taught him how to throw," he said softly, eyes downcast. "He was more of a father to the boy than I was." He shrugged. "There is so much to do."

She offered him a chair. He sat gingerly on the couch, perched forward, checked his boots, making sure he hadn't tracked dirt inside, something that never would've occurred to him had Papa been there. Coffee was served, and he listened carefully as Mary described her dilemma. Leaving Cuba with Papa's papers was no problem, but CNC refused to give her an exit permit for his original works of art. Nothing of cultural value leaving the island had been the council's dictum ever since its inception so that gringos and *gusanos* would not rob Cuba of her national treasures, her heritage. A good idea, Fidel told himself, one conceived by Guevara so the revolution could not be labeled *"haute vulgarisme."*

He spread his hands magnanimously. "Live in Cuba, señora. Stay here with his papers and paintings."

She respectfully declined, saying she could not settle her husband's estate here. Most of the work had to be done in New York because of Ernest's literary affairs. They toured the house, and she pointed out that taking the paintings wouldn't really affect the quiet beauty of La Finca Vigía. Finally, he gave in, called CNC, ordered them to break the rules and accommodate the señora. After all, Papa had loved her. It was the least he could do.

They ended up in the tower, disturbing the cats who gave them baleful looks before sauntering out. Fidel realized he'd never been in Papa's office before, was amazed by the view, stood there for a long time, taking it all in. *¡Caramba!* you can see from the Gulf Stream to Havana, how could he work here with such a panorama? He smiled sadly.

"He loved it here," she whispered.

"I don't understand how he could leave, señora, I don't understand how—"

"He could take his own life?"

"Sí."

She spoke of mental problems, delusions of persecution, the juices had all dried up, he couldn't even write a sentence anymore, he was dying, merely shuffling from day to day, he couldn't live that way.

Confused, Fidel protested. "Begging the señora's pardon, we spoke two days before his death. He sounded so strong and happy."

"He called *you?*"

"Of course, señora, he was celebrating, he wanted me to know he'd finished the book."

"What book?" she cried, shocked.

"You know, the book, the novel about Cuba."

"No, no, there was—" Flustered, she shook her head, had to sit down. "There was no novel about Cuba, Ernest wasn't working on *anything!*"

A stunned silence.

Astonished, Fidel turned away, couldn't face her. Señor Papa never told her, he reasoned, but surely she would've found the manuscript, she— His eyes narrowed. He exhaled in a great rush. Not if someone *else* got there first. Not if they took it. Not if they destroyed it.

After they murdered him.

"Con permiso, señora," he said quietly, "who was it that found Papa's body?"

"I did."

"Was there any sign that someone else had been there? Was anything out of place?"

"No!" she exclaimed. "What are you suggesting?"

He blushed, threw up his hands. "Nothing, señora, nothing at all. I'm just curious." He stroked his beard and leaned forward, his eyes intense and riveting. "Did the police investigate his death? Perform an autopsy?"

"Why bother?" she asked, her voice a thin line of despair. "There was no need."

Of course not, he told himself, turning away again. They were in league with the assassins, they covered up the crime. Papa mentioned the feds when you talked to him on the phone, you should've listened to him, you should've taken him more seriously. He gazed out at the Gulf Stream, now convinced that Papa did not commit suicide. It was too illogical. Quite simply, they killed him because he saved my life.

A thought came to mind, a thought he never would've entertained way back in the Sierra Maestra.

Revenge.

Es verdad, chico, you are no stranger to vengeance either, not anymore. What was it that Señor Papa said a long time ago? If you want to survive, always hit them harder than they hit you. So okay, okay *bueno,* gringo animals, just so you know—

Two can play the assassination game.